Praise for *Pos*

'A fresh, funny new vo￼ ￼ ￼ ￼ ￼ you laugh and then cry in the turn of a page'

Marian Keyes

'An accomplished addition to the genre, a heart-warming take on modern Ireland that veers toward more serious topics and themes while retaining its sense of humour and upbeat pace . . . at times the novel reads like a Dublin version of *Sex and the City*'

Weekend Review, Irish Independent

'A touching story that reminds us all that love's never as simple as it sounds'   *Woman*

'Ella Griffin's hugely enjoyable debut . . . deftly mixes light and shade, humour and conflict . . . Griffin puts a fresh spin on the having-it-all conundrum of juggling relationships and caring for children and parents with the demands of a career'   *Irish Sunday Independent*

'This thrilling story of romance and deceit is too good to put down'   *Closer*

'Love in all its guises fill the pages of this lively novel'

Choice

'As debut novels go this is one stomping entry into the world of storytelling. Like all good rom-coms, *Postcards from the Heart* is a love story with a twist, but it's also got the added element of wit, humour and the odd tear here and there. A fabulous read'   *RTE Guide*

Ella Griffin was born in Dublin. She was an award-winning advertising copywriter before she took the leap into fiction.

She has written four novels since 2011. She loves making readers laugh and cry (sometimes on the same page.)

Ella lives with her husband in County Wicklow in Ireland.

You can find Ella at Facebook/EllaGriffinAuthor @EllaGriffin1 and @ella_griffin_writer

Also by Ella Griffin

The Heart Whisperer
The Flower Arrangement
The Memory Shop

Postcards from the Heart

ELLA GRIFFIN

ORION

An Orion paperback

First published in Great Britain in 2011
by Orion
This paperback edition published in 2020
by Orion Books Ltd,
Carmelite House, 50 Victoria Embankment
London EC4Y 0DZ

An Hachette UK company

1 3 5 7 9 10 8 6 4 2

A CIP catalogue record for this book
is available from the British Library.

ISBN 978-1-3987-0016-1

Typeset at The Spartan Press Ltd,
Lymington, Hants

Printed and bound in Great Britain by Clays Ltd,
Elcograf S.p.A.

www.orionbooks.co.uk

For Neil, who changed everything.

Acknowledgements

If you are going to write a novel, you'll probably find, like I did, that words are only half the story. You'll also need some (or all) of the following.

A friend who will meet you in a Japanese restaurant on George's Street every week and listen to you going on about all the reasons why you'd love to write but can't. Someone who will resist the urge to stuff California Rolls into her ears and, instead, look at you kindly and say: 'I'm going to hold on to your dream of writing a book until you're able to hold on to it yourself.' (Thank you, Morag Prunty).

Another friend who will listen to raggedy bits of your book in its early stages and say nice things about it. And take time out from her incredibly busy life to read your first draft (165,000 words of which around 164,000 are misspelled). And help you to find a brilliant agent (see below). And give you a really lovely quote for your cover. (Thank you, Marian Keyes).

A few kindred spirits who would genuinely prefer to sit around someone's kitchen scribbling things down and reading them out than going to the pub. (Thank you, Ailish Connolly, Suzanne Power, Karen Hand and Lucy Masterson).

Some writing classes. (Thank you, Dorothy Carpenter and Claire Boylan. Both, sadly, gone but not forgotten).

Someone to help you with a bit of research. (Thank you, John Lynn). Someone to get you back onto the writing horse when you fall off. (Thank you, Shiera O'Brien). And some kindly perfectionists to help out when you're editing. (Thank you, Wendy Williams, Nikki Walsh, Helena Mulkerns and Alison Walsh).

It definitely helps to have a charming and brilliant agent. (Thank you, Jonathan Lloyd). A kind and insightful editor. (Thank you, Kate Mills). And a publishing house that feels like home. (Thank you to everyone at Orion, especially Susan Lamb and Jade Chandler).

You may be able to finish your novel without someone who will support and encourage you in hundreds of little ways and quite a few very big ones. Someone who will leave a rose from the garden in your waterglass and make you Minestrone from scratch. And unstick you every time you get stuck. And proof your drafts on trains and planes and text you to say he's laughing at the funny bits, sixth time around. But this is the person I needed most. (Thank you, Neil Cubley, for everything. Especially the Banksy postcard of the little girl letting go of the heart-shaped balloon. You're next.)

*'If love is the answer,
could you please rephrase the question?'*

Lily Tomlin

Part One

It was only nine in the morning but every other man on Grafton Street was carrying flowers. Saffy loved the way Valentine's Day brought out the romantic in the most unlikely people. Like the grumpy-looking businessman clutching a bunch of lilies who was snapping instructions into his mobile phone outside Bewley's. And the goth in the Infected Malignity sweatshirt she caught taking a sneaky sniff of the single red rose he'd just bought from the flower stall on the corner of Duke Street.

Whatever Greg sent her, she knew it wouldn't involve a red rose. Roses were what everybody else did on Valentine's Day. Greg liked to do things differently. In the past he'd sent her flowering cacti and plumes of black orchids and, last year, an enormous Venus fly trap. It was actually quite pretty but there weren't many flies around in February and it had died after Saffy fed it some smoked salmon from a bagel.

Komodo's philosophy, 'Expect the Unexpected' was scrawled on a wall in reception below a massive steel cut-out of the agency logo – a flesh-eating lizard. It was remarkably life-like and it scared everyone, except Ciara, the receptionist, who couldn't see it because she was sitting beneath it. But today, Saffy didn't even notice it because taking up most of the huge reception desk was the most gorgeous bouquet of roses she'd ever seen, and Ciara was waving her over. Her peroxide head appeared, briefly, over the gleaming alps of tissue paper and cellophane.

'Saffy!' she gasped, waving her spinhaler. 'Can you get these bloody flowers out of here before I . . . ?' She ducked down to answer the phone. 'Hhhello, Komodo Advertising,' she wheezed. 'Can I hhhelp you?'

Saffy grinned. Greg hadn't sent a single red rose. He'd sent what looked like at least three dozen. She hurried over, leaned down and breathed in their sweet, peppery scent. There was a tiny white envelope tucked in between the velvety crimson heads.

The spinhaler shot up again. 'Hhhold on! The roses are for Marsh. Probably from Marsh. She's the only person who loves herself enough.' Ciara pointed at an even larger bouquet that was lurking in the corner behind her desk. 'Those are for you. I think I'm allergic to the hhhhuge hhhairy purple one.'

'Got a secret admirer?' Simon smirked when Saffy struggled past him on the way to her office lugging the flowers. 'Is it Tim Burton?'

'Hey, Babe! What are you wearing?'

Even after six years, something in Saffy softly imploded when she heard that voice. Greg could make the instructions for an IKEA flat-pack sound sexy. When he used to do radio ads, before he got too famous, the Advertising Standards Authority had once received forty-seven complaints that his disclaimer on a bank ad – 'interest rates may rise as well as fall' – was too suggestive.

She looked down at her fitted white shirt and grey pinstriped DKNY trousers. She was wearing her favourite Kurt Geiger court shoes but Greg didn't like her in heels, not unless she was sitting or lying down.

'Can I tell you what I'm *not* wearing? It might be a bit more exciting.'

He laughed. 'Tell you what, tell me what you're going to wear when I take you out to dinner tonight instead.'

They hadn't gone out on Valentine's night in years. It was hard to do the whole romantic staring-into-each-other's-eyes thing when most of the women in the room were trying to stare into Greg's eyes too and the ones that weren't were taking pictures of him on their camera phones.

'You sure you don't just want to stay at home and eat scallops and drink a nice bottle of wine?' There was some Prosecco chilling in the fridge and she'd sprinkled handfuls of silk rose petals on the bed before she left this morning.

'I'm sure. So dress up. Okay?'

Saffy smiled. 'Okay.' If she worked through lunch she could

leave early and have her hair blow-dried and pick up her cream dress from the dry cleaner's.

'Hey, did you get my flowers?'

'Oh God, sorry! I did. Thank you! They're absolutely um . . .'

She stared at the bouquet, searching for the right word – searching for any word, really. The centrepiece was a purple thistle roughly the size of a baby's head. It was surrounded by a menacing thicket of birds of paradise and what looked like an entire vegetable patch of ornamental cabbages.

'They're um . . . amazing. I love them.'

'Yeah? Well, the whole "dozen red roses" Valentine's thing's such a cliché. I told the guy at the flower place to push the boathouse.'

Greg had a habit of getting common sayings confused. Somehow he managed to twist them so that they made a weird kind of sense. Like 'the blonde leading the blonde' and the truly inspired 'putting the car before the horse'.

'Well,' Saffy said truthfully, 'he *really* went overboard.'

She could hear voices in the background. Greg was on the set of *The Station*, a daytime soap about a team of Dublin firefighters. There was the wise older one and the troubled young one and the gay one and the pneumatic female one. Greg was Mac Malone, the heroic one, the one who was plastered across most teenage girls' bedroom walls.

'Listen, Saff, I'm probably going to be shooting till at least seven and I've booked the restaurant for eight so I'll see you there. And there's something I want to ask you tonight, something pretty important . . . hang on—' He broke off. 'Dude, I'm on the phone here . . . Well, tell her I'll be there in a minute. And tell her I'm not carrying that whale down that ladder . . . Yeah? Well, one of the stunt guys will have to do it. Sorry, Babe. What was I saying?'

'You were saying you've got something to ask me . . .'

'Yeah,' he said, his voice dropping a delicious half-octave. 'I do have something to ask you—'

There was a scuffle and another voice came on the line. 'This is Robert, the first AD. I've got something to ask you, too. Can you call back when there isn't a half-naked woman in a pregnant

5

suit hanging off a shagging hundred-foot ladder waiting for Mr Gleeson to do his bloody job?'

Saffy tried to focus on writing an Avondale Foods contact report but her mind had other ideas and they didn't involve cheese. Greg had something to ask her. What *was* it? Her heart bumped against her ribcage like a trapped balloon. Could *it* possibly be *it*? She smiled at the giant thistle for a bit. She stood up and went over to sniff one of the dinky little pink cabbages. It smelled, unexpectedly, of cabbage. Then she sat back down at her desk. This was ridiculous. She was the most level-headed person she knew and she was not going to get carried away.

Greg had something to ask her, that was all. He asked her things all the time. Last night, when they were watching 24, he'd asked her if you could have a general anaesthetic when you had a tattoo, whether she thought Kiefer Sutherland used Botox and why dogs didn't have bellybuttons.

She forced herself back to the contact report and, when it was finished, she hit Send. She was allowing herself another sneaky peek at the flowers then she suddenly realised that she had forgotten to spell-check.

She had referred to the client, Harry as 'Hairy'. Twice. And put 'client to pervert' instead of 'revert' and typed her name (her *own* name) as *Sassy*. Luckily the email was still in her outbox and she managed to cancel it. But it was a close call.

She shoved the flowers out of sight behind her filing cabinet and shoved Greg out of her mind. If she got all her contact reports done in the next two hours she'd let herself think about him again at lunchtime. She froze. *Lunchtime!* She had completely forgotten that she was supposed to meet her mother for lunch. She couldn't put her off again. She hadn't seen her since Christmas.

The poster was bright red with polite white type. *If love is the answer, can you rephrase the bloody question?* It wasn't exactly a good sign but at least it was an improvement on yesterday's version: *Do I look like a fucking people person?*

Ant, Komodo's Creative Director, refused to speak directly to anyone at the agency except his Art Director, Vicky. The rest of them had to guess his mood from the gnomic messages that appeared on the door of their office every day. Actually, there wasn't too much guesswork involved. His mood was generally bad but he hadn't been hired for his social skills.

Anthony Savage had written 'The geeks shall inherit the earth' viral for Compushop. And the Axis Tyres radio ads that used out-takes from politicians' speeches with the endline, 'Get a grip'. And the road safety posters with portraits of a beautiful paraplegic girl and the line, 'You drink therefore I am.' His work was advertising gold.

The office was divided in two by a line of black gaffer tape that ran along the carpet, up the wall and across the ceiling. Vicky's half was a temple to the Goddess 'Girly'. Her computer was festooned with flower lights. Her desk was littered with make-up and scented candles and pots of sparkly pens and folders with fun fur covers. The floor was barely visible under piles of books and magazines.

Ant's half contained Ant himself, his desk, his chair and his waste-paper basket. The only objects on his desk were his computer and a box of Smints. The only things on the floor were his Camper shoes, lined up with mathematical precision, exactly parallel to his chair.

'Hey, Saffy.' Vicky was eating Hula Hoops off her fingers. She was wearing a red leotard and a long white traily skirt with stripy red-and-black tights and biker boots. Vicky was about thirty-five years too old to dress like a five-year-old but somehow she made it work.

'Hi, guys. Just wondering how you're getting on with the cheese print? No pressure . . .'

Ant didn't even bother to look up from his Sudoku. He was in his thirties with a shaved head and a small, round, permanently pinched face that made him look like a cross between an old man and a bad-tempered baby. He was dressed, as always, in black and he wasn't eating anything. The only thing Saffy had ever seen Ant put into his mouth apart from Smints and Guinness was a roll-up.

'Tell the suit to fuck off and die,' he muttered to Vicky.

7

'Easy, Tiger!' Vicky stood up and brushed some Hula Hoop crumbs from her long dark hair. 'Saffy is our friend, remember?'

She spread some marker roughs out over the clutter on her desk. Saffy stared at them. There was no way she could show these to the Avondale client. In one, she could just make out what appeared to be the face of Jesus carved from a lump of cheese. The headline was: *Avondale. The Face of Cheeses.*

In another, Jesus was holding a cheese sandwich and a mug of tea under the line: *Avondale. A Last Supper to Remember.*

There were more. The worst one had a beaming Jesus with a piece of bread on the end of skewer. *Avondale. What Would Jesus Fondue?*

Komodo had a reputation for unconventional work and the agency philosophy was 'expect the unexpected', but this was taking it a bit literally.

'Guys,' she said carefully, 'I can see where you're coming from with the Jesus/cheeses thing but—'

Vicky cut her off with a 'trust me' smile. She always managed to rein Ant in just enough to get the work approved. 'We're just throwing ideas around. We'll keep going. We'll have loads more options to show you on Monday.'

'This isn't an advertising agency,' Ant hissed. 'It's hell with fluorescent lighting.'

2

'This is nice.' Her mother picked out a sheer lemon bra with a double row of bright pink satin ruffles and held it up against Saffy. 'This is *lovely*.'

Lovely? If you were a teenage, colour-blind hooker, possibly.

'Um.' Saffy shook her head. 'I don't think it's really me.'

'Oh, Sadbh!' Saffy's scalp prickled with annoyance. She hated her full name. 'We've got to get you out of those neutrals. You need a bit more – what do they call it in that ad? – *va-va-voom*. And fashion tip: if God wanted us to wear glasses, he wouldn't have given us contacts.'

It had seemed like a good idea to take her mother shopping instead of to a restaurant. Saffy had thought she could sidestep Jill's attempt at a girly heart-to-heart *and* buy something to wear under her cream dress. Something sweet and sexy to surprise Greg with. Her mother had been delighted. 'I can't remember the last time we went shopping for you! This will be *fun*!'

Unfortunately, Saffy could remember. It had been for her debs dress. There had been tears (Jill's) tantrums (also Jill's) and humiliation (hers). She had wanted an elegant navy cocktail dress with spaghetti straps. She ended up in pink satin with a puffball skirt, pink lace tights and a matching shrug. She was still dreading the pictures popping up on Facebook.

The lingerie department of Brown Thomas was jammed with loved-up couples canoodling among the rails of suspenders and French knickers.

'You'd look gorgeous in this!' Jill tucked a leopard-print bra under her arm. 'I wonder if they have it in a thirty-four A.'

There was nothing like your mother announcing your bra-size to a small crowd to make you wish you hadn't been born. An assistant was hovering. 'If you and your friend need any help, just let me know,' she said with a smile.

Saffy hated it when people mistook them for friends or, even worse, sisters. Her mother, of course, loved it. But luckily she hadn't heard. She had ascended directly to retail heaven. She was rifling through a rail of clattery hangers. Her blonde hair was escaping from her messy topknot. Her face glowed and her blue eyes sparkled. She had been a model, briefly, back in the seventies and she had the cheekbones and that coltish, prancing walk to show for it. She also had an amazing figure for fifty-three and she could still turn heads but did she *have* to do it in a clingy coral wraparound dress and purple suede boots?

Saffy sneaked a look at herself in a gilt-framed mirror. On the downside, she didn't have her mother's bone structure or her traffic-stopping curves. On the upside, what was so great about stopping traffic? Women disliked you, men expected way too much of you, and, somewhere along the line, you became addicted to all the attention. She suspected that was why her mother always dressed so that she was the most visible person in the room.

Her own grey DKNY pinstriped suit was simple but classic. Her hair, the caramel side of brown, was shoulder-length and feather-cut to flatter her narrow face. Her skin was too pale but, with just the right shade of foundation, it could be persuaded to do a good impersonation of creamy. It was hard to see them when she was wearing her glasses but her eyes were wide greeny brown. She would have liked narrower hips and bigger breasts but wouldn't everybody? Everybody with breasts to begin with, obviously.

At a film premiere once, a journalist had mistaken her for Bono's wife. Ali Hewson was everything Saffy wanted to be: natural, elegant, understated, happily married to a famous man but content to stay out of the limelight, wouldn't be caught dead in purple boots.

'So, tell me,' her mother took her arm and steered her towards the Myla section, 'how are things with Greg?'

'Things are great,' Saffy said smoothly. This was the conversation she had been trying to avoid. 'How are things with Len?'

When she was small her mother used to tell her that you had to kiss a lot of frogs before you found a prince and apparently she was right. Len was the latest in a long line of frogs that stretched back for as long as Saffy could remember.

Apart from the hand-knitted jumper, the passion for veganism and the unhygienic-looking beard, there was nothing really wrong with him. Saffy had met him only twice and she probably wouldn't meet him again. The frogs never lasted very long.

'Oh, Len.' Jill fingered the marabou trim on a white baby-doll and sighed. 'He means well but I'm getting a bit tired of the whole "meat is murder" thing. I can't remember the last time I had a bacon sandwich and I've had to put away all my leather shoes except these.' She gave one boot a loving pat. 'I told him they were mock suede. He's coming round later to cook me a five-bean stew, which is lovely, I suppose, but it's not exactly an aphrodisiac.'

She put the baby-doll back on the rack wistfully. 'What about you? Any Valentine's plans?'

'I think we're going out to dinner,' Saffy said vaguely.

'Ooh! Where?'

'365. It's—'

'I know what it *is*! It's fabulous. I read the review in the *Irish Times*. You're a lucky girl.' She sighed. 'I don't think you have any idea how lucky you are but . . .'

Saffy knew what was coming. 'Wow!' She snatched a hanger at random and held it up. 'You should try this on.' It was a red, fishnet basque.

Her mother looked straight through it. 'Sadbh, don't you think maybe it's time you and Greg got married because it's been—'

'Because it's been what?' Saffy snapped. 'Six weeks since you last asked?'

'There's no need to bite my head off.'

Saffy tried to backtrack. Her mother loved a scene, especially a public one. 'Look, I'm sorry, let's just change the subject . . .' But it was too late. Jill was off.

'No, *I'm* sorry! *I'm* sorry if it's a crime to show the slightest interest in my only daughter.'

It wasn't Saffy's fault that she was an only child. As a matter of fact, she would have loved brothers and sisters. The more the better. Anything that took the blinding spotlight of Jill's attention off her. Anything that stopped her mother expecting an access-all-areas pass to her personal life.

'*I'm sorry*,' Jill pointed a small metal hanger at her accusingly, 'if I want you to be happy and secure. I'm sorry if I don't want you to wake up when you're fifty, alone and—'

'I am happy! I am secure! And I won't be fifty for seventeen years!' Saffy's voice came out louder than she'd intended. Quite a lot louder. Now *she* was the one turning heads.

'And I'm *sorry*,' Jill said dramatically, 'for whatever I've done to make you shout at me in public! Something I hope *your* daughter never does to you!' She stalked around a circular red-velvet banquette towards a wall of glass cabinets.

She needn't have bothered hoping. Saffy wasn't going to have children. She had decided that long ago. Her parents weren't exactly an ad for happy families.

She had never even seen a picture of her father. If there had been any, Jill had destroyed them long ago. The only thing she had to remember him by was her full name, *Sadbh*. He had disappeared long before she had a chance to call him something equally horrible back. Even Irish people, who were *supposed* to know that 'Sadbh' rhymed with 'drive', moved the lumpy combination of consonants around in their mouths carefully, as though they were afraid it might chip a tooth.

Rob Reilly had been more than twice her mother's age when they met, and he'd been married. When Jill got pregnant, he had left his wife and they had moved from Bristol to Dublin. Then, when Saffy was two, he had, apparently, woken up one morning and changed his mind.

He had walked out and gone back to his wife. Jill rarely talked about it but, from the little she said, Saffy knew that her mother couldn't go home. Her parents had told her that, if she had a baby with a married man, she needn't bother coming back.

People said you couldn't miss what you never had but people were wrong. Even when she was too small to understand why, Saffy got a pinch in her chest when she saw a man swinging a little girl up onto his shoulders or taking her hand to cross the street.

For some reason, she had missed her father most when she was a teenager. It was the ordinary things that always got to her. A razor jammed into the toothbrush cup in someone else's bathroom. A man at the school gate scanning the crowd of kids for a face that wasn't hers. Sitting, invisible, in the back of the car while a friend bickered with her dad on the way home from a disco. The words 'Father Christmas'. The utter pointlessness of Father's Day.

She didn't know where her father was or why he had left. And she couldn't change the fact that he didn't want to be part of her life but she could change the horrible name he'd given her and, by the time she was twelve, nobody except her mother called her *Sadbh*.

The crowd parted now and she saw Jill on the other side of the shop glaring into a glass cabinet, pretending to be interested in a display of seamed stockings and showgirl tassels. For a second, Saffy almost felt sorry for her.

Her mother had done so much. She had learned to drive and to type and to soften her English accent so it didn't stand out so much. She had turned the grotty flats they lived in into homes. She had cleaned offices and typed dissertations till Saffy was at school, leaving her with a neighbour or bringing her with her in her pushchair. Then she had taken a part-time job in an antique shop and learned everything she could about the business. She had saved enough to buy a house. But no matter how much she did, her life would always be defined by all the 'if onlys'.

If only she hadn't fallen for Rob Reilly. If only she hadn't believed him when he said he'd look after them. If only she had been careful. If only she hadn't been caught. All the 'if onlys', Saffy realised when she was fourteen, added up to one big one: if only *she* hadn't been born.

Jill was determined that Saffy would get all the things she'd missed out on by being a single mother: college, a career, travel. Saffy had ticked all those boxes but now her mother was holding her breath, waiting for her to tick the biggest box of all. The one that contained the big white dress and the happy-ever-after *she* had never had.

But she was going to have to keep holding her breath. Because having a child didn't mean you got to live your life over through somebody else. That wasn't how it worked.

Marsh was sitting at the huge glass table in her office, staring at a document and ignoring Simon who was sitting opposite, staring at the triangle of creamy skin and the lacy edge of a white bra that showed beneath her soft, perfectly cut, red Nicole Farhi jacket.

Her office looked like a set from *Interiors* magazine. It was huge and elegant with a wall of windows that overlooked the Rotunda at the Mansion House. There was a pale silk carpet and a red leather Eames chair and a grey velvet sofa under a floating glass shelf with a display of glass and metal advertising awards. The roses, now arranged in a massive pewter vase, were, Saffy saw, the same Pantone reference as her suit.

Marsh looked up at Saffy. 'You're late,' she said, 'again.'

Simon didn't bother hiding a smile. Technically, as they were both Senior Account Executives, Saffy and Simon were equals. But, frankly, she couldn't see the point of him and he seemed to think that his job description included undermining her.

It didn't help that Marsh kept hinting that, one of these days, she would take an executive role and make one of them Managing Director. Or that she played them off against one another, making them compete for every scrap of business.

Saffy could wipe the floor with Simon when it came to writing a brief but he was smooth and handsome and sporty and he could wipe the floor right back when it came to flirting with female clients and letting male clients beat him at golf. She was slightly ahead of him in billings but, with Simon, you had to keep looking over your shoulder.

Saffy sat down as far away from him as possible. 'Sorry, Marsh.'

'Do you know what "punctual" means?'

Saffy did. But she was guessing Marsh didn't want the Oxford English definition.

Marsh flicked her glossy hair and gave a tight smile. 'Punctual means never having to say you're sorry.'

Marsh didn't do late or mistakes or shoddy or second-rate.

She did perfect. Personally, professionally and (as far as Saffy could tell after three years) perpetually. She was one of a handful of women who'd made it to the very top of the advertising ladder and the only one to have done it in five-inch heels with Teri Hatcher's hair, Victoria Beckham's body and Carrie Bradshaw's wardrobe.

She could have passed for thirty but Ciara swore that she had seen her passport and that she was forty-five. But then Ciara also swore that Marsh drank the blood of teenage boys, never wore underwear and kept a piece of chamois leather in her drawer and used it to polish her shins.

Saffy slid into a chair beside the Media Manager. Mike was in his forties but could have passed for sixty. There was the ghost of a soup stain on his yellow tie. His slacks had ridden up and he was wearing Santa socks. In February.

Marsh stood up and opened a fresh flipchart and wrote the words 'White Feather' neatly at the top of the page. Her marker squeaked like a frightened mouse.

'This is one of our most important accounts, right? And this,' she ripped the page off, screwed it into a ball and threw it on the floor, 'is what we're doing with it.'

Saffy exhaled. This wasn't her problem. White Feather was a sanpro brand and most of its sizable budget was giveaways and money-off promotions. It was Simon's baby and his Adam's apple, she saw, was bobbing like a yo-yo.

'I ran into Dermot Clancy at a Marketing Society dinner last night.' Marsh paced around the table. Her nude leather Louboutains left a trail of tiny punch marks in the carpet. 'He is not a happy bunny.'

This was hardly news. Dermot Clancy *always* looked like an unhappy bunny. He had candyfloss white hair and pale rabbity eyes and he nibbled things. Biros, his fingernails, the corners of presentation boards. His indecision was legendary. A previous agency had nicknamed him 'Nervous Dermot'.

'Market share is down by twenty-three per cent in the last six months.' March eyeballed them, one by one. 'On. Our. Watch. And he's thinking about putting White Feather out to pitch.'

The air went dead. This wasn't just Simon's problem any

more. Losing a two-million-euro account in a recession could send Komodo to the wall. And, even if it didn't, it would start a domino effect. A big loss always shook every client's faith in an agency. Other accounts would leave 'like rats', as Greg once said, 'deserting a stinking ship'.

'Don't ask me how.' Marsh narrowed her eyes suggestively. 'I managed to persuade Dermot to give us one last chance. But I did. We have three weeks to come up with a new positioning strategy, produce concepts and get his buy-in.' She glanced at the tiny Rolex on her slender wrist. 'Three weeks! Starting. From. Now!'

She jabbed the air with her marker waiting for ideas but nobody wanted to be the first to get shot down. Saffy's stomach rumbled. Mike uncrossed his legs and his socks played a faraway snatch of 'Rudolf the Red-Nosed Reindeer'. He tried to cover it with a cough.

Simon leaned back in his chair. His body language was nonchalant but his hands were shaking and his handsome face had gone a strange shade of puce.

'I saw this coming, Marsh. I've been trying to persuade Dermot to increase his budget since January. The competition has really upped its game. The product is tired. The packaging needs an update and we need a better class of giveaway – an item with a really high perceived value, like a DVD, one that really ties in with the brand.'

Marsh wrote the letters 'DVD' on the flipchart. 'Like?'

'Like, I don't know, say, *28 Days*, which would be perfect because the average woman's cycle is, you know, twenty-eight days.'

'Is that the one with Sandra Bullock as the alcoholic?' Mike asked. 'That's a brilliant film.'

'Yeah.' Simon nodded. 'And we could follow it up with *28 Days Later*.'

'Possibly the best zombie movie ever made!' Mike shook his head in awe.

Marsh held up a hand on which she was wearing the output of a small diamond mine. 'You think a woman who is having *her period* has the remotest interest in alcoholics and zombies?' She turned to Saffy. 'Save me from these idiots.'

'This isn't about budget or packaging,' Saffy said. 'The reason market share is nose-diving is that White Feather is stuck in the Dark Ages. Look at the endline: "Your secret is safe with us." It's just so patronising.'

'It's a perfectly good endline,' Simon snorted. 'It's been around for fifty years.'

'Exactly. And if we were trying to attract the Stepford Wives it would be fine. But we're not. We're trying to attract young, sexy, confident twenty-first-century women. And they're not remotely interested in cheap on-pack giveaways. They're looking for an emotional connection. I think we should go back with a total re-brand on TV, online, cinema and outdoor.'

'Right,' Simon chipped in. 'What the world really needs is another clichéd sanpro ad with a girl in white jeans doing handstands and being pulled along on roller-skates by a Great Dane.'

'No,' Saffy shot back, 'what the world needs, what Nervous Dermot needs, is a challenging campaign idea that redefines the whole sector.'

'And I suppose you have that idea?' Simon said.

Saffy did. And though she felt a bit guilty for kicking him when he was down, this was her chance to air it. It had come to her when she was looking through a photography book in Ant and Vicky's office a few weeks back. She had stopped at a Duane Michals shot of a handsome, half-dressed male angel sitting on a bed watching a woman sleeping. It was just so right. But if she got carried away, she'd blow it. Marsh had to think it was her idea, too.

'Well, I don't have it all worked out, and I'm just thinking out loud here, but the brand essence is "protection" and the product has wings. What about, I don't know,' she gave it a few moments to make it look as if this was occurring to her for the first time, 'what about a White Feather angel who protects women at the time of the month when they're feeling most vulnerable?'

'An angel,' Marsh said thoughtfully. 'A *winged protector*.'

Saffy nodded. That was exactly where she was leading her.

'That's it! There's the brand personality. Women will love it! And we can bring it alive with guerrilla marketing. Have a guy dressed as an angel giving out samples at Dart stations.'

Marsh snapped the lid back on the marker. 'Now this,' she said, 'is why I pay you that ridiculously large salary. Simon, get all the White Feather research over to Saffy. You're off the account unless she asks for your help, which I'm guessing she won't. Mike start digging out figures on women, sixteen to forty-five. Saffy, I'd like the brief on my desk before you leave today.'

Today? That was impossible.

'Nice one, Saffy.' Simon looked gutted but he managed a nasty little smile as they stood up to leave. 'Hope you didn't have anything special planned for Valentine's night.'

Simon had dumped three huge boxes of White Feather documents in Saffy's office. She dragged them up to the boardroom, spread them all out on the huge glass table and started to work through the research. By five, she was snowblind and the brief wasn't even halfway there. She wanted to call Greg to tell him that maybe dinner wasn't a good idea but he was shooting so she guessed he'd have his phone switched off.

She got up and poured herself a cup of coffee and then closed the blinds and flicked on the boardroom monitor to watch the Valentine's episode of *The Station*. She should have been used to seeing Greg on TV but she wasn't, not completely. Maybe it would be different when he moved over into film but the series was set in real time. It was like a parallel life that he was living, one where she didn't exist. Saffy tried not to let it get to her but she didn't like watching him in love scenes with other women, especially when they were with Mia, the female fire-fighter who had been involved with him, on and off, for nearly as long as she had.

She'd half-admitted it to Greg once but he'd gone off on a tangent about the storyline. 'I keep telling the writers they need to add more meat to the whole Mac and Mia thing, Babe. It's not going anywhere. It's just a sexual thing. They don't really have anything in common. They hardly ever talk, have you noticed that?'

She had. They were usually too busy sticking their tongues down one another's throats and peeling off one another's uniforms to say much. And for some reason, she didn't find that reassuring.

The credits ended and there he was, striding through the billowing smoke carrying a small, limp body wrapped in a blanket. It could be a dead dog or even a child but it was hard to care too much either way when the camera moved in for a close up of Mac Malone.

Journalists, especially female ones, ran out of words when they tried to describe that face. His jaw was 'strong and clean' or 'square and strong' or 'clean and strong'. His eyes were 'raisin' or 'toffee', though a woman from the *Clare Champion* had once dug deeper and came up with 'Valhrona 70 per cent'. There wasn't really anywhere to go with his hair, which was black, but sometimes 'coal' or 'tar' or 'soot' was tagged on. From time to time the debate about his height reared its head but the general consensus was that size wasn't important. Not when you looked like Greg Gleeson.

Right now his hair was damp and stuck attractively to his sweaty, sooty forehead. One sleeve of his uniform was torn off to reveal a broad shoulder and a tanned, muscled arm.

The other fire-fighters hung their heads as Mac carried the body past them. Mia put down her hose and called after him but he shook his head and kept walking.

Frank, *The Station*'s craggy fire-chief, put his arm around her. 'Let him go,' he said, stroking her mane of highly flammable-looking hair. 'He needs to be alone.' Mia bit her trembling glossy lip. 'You don't understand, Frank. Even when Mac is surrounded by people, he's always alone.' The ads came on.

The Station made *Gossip Girl* look like *The Wire*, but most people weren't looking for gritty reality. They were looking for escape and *The Station* served it up to them three times a week. It came with an out-of-control blaze, usually involving children, half-naked women or pets, but that was just a backdrop for the real drama: the latest instalment of the smouldering love triangle between Mac, Mia and the married station fire-chief, Frank. And plenty of soft-focus shots of Mac soaping the soot off his six-pack in the shower.

The weird thing was, *The Station* wouldn't exist if it weren't for Saffy. She was the one who had cast Greg in the Ice Bar ad that had inspired the entire series. *Hunky fireman rescues pretty girl and her Ice Bar from a burning building, then dumps her, steals the ice cream and eats it himself.*

Greg had nearly missed the audition. He had turned up late with a straggly goatee and the casting director had told him to go home. Saffy was outside taking a phone call when he was leaving. All the actors they'd seen were taller. A couple were better looking. But there was something about Greg, something a smitten journalist later christened 'Elvis dust', that made her stop him and send him next door to the Spar for a disposable razor. Then she had convinced the director and the creatives to hang around to get him on tape.

And, when he looked into the camera as if he would like to have sex with it soon and often and then fall asleep with his arms around it and delivered the line, 'of all the bars in all the world she had to be eating this one', nobody needed any more convincing. He was their guy.

Ice Bar sales went through the roof. Grown women vandalised bus shelters to get their hands on a poster of Greg. One of the tabloids put him on the front page with the headline, 'Sex on a Stick'. Then someone in a TV production company sat down and rushed off the pilot of a fire station drama and offered him the part of Mac Malone.

None of this surprised Saffy. What surprised her, back then, was that he remembered her name and tracked down her number and called her and kept calling her and asked her out to dinner. And that he hung on her every word. And kissed her in the restaurant, in the taxi on the way home, outside her apartment, inside her apartment and pretty much everywhere else. And that he kept asking her out until it finally sank in. He wasn't just their guy. He was *her* guy, too.

She always thought that those songs about people watching one another sleep were kind of creepy but during those first few months she woke up every other night and lay there looking at

Greg. And every time he walked into a room, she had a feeling of completion; as if he was filling a space she hadn't realised was there.

Not one but two of her exes had bought her *Men Are From Mars, Women Are From Venus*: Ciaran – the accountant with the webbed toes – and Gordon – the graphic designer who could only go to the toilet in his own apartment. Saffy was a 'problem solver' but the book explained that you weren't supposed to help men solve their problems. If you innocently recommended a reputable plastic surgeon or a couple of sessions with a hypnotherapist, they would (and did) disappear off to their caves.

Greg didn't seem to have a cave. He wanted her advice. He asked for it and then he listened to it. She helped him to find the right agent. She knew when it was time to push for a raise. She steered him away from the dodgy plot twists that *The Station* writers floated when the ratings wobbled. Having Mac cross-dress or drink-drive or turn into a coke fiend might have pulled in the ratings for a while but Saffy knew enough about marketing to know that Mac's Unique Selling Point was that he was a hero. And she made sure that Greg hung onto it.

'Couldn't have done it without you, Babe!' he said from the podium after he won his first Irish Film and Television Award, and her heart had doubled in size because she knew it was true.

The Station came back on again. Mia, a pint-sized pneumatic twenty-five-year-old that the papers like to call a 'flame-haired fox', was wriggling out of her uniform in the communal changing room. As she shrugged her jacket off to reveal a lacy balconette bra, the door swung open and Mac burst in. He had an uncanny knack of appearing whenever Mia undressed.

He turned to leave but Mia took his arm. 'Don't blame yourself, Mac. You did everything you could to save that little girl.' He pulled away and paced around the room for a while then punched a hole in a surprisingly flimsy metal locker with his fist. 'It's no use. I can't do this any more!'

'You don't get to choose to be a fire-fighter. You're born to do it. Stop listening to your fears.' Mia thumped her tiny fist against her improbably huge chest. 'Listen to your heart!'

'No, I can't do *this*. I can't keep hiding the way I feel about *you*.'

The camera moved in for a two-shot. There was a lone, wiry hair sticking out from Greg's left eyebrow like a question mark. Saffy would have to get him to have a word with Make-up. She picked up her coffee.

'Mia,' Mac said, 'will you marry me?'

Saffy took a sip full of air. The coffee that she missed splashed down the front of her shirt. *What?* This episode had been recorded sometime last week. Why hadn't Greg told her about this? She stared at the screen in disbelief as Mia's hands flew to her face.

'Oh, Mac! Do you mean it? Do you really mean it?'

Mac dropped on one knee and opened his hand. There, on his soot-stained palm was a huge diamond solitaire. The credits rolled. Apparently he did.

3

22 *Seacrest Road*
Dublin 2

14 February

Dear Ms Kemp,
You get hundreds of letters like this every day, right? And the rule is that you don't accept unsolicited manuscripts.

I know rules are rules but, like Yoda says, 'Do or do not do. There is no try.' So I'm sending you the first chunk of my novel, Doubles or Quits, *on the off chance that this is the one that slips through. The exception that proves the rule.*

Like the hundred other hopefuls that will write to you this week I always thought I had a book in me. I imagined it would be a gripping thriller played out in the back streets of Naples or a doomed love affair set against the backdrop of war-torn Iraq.

But when I sat down to write it, it turned out to be about a single dad trying to bring up his six-year-old twins against a backdrop of toddler groups, jam and pet-hair-encrusted Babygros and Barney *videos.*

So far, I have written 30,000 words and I think I have about another 60,000 to write. I'm hoping to finish it before the end of the summer so I can move on to the next one. (I'm hoping it will be a tale of a craggy, career-driven US Senator who must choose between his movie-star mistress and his career in Washington. But it is probably going to be a story about a bespectacled Fiat Punto-driving teacher with a wife and two kids who must choose between tomato or banana sandwiches in suburban Dublin.)

If you have the time, I would be very grateful if you could read just one page of Doubles or Quits *and let me know if I'm wasting my time. If I am, just send it back to me in the enclosed envelope. I can use it to line the bottom of Brendan's cage.*

Yours,
Conor Fahey

P.S. In case you're worried by the last bit, Brendan is a hamster. He's brown and white and nocturnal. A detail they neglected to mention when I bought him for my kids!

Jesus. He sounded desperate and he sounded like an idiot but he just didn't have the energy to write it again. This was his third attempt. He pressed Print, jiggled the cable and mentally crossed his fingers.

The phone rang and Jess came running out of the kitchen. Conor's desk was tucked into the alcove under the stairs and his chair was blocking her route to the phone. She caught her bare foot in the printer cable and the ancient machine, balanced on the stairs, bounced down a few steps and landed in a plastic laundry basket full of towels and toys.

'Shit! Shit! Shit!' She yanked her foot free and tried to squeeze past him. The hall was so narrow that she had to climb over his lap. He grabbed her so that she was straddling him.

'Hey, this is a nice surprise. A Valentine's lap dance!'

She was wearing one of his jumpers and a pair of ancient tracksuit bottoms. Her long blonde hair whipped across his face. It smelled faintly of coconut and strongly of fish fingers.

'Let me go!' She tried to climb over him but he held on tight. 'I've got to take that call.'

Conor buried his face in her neck and kissed the small hollow beneath her collarbone. The phone stopped ringing.

'You bastard! That was probably Miles extending my deadline.'

'Jess, when has Miles *ever* extended a deadline?'

She stopped struggling to glare at him. She had a small clump of what he hoped was Nutella caught in her fringe.

'I'm never speaking to you again,' she said.

'You're speaking to me now,' he pointed out. 'Look, it's nearly eight. It's Valentine's night. Even Miles must have somewhere to go on Valentine's night. Somebody must love him, right?'

He ran his hands down her back. She wasn't wearing a bra.

'I'll extend your deadline. You have till Monday. Okay?'

'It's *not* okay,' she complained, but her back arched and she put her arms around him.

'Are you having sex?' Lizzie was standing at the kitchen door squinting at them. She wasn't wearing her glasses. She had a half-eaten fish finger in one hand and a struggling hamster in the other.

'Put Brendan down,' Conor and Jess said, together. Lizzie dropped him and he scampered up the hall and dived into the laundry basket.

'They're not having sex.' Luke, Lizzie's twin, appeared behind her. He was wearing Lizzie's glasses. They magnified his huge blue eyes to almost scary proportions.

'The man can't put the penis in the lady when she's wearing pants.'

Sometimes, when he looked at the twins, Conor remembered that joke about the trouble with the gene pool. The one about the fact that there are no lifeguards. Luke was a miniature version of Jess, a golden boy. Straight, heavy, honey-coloured hair; deep blue, long-lashed eyes, and that olive skin that looked faintly tanned, even in winter. Lizzie had the full Fahey genetic package. His wiry black curls, his freckles, his long-sighted grey eyes, his pale Irish skin and what his mother optimistically called his 'big-boned build'.

But the funny thing was that Conor thought they were equally beautiful. In fact, apart from Jess, they were the two most beautiful people he had ever seen.

Jess climbed off his lap. 'You're right, Luke, we're *not* having sex. Daddy wouldn't let me answer the phone so we're never having sex ever again.'

Conor grabbed the back of her tracksuit bottoms as she walked away. The elastic broke and they fell around her knees.

'Mummy isn't *wearing* any pants,' Lizzie said.

People stared at Jess all the time. They couldn't help themselves. It made sense to Conor when he read that beauty was about symmetry because her face was like a perfect equation that their eyes needed to solve.

He'd catch them adding her up, feature by feature. The navy

velvet of her eyes plus the delicate line of her cheekbone multiplied by the curve of her bottom lip divided by those endless legs. Then they'd factor him into the sum and he knew they were trying to figure out how he fit in. He knew it because he was still trying to figure it out for himself.

They had met eight years ago at the *Irish Voice*. He was on News when she joined Features. She had smiled at him a couple of times in the lift but he didn't take it personally. Women who looked like that usually had a lot to smile about.

Then, one lunchtime, in the coffee shop next to the office, she had forgotten her purse so she couldn't pay for her sandwich. He paid for it and then, when she saw that he didn't have enough to pay for his own lunch, she offered to share it.

That night they shared dinner and the next morning they shared breakfast. He kept waiting for it to end. But three months later, she was still tumbling into his bed and using his toothbrush and borrowing his clothes and then she was sitting on his lap in a sunny park with a pregnancy test in her hand and it was positive.

It was the same week the paper folded. And, even though they were broke and unemployed and way too young to be starting a family, Conor felt blessed. So what if everyone who saw them together was wondering what she was doing with him? He got to wake up with her every morning. And that was all that mattered.

'You must be hung like a horse, mate,' a guy called after them once, when they were walking past a pub.

'Wow!' Jess shot right back. 'When did you find out you were psychic?'

Jess changed into a pair of jeans, pointed the twins back at their half-eaten dinners and sat down to try to finish her piece for *Looks* magazine. If she mailed it now she could pretend to Miles that there had been a problem with her dial-up internet connection. Again.

It was just a puff piece that ran in every issue, an excuse to name-check the advertisers who had booked full-page ads.

If 'you are what you wear', be oh-so-sweet and a-little-bit-naughty in a pretty daisy print underwired bra and matching thong from Cocotte, available exclusively at Brown Thomas.

Lizzie was making little mountains of salt in her tomato sauce. Luke had abandoned his fish fingers and was eating Coco Pops out of a box that had been on the table since breakfast.

'Don't do that,' Jess said at nobody in particular.

Relight his fire with the heady fragrance of a Persian Passion Candle from The Bedroom Store. Let the scent of jasmine, lily of the valley and vanilla seduce him. Then lie back and think of The Arabian Nights.

She had another seven products to get through, starting with lipgloss. It was going to be a long night.

Conor sealed the envelope, addressed it to 'Douglas, Kemp & Troy', unplugged the printer and stashed his chair, sideways, under the desk so it didn't stick out. He daydreamed about converting the attic into an office but Jess was right. Even if they had the money, which they didn't, it would be insane to spend it on improving their landlord's house. He rounded up the twins, hurried them into their coats and boots and sent Luke back into the kitchen to get Jess.

'Daddy's got something to show you.'

'Tell him to show it to someone else. I'm not interested and I'm in the middle of something.'

'Come on!' Conor called. 'This will take five minutes!'

'I don't *have* five minutes, Conor.' She rolled her eyes but she shut her laptop and went out to the hall.

'Please tell me this isn't some kind of soppy Valentine's thing. You know I hate all that Hallmark holiday crap.'

'Mummy said "crap",' Luke said.

'She said "shit" *three* times before,' Lizzie gloated. 'You weren't there.'

It was starting to rain. Jess could hear the distant, comforting honk of a foghorn from the East Wall. A fine mist blurred the ends of the terrace of tiny two-up two-downs. They could have rented a much bigger house in the suburbs but she loved living near the sea, even if they were closer to the Poolbeg power station than to Sandymount Green.

The twins ran ahead, excited, jumping on one another's shadows under the yellow streetlights. Luke switched on his torch when they came to the sandy track that led down to the sea. The ground was littered with cans and broken glass and chip bags. Jess swore when she stepped on a used condom.

'Well, this is *very* romantic.' She took Conor's arm. 'Promise me you're not going to ask me to marry you in front of the twins. Or behind them. Because the answer will be "no". You know how I feel about the M word. The answer will *always* be "no".'

'Christ! What was that?' Conor stopped suddenly.

'What?' Her eyes widened. She looked up at him.

'Shhh! There it is again!' He clutched his chest. 'It was the sound of my heart. Breaking.'

The tide was out and the vast, flat stretch of sand was deserted except for a cloud of seagulls that rose, hovered and landed again as they passed. Dublin was spread out in a long, low crescent of glittering lights that stretched from Dun Laoghaire all the way to Howth. A huge container ship, lit up like Christmas, was sailing out of the port.

The crumbling white walls of the derelict swimming pool were just ahead. Luke shone a torch up and Lizzie called out, 'Ta-dah.'

Jess covered her mouth with her hand. Three 'shits' and one 'crap' was enough for one night. The red, spray-painted heart was at least three feet wide and nearly as high. There was a wonky gold 'J' in the centre.

'I did the J,' Lizzie called. 'Daddy helped me.'

'I watched out for the Guards,' Luke said proudly.

'Conor, you're supposed to be a teacher.' Jess shook her head. 'I can't believe you're turning our kids into vandals.' But the corners of her lovely mouth were lifting.

'We love you! We love you!' Luke and Lizzie danced like mad things and the torch beam danced on the painted heart above them.

'Well, the next time, maybe you can just *say* that instead of defacing public property and—'

'Shut up,' Conor laughed. And, just in case she didn't, he shut her up with a kiss.

Whoever decided these things had decided that floodlight was the new candlelight, and 365 was lit up like a football stadium. On the way to the table, Saffy saw not just the faces but the actual pores of everyone who was anyone in Dublin. Musicians, actors, models, rugby players, TV presenters. All present, all perfectly paired.

The dishes were printed on heart-shaped balloons that bobbed near the ceiling. Everything seemed to involve 'breasts' and 'legs' and 'shoulders' and 'loins', which was pretty much the dress code for every woman in the room except Saffy. Heads swivelled as she crossed the huge white room to the table. She couldn't have stood out more if she was naked. She was wearing her pinstriped business suit and carrying her briefcase.

It had taken her till twenty to eight to finish the White Feather brief. Going home to change was out of the question. She had dashed around to Swiftclean to try to retrieve her cream dress. The lights were on but the door was locked and the man inside had ducked behind the electronic rail when she banged on the window. But she was too upset about what had happened on *The Station* to care.

It was stupid to take it personally when your boyfriend proposed to another woman on national television, she knew it was stupid. Mac was a fictional character. Mia was practically a cartoon, for God's sake.

But for some reason, seeing Greg down on one knee like that, saying those words that she had been waiting for him to say for six years, had really thrown her off balance. *What if this was as close as you're ever going to get to seeing him propose?* a little voice inside kept asking. *What if you have to watch Mac and Mia getting married and moving on with their lives while you and Greg stay stuck exactly where you are?*

She was relieved to see that Greg wasn't at the table. She needed to pull herself together before he arrived.

A waitress came and told her that Greg had called to say he was running late. She opened a bottle of champagne and poured a glass. Saffy drank it quickly and had another one. By the time she was halfway through the third, the knot of tension in her stomach was beginning to dissolve and she was starting to feel a lot better. Until the hiccups started.

The first one was so loud that the woman at the next table jumped. Saffy looked around, as though she had no idea where it had come from. When she felt the second one rushing up her windpipe she rummaged in her briefcase for her mobile and pretended to be reading a text. But it was hard to look convincing when the hiccups were jerking her around like a puppet.

'Hey! You can't do that in here.'

A tall guy with a liony tangle of red-blonde hair was leaning over the table. The accent said 'Australia'. The hair and the tan said 'surfer dude'. The white jacket and checked trousers said 'kitchen staff'.

Saffy looked up at him. 'Are you asking me to leave for hic . . . hiccupping?'

'Hiccups are allowed. Mobiles aren't. Nothing personal. Your Crazy Frog ring tone would ruin the romantic vibe.'

'My ring . . . tone is . . . hic . . . wind chimes . . . and it's on . . . hic . . . silent.'

He took her phone and switched it off. Then he pulled out a chair and sat down opposite her.

She looked around. Were staff *allowed* to act like this? 'What are you – hic – doing?'

'I'm going to *hic*-help you.'

Saffy opened her mouth to tell him she didn't need help but a rapid burst of hiccups escaped before she could say it.

'You want to sit here sounding like a drive-by shooting, be my guest.'

She shook her head.

'Okay darl'. We're going to do some yoga breathing. Take a big big one. And hold it for forty seconds.'

She managed to snatch a gasp between hiccups.

'Great. Now stick your tongue out and put your fingers in your ears.'

She was being punked. This was the only explanation. She couldn't see a film crew but there must be a hidden camera somewhere. She let her breath go. It rattled out like corn popping in a pot.

The Kitchen Guy laughed. 'Listen, I learned this technique at an ashram in India. It has an eighty per cent success rate but you have to do what you're told. Let's try again.'

Saffy took another breath, plugged her ears with her fingers and stuck her tongue out. The chatter and clatter of cutlery stopped and she was listening to the hum of her blood and the hammer of her heart.

'That's the girl.' He leaned over and pinched the tip of her nose hard. Tears shot into and then out of her eyes. It was the longest forty seconds of her life but when it was over the hiccups were gone.

She blotted her eyes with a napkin. 'Thank you, but was the nose-holding thing really necessary?'

'I could have kissed you instead.' He shrugged. 'That has a hundred per cent success rate.'

She stared at him. 'Are you on *drugs*?'

He brushed the front of his jacket. 'Nah. That's icing sugar and I'm guessing that's . . .' He leaned over and took a look at the front of her shirt. 'Coffee, right? You want a bowl of white vinegar and warm water to get it off? Or is it part of the anti-Valentine's look, which I like, by the way.'

He pulled the bottle out of the ice bucket and refilled her glass. 'It's a rare and beautiful thing for a woman not to try too hard. Specially tonight.'

'Thanks,' Saffy said coldly. 'Now I think you'd better go. Because one, I have a boyfriend and two, aren't you supposed to be in the kitchen julienning carrots instead of hitting on the customers?'

He laughed. 'I'm sorry. I'm not laughing at you, I'm laughing with you.'

'Really? Because I'm not laughing.'

'Yeah, I can see that. You look kinda stroppy. Is it cos he's late?'

'He's not late. He's delayed.'

'But you're pissed off with him, right? Didn't get the dozen red today then?'

'No. I mean, yes, I did get flowers.' Saffy tried to catch the maître d's eye. Why wasn't someone *removing* this guy?

'Look, can you please—'

''Fraid not. House policy. We can't have beautiful women in,' he looked her up and down, 'revealing *business attire* sitting on their own on Valentine's night. It's too distracting for all the blokes.'

He topped up her glass again. 'So how long have you and this *boyfriend* been together?'

Saffy stared into the middle distance. Maybe if she ignored him he'd go away.

'A year? Two? Five?'

'None of your business.'

'So, more than five, then.' He leaned forward and took her hand. 'And he still hasn't put a rock on it. That explains the strop. Like a friend of mine once said, relationships are like sharks: they have to keep moving or they die in the water. I'm Doug, by the way. And you are . . . ?'

'Going to start screaming,' she said, 'unless you let go of my hand right now.'

He shrugged and stood up just as she heard a whisper run around the room. She looked over her shoulder and saw Greg by the door. He was wearing dark jeans and a very tight white T-shirt with a black leather jacket. He looked like a French movie star from the fifties.

Somebody started clapping and then a ripple of applause broke out and a few people stood up to shake his hand as he made his way to the table.

'Congratulations, Gleeson!' A tipsy newsreader called. 'You're finally making an honest woman out of Mia!'

There was some cheering and wolf-whistling.

'Thanks, guys. It's a tough job but someone had to do it!' Greg made a mock bow. 'Sorry I'm late, Babe.' He was holding a wilting red rose wrapped in plastic.

'Is that for me? Thank you! It's lovely,' Saffy gushed for Kitchen Guy's benefit.

'What? No, I got it from a fan. She tailed my taxi on a pushbike all the way from the studio. Bless!'

He handed the rose to Kitchen Guy. 'Bin this, will you, dude?' He picked up the champagne bottle, which was nearly empty. 'And bring another bottle of that. Hey.' He kissed Saffy and sat down. 'Look at you! You look . . .' He took in her suit.

'Like I came straight from work?' she said. 'I know. I did. I meant to go home and get changed but I ran out of time.'

'You look hot.'

'Really?'

'Yeah. You look hot *as in hot* but also, you know, *hot*. Why don't you take your jacket off?'

'I can't. I spilled coffee on my shirt.'

'You have one of those days?'

'Mmmm.' She didn't want to talk about her mother's tantrum in BTs or the marathon White Feather work session or the humiliating hiccups or the arrogant Aussie guy or the fact that Greg hadn't even bothered telling her that Mac was going to propose on *The Station*. And she especially didn't want to talk about the way he'd acted when everyone congratulated him just now. As if Mia were real and she was the fictional character.

Greg craned his neck to read a balloon menu. 'Man, I'm starving. The catering van was a heart attack on wheels, today, so I've been saving myself. Okay . . . I'm going to have the scallops to start. Then I'm going to have the chicken . . . shit!'

'Oh my God! You're Greg Gleeson.' A very busty girl in a low-cut purple dress was bearing down on the table.

Why did they always say this, Saffy wondered, as if he didn't know who he was?

The girl was twiddling her long flicky hair and batting her eyelashes, pretending to be nervous like they always did.

'I hope I'm not interrupting. I told my boyfriend it was you but he wouldn't believe me! I had to come over and tell you that I cried for a full hour when you proposed to Mia. I'm so happy for both of you! And I love your work. And I think you're going to be the next Colin Farrell. And I'd do *anything* for an autograph.' She was acting as if Saffy was invisible. They always did this, too.

Greg switched on a high-beam, Mac Malone grin. 'No problem. What's your name, Babe?'

'Oh my God!' She added a full body wiggle to the hair flicking. 'Your voice is even sexier in real life than it is on TV. It's Madeline. But make it to Maddy.' She leaned right over so that her massive breasts were grazing his ear. 'That's Maddy with a double "D".'

Women like Maddy with a double 'D' were the reason Greg had come ninth in The Goss 'Sexiest Man of the Year Awards' and been voted Ireland's fifth most eligible man in a Weekend Trend survey. And Saffy was the one who usually reminded him to be pleasant to them. But right now she was having trouble remembering that.

'Thank you!' Maddy with a double 'D' took the napkin Greg had autographed and bent down again to kiss his cheek. 'I meant what I said,' Saffy heard her whisper. 'I'd do *absolutely anything*.'

'Would you leave us alone?' Saffy said quietly. 'Would you go back to your own table and hit on your own boyfriend?'

Greg raised an eyebrow after she'd left. 'You okay?'

She wasn't but this wasn't the time and it definitely wasn't the place to talk about it. Rule Number One of going out with a famous person was always look happy in public.

She managed to pull a smile out of somewhere. 'I'm just a bit tired. I'll be fine in a minute.'

Greg had meant it when he said he was hungry. He polished off his scallops then hers. He had his chicken breast and her duck leg and both of their vegetable medleys. Saffy couldn't eat a thing. She was doing her best not to let it, but watching him sitting there scoffing everything as if there was nothing wrong irritated her. She hadn't *told* him that there was anything wrong but, after six years, surely he should know.

When the second bottle of champagne was nearly empty, a commercials producer who always called Saffy 'Sandy' sent over another one with a note that said, 'Congrats, Mac!' And Saffy had to pretend to toast him when really she would have liked to pour it down the back of his neck. But after another glass, she was glad of it.

The champagne was taking the edge off her mood. She was feeling pleasantly drunk. She could nod and half-listen while Greg talked about an indie director who was planning to re-make *The Quiet Man* as an anime feature and a blogger who claimed to have been Brad Pitt's bottom double in *Benjamin Button* and a rumour that the continuity girl on *The Station* was a hermaphrodite.

'. . . an electrician heard the sound of a Philishave coming from one of the cubicles in the honey wagon the other day,' he was saying now. 'I wouldn't have bought it but the dude recorded it on his phone.'

A waiter came to clear their plates. 'Hey, what's on your mind? You're very quiet, Babe.' Greg grinned. 'You're wondering what I'm going to ask you, aren't you?'

She hadn't been but she was now.

The waiter reappeared. 'Dessert?'

Saffy shook her head.

'Come on, Saff, you've got to have the pineapple and passion fruit soufflé.'

Something about the way Greg said it and the way he was smiling at her seemed loaded. 'It's amazing. If you don't, you'll regret it.'

Her heart began to bump around under her shirt. Everything seemed to slow down. She caught her breath. *Regret it*. Could that mean what she thought it meant?

'Okay, I will.' Hiding a ring in a dessert was *exactly* the kind of thing Greg would do. 'I mean I will *have* it, not regret it!'

Saffy sectioned her soufflé surgically with her spoon while Greg demolished his double chocolate and nut bombe and told her a long story about some Hollywood legend. She was too distracted to take in which one.

'. . . is at a press conference in China and a journo's mobile rings and he gets really pissed off . . .'

She pushed the pineapple pieces to one side and made a little pile of the passion fruit seeds.

'. . . and then it rings again and the dude walks over and grabs it and says "*Konnichiwa*". It's the Chinese for "hello".'

Saffy thought it might be the Japanese, actually, but that wasn't important right now. She spooned the soufflé into her mouth, rinsing each mouthful carefully with sips of champagne. Her tongue darted round her mouth, searching for metal.

'And the journalists are falling around laughing and he says into the phone, "This is the second-highest-paid actor on the planet. How are you doing? We're just having a press conference here. Is there something I can do for you?"'

There was nothing in her mouth except air.

'Greg, what is it you want to ask me?' It wasn't Saffy talking. She wasn't normally this impatient. This was the champagne, and the champagne couldn't wait any longer.

He licked some chocolate off his spoon, grinned and put it down. Then he reached into the inside pocket of his leather jacket and took out his iPhone. She was expecting a jeweller's box but maybe he had taken a picture of a ring. Maybe he'd taken pictures of a whole lot of rings so she could choose one.

He opened his Gmail and began to read: '*Sending this from terrace of Chateau Marmont in LA.*'

Was this a speech? Or maybe a poem? Saffy's mind charged ahead, fuelled by the champagne, trying to find words that rhymed with LA. *Today? Hurray? Crochet? Bidet?*

'*Just out of meeting with casting agent Gordon Driers. He wants to test you for lead in Western based on Elmore Leonard story. Top Irish actor was pencilled but has dropped out due to creative differences.*' He flashed her a knowing look. 'I'm thinking Colin Farrell. Or maybe Cillian Murphy.'

Saffy was confused. Why was he reading her a work email? And how was he going to get from this to the 'will you marry me?' bit?

'Or,' he tapped his chin, 'it could be Rhys-Myers. Apparently that dude's pretty high maintenance.' He went back to the email. '*Screen test should be around mid-May. Driers will cover flight and suite at Chateau Marmont. Happy days. Lauren.*'

He beamed at her. 'This is it, Babe. If I get this part, I'm all over Hollywood. I *really will be* the next Colin Farrell.'

She got it. He wanted her to come to LA and then they'd go to Vegas and get married in one of those tacky little wedding chapels.

'Saffy,' he took her hand and looked at her, 'I don't want to do this on my own.'

She put her other hand to her mouth. This was it.

'Will you come with me? I'll pay for your flight. You'll have to take a week or ten days off work but think about it. LA, baby! Hanging at the Chateau. Mulholland Drive. Venice Beach. I've Googled this Driers guy. He's buddies with everyone. We can party with Penelope Cruz and Nicole Kidman and Tom Cruise. Though probably not at the same time.'

He saw her face. 'What's the matter?'

'Nothing's the matter really . . .' *Please*. She begged the champagne. *Please. Don't. Say. Anything.*

He looked confused. 'This is what we've been waiting for. This is Hollywood! I thought you'd be happy.'

'And I thought,' the champagne said, before she could stop it, 'that you were going to ask me to marry you.'

'Marry you?' He was amazed. He was genuinely amazed. 'But . . .'

'But what?'

She was having what Greg called an 'outer body experience', floating above the table, looking down, but with no control over what the champagne was going to say next.

'We've been together longer than Mac and Mia, Greg. And we're real people. Why would that be such a crazy thing to do?'

'Saffy, take a chill pill, would you? And keep the volume down. You're making a scene. Look, is this about having kids? Because, like I've said before, I'm not sure I'm ever going to do that. I'm basically just a big kid myself and—'

'It's not about kids. You know I don't want kids. But I *do* want a family. I want *us* to be a family. And it's been six years, Greg. And we're not *going* anywhere.'

'We're going to LA.' He grinned. 'Aren't we?'

She stared at him. He was a bit fuzzy at the edges but he was serious.

'No, we're not. I'm not going anywhere with you unless you want to take things to the next stage.'

What was the champagne saying? And how could she make it shut up?

'Look, you can't just hit me with this like a bowl from the blue, Babe.' He shook his head. 'This is big stuff. We need to talk it through and—'

'A *bolt* from the blue? I've been waiting for you to ask me to marry me for *years*, Greg, *years and years and years*. And I'm sorry but I can't go on like this, pretending that it doesn't matter.' It was true, she realised. And it was a relief to say it. 'Relationships are like sharks: they have to keep moving or they die.'

Greg smiled nervously and tried to take her hand. 'Who says? Maybe they're like sloths. Sloths hardly move and they can live till they're in their forties. I saw a documentary on Discovery.'

The couple at the next table had stopped spoon-feeding one another dessert to watch them. A woman in a green dress leaned around a pillar to take a picture with her camera phone.

Saffy pulled her hand away. 'I'm sorry, but I'm not a sluth.' The champagne was running out of steam now, or bubbles, or whatever made it bolshy. 'I mean a slosh. And I don't want to be forty and shingle.' She reached for her glass but Greg got there first.

'I've had enough,' he said in a furious whisper. 'And so have you. We're out of here. I'm taking you home.' He looked around for a waiter.

'I'm not going home with you!' Saffy told Greg and the fifteen other people who appeared to be listening in. 'I'm not going anywhere with you unless you want to marry me.'

'Don't twist my words, Saffy. I never said I wouldn't marry you.'

'Okay. Well, will you? Yes or no?'

'No.' his face was white with anger. 'I'm not playing this game.' He scribbled in the air for the bill.

The last of the champagne drained away and the 'no' hit Saffy like a wrecker ball. She was suddenly exhausted. What had she done? And what was she supposed to do next?

'Well.' She got to her feet and retrieved her briefcase. 'At least now I know where I stand.'

Remembering *how* to stand was the problem. The room was whirling and she felt as if she was trying to balance on a tangle of legs, though that was impossible because she only had two. She made a lunge for the door and managed, somehow, to reach it without falling off her shoes.

It was lashing rain outside and people had ducked into the doorways along Parliament Street for shelter but Saffy didn't care. She half-ran as far as the Quays hoping to hail a cab but they all sailed past full.

The air was cold but her face was burning and her heart was beating double time. What had just happened back there?

She didn't get drunk in public. She didn't do scenes. She wanted to turn around and go back and make this have a different ending. But by now her hair was plastered to her head. And everybody had seen her storm out. She couldn't face the walk of shame back through the brightly lit restaurant. She needed to go home and sober up. Everything would look better in the morning.

A cab pulled over to let a couple out and she climbed inside.

'Cheer up, love,' the driver said. 'It might never happen.'

The trouble was, he was probably right.

4

Water was dripping from Greg's eyebrows. 'Happy fucking Valentine's Day.' He squelched past Conor, leaving small puddles on the carpet.

Shit! Conor thought. *He's going to see the book!* The envelope addressed to 'Douglas, Kemp & Troy' was on the desk in the alcove. He grabbed a tea towel from the laundry basket and threw it to Greg.

Then, while he was drying his hair, he slipped into the kitchen and shoved the envelope under the table. Greg followed, kicking off his sodden boots and knocking over a plastic bucket full of Lego. Tiny red and white bricks bounced around the floor.

'Man, what a mess.'

For a second, Conor thought he was talking about the chaotic kitchen with its shabby units and peeling lino but he wasn't.

'First Saffy turns up to dinner in a business suit. Then she gets completely hammered. Then she asks me to marry her. Then she storms off. Then I sit there looking like a prat on my own till they bring the bill. Then, of course, there are no fucking taxis. So I have to walk all the way here in the pouring rain.'

He gazed down at his ruined boots. 'Look at that: three hundred euro worth of Prada down the drain.'

Conor was confused. 'Saffy *proposed*?' If she had, why wasn't she here too?

'That's what I'm telling you.' Greg took off his leather jacket and hung it carefully on the back of a chair, and then he peeled off his wet T-shirt and his jeans.

'Are you sure?' The idea of cautious, careful Saffy drunk and falling on one knee in a restaurant made absolutely no sense. She was one of the most reserved people Conor knew.

'Yeah, I'm sure.' Greg was down to his white trunks. 'But hey, if you don't believe me you could always ask one of the hundred and fifty people who were videoing it on their phones.'

'But where is she now?'

Greg dabbed at his muscled six-pack with the tea towel. 'I don't know. She stormed off. On her way back to the apartment, I guess.'

'You guess? Shouldn't you call her and check? If there are no taxis out there—'

'Are you kidding me? I'm not calling her till she cools off. I've never seen her like this before. Man, she was like the Antichrist. I can't call her, anyway. My phone got wet. I think it's screwed.' He pulled it out of his jacket and put it on the radiator. 'Shit! No wonder it's freezing. Your heating's not on. Lend me your dressing gown, will you?'

'What?'

'Come on, man, I can't afford to get the flu, and you still owe me for talking Rachel Kennedy into going to that gig at Slane Castle with you.'

'That was fifteen years ago.' Conor handed the dressing gown over. 'And you got off with her, remember?'

'Oh yeah,' Greg nodded, 'I remember! Did I ever tell you she tracked me down on Facebook a few years back and offered to—'

'Yep,' Conor said, 'you did.' He felt ridiculous standing in his own kitchen in his boxer shorts with another man.

Greg padded over to the fridge. 'Tell me there's something to drink in here that isn't Sunny Delight.'

'Milk?'

Greg rolled his eyes. 'How can we stay up all night talking when there's nothing to drink?'

'We're not staying up all night,' Conor said. Jess was upstairs in their warm bed waiting for him.

Greg sighed. 'I give up. Just get me a duvet and I'll hit the sofa bed.'

'Shit, the kids broke it. If you're stuck I suppose Lizzie can sleep with us and I can put you in with Luke.'

'Great. Valentine's night in a bunk bed. How sexy is that? And speaking of sexy . . .' He grinned and pointed at Conor's chest. 'I'm loving the moobs.'

*

'What's he doing here?' Jess was sitting up in bed, her hair falling over her bare shoulders. She scrabbled for the alarm clock on the bedside table, knocking it over and toppling a stack of old newspapers and the pile of seashells the twins had collected on the beach. Conor's favourite grey T-shirt was underneath. He'd given it up for lost.

'They've had a row. He says she asked him to marry her and he turned her down.'

Jess tried to open the drawer of her bedside table but it was jammed shut. 'Right. In his dreams,' she snorted. 'Is he drunk or something?'

'No. But he says Saffy is. She caused a scene in a restaurant and stormed off home.'

'Saffy? A scene? That's kind of oxymoronic. And there's only *one* moron in that relationship. I'd better call her.'

She switched on the lamp and rummaged in her bag for her phone. 'God, it's after one. I'll call her in the morning. But if she's gone back to Trump Towers, what's he doing here?'

'Trump Towers' was Jess's nickname for Saffy and Greg's apartment. The living room was only fractionally smaller than their entire house.

'He wants to give her time to cool down. He needs a place to stay.'

Jess groaned. 'What's wrong with a hotel?'

'It's Valentine's night, Jess. He'll never get a room.'

'Okay, fine. As long as he doesn't keep you up. You were in the middle of something.' Jess pulled the covers back. 'Remember?'

He did remember. And if he hadn't, seeing her naked would have reminded him.

'Jess, the thing is the sofa bed's banjaxed and I've had to put Greg in with Luke. So we've got company.'

Lizzie appeared at the door in her Dora the Explorer pyjamas. She blinked sleepily. She couldn't see a thing without her glasses. Conor scooped her up and carried her over to the bed.

'Daddy's friend Greg is in our room,' she yawned, 'and he says Brendan is a "disgusting little rat".'

Jess put her arms out and gathered her daughter in, tucking

the covers around her. She gave Conor a dirty look. 'Yeah? Well, it takes one to know one.'

Saffy woke up face down on the bed. Her head was so sore that her hair hurt. She was wearing her bra, her trousers and one shoe. There was something stuck to her face. For a horrible moment, she thought it was a scab. She picked at it and a dried rose petal floated down and landed on her lap. A man in the penthouse opposite was standing at his balcony eating cereal and watching her like television. He waved his spoon.

She dived for the floor, found the remote control and managed to close the blinds then she crawled back onto the bed. She lay down carefully and stared up at the huge black chandelier. She had often thought that if it fell, it could easily kill a person. She willed it to fall on her now because, if it did, she wouldn't have to deal with her hangover or her headache or what had happened last night.

She covered her eyes with her hands. Had she really asked Greg to marry her? And had he said 'no'? She called his name in a wobbly whisper and then as loudly as she could without causing her brain to short-circuit with pain. But she knew from the stillness of the apartment that he wasn't there.

She sat up again and scrabbled around for her phone. It was five past ten. There were no missed calls. No new texts. She called Greg, her heart in her dry mouth, unsure what she would say when he answered. But he didn't. It went straight to message.

Rain clattered against the floor-to-ceiling windows. The Great Dane in the apartment below was howling at the seagulls outside. The woman above was playing Abba and doing the hovering. But the silence from her mobile, the sound of Greg *not* calling her, was the loudest sound of all.

Greg was sitting at the kitchen table eating the last Petit Filou. Luke was going to freak out, Conor thought. It was the only thing he would eat in the morning.

'Man, you have no idea how close I came to topping that rodent last night,' Greg groaned. 'Does the little bollox ever sleep?'

'It's a Syrian hamster.' Lizzie slid in beside him. 'It's nocturnal. And it's not an "it"'. It's a "he". And his name is Brendan and—'

'Lighten up, Speccy Four Eyes.' He hit her on the head with a cereal box. 'And do something about that dog breath before you grow up and have to kiss someone.'

Lizzie giggled. Conor shoved some bread into the toaster for Luke, though he almost certainly wasn't going to eat it. It always amazed Conor that kids liked Greg so much, even when he was being obnoxious. It was probably because he didn't talk down to them. 'He doesn't have to,' Jess had said when he told her his theory; 'he's practically the same height.'

She came into the kitchen now wearing an old, very thread-bare bathrobe. Her hair was wet.

'If I were you,' she leaned over and stole Greg's coffee, 'I wouldn't be sitting around shooting the breeze. I'd be phoning Saffy right now to apologise because whatever happened last night, trust me, it was your fault.'

'If I were *you*.' Greg grinned. 'I wouldn't be wearing that bathrobe. I'd be taking a long, soapy shower and playing with my—'

'You see *this*.' Jess shook her head. 'This is why no woman, and especially not a smart, beautiful one like Saffy, would *ever* propose to you.' She turned to Conor. 'Remind me why you're friends with this idiot.'

Lizzie tried to put her hands over Greg's ears. 'Don't listen. She's always quite grumpy in the morning.'

He stole a piece of her toast. 'Don't worry about me, Lizzie-baby. It's all water off a dog's back.'

'Conor?' Saffy's voice was shaky. 'Greg's disappeared. I've been calling him for hours but he's got his mobile switched off and he never switches it off in case his agent rings.'

The phone cord was caught around the banisters. Conor had to half-squat to hold the receiver to his ear. 'I wouldn't worry about it, Saffy—'

'But I am worried. We went out to dinner and we . . . we left separately and he's never not come home before. I think something has happened to him.'

'Nothing's happened to him.'

'Do you think I should call the hospitals? How long do you have to wait before someone is a missing person?'

'He's not a missing person, Saffy. He's here. He stayed over.'

'Thank God! Is he okay?'

'He's fine.' Conor was getting a cramp crouching like this. He tried to untangle the cord with his free hand. 'Well, as fine as anyone who has sat through two episodes of *He-Man and the Masters of the Universe*.'

'Who-man?'

'He-Man. Prince of Eternia. Defender of the secrets of Castle Grayskull. You know, the cartoon?' Too late, Conor realised that this was probably too much information.

'He's . . . he's watching a cartoon?' Saffy had imagined Greg being mugged or stabbed or left for dead after a hit-and-run, or in a darkened room searching his soul. It hadn't occurred to her to imagine him watching children's television.

She had thought her body was too dehydrated to produce tears but she was wrong. How could he be so heartless? He must have *known* she'd be going out of her mind with worry.

'It's okay,' Conor said helplessly. He was terrible at this. This was Jess's department. 'Shhh! It's okay, really.'

Greg came out into the hall. 'Man,' he said, 'that sorceress is hot. Have you seen those skimpy little shorts? They didn't have cartoons like that when I was a kid.'

It's Saffy, Conor mouthed.

'Is she still . . . ?' Greg mimed a rapid circle with one finger by his ear.

'Greg wants a word,' Conor said, yanking at the cord so he could pass the phone to Greg. 'I'll pass him over.'

'No!' Saffy said in a strangled voice. 'Don't. I don't want to talk to him. And I don't want him to come back to the apartment. Can you tell him that when he's not too busy watching the TV? And can you ask Jess to come over? Please. Thanks Conor.' She hung up.

Greg reached for the receiver. 'You guys must be the only people on the planet who don't have a hands-free.'

*

Everything in Saffy and Greg's apartment was white or expensive or delicate or all three. It fried Jess's head just thinking about the sort of damage Luke could cause without even trying. But he had thrown a huge wobbler after Greg ate his Petit Filou and she didn't have time to talk him down so she put him on the back of her bike and hoped that Saffy would understand. She pedalled along the sea road into the horizontal rain. She probably wouldn't. People who didn't have children rarely did.

Jess could laugh now, thinking about the picnic Greg and Saffy had organised for Luke and Lizzie's second birthday, though it hadn't been funny at the time. Not unless your idea of fun was hoofing two heavy toddlers and the world's heaviest picnic hamper up a vertical track to the top of Howth Head.

The hamper, it turned out, contained two bottles of champagne, a couple of jars of duck confit, a couple of kinds of smelly cheese and a box of chocolate truffles. Nothing for the kids to eat or drink. Not even *water*. Luckily there was a bag of ice that was beginning to defrost and she had found an old packet of Tuc Crackers in the bottom of her bag.

She could still remember the look on Saffy's face when Lizzie had to use the champagne bucket as a potty. And the amazement in her voice the time Jess had turned down backstage passes for a Madonna concert. 'You're seriously going to give up on the chance to meet the most famous woman in the world to stay at home and mash carrots and change nappies?'

'Mother Teresa is the most famous woman in the world,' Jess had said. 'But I'll have a word with them about pulling their weight. There's something selfish about infants who won't pitch in and change their own nappies and mash their own carrots once in a while.'

It was kind of a miracle that Saffy and Jess were friends really and it might not have happened without Conor and Greg. But Jess was so glad it had. The whole BF thing had bypassed her at school and college. For some reason, other girls were always cagey around her, as if they thought she was going to steal their boyfriends.

Finally finding someone she could really talk to in her twenties was a lovely surprise. Even if most of their conversations turned out to be parallel monologues where she let off steam about bed-wetting and lice treatments and Saffy rattled on about advertising agency politics and Greg's career.

Saffy was a bit buttoned up and she acted as if life was an exam she was desperately trying to pass, but deep down, she was one of the sweetest people Jess had ever met and if that idiot Greg hurt a hair on her head or a ventricle in her heart, she was going to have to do a Tony Soprano on him.

Luke snuggled closer into her back. 'Where are we going?' he said into her ear. His voice was still a bit husky from tears but she could tell that the worst of his upset was over. 'The rain got into my memory and I forgot.'

'We're going to have a sleepover with Saffy and we have to cheer her up, okay?' she told him, over her shoulder.

'Okay. I brought a DVD and I could show her my verruca. I thought it went away but it didn't.'

She had to stand up on the pedals to get up the hill at Irishtown. She loved the way the extra forty-six and a half pounds of her son made every muscle in her calves work harder.

'Does Saffy like hamsters?' Luke enquired when they were in the smoked-glass lift on the way up to the apartment.

'I'm not sure but probably not . . .' Jess spotted something moving in his coat pocket.

You were never going to have a perfect life with children, she thought, zipping Brendan into her bag. But you sure as hell weren't going to have a dull one.

Saffy was dressed in cream jeans and a pale sweater but she looked, Jess thought, as if she had been recently exhumed.

'I brought *SpongeBob*!' Luke darted past her and scooted along the vast polished maple floor in his Heelies. He fed the DVD into the player, flicked on the TV, jumped down onto the white leather sunken sofa and began to bounce.

Jess followed Saffy into the bedroom. White blinds were drawn over the floor-to-ceiling windows. The carpet was white. The white walls were bare except for a huge off-white painting. It was like something from an episode of *Star Trek*. You expected a woman in flowing robes to wander out and say,

'Welcome to our planet. There is no need for war or strife here. All is harmony.'

Except all wasn't harmony. Saffy had climbed into bed, fully dressed, and was curled up, sobbing into the duvet. Jess took off her shoes and climbed in too.

'It's okay,' she said, though she wasn't sure that it was. She had only seen Saffy crying twice in six years. Once when she caught her finger on a car door and once when they all watched the DVD of *Titanic*. She had never seen her crying properly.

'You poor thing. Tell me what happened?' She stroked Saffy's back. Her jumper was incredibly soft. Saffy's clothes always looked ordinary but they usually turned out to be made from something incredibly expensive that came from silkworms or the underbellies of goats. 'Come on, just let it all out.'

Saffy took a shuddering breath. 'I don't really know what happened. I think something kind of flipped inside me when I saw him proposing on *The Station*. And I tried not to let it get to me. I mean, it's just a stupid soap opera. I know that. But then, when Greg came into the restaurant and everyone started congratulating him about getting engaged to Mia, it was just too much.'

'What? Who's Mia?' Jess didn't watch *The Station*.

'She's a character in the series. She's awful. She has masses of red hair and plastic nails and horrible implants, but for some reason it's okay for him to marry *her* but not me.'

'Come on, Saffy,' Jess said gently. 'She's a fictional character. And Greg doesn't write *The Station*. I'm sure it wasn't his idea . . .'

'But it was so humiliating, Jess. And now I'm supposed to watch the whole country cheering him on while he goes through some huge TV wedding and I can't. Not while I'm stuck in this relationship limbo where he can leave me for someone else anytime.'

'But why would he leave you? He loves you, you know that.'

'If he loved me, he would have come home last night.' Saffy's voice was ragged. 'He would have called me to tell me where he was. Instead of lying around watching cartoons while I was imagining him on life support. Why is he treating me like this? What's wrong with him?'

Where was Jess supposed to begin? Greg was vain and self-obsessed and vertically challenged. He had his chest waxed and used moisturiser and hair serum and words like 'dude' and 'chillax'. But she seemed to be the only woman in Ireland who didn't find him irresistible.

'I think I asked him to marry me.' Saffy covered her face with her hands. 'And I think he said "no". Actually, what he said when I, you know, kind of asked him was: "No, I'm not playing this game." Do you think that was an actual "no"?'

'I think this is all a misunderstanding,' Jess said. 'I'm sure it is.'

'But you didn't see his face, Jess, when I said it. He looked horrified.'

Jess would have liked to have seen his face and slapped it hard. Greg should be down on his hands and knees thanking whatever it was he worshipped (apart from himself) that a woman like Saffy wanted him at all.

'Maybe you just caught him off guard,' she said tactfully.

'After *six* years? Come on, Jess. *Six* years.'

'Conor and I have been together for *eight* years. And I have a heart attack every time he brings marriage up. Some people have a problem with the whole institution, Saffy.'

Saffy should have known there was no point in talking to Jess about this. She was the last person in the world who would understand. Women weren't flinging themselves at Conor on a daily basis. She wasn't looking into a near future where she'd have to compete with Kate Beckinsale or Natalie Portman. And, even if she did, she'd probably win. When you were as beautiful as Jess, you didn't have to be insecure.

'You know it's possible,' she was saying now, 'to want to spend the rest of your life with someone without wanting to sign it over to them.'

'But why would I *want* to spend the rest of my life with someone who can just walk out any time?'

'Look,' Jess said gently, 'maybe this isn't really about you and Greg. Maybe it's about your parents. And maybe you think things would have turned out differently if they had married, but you'll never know that. If your dad was going to walk, he'd probably have walked anyway. A marriage licence wouldn't have made any difference.'

Her *dad*. People who had *dads* used that word when they talked about hers. They didn't understand that you weren't born with a *dad*. You were born with a father. He *became* your dad over hundreds of thousands of tiny moments. The bedtime stories he told you. The songs he sang in the car. The water wings he blew up. The money the Tooth Fairy left under your pillow. The pictures of you he kept in his wallet.

'Well, apparently it did make a difference.' She closed her eyes so she wouldn't have to look at Jess. 'Because when my *father* walked out on us he walked back to his *wife.*'

Luke appeared at the door and came over to the bed, dragging his Heelies along the carpet. 'Look, a madpie.' He pointed at a seagull perched on the rail of the balcony outside the window. 'Can I give him some of my crisps?' Jess put her finger over her lips and shook her head.

Luke blinked his huge blue eyes solemnly. He looked, she thought, like an angel. Why couldn't Saffy open her eyes and see that this was what it was all about?

Standing in a church or register office in a big white meringue repeating a lot of legal mumbo-jumbo didn't mean anything. Wanting children together, staying together to raise them, that was what love was really about. That was what it was *for*.

'Is she asleep?' Luke whispered, leaning over to have a look at Saffy. 'Can I give *her* some of my crisps?'

'No, I'm not asleep.' Saffy opened her eyes. His breath smelled of Sour Cream & Onion and it was turning her stomach.

'She's just sad,' Jess said.

'Why is she sad?'

'Well, you know I explained that boys and girls are different?' Jess wiped his mouth with her sleeve. 'Sometimes that can make things pretty difficult.'

'Boys have a penis,' Luke explained to Saffy. 'Girls have a china.'

'Vagina, Luke,' Jess corrected. 'But that's usually the cause of the problem.' She smiled wryly at Saffy. 'Out of the mouths of babes . . .'

Out of the mouth of babes comes what? Saffy wanted to howl. *Apart from drool and half-eaten Pringles?*

'Oh man!' Greg shook his head. 'What is that?'

'Spagausages.' Conor put the saucepan on the table. 'Spaghetti, cocktail sausages, tomato ketchup, spoon of sugar. Lizzie's favourite.'

Lizzie peered at it. A lick of steam fogged up her glasses. 'I don't like it. It's moving like worms.'

Conor shoved a sausage in his mouth to stop himself snapping at her. She'd been siding with Greg all day. He had sprawled on the sofa reading the papers and channel-hopping while she had hovered around him, bringing him eggcups of orange squash and plates of pretend cake and agreeing with everything he said. Apparently, she, too, thought that Sean Penn was overrated, that the GI Diet was a load of bollocks and that Elizabeth Hurley was kind of fit for an old bird.

'Come on, Lizzie, you love this,' he coaxed.

'Why don't I order us all a Japanese takeout?' Greg said. 'Which do you prefer, Liz, sushi or sashimi?'

Lizzie stroked her Rainbow Pastel Unicorn and considered this. 'Probably, I like them both.'

When it arrived, he put her in charge of the wasabe and set it all out on plates. She listened patiently while he explained what everything was and then she said, 'Can I try the raw eel one, please?' This was the child who had to be bribed to finish a fish finger.

But Conor didn't know why he was surprised. His best friend had always had this effect on girls. If he hadn't, they probably wouldn't be friends at all.

Conor had always been bigger than the other kids but, in the last year of junior school, the Fahey DNA had kicked in and he'd grown eleven inches and put on thirty pounds. Boys who had been his friends since Infants started to call him 'Bigfoot'. But at least he still had friends.

At secondary school he was an outsider from the start. He

never had a chance to make friends. He was taller and bigger than every boy in the year and it didn't take a member of Junior Mensa to change his name from 'Fahey' to 'Fatty'. He could have stood up for himself but he didn't have the heart for fighting. He kept his head down and pretended he was a loner, and he would have been if it hadn't been for Greg.

Even from a distance, Conor could see that things were even worse for Greg. He was the smallest boy in his year and the best-looking boy in the entire school. In week one, the other boys called him 'Titch'. But, by week two, when a girl who was three years older than him had been suspended for writing his name 114 times down the leg of a desk, they were calling him 'Bitch'.

The more the girls chased after Greg the more the boys chased him too. They were always cornering him and giving him a bloody nose or sticking his head down the toilet.

One afternoon, when Conor was sitting in the bike shed eating his lunch on his own, Greg was chased and pushed up against the bike railings by a boy called Johnny Kelly. Kelly looked around for a weapon and the nearest thing to hand was Conor's tuna and sweetcorn bap. He grabbed it and mashed it into Greg's face. Before he realised what he was doing, Conor had knocked Kelly over and was sitting on his chest surrounded by a circle of cheering boys. It was the violence against his sandwich as much as the attack on Greg that had set him off, but twenty years later, here they were, still friends.

Greg was what Conor's dad liked to call 'up himself', and he was possibly the least self-aware person on the planet, but Conor loved him. You couldn't not, because he could be the most kind-hearted, charming, generous person when he wanted to be.

He spoiled the kids at Christmas and he was always inviting Conor and Jess to openings and offering them tickets to plays and gigs and asking them out to restaurants they couldn't possibly afford. He'd offered to pay for babysitters and, when they wouldn't accept, he and Saffy got into the habit of showing up every few weeks with exotic takeaways and expensive wine.

Once in a while, they'd all go out to Sunday lunch at the little Italian place in Sandycove that Jess liked because the food was cheap and the waiters made a fuss of the kids. Probably, Conor knew, because, after he'd insisted on paying the bill, Greg left them an enormous tip.

He would never forget the time he'd asked Greg for a loan of five hundred euro when the twins were small. Even with his salary from St Peter's and Jess's occasional freelance cheque they were struggling to make the rent every month and he had no idea how they were going to afford two new car seats and get through Christmas. He hadn't told Jess; she'd had enough to worry about.

Greg had written him a cheque. But when Conor went to cash it, he thought there had been a mistake. It wasn't for five hundred euro. It was for five grand.

'Don't sweat it, man,' Greg had said when he called him. 'I'm raking it in with this *Station* gig. And I don't want it back, okay? We're mates. That's what mates are for.'

Conor looked at him now, sprawled on the sofa watching *Lock, Stock and Two Smoking Barrels* while Lizzie took pictures of him with his iPhone.

'Man, this is horseshit,' he was telling her. 'Me and your dad are going to come up with a much better idea for a gangster movie. And then he's going to write it and I'm going to play the lead and probably direct it.'

'Can I be in it?'

Greg shrugged. 'If you're pretty enough. If not, you can produce it.'

Conor and Greg had been meeting every other week since college to work on a screenplay. They had written a few short treatments back in the early days but now it was really just an excuse to drink a few pints and play pool. Nothing had ever come of it and nothing ever would.

Conor stood up to clear the dishes away. Greg would freak if he found out that Conor was working on a novel behind his back. But the chances of anyone at Douglas, Kemp & Troy even reading his letter were slim to nothing, so it wasn't very likely that he'd ever know.

*

Conor carried Lizzie upstairs and helped her out of her clothes and into her pyjamas.

'Is Greg married?'

'No, he's not. But he's going out with Saffy, you know that.'

'Can I marry him, when I grow up?'

Conor looked down at her little worried face. He had a sudden flash of the woman she'd be someday and his heart clenched like a fist. He didn't think he could bear it if anyone hurt her.

'Let's talk about that closer to the time, okay?'

When he came back downstairs, Greg was talking on the phone. He went into the kitchen and closed the door to give him some privacy.

He was sitting at the table marking essays when Greg came back to get a beer.

'So how did that go? Have you and Saffy sorted things out?'

Greg pulled the tab on a can of Sapporo. 'I wasn't talking to Saffy. That was Lauren, my agent, calling from LA.'

'Well, I think you should call Saffy,' Conor said, 'sooner rather than later because—'

'She said *not* to call her.' Greg picked one of the sausages out of the saucepan Conor had left on the cooker and ate it. 'Remember? Or go back to the apartment. And that's pretty much what Lauren said too.'

'I'm sure she didn't mean it, Greg.'

In fact, Lauren had been pretty clear. 'Getting married at this point would be bloody professional hara-kiri,' she'd said. 'I've packaged you out here as young, hot and single, Greg, and a wedding ring is not part of that package.'

Greg guessed Harry Kiri was some failed actor or something, but he didn't want to ask.

'You think Angelina isn't putting pressure on Brad?' Lauren asked. 'You think that Gisele didn't try this on with Leonardo? You think some woman didn't try to poison that pot-bellied pig of George Clooney's so she could drag him up the aisle?

'You want to put the kibosh on Hollywood, go right ahead. Get married. But if you don't, if you want me to get your foot in the door, you're going to have to play hardball with Saffy. Check into a hotel. Call her bluff. Let her come running back to you and then take her back on your terms.'

'Greg.' Conor was frowning. 'If you're not going back to the apartment what are you going to do?'

'Don't worry, man. One more night in rodent central is about as much as I can take. I'll be out of your hair tomorrow. You can get Jess to pack a bag for me at the apartment and I'll check into a hotel. Lauren says Saffy needs a couple of days on her own to get a few things straight.'

'What things?'

'One,' Greg said, 'she can't flip out like that in public ever again. And two, this whole marriage thing is a deal-breaker. I'm not saying I won't marry her at some point but it's got to be on my terms. Those were Lauren's exact words.'

'Lauren is a businesswoman not a psychotherapist. She's not interested in your happiness she's only interested in her commission . . .'

Greg crumpled the Sapporo can and tossed it into a black refuse sack that they used as a bin.

'Cheers for the concern, but I've made up my mind and I'm not changing it. I have to focus on my career. Hollywood is only going to come knocking once and I'm not going to let anything screw it up. Okay?'

'Okay.' Conor went back to an essay by a second-year who was under the impression that Ireland's most important writer had been called 'James Joys'. If Saffy hadn't come along, Greg wouldn't have a career to focus on – he'd still be living in that crummy bedsit in Ranelagh, auditioning for crappy commercials and Christmas pantos and going out with airheads.

Maybe Greg didn't remember how empty his life had been before he met Saffy. Maybe he had forgotten just how good for him she had been. And maybe he thought that getting a part in a movie would be the best thing that could ever happen to him.

But he was wrong. The best thing had already happened. And it was Saffy. It scared Conor to watch his friend going out on a limb like this and risking losing her. She was smart and pretty and kind and she loved him. Jesus! She must really, really love him to want to spend the rest of her life with him. Because Conor loved him, but another twenty-four hours was about as much as he could take.

Saffy spent most of Sunday watching *Grey's Anatomy* on her laptop in bed and pretending not to cry while Jess and Luke tiptoed around and played silent Snap, which involved waving your arms around and doing a dance when you got a matching pair.

At about five Conor called to ask Jess to ask her to pack a bag for Greg. When Jess told her what she was doing, Saffy locked herself in the bathroom. She couldn't bear to watch. She ran the shower and all the taps but she could still hear Jess moving around the walk-in wardrobe next door.

She sat on the side of the bath while the room filled up with steam. Forty-eight hours ago she had been planning a Valentine's night in with Greg. And, until a few minutes ago, she had still thought that somehow everything would be okay. That he would walk back in and they'd talk and sort it all out. When she had told him not to come back to the apartment she hadn't meant *indefinitely*.

Was this what he wanted? To move out for good? Was this how six whole years of her life were going to end? Not with a bang but with the sound of drawers opening and closing and a six-year-old singing the theme song from 'Spongebob Squarepants'.

5

It was still dark when Jess heard Conor getting up. She was glad to be back in her own bed. She hadn't slept properly at Saffy's. She never slept properly unless Conor was there.

'The good news is, there are clean shirts,' she said sleepily. 'The bad news is they're not ironed.'

He leaned over the bed and nuzzled her ear. 'I'm already dressed.'

'That's a shame,' she stretched, 'because I've missed you.'

He pulled away. 'Don't tempt me. I've got to go or we'll all be late for school. I forgot to tell you, Lizzie must have let Brendan out of his cage again. Can you check to see if he's gone up the back of the fridge? And can you post my manuscript? It's in the kitchen.'

'Sure.' Jess snuggled back down for a five-minute doze.

'And no sneaky peeking.' He kissed her shoulder.

'Not even a single page?'

'Nope. Not till I know it's worth reading.'

When Jess woke again, it was nearly eleven. She pulled on a pair of jeans and one of Conor's fleeces and dragged herself downstairs. She had meant to finish her 'Looks' piece over the weekend but she had spent most of the time over at Saffy's and she hadn't had a chance.

Conor had left an envelope on a chair with a ten euro note. The breakfast dishes were still on the kitchen table. She pushed them out of the way and set up her laptop. There was an email from Miles saying she had better have her copy in for twelve. 'Or,' it ended, 'bloody else.'

She poured herself a cup of cold coffee, found her notes under a pile of newspapers and got started.

Make every day Bloomsday with freeze-dried flower heads from Wild Things on Dame Street. String them on threads to make delicate garlands to drape over the bedposts.

Somewhere, James Joyce was revolving in his grave. At five to twelve, she had only one more piece to go. She nibbled on a jammy toast crust and begged her soggy brain to cooperate. Something was tickling her lip and then it was inside her mouth, moving around. It felt like, it *was*, a fly.

She spat it out and jumped up, knocking over the coffee pot and a jar of jam that smashed into a hundred sticky splinters. She grabbed her laptop and turned it upside down. A few drops of coffee dripped from between the keys, but it seemed to have escaped the worst. Which was more than she could say for Conor's envelope. She grabbed a tea towel and managed to soak up the coffee. The jam was a trickier. It had already collected a blur of Brendan's fur from the kitchen floor. Jess swore as she tried to dab it off. She didn't have time for this. She had – oh God – she had exactly two minutes before her deadline. She stuffed the envelope into her bag. It would have to do.

Conor tried to tune out the sound of thirty sniggering seventeen-year-olds so he could listen to Graham Turvey murdering his favourite Patrick Kavanagh poem.

'The b . . . bicyles go b . . . by in twos and threes.'

Christ. This was painful. 'Take your time,' Conor said gently.

'There's a . . . d . . . dance at Billy Brennan's b . . . b . . . barn tonight.'

The heat was up way too high but if Conor took off his jumper, the class would switch their attention from Graham's stutter to the damp patches under his arms. They weren't remotely interested in poetry. All they really wanted to do was get off with one another. The funny thing was, that was what Kavanagh's poem was about, *teenagers getting off with one another*. But Conor was never going to get them to listen for long enough to explain that.

Graham Turvey stammered his way through to the end, closed his book and collapsed back down into his seat as if he'd been shot.

'Any thoughts on what Kavanagh is writing about here?' Conor asked the room.

Nobody was listening. Ronan O'Keefe and Ciaran Gorman

were flicking pellets of chewed paper at one another. Alan MacSorely was drawing a cow wearing three bras on the cover of his folder. Lesley Duffy was poking her tongue around her mouth, apparently imitating an act of oral sex for Wayne Cross.

'The bicycles go by in twos and threes . . .' Conor had to raise his voice to be heard. 'What does that suggest, Ronan?'

'They didn't have cars, Mr Fahey.'

'Quiet, everybody!' Conor read from his notes. 'That nobody is alone except the poet seems to suggest that he is aloof. Not part of things. Would you agree, Cross?'

Wayne stopped leering at Lesley and swivelled his shaved head in Conor's direction. 'A loof? Yeah, Mr Fatty,' a slow grin spread across his meaty face, 'I would.'

What were you supposed to do when they called you names to your face? Conor hadn't known when he was a child and he didn't know now. The roots of his hair fizzed with shame, but all he could do was pretend he hadn't heard.

Greg lay back in the big leather chair and closed his eyes.

'So, did you hear about Damo from BoyzRus? There's a rumour that he might be joining the cast!' Cathy, the head of Make-up, leaned over to look at his face. Her breath had an eggy whiff. 'Jesus, Greg! What happened to your skin?'

Two broken nights of sleep in a bunk bed was what had happened to it. Followed by another night in an overheated hotel listening to buses thundering by at five-minute intervals. Greg had eventually managed to get to sleep after a half a dozen vodka miniatures from the minibar but spirits played havoc with his pores.

He wondered just how long it was going to take Saffy to get this whole wedding idea out of her system so he could move back into the apartment. If it was more than another couple of days he might have to look into a non-surgical face lift.

Cathy began rubbing concealer under his eyes with her fingers. 'Come back after you're through shooting your first scene,' she said, 'and I'll make you my emergency oatmeal and honey facemask.'

'Can you use a brush?' Greg winced. 'Your fingers smell of

bacon. And can you please have a mint or something? Your breath is killing me here.'

'Sure.' Cathy flushed. 'Give me a minute. I'll just go and scrub up and nip to the dental hygienist.' She stalked off.

Greg sat up. The hairdressers were looking at him like he'd murdered Bambi. 'Oh come on, what's her problem?' He didn't need this right now.

Tanya, the junior make-up girl, came over. She was a Kelly Osborne look-alike who dyed the tips of her black fringe a different colour every day. Everyone knew she had huge crush on Greg.

'You just lie back,' she warmed a tube of Elizabeth Arden 8 Hour Cream with a hair dryer 'and let me, like, hydrate you.' She would be quite pretty, Greg thought, if she lost a few pounds. He wondered if she had any spare tights.

The Station was shot on location in a vast, draughty warehouse that was impossible to heat. The crew all wore beanie hats and fleeces beneath their baggy jeans and puffa jackets but Greg was nearly always wet or half naked, often both. The writers took every opportunity to showcase his legendary six-pack.

He had once been hospitalised with pleurisy after twenty-four takes of a scene in the communal shower where Dan, one of the other fire-fighters, broke down and admitted he had feelings for Mac. Pretty much every episode involved striding around bare-chested. The cast weren't allowed to wear thermals so Greg had started wearing tights under his uniform trousers. He couldn't ask Conor to get Jess to pick up a pair when she was packing his bag at the apartment. And if he asked Wardrobe, he'd never live it down.

He was already freezing his ass off and he still had his clothes on. His first scene was the second part of the scuffle with Frank, the fire-chief, after he finds out that Mac has proposed to Mia. There was going to be a lot of rolling around on the wet floor and he was going to have his jacket torn off.

Tanya was patting fake blood very gently onto his cheekbone with her fingertips. He opened his eyes. 'Listen, do you have any spare tights?' he whispered.

'No. But I could ask Wardrobe,' Tanya whispered back.

Greg shook his head.

She smiled. 'I might have some hold-ups in my bag.'

'Can I have them?'

She peeped at him coyly through the pink tips of her fringe. 'Course you can. You can have anything you want.'

The poster on Ant's door said: *I'm busy right now. Can I ignore you some other time?*

Ant was out but Vicky was hunched over her screen wearing what looked like a rumpled blue nightie. She had a different shade of sparkly nail varnish on each finger.

'Saffy, what happened to your eyes? Are you okay?'

Saffy had used nearly half a tube of Touche Eclat trying to disguise the fact that she'd been crying on and off for nearly sixty hours. But obviously it wasn't enough. 'Hay fever.'

Vicky shook her head. 'Is there hay? Already? That was quick. Did you and Greg have the most romantic weekend ever?'

Saffy made a non-committal sound. As long as she didn't talk about what had happened, she could pretend to herself that it hadn't. 'What about you and Josh?'

'I booked that lovely Moroccan place for a romantic Valentine's dinner but Little Lindsay had an asthma attack, and he had to cancel.'

Vicky's boyfriend Josh was divorced and 'Little Lindsay' was eighteen but Josh was always having to run back to his ex-wife's to sort out some domestic crisis or other.

'Oh, well,' Vicky said with a sigh, 'I suppose we can't all have Mr Perfect Greg Gleeson, can we?'

'No.' Saffy bit her lip and stared at the new Avondale layouts Vicky had pinned to the wall. 'We can't.'

This time, the posters were bang on brief. Jesus was nowhere to be seen. He'd been replaced with kitsch chocolate-box pictures. A fluffy kitten in a pink, heart-shaped basket had the line: *Think this is cheesy? Wait till you try our Mature Cheddar.* Two cute puppies were tangled in a ball of pink wool above a line that said: *Think this is cheesy? Wait till you try our Smoked Applewood.*

'Ant's thinking of chat-up lines for the radio,' Vicky said.

'Really cheesy ones like: "Are you wearing window cleaner? Because I can see myself in your pants." We were wondering if we could get Greg to do the voiceover. He'd be perfect. I know we probably can't afford him but maybe you could persuade him to . . .'

Before Saffy had to explain that this wasn't such a great idea Ciara popped her head around the door. 'What's a conniption?'

'I think it's a kind of hysterical fit,' Vicky said.

'I thought so. Can you come out to reception, Saffy? Because there's a woman out there in amazing boots who says she's your mother and I think she's having one.'

Jill had never been to Komodo before. In fact, she'd only been to the apartment a handful of times. Saffy had never encouraged her because, if she did, she'd be there 24/7. Now she was pacing back and forth dramatically in front of the automatic doors, which were hissing open and closed as she passed. What was she doing here? Saffy had seen her three days ago and she wasn't planning to see her again till the middle of March.

Seeing her here now gave her the same feeling of claustrophobia she'd had as a teenager when Jill would come into her room, perch on the end of the bed and say 'tell me everything', and Saffy, who knew she was supposed to talk about boys and crushes and clothes, would pretend to misunderstand and talk about homework and exams because the only thing she really wanted to tell her mother was to go away.

Jill stopped pacing and gave her a quick, fierce hug. 'Sadbh, I'm so sorry. I feel just terrible.' She didn't look terrible at all. She just looked overdressed. Her hair was in a kind of snood thing and she was wearing a nipped-in military coat and thigh-high black riding boots. All she was missing was a horse.

Saffy put her hand on her mother's back and began to move her towards the doors. She couldn't cope with this, not today.

'Look, I don't know what this is about, Mum, but I'm sorry, it's going to have to wait till later because I'm right in the middle of a presentation.'

Jill dug in her heels. 'I can't stop thinking about that terrible thing I said to you on Friday.' She peeled off one of her black leather gloves and dabbed at her eyes with a tissue. 'About you waking up when you were fifty, on your own . . .'

'It doesn't matter, really; I'd forgotten all about it.'

'It's so like you to put on a brave face, but you don't have to do that. I know you're devastated. I'm here if you need to talk.'

The arrogance of it. What her mother thought or said had lost the power to devastate Saffy long ago. She rolled her eyes. 'There's nothing to talk *about*.'

Jill pulled a newspaper out of her bag. 'But, Sadbh, what about this?'

Half of the front page of the paper was taken up with a picture that had been taken at a movie premiere. Greg was wearing a tuxedo and pointing a finger and thumb at the camera like a gun. Saffy was doing that head-ducking thing she always had to do when they were photographed together and she was wearing a green satin Whistles dress that she now realised made her look like a courgette.

The dress was bad but the headline was worse: VALENTINE'S DAY WASH-OUT FOR SOAP STAR GREG.

Last Friday, *The Station*'s heart-throb Mac Malone popped the question to flame-haired fox Mia. But later that night, in exclusive Dublin eatery 365, the course of true love did not run smooth for actor Greg Gleeson and real-life partner Sadbh Martin.

While the couple tucked into a €70-a-head champagne dinner, a blazing row broke out. The hunky TV fireman did his best to quench it but Ms Martin stunned fellow diners by storming out, leaving Gleeson to finish his bubbly alone.

A source close to the couple revealed that Gleeson, who is tipped to play the lead in a Hollywood movie later this year, has moved out of their luxury penthouse apartment and into a suite at the sumptuous Davison Hotel.

It looks like one of showbiz's longest-running relationships has gone down in flames.

Saffy pushed the paper away and, with the last of the strength she had been holding onto to get her through the day, she propelled her mother out through the glass doors and onto Schoolhouse Lane. A man was unstrapping a toddler from a pushchair outside the car park. A courier was leaning on his pushbike on the corner smoking a cigarette.

'I'm going to go now, Mum.' Saffy's voice was steady but the corners of her mouth were trembling. 'And I don't want you to ring me or call around, okay?'

'But, Sadbh, I want to help. I can move in to the apartment for a few days. Or sit Greg down and give him a talking to or—'

'I don't want help. I want you to back off!' Saffy's voice had risen to a kind of shouty wail. The man and the courier both turned to stare. 'Why can't you understand that? For once in your life why can't you just back off and leave me alone!'

She turned and hurried back into the building, crossed the reception area and disappeared through a door on the other side.

The man and the toddler went into the car park. The courier flicked his cigarette away and climbed onto his bike and cycled off towards Kildare Street and Jill was the only one left. She was still staring at the glass doors, unable to move, her face red, as if she had been slapped.

They had been so close when Sadbh was small. Then, when she hit fourteen, she had stuck a 'keep out' sign on her bedroom door. And she had been wearing an invisible sign on her forehead ever since.

Jill had tried to ignore it because she wasn't just her mother; she was the only family Sadbh had. But maybe it was time she finally got the message. Her daughter was never going to let her back in.

'Thanks for meeting me.' Saffy sat down beside Greg. He looked gorgeous but grim, she thought – sort of puffy and gaunt at the same time. For some reason, that made her feel better because maybe it meant that he missed her.

They were sitting on a bench in the Iveagh Gardens. Greg hoped it was clean. Jess had only packed two pairs of jeans for him and the other pair had been mislaid in the hotel laundry. Saffy had wanted to meet him in St Stephen's Green but that was way too public and he didn't want to be papped in case his agent saw the picture.

When he'd rung Lauren to tell her that Saffy had texted she

had sort of cackled and instructed him to let her stew for a couple of days before texting back.

'And, Greg,' she had warned him, 'this is a negotiation. So listen to your Auntie Lauren. You have to know, going in, that you probably won't get what you want in round one. If you want her to come running back to you, you have to play it cool. Listen to what she has to say. Ignore it. Set out your terms. Walk away. Trust me. It works every time. Do you think you can do that?'

Greg thought he could but he couldn't wait a few days to do it. He had texted Saffy the minute Lauren had hung up. It was good to see her. She looked so sweet and serious in her navy coat, with her hair pulled back into a pony-tail. He wanted to wrap his arms around her but he managed to stop himself. He was supposed to be playing it cool.

'Listen, I'm sorry about what happened on Friday,' she was saying nervously. 'I shouldn't have lost it in front of all those people like that.'

'No,' Greg said. He stared off at a statue of topless girl kneeling in front of the fountain and tried to look stern. Why was it art when it was stuck on a bit of grass, he wondered, but porn when it was on the flat-screen in his hotel room?

Saffy waited to see if *he'd* say he was sorry for something but he didn't. This wasn't going as well as she'd hoped. Maybe it wasn't such a good idea. But after another two days of silence, she'd felt that one of them had to break the deadlock. It should have been Greg. She had called him after she'd walked out of the restaurant. It was his turn to call *her*. But what did it matter whose turn it was?

Seeing the article in the paper with the end of their relationship spelled out in black and white had made her realise that one of them had to salvage things before it got any worse, while there was still time.

Jess had been right. It was probably just a misunderstanding. She had gone over the conversation a hundred times in her head. He hadn't said he didn't want to marry her. Well, he hadn't used those exact words. He had said, *No, I'm not going to play this game.* She was reacting to something he hadn't said.

When she texted him to suggest meeting, he'd texted right back, which was a good sign. And he had been really pleased to see her; she'd seen it in his eyes. But now he wouldn't look at her. He kept glaring around at things – trees and statues and fountains.

'Greg, I think both of us overreacted on Friday and I know you weren't expecting me to,' she took a breath, 'you know, bring up getting married. And that's understandable because we've never talked about it before. But now that it's out there do you think that maybe it's time?'

Greg stared hard at a sausage dog taking a shit on the gravel. 'Time to talk about it?'

'Well, yes, of course to talk about it.' She looked at him hopefully. 'But, you know, also time to *do* it . . .'

Greg replayed Lauren's instructions in his head. Cool. Listen. Ignore. State terms. Walk away. He shook his head. 'No.'

Saffy stared at him. Had she just asked him to marry her again? And had he just said 'no'?

'You have to give up on this whole wedding thing, Babe. I can't take you back if you don't.'

He took a quick peek at her. Her face was always pale but it was paler now than he'd ever seen it.

'You can't take *me* back? Is that what you think this is, Greg, *me* asking *you* to take me back?'

'Well, yeah.' He gazed down at his boots. He'd replaced the pair he'd ruined on Valentine's night but he much preferred the old ones.

'My God, you are so deluded. This is me trying to save our relationship for *us*. For both of us. Because I thought it mattered to *both of us*.' She stood up. 'I'm tired of trying. If you want to try you know where I am, but I'm done.' She walked away.

Greg watched her go. Apart from the fact that *he* was supposed to be walking away, he thought, it had gone pretty much to plan. Now all he had to do was wait for her to come running back.

6

It was a week since the Iveagh Gardens. A week without a single text message or call from Greg. A week since Saffy had bothered putting in her contact lenses or doing a workout or washing a dish or eating anything that didn't involve fat, chocolate, alcohol or (in the case of the entire M & S trifle) all three. This morning she'd had a chocolate Creme Egg and a packet of Smoky Bacon Hula Hoops for breakfast. The weird thing was, she'd lost seven pounds.

For the first time in as long as she could remember, she weighed less than nine stone.

Yesterday, Vicky had tried to make her eat half of her tofu sandwich in the kitchen at lunchtime. 'You need to eat some proper food, Saffy. You're fading away.'

'Every cloud has a silver lining.' Ciara had looked at her approvingly. 'I think you look fabulous. If you keep this up you're going to turn into a really skinny person like Keira Knightley.'

Except, Saffy had thought bitterly, without Keira Knightley's face or hair or clothes or life.

'Every cloud has a silver lining,' Saffy had heard Ant mutter to Vicky, 'except for the mushroom-shaped ones, which have a lining of Iridium & Strontium 90.'

The fact was it didn't matter how skinny she was if Greg never called her again. If all she did was work and then come home to an empty apartment and drink red wine and eat cold pizza out of the box. She used to be the kind of person who folded sheets before putting them in the laundry basket. Now she didn't even bother changing them.

The apartment was filthy. Her clothes lay where they had fallen. The kitchen sink was overflowing with dishes. She had a horrible feeling something might be living in the kitchen. Sometimes, in the middle of the night, she could hear it scratching around in there.

She had cancelled the cleaner. She could just about manage to get up and shower and dress every morning so she could keep up the pretence of coping at work but every time she came home she fell to pieces. And if someone saw her in this state, the cleaner, Jess, especially her mother, she knew she wouldn't be able to keep pretending. She would fall to pieces permanently.

She hadn't meant to but she had pushed herself and Greg over a line. They couldn't go back to the way they'd been before and they couldn't go forward unless he was going to marry her. And he wasn't. He'd made that pretty clear.

She was going to have to get over him. But how was she supposed to do that when he was everywhere she looked? She wouldn't open Facebook or look at the tabloids in case she saw his picture but she couldn't avoid him at the apartment. His ghost was in every corner. Lathering up for a shave, like a Gillette ad, and sleeping on the sofa in a pool of sunshine, like a Habitat ad, and wandering around in his underwear, like a Calvin Klein ad.

She tried to shut him out with red wine and television. Most of the time, she didn't even bother changing channels. She'd stay on the sofa till she was tired enough to crawl into bed. She sat through *An Nuacht* and *Greyhound Racing* and *Wife Swap* and *Tellybingo* . . . She didn't care what she was watching as long as she knew Greg wasn't going to appear in it.

Saffy dropped her coat on the chair, dumped her pizza box on the coffee table and went out to the kitchen to open a bottle of wine. The pizza box must have landed on the remote because when she came back into the living room, *The Station* was on and Greg's half-naked body was emerging from a steamy shower on the 63-inch flat-screen TV.

She took off her glasses and covered her eyes and rummaged for the remote under the pizza box but she couldn't help it, she had to open her fingers for one little look at his broad shoulders and his strong arms and his huge . . . rattlesnake tattoo. My God. She took her hand away from her eyes. When did Greg get a tattoo?

The camera pulled out for a wider shot and the steam cleared and she realised that it wasn't Greg at all. It was a tall blond guy; she vaguely recognised him from some boy band or other. He began to dry himself with a tiny white towel just as Mia walked in.

'Oops!' Mia pouted through about an inch of pink lip-gloss. 'I was looking for someone. You must be the new rookie.'

'I'm Finn.' He grinned and looked her up and down. 'I've been looking for someone too. But I think I just found her.'

Saffy sloshed some wine into a glass and opened the pizza box. Now that it was on she might as well keep watching. The thought of seeing Greg, even for a few seconds, was too hard to resist. It was quite a while before he appeared. There was a long scene where the new guy and Mia went into a burning convent to rescue a very young, very pretty nun. Then there was an ad break. Then there was a shorter scene where Mia ran back into the building to save an old blind nun and then Finn saved her from an exploding gas cylinder and carried her outside to the fire engine and there, finally, was Greg. He was pointing his hose at the blaze but his eyes were locked on Mia and Finn.

Saffy's heart banked like a descending plane. He looked so handsome and so familiar and . . . so incredibly angry. The camera moved in for a close-up. His jaw was clenched, a tiny blue vein she'd never noticed on his temple was throbbing weirdly and his eyes were murderous. If he was acting, he deserved an Oscar.

The pool hall was in a basement on Drury Street. It still had the same smell Greg remembered from their college days: a mushroomy fug of wet anorak and BO and stale beer and damp carpet. A grumpy girl with a lot of face piercings put down her copy of *The Bhagavadgita* and poured his pint.

After about five minutes, Conor appeared out of the murk in a navy Shetland jumper and baggy grey wool trousers and a bicycle helmet. His entire outfit, Greg thought, probably cost less than the AussieBum trunks he'd just bought in Brown Thomas.

He'd blown €3,000 on new clothes but what was he supposed to do? He'd been living in the same stuff now for nearly two weeks and he couldn't risk going back to the apartment in case he bumped into Saffy. When was she going to come running back, like Lauren said she would?

He wished she'd hurry up. He missed her, and living in the hotel was hell. He'd overdosed on porn, room service and cashew nuts. His suite was luxurious but he was getting cabin fever. Every time he went out women kept trying to hit on him. With Saffy there as a buffer, female fans could be pretty full-on; but without her around . . . man, they were a whole new ball game.

At the opening night of a really boring play at the Gate he had been pursued by a woman in a horrible leper-skin dress. When he got back to his room, he'd found a pair of panties in his jacket pocket with a mobile phone number written on them in lipstick. He'd had to wrap them in the shower cap and dump them in a litterbin the next time he went out. If he hadn't, some flunky would have found them in the waste-paper basket and flogged them to a tabloid.

Conor took off his bicycle clips and stashed his satchel under a stool. Greg had already bought him a pint. He really shouldn't drink it. He was trying to get up at five-thirty every morning to get a couple of hours' writing done before school. Jess had thought that when he sent off the first 30,000 words, he'd sit back and wait to hear from the agent. But she didn't get it. He might have to send it to ten agents before he heard anything, if he heard anything. And whatever happened, he was going to finish this book because he was certainly never going to write a movie script with Greg.

He took Syd Field's *Screenplay* out of his satchel and put it on the bar along with a notebook that he knew they wouldn't open. Conor had stopped throwing out ideas a long time ago. Greg just shot them down and, when *he* had an idea of his own, it usually turned out to belong to somebody else.

'A rich, handsome dude hires a hooker then falls for her.' (He already had, in *Pretty Woman*.) 'A Mafia dude goes into therapy.' (*Analyse This*, *Analyse That* and *The Sopranos*.) He hadn't actually come up with 'A talking pig learns to herd sheep and saves the day', but it was probably only a matter of time.

Conor waited for Greg to sign autographs for a couple of

star-struck girls in school uniforms. At least they weren't from St Peter's so he didn't have to report them.

Greg broke and potted four solids, one by one. 'You won't believe what the kids at school did today.' Conor chalked his cue. 'They rolled my bicycle wheels through dog shit. They must have carried the bike over to the park to find the shit. Dogs aren't allowed on the school grounds.'

'Maybe they carried the shit over to the bike.' Greg pocketed the white.

Conor sank three stripes and then snookered himself and hit a solid.

'Speaking of shit.' Greg leaned over to take his two shots. 'I've been dealing with a bit of it myself. This asshole Damian Doyle was supposed to be in three episodes of *The Station*, but now they're talking about writing him in to the next series. You probably never heard of him, right?'

'Damo? From BoyzRus? Are you kidding? "I'll Fly You To Forever" is the ringtone on half the mobiles I confiscate. He's huge.'

He was huge. At least six foot four. Greg had spent the whole week trying to avoid standing near him in case anyone took a picture. What the fuck was going on in Production? First they'd hit him with the proposal thing. Now that seemed to have gone cold and there was a whole new sub-plot that revolved around this meat puppet who couldn't act.

He prowled around the table. 'If he affects my storyline in any way, shape or form, I'm out of there. And it'll be "hasta manana, baby" for the whole series.'

'I think you mean "hasta la vista",' Conor said.

'Whatever.' The last two solids went down like a dream. 'But we've got to get the finger out to get this screenplay written, man, because once I get to Hollywood I'll be hanging out with all the greats. Martin Scorsese and Stanley Kubrick will be fighting over our script.'

He potted the black. Stanley Kubrick was dead but Conor didn't need to tell Greg that. What he needed to tell him was that he was happy to play pool every other week but he wasn't interested in writing a screenplay any more. He needed to come clean about the book.

But he couldn't. Greg would want to see what he'd written so far. He'd want to change it *into* a screenplay. He'd want to turn the single dad into a racing driver or a stunt pilot or a brain surgeon. Conor felt sick just thinking about it.

7

Saffy got to her desk every morning at seven. She stayed through lunch. She was the last to leave. And sometimes, when she was writing a contact report or tweaking a production schedule or working on a keynote presentation, she could forget about Greg for a whole minute. She was actually thinking about him when Marsh popped her head around the door but she pretended to be reading a research document about gender differences in new media use.

'Who's a clever girl?'

Saffy thought this might be a trick question. You never knew with Marsh. But it turned out that Avondale loved Ant and Vicky's print campaign so much that they'd found an extra three hundred thousand for a TV ad.

Marsh smiled. Her lips looked different. Or maybe it was her teeth. Or her cheeks. She was wearing flirty little brown tailored shorts and a boyfriend jacket and her long hair was loose. She was the only person Saffy knew who seemed to be ageing in reverse.

'Simon was hoping you'd fall to pieces after that messy break-up but I knew you'd play a blinder and I was right. You're like that little Duracell bunny. You keep going and going. If you keep it up, this time next year, you could be in my shoes.'

Saffy looked down at her Jimmy Choo ankle boots. They were at least two sizes too small but they were so beautiful that she was willing to give them a try.

Marsh picked up a document off the desk and scanned it, then put it down again. 'Would you like to rub his face in it over a nice long lunch to celebrate the Avondale coup? Client and agency. Thursday is good for me. I'm thinking that new place, 365.'

Saffy was thinking 'last', 'place', 'on' and 'earth', in that order. The idea of going back to 365 after what had happened there on

Valentine's night was too horrible for words. But she forced herself to say, 'Sounds good.'

Harry Burke, the MD of Avondale, was a captain of industry with a golfing tan and, as Simon put it, 'an eye for the ladies'. Ali, his Marketing Manager, was warm, blonde and middle-aged, with a drink problem and the loudest laugh Saffy had ever heard. She was already hooting before the wine had arrived.

'Holy mackerel!' She pointed to a painting of a naked woman carrying on with a fish.

Saffy bit her lip. The last time she had seen that painting, she had been sitting under it waiting for Greg to arrive.

Vicky peered at it. 'I think that's supposed to be a sardine. Or a very skinny sea bass.'

'It's a load of old cod!' Harry pronounced. And everyone, except Ant, pretended this was the funniest thing they'd ever heard. It was going to be a very, long lunch.

There was champagne, then wine, then dessert wine, and by the time Ali had ordered the second round of Bellinis, they were the only people left in the restaurant. Mike was asleep. He had loosened his tie and slipped off his shoes. His socks had matching big-toe holes. His wife, Saffy thought enviously, must have stopped seeing the holes. That's what marriage was all about. Loving somebody so much, for so long, that you didn't notice the holes any more.

Marsh was leaning against Simon in a Missoni dress, like a prettily wilting flower. 'Have you ever kissed someone so hard,' she was saying, 'that their lips bled?'

Harry had his arm around the back of Vicky's chair and was telling her that she reminded him of Kate Bush . . . 'Marvellous pair of lungs,' Saffy heard him saying. 'Lovely in a leotard.'

Ali, who was the drunkest person at the table, but only by a fraction, was talking to Ant about dead people.

'Where do they go?' She waved her arms. 'What do they do all day?'

If Ant knew the answer, he wasn't saying.

'The nuns at school used to say when people died, they could watch over you.' Ali mimed glasses and goggled at Ant. 'And I always remember that. And when I'm on the loo or in the bath I think all the dead people I know can see me.' She giggled. 'My granny and my grandad and my Uncle Finbarr and now my poor Mammy and Daddy.' Her eyes filled with sudden tears.

'You're not really an adult,' she swung around to Saffy, 'until your parents die. You could be twenty or fifty or ninety the day they're both gone, that's the day you know you are truly alone. Is you mammy dead?'

Saffy shook her head.

'You're lucky. What about your daddy?'

Saffy hesitated. She never knew what to say when people asked her that. Her father hadn't tried to contact her mother in over thirty years. If he wasn't dead, he might as well be. But even though she didn't know him and she didn't owe him anything, and even though it would have been easier to say that he *was* dead instead of admitting that she had no idea, she had never been able to do it.

'I'm not sure . . .' she began, but Ali had already forgotten the question.

'I know! Let's play porn star names!' She beamed around the table. 'Okay! You take the name of your first cuddly toy and the street where you grew up. So I'm Fluffy Stillorgan.' She hooted and pointed a wobbly finger at Ant. 'What are you?' Ant mouthed something to Vicky. It looked to Saffy like 'suicidal' or possibly 'homicidal'.

She escaped to the Ladies and locked herself into a cubicle. She put the lid down on the loo and sat with her head in her hands. The longer she stayed here, the less time she'd have to spend out there surrounded by memories of that horrible night with Greg.

She doubted whether her grandparents and her mother's brother and her father would be lining up to get into the cubicle, even if they were dead. She wasn't sure what people did beyond the grave but she was pretty sure they didn't queue up to watch her using the bathroom.

She stayed there for as long as she thought she could get away with and then got up and washed her hands and splashed her face with cold water. She had drunk far too much but you couldn't *not* drink with clients and you couldn't leave till they stood up or fell over. She wished they'd do one or the other soon. She needed to get home and get into bed and get some sleep. The White Feather pitch was at seven thirty in the morning in a field in the middle of Wicklow and she planned to get up at five to rehearse her presentation.

There was someone watching Saffy come out of the Ladies but it wasn't a dead person. It was the Kitchen Guy from Valentine's night. He was dressed in ripped jeans and a T-shirt instead of a chef's outfit but he was still wearing the same cocky smile. He put his arm up to stop her going by.

'Had any hiccups lately?'

'No, thanks. I've been hiccup-free.' Saffy looked at his arm, pointedly. It was a nice arm, tanned and muscled, with one of those annoying little threads celebrities wore around the wrist, but it was in her way.

'So, when are we going to have dinner?' He grinned.

'I don't think my boyfriend would like that.'

'Nice try, darl, but I happen to know your *boyfriend* is history. We got a name-check in the death notice: "Exclusive eatery 365". Come on. It's just dinner. What have you got to lose?'

'Let's talk about what you have to lose?' she said. 'Like your *job*.'

'You're right. We're not supposed to hit on the customers though I think my boss might make an exception in your case.' But he let her pass.

Ali had moved from porn star names to 'kiss, shag or marry'.

'I'd kish *you*,' she slurred, blowing Saffy a kiss, 'and shag Ant and marry Simon.'

'Ant is celibate,' Simon sniggered 'But that's probably not by choice.'

'You can shag *me* instead,' Harry quipped.

'I've already shagged you,' Ali hooted. 'Lots of times. You don't count.'

Marsh flashed Saffy a look. This was the kind of classified

information that could lose an account. Vicky came to the rescue.

'I'd kiss you, Harry!' she interrupted. 'And . . . and I'd . . . em . . . you know, Mike. But only if your wife was okay about it. And I'd marry, um, Ant.'

Harry looked pleased. Mike looked mortified. Ant looked surprised. With any luck, nobody would remember what Ali had said about Harry. Especially not Harry.

'I'm sorry, madam,' the sleek French woman behind the desk looked at Saffy coolly. 'There's a problem with your card.'

'Are you sure?'

'I've tried it twice.'

'I'll write a cheque.' Saffy rummaged in her bag.

'It's not our policy. I'll have to ask the owner.' She disappeared into the kitchen and returned, a few moments later, with Kitchen Guy.

'Is there a problem?' he asked her.

'I'm waiting to talk to your boss.'

'You're talking to him.' He put his hands over his ears. 'But he's not listening because he's obliged, by law, to cut up dodgy credit cards.'

'*You're* the owner! *You*?' She didn't have time to feel embarrassed about what she'd said about him being fired. 'Please don't do that. I'm here with an important client.' Marsh would freak out if there was a problem with the bill. 'I'll come back later with cash.'

The French woman produced a pair of kitchen shears.

Saffy panicked. 'Look, I'll go out for dinner with you. Here, I'll give you my phone number.'

'Don't want it. Dinner tonight.' He grinned and waved the shears. 'Or the card gets it.'

♥ 8 ♥

The 'Stilettos Strip Club' sign buckled and began to melt. A ball of fire shot up into the air. A topless girl leaned out of an upstairs window and screamed. Damo Doyle leaped out of the fire truck and ran towards the building. A chorus of screams and cheers broke out from a crowd of women who were watching the shoot.

'Cut!' The director, Roisin, turned to the First Assistant Director. 'Robert, I can see her left nipple. We need to put her into a bra or re-look at the smoke. And can you get those fans to shut up.'

'Quiet on set!' Robert roared.

The women shouted back. 'Damo! Damo! Damo!'

Damo Doyle hurried over. 'Roisin! So sorry about this. I'll go and sort them out.'

Greg watched as Damo strode towards the barrier that kept the public off the set. The crowd stopped chanting and began to sing, 'Come on, Damo, light my fire!'

The wardrobe girls came running to wrap sleeping bags around half a dozen extras in stripper shoes and tasselled bikinis. Roisin was checking video assist. She was a small, wiry woman in her thirties who was new to the series. If it wasn't for the pigtails sticking out of her beanie hat, Greg thought, she could have passed for a guy.

'Roisin, sweetheart.' He put a friendly arm around her shoulder. 'We need to talk.'

'Not a good time, Greg. I've got to get this scene in the can before lunch or we'll run into overtime.'

Greg nodded. 'That's what we need to talk about. This Doyle guy, Roisin. He's screwing with everyone's performance. How are we supposed to work under these conditions?'

She didn't even look at him. 'Okay, Robert, let's try the dry ice machine to the right of the window and see if that solves the nipple thing.'

Greg took his arm away. 'What the fuck's going on here anyway?' he said quietly. 'I'm a professional actor. I'm the highest paid person on this show. What am I doing humping hose while this white smoke does all the action stuff?' *White smoke* was fire-station talk for a newbie, which was the kind of thing a blow-in like Doyle wouldn't know. 'And what's happening to the Mac and Mia storyline? Why has it gone on ice?'

Roisin turned to face him. 'I don't tell the writers what to do, Greg. I tell the actors what to do. And I'm telling you to please go back to your first position so I can do my job.'

'Your job? If you were doing your job we would have wrapped this scene an hour ago.'

She folded her arms. 'What about *your* job, Greg? Have a look at yourself on video assist, will you? You're the reason we're on our twenty-second take. Every time you're in a shot with Damo you start twitching like Anthony Perkins in *Psycho*.'

Robert tried and failed to stifle a snort of laughter and walked away.

'My character's *supposed* to be angry with his character.' Greg didn't mean to shout; it just came out that way. 'I'm *acting*, you silly little cow.'

'Really, Greg,' Rosin said very quietly. 'And are you acting *now*?'

Whatever Doyle said to the screaming girls worked. They shut up. Greg got to stand around pointing his hose while Damo ran into the blaze and returned carrying the topless girl in his arms. Then Greg got to hump a lot of hose while Damo's character, Finn, butchered a scene that was rightfully his.

EXT. STILETTOS STRIP CLUB – DAY

FINN carries JOSIE, a topless stripper, to a safe distance from the burning club. He puts her down. Other half-naked strippers stand in shock, watching the blaze. JOSIE stands, shivering, looking at the burning building. Finn takes off his uniform jacket. He puts it around her shoulders.

79

FINN
Here. You can't stand there half-naked.

JOSIE squints at him through the smoke.

JOSIE *(sarcastically)*
I'm a stripper, sweetheart. Half-naked's my uniform.

FINN *(gruffly)*
Yeah, well. It's probably a lot warmer at work than it is out here.

JOSIE turns to look at the burning club.

JOSIE *(laughing)*
It is now.

FINN *(gently)*
It's okay to be scared.

*JOSIE'S laughter turns to tears and she breaks down.
She clings to FINN, sobbing.*

FINN *(tenderly)*
Let it all out, sweetheart. I'm not going anywhere.

Roisin did it in only one take, which Greg knew was supposed to be a dig at him.

'Dudes, I just want to say thanks for being so patient with the fans,' Damo shouted to the crew after she had called a wrap for lunch. 'And with me. I'm not just *The Station* rookie, I'm a rookie when it comes to acting too and I know it's been a pretty frustrating morning for all of you.'

The actress who played the stripper giggled and gave him a suggestive look. 'It was certainly *frustrating* for me!'

Greg heaped his plate with roast lamb and potatoes and took it up to the top deck of the catering bus. He got the feeling that everyone was giving him a wide birth and he was relieved. But, after about ten minutes, Damo Doyle appeared, making a big show of ducking his huge blond head so he didn't whack it on the ceiling.

Someone had left the *Irish Times* cryptic crossword on the

table. It was filled in except for one clue. Greg stared down at it, pretending to be lost in thought. *Seven down. A number of fingers. Five letters.*

'Hey, mind if I sit with you?' Damo put his tray on Greg's table.

Greg shrugged. He had managed to avoid talking to Damo for the last week but he supposed it had to happen sometime. Damo slid into the seat and began to fork his salad into his mouth, stopping between mouthfuls to stare at him and shake his head and grin.

'What?' Greg said after a while.

'I can't believe I'm sitting here with Greg Gleeson. Dude, I grew up watching you! Mac Malone was my total fucking hero!'

Grew up? The show had only been running for six years.

'I love your work, man. You've been a real inspiration to me.' Damo's eyes were so blue they were almost violet. He had to be wearing contacts, Greg reckoned. Really good ones. And eyelash extensions. 'You ever thought of moving over into film?'

Greg leaned back and tapped his biro on the paper. 'Matter of fact, I'm up for the lead in an Elmore Leonard movie. Should be hearing any day now.'

'Elmore Leonard!' Damo shook his head like a retriever puppy after a swim. 'That dude's got the chops.'

Right, Greg thought. *This dumb-ass hadn't a clue who Elmore Leonard was.* This was going to be fun.

'It's based on a short story . . . Jury's out on which one. I'm guessing it's "The Tonto Woman"!'

Damo nearly choked on a French bean. 'Dude, I love that story!'

'Yeah?' Greg said. *Right. Like he'd ever read it. Like he could even read!*

'I think they've made a short movie of it already, though. Haven't seen it but it was nominated for an Oscar.'

'Really?' Greg frowned.

'Man, "Tonto Woman" is incredible! The part where the husband rejects her when she comes back with the Indian tattoos on her face? That was so awesome that I wrote a song about it.' Damo closed his eyes and began to sing:

I read between the blue lines,
Yeah, I saw the signs
of why you're blue,
Ooh,
Tonto Woman, that's when I fell for you.

There was a burst of cheering from below. Somebody shouted, 'More!'

'The word is that Colin Farrell was really interested but it didn't work out,' Greg said before Damo could oblige. 'Guy's come a long way since *Ballykissangel.*'

Damo nodded. '*BallyK* was before my time. But that dude's a legend.'

Greg nodded. 'Yeah, well, we'll probably party when I'm in LA in May.'

'Hey! BoyzRus are doing a tour in the States in May. You, me and the Farreller should hook up.'

The Farreller? Who did this muppet think he was? 'Well,' Greg looked back down at the crossword again, 'Colin's a pretty busy guy.'

'I don't think he's doing much partying these days though. I heard a rumour a while back that he might be a friend of Bill's.'

'Bill Clinton?' It hadn't even occurred to Greg that he'd get to hang out with the Clintons in Hollywood. The whole thing just got better and better.

Damo laughed. ' "Friend of Bill" is code for a dude who's in AA. Anyway, all work and no play . . .'

He stood up, put his plate on his tray and glanced down at Greg's crossword. 'Seven down? A number of fingers? Five letters? That's "frost"!'

'I don't think so.'

'A number of fingers? Frost? It makes your fingers numb, get it?'

Greg had never phoned GOD before. Glen O'Donnell was the Executive Producer of *The Station* but everyone called him 'God' and it wasn't just because of his initials. GOD was all-powerful.

All of their fates were in his hands. 'Glen, how's it going? It's Greg here.'

'Greg *who*?'

'Greg Gleeson? Glen, I'm calling you directly because I have a couple of concerns about *The Station* that I'd like to share with you.'

'*Concerns?*' GOD made it sound like he'd said 'haemorrhoids'.

'Glen, you're obviously not aware of the detrimental effect that Damo Doyle is having on our shooting schedule—'

'Firstly,' GOD cut in, 'I am aware of *everything*. And secondly, *you* are obviously not aware, Greg, of the effect that Mr Doyle is having on our ratings.'

Greg's voice began to wobble. 'Look, my point is that we're probably going into overtime again for the third day in a row, which is probably costing—'

'My point, *Greg*, is that since Mr Doyle joined the series two week ago our viewing figures have gone over the half a million mark for the first time. Ever.'

Greg swallowed so hard he thought he was going to choke on his Adam's apple. That was 50,000 more than the episode where Mac had ended up on life support.

'Any more *concerns* you would like to share with me, Greg?' GOD said. 'Before you get back on set and do your *job*?'

Greg's chest was pounding. He wondered if he was having a heart attack. He read over his lines for the next scene again. He couldn't believe it. His character, Mac, was supposed to confront Damo's character, Finn, and tell him to stay away from Mia. He couldn't be one hundred per cent sure, but he had a sinking feeling that *The Station* love triangle was going to continue with Finn instead of him.

Who do you think you are? Mac was supposed to shout at Finn. *You can't just walk in here and take what's mine.*

Was this some kind of joke? Did the writers *know* how freaked out he was? Were they trying to screw with his head? Was everyone in on this? Were they all laughing at him behind his back? What was he supposed to do? He couldn't call Lauren.

It was only six a.m. in LA. Conor would be at school. He was supposed to be leaving Saffy to sweat it out. But fuck that. He had to talk to her. She would know what to do. She'd help him get his mojo back. She always did.

He called her mobile but it was switched off. Then he tried Komodo. He didn't want to get into some long thing with Ciara the receptionist, so he disguised his voice. He made it older and put on a Cork accent or maybe it was a Kerry accent. They all sounded the same to him.

'She's out to lunch,' Ciara said. 'They're all out to lunch. Greg, are you okay? You sound Jamaican and, I don't know, sort of unhinged.'

The script said that Mac and Finn were supposed to 'face one another down' outside the burned-out strip club. But this wasn't as easy as it looked on paper. When Greg tried to face Damo down, he ended up staring at his ribcage.

Roisin called a fifteen-minute break and, after a long, muttered conversation with Robert, she came out from behind the camera.

'Guys, I'm having a problem getting you both in shot,' she said quietly.

'Get him to sit down,' Greg hissed.

Rosin looked around the blocked-off street where they were shooting. 'Sit down where, exactly?'

'What about bringing a car into shot,' Damo said loudly. 'I can lean against it; that would solve the height problem.'

'We can't have a car because of continuity.' Roisin was avoiding Greg's eyes. 'Look, I'm sorry. We should have foreseen that there would be problems framing you both in medium close-up. And you will be in a lot of scenes together in the future so I'm going to organise some shoe lifts for you, Greg, but they'll take a few days, so I've talked to Wardrobe and they've come up with a short-term solution.'

As if on cue, a girl from Wardrobe ran up, panting, holding a pair of shoes.

'You're taking the piss.' Greg looked from the gold peep-toe stilettos to Roisin's face and back again.

'They're all we've got, Greg.' She bit her lip. 'They're your size. They won't be in shot, I swear.'

One of the sparks wolf-whistled.

'I know it's not ideal. But we've only got about ten minutes before we lose the light. Please . . .' Roisin put her hand on his arm. 'Please?'

Greg shook her hand away. 'Take your hands off me, you poisonous little dyke,' he shouted.

The set suddenly went very quiet.

'You wouldn't pull this on Colin Farrell.' Facing Roisin down was easy. She was at least two inches smaller than him.

'He's five foot ten,' Roisin said quietly. 'I wouldn't have to.'

'Dude's closer to five nine, if you ask me,' Damo said.

Greg turned on him. 'Nobody asked you! Fuck you!' He rounded on the crew and the extras and the fans. 'Fuck all of you!' he yelled.

Then he walked. He walked past the generator and the catering truck. A cheer went up as he passed through the barrier.

A woman in a pink puffa jacket stuck out a pen and a piece of paper for him to autograph but Greg kept walking and, as he walked, he held his breath and waited for someone to shout 'cut!' but it didn't happen.

The deal was starter, main course, dessert and no more than four hours, but Saffy was already wishing she had haggled Doug, Kitchen Guy, down to three. She had presumed that they were just going to stay in 365 but he steered her out onto Dawson Street.

'Where I'd really like to take you for your first course,' he said, 'is Vertigo on the roof of the Banyan Tree in Bangkok. Scallops with toasted hazelnut and coriander butter. A view to break your heart.' He grinned. 'That's presuming you have one.'

'I hope you're better at surfing than you are at flirting.' Saffy rolled her eyes. 'Because if you're not, you're going to make some shark very happy.'

But Doug was impervious. 'Main course would have to be Tetsuya's in Sydney. Spatchcock chicken with foie gras and gobo root, you guys call it burdock . . .'

They were passing the Sony shop on Grafton Street. He droned on but Saffy had stopped listening. She was staring at Greg. His face was in the corner of every screen in the window. A female newsreader with a stern expression and a helmet of shiny black hair was talking earnestly to camera. Greg could be dead, Saffy realised. He could have died in some tragic accident and she would be the last person to find out.

She waited to feel sad but, instead, she just felt blurry and numb. It was his fault that she had to go to dinner with this idiot. They had a joint credit card. She was pretty sure that the reason it had been rejected was because Greg had maxed it out. If he hadn't, she'd be at home now watching the news and she'd know if he was dead or not.

She tuned back into Doug FM. '. . . dessert,' he was saying. 'Decisions, decisions! Okay, my money's going on Los Caracoles in Barcelona. Best *Crema Catalana* on the planet. After a meal like that you'd be eating out of my hands.' The end of every sentence lifted slightly, so even statements sounded like questions. 'Eading oudda my hens?'

'Please tell me you don't talk with your mouth full,' Saffy said.

'Depends on what it's full of.' He flashed her that cocky grin again. This just might, Saffy realised, be the longest four hours of her life.

La Boheme was on a side street near Trinity College. The sign on the door said 'closed'. Saffy had been there on a date once with Ciaran of the webbed toes. Then it had been candlelit and full of dark corners; in daylight, it looked shabby. The carpet was worn. The velvet drapes were dusty. The tables, without their starched cloths, were just circles of chipped MDF.

Three waiters in dress shirts were playing cards in the corner by the piano. Doug pointed Saffy at a table by the window and went over to talk to them in what, even she had to concede, was pretty impressive French. He came back with a big bowl, a small knife, a chilli, a lemon and a bottle of white wine.

'No wine.' Saffy held up her hand. 'I'll just have water.' She didn't know how much she'd had to drink at lunch but she did know that it was too much.

Doug strolled over to a fishtank by the window, rolled up the sleeve of his jacket, stuck his hand in and rummaged around under a tragic-looking lobster. He pulled out a handful of oysters and brought them back, dripping, to the table.

He split the chilli and took out the seeds and rolled the lemon on the table and poked a hole in it. Then he prised open an oyster, squeezed in some juice, sprinkled a few chilli seeds onto it and handed it over.

If he thought she was going to perform some sort of erotic oyster-eating act, he could think again. She grabbed it and tossed it down. It was fleshy and wet and salty and incredibly hot. There wasn't any water so she had to gulp down the glass of wine he handed her.

'Muscadet.' Doug took a pull straight from the bottle. 'Technically a dessert wine. Bonzer with shellfish.'

She had no idea what 'bonzer' meant but it was good. She picked up a second oyster and reached for the knife.

He grinned. 'Let's shuck.'

'You have three new messages.'

'Hi, Greg, Paul Dunn here from the Irish Mail. *Heard there was a situation at* The Station *earlier. We're running a piece in tomorrow's paper. We'd like your side of the story. Call me.'*

'Oh hiya, Greg, sweetie, it's Greta from Venom Models. Just to remind you that it's our fifth birthday party in the POD tonight and you're on the VIP guest list. It's going to be a lot of fun, so don't miss it! Byeeeee!'

Please. Greg ripped the tissue paper off a bottle of Jack Daniel's with his thumbnail. *Please* let the last voicemail be Saffy. *Please.* He had been calling every hour but her phone was still switched off.

'Greg! Are you okay? Please call me and let me know! I've been so worried about you! It's chaos here. Everybody's in shock. I've got to talk to you. Oh, it's Tanya Casey, by the way. From Make-up.'

He poured some JD into a glass. He'd picked it up on the way back to the hotel. He didn't need some room-service flunkie selling a 'Greg Gleeson Drowns His Sorrows' story to a vulture like Paul Dunn. What he did need was to get pissed. Very, very pissed. But first, he needed to find out what had happened after he'd walked. 'Oh my God! Greg!' Tanya had to shout over the background noise. 'I hope it was okay to call you. I got your number off Roisin's call sheet.'

It wasn't okay. But this wasn't a good time to point that out. 'You said you had to talk to me?' he said gruffly.

'Greg, it's all, like, so crazy. The shoot's been called off. The cast and crew are here at the Gravedigger's in Glasnevin and everyone is getting really hammered and the rumours are, like, flying. You wouldn't believe what they're saying . . .'

He tried to keep his voice level. 'Try me.'

'What? I can't hear you . . . it's so noisy in here. Why don't you tell me where you are and I'll, like, come and meet you.'

Doug's accent was beginning to hurt Saffy's head and his ego appeared to be made of Teflon. He thought her put-downs were hilarious. It was exhausting. She was so tired she could barely stand by the time they left La Boheme. He took her arm and led her across four lanes of traffic to a burger joint called Nick's.

The place was packed with teenagers and a gang of English blokes on a stag party. Doug ordered two cheeseburgers, a bottle of water and two paper cups.

'I don't eat burgers and I'm not hungry.' Saffy sank into a yellow moulded plastic seat and put her elbows on the red Formica table. The black and white floor tiles moved in and out of focus like a bad optical illusion under her feet. Maybe more food was a good idea.

Doug took something out of his jacket and fumbled around under the table, then he passed her a paper cup of wine. 'Casa Santos Lima, Touriz 2002, don't shout about it or everyone will want some. Cheers!' He picked up his burger. 'So, what was your best meal ever?'

She tried a small nibble of her cheeseburger. The meat was charred. The onions were sticky and sweet. The cheese was crumbly. It was good. It was amazing, in fact. 'I don't know. Dinner in Farrington's probably, when it had two Michelin stars.'

'What did you eat?'

She tried to recall actual dishes but she couldn't. 'Lovely little slivers of things with tiny dots of other things. I don't know. It was nice.'

'You'll remember this meal for the rest of your life.' Doug licked his fingers. 'You'll remember it when you're sitting drooling in your chair in the retirement home.'

She rolled her eyes and took another bite of her burger. 'If it goes on for much longer I will be going straight *to* the retirement home.'

Doug laughed. 'Your turn to ask me a question.'

'I can see you're going to tell me anyway,' Saffy grumbled, 'so go on. What was your best meal ever?'

'2002. I was hitching from Amsterdam to Tarifa to surf. Had all my money stolen in Hamburg. Wound up working in a pickle factory. Spent my last few dollars on the campsite and lived on gherkins for a week.

'When I got paid I went to the fish market and bought a couple of kilos of king prawns, a couple of lemons, some garlic and a bottle of Riesling and a frying pan. Fried them in butter over a camping stove. Ate them with my fingers.'

Saffy swallowed the last mouthful of her burger. She couldn't resist the urge to put him down. Again. 'But you didn't *buy* any butter.'

'Yeah, I know.' He grinned. 'But there was a Swedish girl in the next tent. She had plenty.'

9

Tanya looked like she'd raided the Wardrobe department's stripper rail. She was wearing a tiny, shiny black coat over an even tinier and shinier red dress. Her white lacy ankle socks bunched over a pair of six-inch red stilettos. She stood in the doorway clutching a Hello Kitty lunchbox she was using as a handbag. 'Oh my God! This place is, like, so cool! It must cost megabucks.'

It did. Without breakfast, the suite was setting Greg back five hundred euro a night. Throw in the minibar, meals and parking and he was looking at five grand a week. He wasn't sure how much more the credit card could take.

'Oooh! There's a sound system!' She gazed at him in amazement, as if he'd personally invented hi-fi. 'And a GHD and a DVD and a teenchy, weenchy little fridge! Does it have, like, white wine and everything?'

It did. At twenty euro a pop. Greg hadn't intended offering her a drink, but she was looking at him hopefully from under her blue-tipped fringe. He opened the minibar.

She teetered off to check out the bathroom. 'Oh my God! You've got, like, huge fluffy bathrobes,' she squealed, 'tied up with *ribbons*! And loads of dinky little bottles of Aveda. I *love* Aveda.'

'You can have them.' Greg poured her a glass of wine. Just one glass and she was out of here. Fifteen minutes max.

It took two more mini bottles of Sauvignon Blanc and several hundred pointless digressions to get the full story out of Tanya. After Greg had walked, Roisin had burst into tears and Damo had taken her off to the Wardrobe bus to comfort her. Robert had called a wrap but the crew got shirty and refused to leave until they saw a revised shooting schedule.

The extras wouldn't change out of their costumes because he didn't want to pay them a full day's rate. The Damo fans turned nasty because they hadn't been given the autographs they'd been promised. Then Damo reappeared and announced that he was putting his credit card behind the bar at the Gravediggers and everyone was welcome and there was a stampede for the pub.

'You mentioned some rumours?' Greg tried to sound casual.

Tanya nodded. 'Well, Susan in Wardrobe says that GOD is going to, like, fire Roisin. And you know Eleanor, who everyone thinks is, like, a hermaphrodite, which she isn't. Well, I did her make-up last week for her sister's wedding. She told me she has, like, polycystic ovaries and that's why she has that facial hair and . . .'

Greg had to sit on his hands to stop himself grabbing her and shaking her.

'Anyway, *she* says that what happened to you was, like, destructive dismissal and because the crew are in the same union as you, they'll have to picket the set.'

'Okay.' This was good. This was very good.

Tanya's round, spidery-lashed eyes filled with tears. 'But Robert told Melissa from Catering who told Fran from Hair that the production company has called an emergency meeting with the writers to, like, kill you off.'

'To *kill me off*?'

'Well, not you: Mac Malone.'

Greg took a gulp of whisky. His brain hurt, as if this piece of information was too big to fit into his head. 'They can't kill off Mac Malone. Mac *is The Station*.'

'That's, like, what I said.' Tanya's nose began to run in sympathy with her mascara. She wiped it on the hand-painted cream velvet throw and stared at him pitifully, like a sheep with its leg stuck in a gate.

'I was, like, "No way." I couldn't, like, go on if Mac wasn't part of *The Station*. I know it sounds stupid, but I love Mac. He's the only pure, perfect person in the world. He doesn't, like, deserve to die.'

What was his legal position? Greg wondered. Was there something in his contract about this? He was getting the mother of all tension headaches. He had to get Tanya out of here so he could take it all in. But how was he going to get rid of her? He remembered the Model Agency party at the POD. He'd take her there, lose her, then come back and try to get hold of Lauren in LA.

'The Venom bash, that's, like, the party of the year! Oh my God!' Tanya stopped crying and gazed at him. 'Oh shit!' She snapped open her Hello Kitty case and took a look in a hand mirror shaped like a pair of pouting lips. 'Look at me! I can't go into a roomful of models looking like this!' She began to rummage round in a mesh make-up bag.

She had a point. Greg decided he'd get the cab to drop them at the back in case the press got a shot of them together. He fished an ice cube out of this glass and pressed it against his aching forehead.

'Oooh? Does your head hurt? Here, I'll give you a scalp massage.'

'No!' He stood up. 'It's just a headache. We can pick up some paracetamol on the way.'

She fished inside a matching Hello Kitty purse. 'I've got something that will get rid of that.'

He swallowed the tablets she gave him with a mouthful of whisky and resisted asking if she had anything that would get rid of her.

Before he was discovered in the Ice Bar TV ad, Greg was too broke to afford drugs. Once *The Station* took off, he'd been offered pretty much everything for free. But dope gave him the munchies and he had to watch his six-pack. Coke was out because he didn't need a divided septum. And everything else just seemed a bit hardcore. Plus, he was supposed to be a role model for the kids.

So he didn't know what Tanya had given him but he was beginning to think it wasn't Nurofen. A jet of liquid heat shot up his spine, surged around his head then plunged back down into his stomach. It left a deliciously weird trickling sensation in his scalp, and his eyelashes felt as if they were fizzing. He wondered for a second if he was going to be sick and then he realised that he didn't care. Being sick would be fine. It might even be fun.

'What were those tablets?' He touched Tanya's arm. Her

shiny coat felt slippery and smooth and wet. He wanted to stroke it against his cheek. 'What did I take?'

'Ecstasy.' She had a lovely voice. High and clear and sweet. He hadn't noticed it before. It was beautiful.

Everything, he realised, looking around, was beautiful. His whisky glass had a little golden halo that floated just above it. An orchid in a vase on the bedside table looked so delicious that he wondered how it would taste. There were tiny fireflies of light buzzing around the bedside lamp.

He stood up. His knees felt as they'd been by built by Porsche. He turned around to tell Tanya and caught a glimpse of his own reflection in the mirror. He stopped and stared. Jesus. He was beautiful. How come nobody had told him he was so fucking beautiful? Just looking at himself made him feel kind of gay.

Doug was one of those annoying Australians who treated the world like a giant theme park. He had been everywhere and done everything. Instructor at a diving resort in Malaysia? Check. A year cooking in a street café in Bangkok? Check. Six months busking in Argentina? Check. Tour chef with a female Japanese punk band? Check. Then, apparently, he had just woken up one morning and decided to open a restaurant in Dublin.

'So what's her name?' Nick's was growing on Saffy. The yellow plastic chair was really very comfortable; she was feeling pleasantly mellow and full. She had finished her burger. The four hours were nearly over. Soon, very soon, she would be able to go home and get into bed and sleep.

Doug took her paper cup and poured the last of the wine into it. 'Whose name?'

'I'm reading women between the lines, here. Miss Sweden. Miss Thailand. Miss Japan. I'm sure you didn't just decide to come to Dublin. There had to be a Miss Ireland involved.'

Doug shrugged. 'Her name is Connie Stokes.'

'Wow!' Connie Stokes really *had* been Miss Ireland two years ago. 'And?'

He frowned down at his empty styrofoam burger box. 'And maybe *you* can tell me something. Why is it you can tell a woman straight out that you love her but you're not ready to settle down and she says she's cool with that, then, come Christmas, she's looking at you like a half-chewed twisty when there isn't a ring under the adjectival tree?'

Was this what she had done to Greg? Looked at him like a half-chewed twisty? Whatever a half-chewed twisty was.

'She gave me an ultimatum. And a whole lot of crap about sharks and having to move forward. So I did. I moved out.'

'Well, someone married her,' she said. 'It was all over the tabloids.'

'Yep. Connie got her bloke. Hunted him down. Lassoed him. Hauled him up the aisle. Yee haw!' Doug tapped his paper cup against hers. 'Clink,' he said. 'To crappy-ever-afters. And speaking of *afters*, I hope you've left room for the legendary Doug Lee Dark Chocolate and Blood Orange Soufflé.'

'Oh, come on.' Saffy shook her head. 'We're done here. You said dinner. We've had dinner. I'm shattered. I have to be up in six hours.'

'We agreed starter, main course, dessert. A deal's a deal. My place is only around the corner.'

She checked her watch. It was a bit blurred around the edges. Everything was a bit blurred around the ages. The black and white floor tiles now appeared to be pulsating. She was, she suddenly realised, very, very drunk.

'You have exactly tifty-foo minutes,' she said. 'I mean, fifty-two minutes, and then I'm out of here. I mean there, wherever it is.'

It was Thursday night but Temple Bar was heaving. There was supposed to be a recession but crowds of people were hanging around on the pavements outside every pub, talking and laughing and smoking and flirting their heads off. In the square a tramp with an accordion was murdering 'Galway Girl'. A guy with dreadlocks was applying a henna tattoo to the stomach of a drunken man in a suit. Two women in plastic devil horns were drawing a hopscotch grid on the flagstones with lipstick. Who *were* these people? Saffy wondered. Surely *some* of them had to get up for work in the morning? Apart from the tramp who could, obviously, sleep in.

Doug's apartment was on the third floor of a block on Curved Street. The living room was a schizophrenic mash-up of *Elle Decoration* and *The Great Outdoors*. There was a red velvet sofa, a zebra-skin rug and a massive, unframed oil painting of a naked man on a huge white bed spooning a salmon.

'Self-portrait,' he said. 'Crap, isn't it? I should stick to the physical stuff.' He nodded at the rowing machine, the surfboard, the pile of free weights and the mountain bike with muddy tyres leaning against the exposed brick wall.

He pulled out a bottle of Armagnac, poured her a glass and went into the kitchen, still talking over his shoulder.

'Get that down you. According to some fourteenth-century French cardinal bloke on the label, it cures *hepatitis, gout, canker and restores the paralysed member by massage*.' He laughed. 'Not that I've actually tried that!'

Saffy stepped carefully over a dumb-bell and moved a wetsuit onto the arm of the sofa so she could sit down. Her head was throbbing. She put her glass on the floor and lay back and closed her eyes for minute.

When she opened them again, it was daylight and she wasn't on the sofa any more. She was in a bed and Doug was sleeping next to her and everything smelled of chocolate and oranges.

'Hey! I know, let's walk, like, barefoot on velvet!' The blue tips of her Tanya's fringe gave off a lighter blue haze. Greg wished he had a camera. Or some paints. He wanted to paint her so badly!

She pulled off her shoes and her ankle socks and spread the throw on the floor and stepped onto it and wiggled her toes. They looked like small, fat nuns with little nail faces. Greg giggled.

'Ooohhhhh. You've got to try this. It's, like, better than sex.'

He bent over to take off his socks, too, but a delightful dizziness hit him like a sack of feathers, knocking him to his knees. He collapsed onto his back and lay there, looking up at Tanya's plump, pale calves. Far away was the red horizon of the hem of her dress. Beyond that, he could see a distant flash of frilly white crotch. And suddenly he wasn't feeling so gay any more.

Alanis Morissette was on TV in that Kevin Smith film, the one where she played God. Greg loved that film. He wanted to turn the sound up but his arms and legs were tied to the legs of the bed with bathrobe belts. Tanya was crouched over him on all fours in her underwear with an ice cube between her teeth. She was rubbing it along his thigh, which was a bit strange but also kind of amazing.

There was a sudden, tinny burst of Justin Timberlake's 'Sexyback'. Tanya leaned over and found his iPhone on the bedside table. She put it on speaker and went back to her ice cube.

'Greg, are you there? Why am I on speakerphone?' It was Lauren.

She didn't ask him how he was, but he told her anyway.

'I'm beautiful, Lauren. Just beautiful. And so are you.'

His agent was sixty-something, overweight, with an over-active thyroid and thinning grey hair and she dressed like a bag lady. But she was beautiful. Everyone was beautiful.

'Have you lost your fucking mind, Greg? How dare you call GOD directly? How dare you storm off set and lose the production company a half-day's shooting?'

Greg vaguely remembered feeling angry about *The Station* but it was hard to feel anything other than pleasure as Tanya's head began to bob.

'Hey, Lauren, chill. It's okay.'

'It is so *not* okay, you stupid little shit! If anyone here in LA finds out about what happened today, your chances of getting the Elmore Leonard lead are zero. I've just spent the last half-hour on the phone persuading GOD not to call Harvey Weinstein and get you blacklisted.'

GOD – that was so weird because Alanis Morissette was on the TV screen right now, in a white satin trouser suit, *as* God. *And* she had sung that amazing song *about* God. Man, that was an amazing song. Greg should re-record it. And Lauren should get him a record deal. He tried to remember the words.

'Our next problem is Roisin,' Lauren was saying. 'She's threatening to sue you for outing her in the workplace. If the media get hold of this you'd better grow a beard and find a cross,

Greg, because they will crucify you. So I want you on set, on your hands and knees, when she gets there tomorrow morning. And I want you to kiss her ass like she's Kylie bloody Minogue and she's wearing those little gold shorts! Do you hear me? And do not call GOD again because—'

'What are the words of that song about God?' Greg interrupted. 'The one where he's on a bus and . . .'

'I have no fucking idea. But—'

But it was hard to hear Lauren because Tanya had started singing the Alanis song. Her voice was a bit muffled by the icecube and it was a bit flat but Greg was getting goosebumps all over his body just listening to her. Lauren should sign this girl. They could record a duet together. Like Robbie Williams and Nicole Kidman. But way better.

'Greg?' his agent was saying, 'Greg! You have to listen!'

'Sch! *You* have to listen.' Greg waited for Tanya to get to the chorus and then he joined in.

10

The taxi driver had the heating on full and the window rolled down. Icy gusts of air whipped around Saffy's face and her bare thighs stuck hotly and horribly to the warm leatherette seat. She hadn't been able to find her coat when she pulled her clothes on in the hallway of Doug's apartment. But that wasn't all she'd lost.

She had lost track of seven whole hours. One minute she was sinking into the red velvet sofa while Doug rambled on about gout and canker. The next, she was waking up naked, in his bed, with her contact lenses still in, looking at his broad, tanned back. She had absolutely no idea what had happened in between.

Her head hammered and a ribbon of nausea unfurled in her gut as she did the maths. Seven hours. That was four hundred and twenty minutes. That was, she rummaged for her phone to multiply four hundred and twenty by sixty. It was out of battery. It must have died in the night. But she didn't need a calculator to know that it was *thousands and thousands* of seconds. She put her knuckles to her mouth and pressed so hard that her top teeth began to cut into the inside of her lip. Anything could have happened. *Anything.* The only person who could tell her what *had* happened was Doug. And he was the last person on earth she wanted to ask.

The idea was to turn the White Feather pitch into an experience that Nervous Dermot would never forget. He would turn up for a breakfast meeting at Komodo and be kidnapped by Marsh, and whisked off to a field in Wicklow in a limo. After Saffy had pitched the 'Winged Protector' creative, a male model dressed as an angel would take him on a flight in a hot-air balloon that had been customised with the White Feather logo and the new strapline: *Angels are everywhere.*

It was Saffy's idea and it had seemed like a good one at the time. But that was a time when she could not have imagined turning up nearly an hour late, horribly hung-over, with the guilty horrors: no coat and unsuitable footwear.

Vicky, Nervous Dermot, Marsh and the photographer were huddled by the limo in the drizzle, drinking champagne from styrofoam cups. As Saffy made her way across the cowpat-strewn field, her high heels sinking into the soggy ground, Marsh, who had sensibly worn Prada cork platform wedges, came hurrying to meet her.

'Where the hell have you been?' She pecked Saffy hard on the cheek but this show of friendliness was purely for Nervous Dermot's benefit and the pecking actually hurt. 'You smell like a wino and you look like shit. I have been calling you since six fifteen. Why didn't you answer your phone?'

She took Saffy's arm and frog-marched her towards the limo. She was smiling but her voice wasn't.

'The only way I could stop Dermot leaving was to tell him that your father had a heart attack!'

To Saffy's surprise, tears sprang into her eyes, as if what Marsh had said might be true.

'But my father is . . . I mean . . . I don't really have a father.'

Marsh's fingers dug painfully into her arm. 'Well, you'd better make one up fast. And he'd better be in a coronary unit being prepped for a triple bypass or you won't *really* have a job either.'

Nervous Dermot's nose was twitching and his mouth was a puckered into a clenched 'O' of worry that looked like a cat's bottom.

'Dermot, I'm so sorry I'm late.' Saffy's put her hand out to shake his. 'I've just come from the . . .' Marsh glared at her, '. . . the hospital. I've been there all night with my, em . . . my . . .' Should she say 'father' or 'dad'? Which sounded more convincing?

Before she had to choose, Nervous Dermot stretched his arms out and enveloped her in a huge hug. She buried her head in the beige blur of his raincoat.

He rocked her and patted her back, as if she was a big baby and he was winding her. 'I know. I know. I went through this with my own father a few months ago. It's okay. You can cry if you want to.'

And the funny thing was, she did want to. Even though the heart attack was just a story that Marsh had made up, when she thought about losing the father she'd never even had, she wanted to lie down in the cow shit and cry till the cows came home.

Saffy had rehearsed the White Feather presentation so many times that it practically delivered itself. The fact that she was still slightly drunk probably helped. She thanked Nervous Dermot for being so patient and for giving Komodo a chance to present before he put the account out to pitch. Then she went through some figures on competitive spend. Apart from a slight slur on 'Goliaths' when she was comparing the brand to its giant competitors, it all emerged from her mouth intact.

'You probably think we're going to ask you to double your budget,' she said. And she knew from the way Nervous Dermot's nose twitched that she was right. 'Well, we're not. The reality is, you don't have the resources to outspend the competition. It's your agency's job, *our* job, to help you out-think them instead. How do we do that?'

Marsh was watching her intently, mouthing the words, like a pushy mother at a school play.

'By taking the key benefit – winged protection – and using it to create a brand personality that your target market will find irresistible. A White Feather Angel. A winged protector who is there for every woman any time she needs him.' When she got to the creative rationale, Vicky held up mood boards with beautiful black-and-white shots of male angels. Nervous Dermot frowned and nibbled the rim of his styrofoam cup anxiously but he looked, if not exactly like a happy bunny, like an interested one at least. 'Even in this day and age, every woman wants to believe in angels,' Saffy finished. 'And now she can. Because with White Feather, even though we can't always see them, angels are everywhere!'

While Nervous Dermot was distracted by the presentation, the hot-air balloon with the new logo had been inflated in the next field. At this point, a male model dressed as the White Feather angel was supposed to appear and lead Nervous Dermot over to it. But the angel was nowhere to be seen.

He was crouching under a dripping hedge with a Marlboro Light between his shaking fingers. A blond, curly wig half hid his pretty, pudgy face. He had two refuse sacks draped over his huge white wings and a loincloth clung limply to his badly fake-tanned love handles.

'I'm not going up in that thing.' He flicked his eyes at the hot-air balloon, which was looming impressively behind a stand of trees. 'You can't make me.'

But Saffy had to make him. She had already screwed up once this morning. She couldn't afford to do it again. The agency needed a photograph of Nervous Dermot and Marsh and the angel in the hot-air balloon for *Marketing Weekly*. A publicity shot would link White Feather with Komodo and the angel campaign and it would make it harder for Nervous Dermot not to buy their pitch.

'What's your name?' she asked the angel.

'Geraldo,' he said.

'That's a lovely name,' she said softly. 'Is it Spanish?'

His bottom lip trembled. 'That's me modelling name. Me real name is Patsy.'

Saffy had bought Greg a self-hypnosis CD once because he had to do a scene where Mac rescued a drowning Alsatian and he was afraid of dogs and water. She tried to remember how it went.

'Okay, Patsy. Would you like to learn a simple meditation technique to overcome your fear?'

He shook his head. 'I'm not taking medication.'

'You don't have to take anything. All you have to do is close your eyes and imagine you're in your favourite place.'

'The Dundrum Shopping Centre?'

Saffy frowned. 'Um . . . maybe somewhere out of doors, like a forest or a deserted beach.'

He screwed his eyes up tight. 'Me mam's patio.'

'Perfect. Imagine you're on your mam's patio. It's a beautiful day. You can hear birdsong. A gentle breeze ruffles your hair. The sun is warm on your skin. You're feeling very, very relaxed.'

Patsy sighed and his face softened slightly.

'Now, let your mind move through your body like a rippling stream till it finds your fear. It might be in your head or your heart. Imagine it as a liquid. What colour is it?'

'Taupe,' Patsy said. 'No, wait, eau de Nil.'

'I want you to imagine the stream of your mind unblocking your fear and dissolving it so that it flows freely down through your body, draining away through the soles of your feet—'

'And I want you to imagine,' Marsh had appeared behind her, 'that you are sleeping in a doorway. Because if you don't go up in that balloon right now, you feathery little fuck, I'll see to it, personally, that you never work in this town again.'

Patsy's eyes snapped open.

'Cut the crap,' Marsh hissed, 'and get in the basket.'

Angels were not, as it turned out, everywhere. Not in the wilds of Wicklow anyway. The limo driver was gaunt with long greasy grey hair. Perfect if Saffy needed a stand-in for the Angel of Death. Glen, the photographer, had a round face and if they lost his glasses there was a chance he might look cherubic but he couldn't be up in the balloon dressed as an angel *and* down on the ground taking the shot. That left the crew from the hot-air balloon company. One of them looked like Meatloaf and the other one was a woman in a jumpsuit who looked like a blonde Lara Croft.

Saffy saw Nervous Dermot peeking at his watch. And then, behind him, talking on a mobile phone, she saw her angel. He was in his late thirties, which was on the old side. But angels were immortal, right? His hair was brown but they could put the wig on him. He was tall, six foot two or three, and looked in pretty good shape. There was a fair chance that he'd look okay without his clothes on. As long as he didn't have any tattoos they'd be fine. She took a deep breath and marched up to him. With her heels, it was more of a hobble than an actual march but she did her best. 'Hi! I'm Saffy.'

He put his phone back into the pocket of his jacket.

'Joe.'

'Okay, Joe, how would you like to earn five hundred euro,

cash in hand, for half an hour of your time?' She attempted a bright smile then abandoned it in case her horrible hangover-breath leaked out from between her teeth.

He was way too swarthy to be properly angelic, with heavy brows and a serious five-o'clock shadow. And his nose was very slightly crooked. But it didn't matter. None of it mattered. All that mattered was persuading him to do this. He was her only hope.

'The thing is, I need an angel to go up in the balloon with my boss and my client, and the one I hired has had a panic attack so I'm looking for a stand-in. Wings and a loincloth will be provided.'

He folded his arms, looked down at her with a small quizzical smile, as if he was trying to figure out what species she was. 'Wings and a *what*?'

'A loincloth. To cover your . . .' Saffy wasn't wearing a coat. A minute ago, she had been frozen but now was starting to feel clammy. 'Your, you know,' she said in a small voice, 'loins.'

The smile broadened. 'My *loins*?'

'Six hundred euro. That's my best offer. Come on! That's thirty euro a minute!'

'It's twenty, as a matter of fact. But I'm afraid I'm going to have to turn it down.' He turned away.

'Please!' She plucked at his leather sleeve. 'You're perfect. For the job, I mean.'

'Well, hey.' His accent had a touch of American in it. 'I'm flattered – really – and I'd like to help you, Sally, but the answer is still no.'

She wanted to slap his face but her heels had sunk completely into the mud and she wasn't sure she could reach it. Before she could attempt it, Vicky came running across the field.

'Saffy! We have lift-off. Patsy says he'll go up in the balloon with Nervous Dermot but only if you go instead of Marsh. He thinks you're some kind of new-age therapist.'

Saffy turned back to Joe. '*Well, hey*.' She exaggerated his accent sarcastically. 'Looks like I don't need your help anyway!'

'Except to fly your balloon,' he said. 'I'm the pilot.'

The gas burner roared over her head as the skin of the balloon began to swell. The smell of the fuel caught in the back of Saffy's throat. Her intestines did a couple of quick flips and stretched like a waking snake. With Nervous Dermot, the pilot, Patsy and Patsy's enormous wings packed in around her, the creaking wicket basket felt horribly crowded.

'I can't do this,' she whimpered. 'Please, you have to let me out.' But nobody heard her over the roar of the burner and then it was too late. The balloon felt as if it wasn't moving but the ground seemed to be falling away below them. Nervous Dermot didn't look nervous, he looked exhilarated. 'What's moving us?' he shouted. 'I can't feel any wind.'

'That's because we're moving with it.' The pilot was fiddling with some controls.

'I've been in a chopper.' Nervous Dermot leaned right over for a good look down. 'But this is something else. It has a dream-like quality, doesn't it?'

'It's a fecking nightmare.' Patsy began flinging fistfuls of feathers over the edge of the basket and muttering through gritted teeth, 'I'm on me mam's patio. I'm on me mam's patio.'

Saffy's mouth, which had been parched since she woke up, flooded with saliva. The back of her neck prickled. She clutched the wicker rim of the basket and closed her eyes.

She felt a hand on the small of her back and a voice, close to her ear. It was the pilot. 'Sally! Open your eyes and focus on the horizon, or you're going to be . . .'

She opened her eyes but she couldn't look at the horizon. She stared down his yellow Caterpillar boots instead.

'. . . sick.'

Greg was lying naked in the bath. It was empty but be couldn't manage all that complicated stuff you were supposed to do with taps and water. He was too busy dying.

'Knock! Knock!' Tanya shuffled in, naked except for her red shoes. She yawned, gave him a yeasty kiss on the lips, perched on the toilet and began to pee noisily. 'Have you got a hurty head again? You're very pale. Want me to do your make-up before you go to the studio?'

'I'm-nog-oing . . .' Greg couldn't find whole words. Not ones he recognised, anyway. He tried to arrange the bits he could find to make sense. '. . . chew-ja-studio.'

'But you have to go. You have to kiss Roisin's ass. Your agent said, remember? And you have to be there to stop them killing Mac off.'

He tried to shake his head but it was hurty. It was very, very hurty. 'Jeycan't killim.'

'Are you, like, sure?' Tanya wiped herself and stood up. She went over to the basin but didn't wash her hands. Instead she opened a pot of Greg's Crème De La Mer moisturiser and began to dab little blobs around her eyes.

'Because I, like, read somewhere that a soap character's three times more likely to die a violent death than a real person.'

'Ifjey killim, natings would rosedive.'

Tanya leaned over and put the bath plug in and turned on the tap. 'Remember on *Corrie* when that bloke Richard killed Maxine? About, like, twenty gazillion people watched that.'

She kicked off her shoes and began to climb in on top of him. 'But if you want to pull a sickie, I can, like, pull one too.'

Saffy copied Marsh on the email to *Marketing* magazine. It had a shot of the balloon and a thirty-two-word caption that had taken her, in her hungover state, over an hour to compose.

> Dermot Clancy, Marketing Director of White Feather, and Saffy Martin of Komodo Advertising take to the air with a feathered friend to discuss a new brand campaign that could be ready for take-off.

It wasn't a great shot but the redesigned White Feather logo and the new endline were visible, Patsy looked reasonably angelic and she didn't look too green. Nervous Dermot was grinning. He had loved every moment of the balloon trip. He might have loved it less if he'd known what was on the floor of the wicker basket, but nobody except the pilot had seen Saffy being sick.

She hadn't been sick much, it was only about an eggcup full of brown stuff with little orange flecks. But still. A hot wave of shame broke over her. She had never done *anything* like that before.

Since she'd broken up with Greg, her life had turned into a car crash and the last twenty-four hours were off the scale. Drinking wine in a burger joint. Blacking out. Sleeping with a stranger. Getting sick on someone's shoes. What was happening to her? And when was it going to stop?

Conor had been up till three in the morning combing the house for Brendan. The little bugger hadn't put in an appearance for a while and it didn't look good. He should be at home right now taking the back off the fridge and having one last look in the attic and, even in the absence of a body, organising a hamster funeral, not sitting in the Davison Hotel bar drinking a three-euro-fifty latte. He wouldn't have come at all but Jess had spotted the article in the paper and he thought Greg might do something rash.

BIG MAC TO GO DOWN IN FLAMES

Sources at the nation's favourite soap The Station *today confirmed that Greg Gleeson has quit the series for good. Gleeson walked out after a disagreement with director Roisin Foley yesterday during which he outed her as gay. Mac Malone fans counting on a comeback had their hopes dashed this morning by the devastating news that the hunky fire-fighter is due to die a heroic death. trying to save a premature baby in a blaze at a hospital incubation unit. Gleeson, who has been with the series since day one, was unavailable for comment.*

The picture showed Greg as Mac, looking moody and rugged. He was bare-chested but, inexplicably, still wearing a fireman's helmet and carrying a hose.

The real Greg looked like death, Conor thought. Death with perfect teeth and great hair and expensive clothes was still Death. 'I read about the *Station* thing,' he said carefully. 'Is it written in stone?'

'It might as well be written in shit for all I care.' Greg poked at his Bloody Mary with a celery stalk. When Tanya had finally left his room the previous day, he had fallen back into bed and slept for sixteen hours straight. His body still felt poisoned when he woke up but at least his mind had cleared. *The Station* was history. He had blown it. He couldn't change the past but he wasn't going to blow the future.

'Listen, Conor, I need to give Saffy a ring.'

'I'm glad to hear it. This whole thing has gone on long enough. I've been on the point of telling you to call her all week but you said you—'

Greg groaned. 'Not a *ring*, Conor. A *ring*. A rock? Capiche? I'm going to ask her to marry me.'

Conor's face broke into a huge grin. 'What? That's brilliant!' He jumped up and began pumping Greg's hand up and down so hard that Greg was afraid he was going to cause permanent damage. Then he sat down again. He was still grinning but he looked as if he was going to cry.

'God, Gleeson! I'm feeling a bit emotional here. You really had me worried for a couple of weeks there. I thought you had bought that bullshit your agent was giving you about Hollywood. What made you change you mind?'

Greg was so shaken after the last couple of days that he almost told the truth, which was that since Saffy had walked out of 365 he felt as if someone had shoved his life into a blender and pressed 'pulse'. He wanted her back. He wanted everything to be the way it was before Valentine's night. And if he had to marry her to make that happen, he'd do it.

He jerked his shoulders into what he hoped looked like a nonchalant shrug. 'Screw Lauren. You have to pick your battles. It's not a big deal. If it makes Saffy happy then I'm game.'

'When are you going to ask her?'

'Tomorrow. But I'm in a bit of trouble, man. My card's maxed out. I'm owed two months' money from *The Station*, which I don't think they're in a hurry to pay. And I'm smashed. I blew all my savings when I bought the Merc.'

The SLK, Conor thought, that Greg hardly ever drove. It had been sitting in the underground car park of his apartment block for months because he was afraid that if he brought it out, somebody might key it.

'So.' Greg rubbed his eyes with his fingertips. He looked like he hadn't slept for days. 'You're going to have to front me the cash to buy the ring.'

Conor laughed.

'Something funny about that?' Greg squinted at him.

'Well, as you might have noticed, I'm not exactly loaded.'

'But you have a credit card, right?'

They did. Jess called it their 'crisis card'. They only used it when they really needed a dig-out. Like the time he had to get a last-minute root canal or the Christmas they had to replace the washing machine after Luke boil-washed the turkey.

'It's for emergencies, Greg.'

'This is an emergency.'

'I don't think Jess would see it that way.'

'Well, don't tell her then.'

Conor shook his head. 'I'm sorry. I'd like to help you, really. But I can't.'

Greg stared at him grimly. 'Man, I can't believe you're making me bring this up but I baled you out with five grand when you ran into trouble a few years back.'

Conor flushed. 'I wanted to pay you back but you wouldn't let me. You said—'

'I said I didn't want it back. And I meant it. I still mean it. All I want is a loan of a few grand for a couple of weeks. I'll pay you back long before your next statement arrives – Scots' honour.'

'But you said you were broke.'

'Yeah. But I'm going to sell the Merc.' Greg hadn't thought of this till right now but it was genius. He really was broke. He had been pulling down 15k a month from *The Station* but he had no idea where it had all gone.

'I've put a call in to the garage where I bought it,' he lied. 'They're giving me forty grand, which is day-night robbery, by the way. But they won't pay me till they shift it and I need to get the ring today.'

'Today? But, I don't understand.'

'What part of "to-fucking-day"—' Greg's deep voice had shot

up a half an octave and it had a tremble that Conor had never heard before '—do you not understand?'

Saffy had a dream about her father. Not her actual father, because she had no idea what he looked like. In the dream there was just a figure with a blurry face strapped to a gurney in a hospital cubicle but she knew it was him and she knew he'd had a heart attack and died.

Joe, the balloon pilot, was trying to restart his heart with those paddles they used on *Grey's Anatomy*, but it wasn't working. 'Keep trying!' Saffy was saying, over and over. 'I don't want to lose him! Please, keep trying!'

Joe stood back and shook his head and Nervous Dermot said, 'Call it!' and Patsy, the White Feather angel, looked at his watch and said, 'Time of death: eight a.m.'

When she woke up, her face was wet with tears. *Cause of death: estranged daughter's attempt to win advertising pitch*. She had done plenty of terrible things in the last few weeks but she didn't need a dream to know that lying to Nervous Dermot, pretending that her father was dying, was the worst one.

She couldn't get back to sleep. She lay on her back, staring up at the huge dark shadow of the chandelier, counting up all the things she had lost since Valentine's day. She had lost control in public. She had lost Greg. She had lost her self-esteem and let the apartment turn into a tip. She had lost her coat and seven hours of her life in Doug's apartment. She had nearly lost her job in that field in Wicklow. Then she had lost her dignity in the balloon. She had only ever had a fragile connection with her father, but somehow she had managed to lose that too.

Something was scratching around in the kitchen again. It was probably a rat and it served her right. She had to clean up the apartment and she had to clean up her life. It was time.

Saffy bagged Greg's Gucci loafers, his Nike trainers, his All Star sneakers, his Armani leather jacket, his Dior tux, his Paul Smith suits, his Prada shirts, his Calvin Klein underwear, his G Star T-shirts, his Diesel jeans. She packed away his Police sunglasses and his Creed aftershave and his Erno Laszlo Skin System, his passport, his nail clippers, his dental tape, his memory foam pillow, his bite guard.

The hardest part was clearing away their framed photographs. She fought back tears as she wrapped his up in towels. She boxed his blockbusters and his books on stagecraft and his huge collection of DVDs. She unplugged the Xbox and the PlayStation and wrapped them in bubble wrap. She took down the plaster sculpture of the woman's bottom he'd bought for the bathroom. It was a very nice bottom. Far nicer than hers, in fact, and it would be a relief to have a pee without feeling she had to compete with it.

She dragged all the boxes and bags into the study, then she tackled her clothes, making piles for washing and dry-cleaning. She stripped the bed and sorted the laundry and put the first load in the washing machine. She hoovered and scrubbed and mopped, and when she was finished, she could have eaten her dinner off the kitchen floor. Except that she didn't have any dinner. There was some ancient pizza in the fridge and she found a packet of mini Jaffa cakes in a cupboard but she binned them. She was through with all that.

She sat down at the table to go through the heap of unopened post that had piled up there. She found their last credit card statement. Greg had run up nearly fifteen grand in the last few weeks. The transactions were like a route map of the life he was living without her.

She cleaned out her savings account and cancelled the card. He could pay her off when they sold the apartment. Or not. She didn't care. What he did was his own business. She had to start looking after herself.

She drove to the supermarket and shopped for the first time in weeks, came home, cooked a Tuscan Bean Stew, conditioned her hair, covered it with a plastic bag and put on a face mask. Then she put in her teeth-bleaching shields and got out her yoga mat. She was in downward-facing dog when the phone rang.

'Nyeth?' she said. It came out strangely because of the shields.

'Hello, darl.' It was a man and he had an Australian accent.

'I'm thorry.' She tried her hardest to sound like a recording.

'Thaffy than't thumb to the phone righth now. Pleath leathe your name and number afher the thone.' She hung up.

The phone rang again. Doug was the kind of guy who loved a chase. If she didn't get rid of him now, he would never leave her alone. She pulled out her bleaching shields out and wiped her mouth on her sleeve. Her teeth tasted horrible. 'What do you want?' she said coldly.

'Cheers for sneaking off without even a "hooroo" or a "seeya later, mate".'

'I don't know what a "hooroo" is and I'm sorry but I'm not going to see you later. I'm not going to see you ever again. Goodbye.'

She still had the phone in her hand when it rang again.

'What is it with you?' she said before he had a chance to speak. 'Why can't you get it into your tiny Australian brain that I'm not interested?'

'Saffy?' It was *that* voice.

'Greg!'

'Who were you talking to?'

'I was just, um, talking to the radio. That really annoying Harvey Norman ad was on again.'

'Well, turn it off. And open the door, will you?'

Sometimes, after four or five glasses of wine, Saffy had imagined seeing Greg again. What she hadn't imagined was that she'd be plastered in Age Defying Dead Sea Magnetic Mud with a plastic bag on her head and – from the expression on Greg's face – he hadn't imagined it either. He looked up at her from where he was crouched on the floor in the corridor.

'Babe! What happened to your face? Are you sick?'

He had planned to propose when she opened the door, but this was a moment they were going to remember for the rest of their lives. It didn't seem fair to do it when she looked like this.

'It's a face mask.' Saffy pulled the plastic bag off her head and scrubbed at her face with her knuckles. Flakes of dried green mud drifted down onto her shoulders like Shrek's dandruff. She tried to brush them off.

'What are you doing on the floor?' She had just cleared him out of her life. What was he doing here at all?

'I dropped my key.' Greg slid the engagement ring back into his pocket and stood up. 'And what I'm doing here is taking you out for dinner. No!' He must have seen her face. 'I won't take no for an answer. We need to talk.'

He looked exhausted, Saffy thought. But even with smudges of purple under his eyes he looked so handsome that she felt a quick, sharp tug of longing in her heart. He was wearing a pale blue shirt and black jeans and a soft black suede jacket she had never seen before. He tried to hug her but she backed away.

'You can't afford to take me dinner,' she said. 'I've just had to pay off our credit card. You owe me fifteen thousand euro.'

Greg came into the apartment and closed the door behind him. The place looked weirdly empty, like a show flat or a film set. Where was all his stuff? His books on method acting? His Ronnie Wood print of Jack Nicholson? The framed photograph of him accepting an award from Gabriel Byrne?

He reached out and took Saffy's hands and pulled her towards him. 'That's not all I owe you.' He cupped her chin in his hands so they were face to face. 'I owe you an apology.'

He hadn't shaved for a few days and his hair was longer. He was smiling at her in a gentle, understanding way. He looked a bit like Jesus, an incredibly sexy, expensively dressed Jesus. He smelled so familiar, so good, that Saffy almost caved in but she wouldn't let herself.

She pulled away. 'Greg, you can't not call me for two weeks and then walk back in as if nothing has happened.'

'Something *has* happened. I've missed you.' He pulled her back and buried his face in her neck. 'And I've realised that I can't live without . . . *shit*!'

He jerked back and wiped his mouth with the back of his hand. 'Ugh. What's that *stuff* in your hair?'

'It's protein conditioner,' Saffy said. 'Whatever you do, don't get it in your eyes.'

Saffy showered and dried her hair and put on her oldest jeans and a sweater and a pair of very high black boots. Greg would hate them but she didn't care. She would go to dinner. She owed him that. It would give them a chance to talk about putting the apartment on the market. But if he thought she was going to dance around him making him look taller than her, he could forget it.

When she went back out to the living room, she thought he could probably forget about dinner too. His right eye had swollen up like a ping-pong ball. She made him stand under the light to have a better look.

'That looks pretty nasty. Maybe you should go back to the hotel and call a doctor. Come and have a look.'

He examined his eye in the mirror. Jesus! What was in that stuff? He could hardly see. He should probably go to the hospital right now but he couldn't propose in A & E. He didn't like what Saffy had said about going back to the Davison. The idea of another night at the hotel, another night without her, was just out of the question.

So he channelled his inner Mac Malone. 'Don't worry about me, Babe,' he said gruffly. 'I'm way okay.'

There were roadworks on Grand Canal Street and half of the pavement had been torn up. Saffy kept stumbling in her ridiculously high boots but she refused to take Greg's arm when he offered it.

'Where are we going, Greg? And I don't mean *in life*, okay? I mean right now and is it much further?'

He had planned this line and rehearsed it until it sounded perfect. 'Back in time, Babe. Back to 365. I'm going to take you back to where things started to go wrong and we're going to start all over again.'

Saffy stopped. 'No!' If they went to 365 they might run into Doug. 'I mean, no, I'm not really dressed for it. Let's just go for a coffee or a drink instead.'

Greg was relieved. He'd managed to squeeze an extra couple of hundred out of Conor after he'd paid for the ring but he only had a hundred and fifty left. Enough for dinner but not dinner with champagne.

'You know what? Let's just go home.' He smiled at Saffy in

that Jesus-y way again. Jesus who'd been in a punch-up with Herod or Judas.

'Home? What do you mean home? How can we go *home*? We don't even *live* together any more.'

Greg checked the pavement for dog poo and sank to one knee. Then he held out his hand. In his palm, in a red leather box was the biggest, brightest platinum and diamond solitaire he had been able to find for Conor's ten grand credit limit.

'Saffy, will you marry me?'

11

'Congratulations! That's um, that's amazing news!' Conor tried to sound surprised.

'You didn't know?' Saffy laughed. He realised they had him on speakerphone. 'Greg didn't tell you? That's not like him. He's terrible at keeping secrets.'

Greg chimed in. 'Hey! Don't talk about your fiancé like that. Sorry, I didn't tell you, Conor. Had to keep it under wraps till I was sure she'd say yes!'

These were white lies but they made Conor feel queasy. 'Hang on, here's Jess.' He handed her the phone. 'Saffy and Greg are getting married.'

'*What?*' She pretended to faint and, at the last moment, sat down on the stairs beside him.

'You guys move fast,' she said. Yesterday, the papers said they were "permanently estranged". 'When did this happen?'

'About two hours ago.' Saffy's voice was squeaky with excitement. She sounded as if she'd been inhaling helium. 'Isn't it amazing?'

'It is!' Jess pulled a plastic Spiderman figure out from underneath one bare buttock and made a 'what the hell?' face at Conor. 'It is absolutely amazing. When are you planning to do it?'

'It probably won't be till the end of next year but we want you guys to be part of it, you know, bridesmaid, best man . . .'

'Hey! Watch that! Second-best man!' Greg growled. There was some giggling and a wet, smacking sound that was, Jess realised, probably kissing.

'Ugh!' She handed the phone back to Conor.

'So this is it?' he said. 'For richer for poorer?'

'Yeah, man! This is it!' Greg said. 'In sickness and in hell!'

'Okay, who will we call next?' Greg grinned and clinked her glass of champagne with his. She had never seen him look so happy or so handsome, especially in profile, when she couldn't see his swollen eye. 'How about your mother?'

Her mother was probably still sulking after their scene outside the agency the other day. But the minute she heard the news, she'd swing into action and try to hijack the whole thing. Saffy couldn't bear that, not just yet.

She shook her head. 'Let's call your family first.'

Saffy lay awake after Greg had drifted off. Her body was fizzing with adrenalin; her mind was swinging between excitement, disbelief and relief. She kept turning the ring around and around on her finger with her thumb, trying to learn the size and shape of it in the dark, trying to take in what it meant. It had all happened so quickly. In the time it took them to say six words, they had settled the rest of their lives. A few hours ago, she had finally given up on Greg but now they were starting all over again.

A tear streaked down her temple and trickled into her hair. Living without Greg had been a nightmare. She hadn't been herself. She had been hopeless in every way she could have imagined and some ways she couldn't. But the nightmare was over. Greg was back and he wasn't going anywhere. She touched his shoulder. He murmured in his sleep, something about God being on a bus.

She slipped out of bed quietly and went over to the window. It was still dark outside. Grand Canal Street was empty except for a taxi waiting at the lights. Dublin was still asleep and she should go back to bed. She had to be at work in a couple of hours but she didn't want to go to sleep. She smiled at her reflection in the window. This was where her happy-ever-after started and she didn't want to miss a single second of it.

Saffy wanted to tell Vicky the news first but Ciara could spot an engagement ring at several hundred feet. She clocked it the minute Saffy walked into reception.

'Now that is a whopper!' She grinned. 'And I'm guessing you didn't get it with fries at Burger King.'

'Is it too big?' The diamond was massive; way bigger than

Saffy would have chosen for herself and it was on a raised setting that kept snagging on everything.

'Well, I know what Marsh would say.' Ciara raised one shoulder coquettishly and did a perfect impersonation of their boss. 'There's no such thing as *too big* when it comes to rocks or—' She was interrupted by the phone. 'Komodo, can I help you?'

Ciara had promised not to tell anyone, but by the time Saffy got to her office, Marsh had sent around an email asking everyone to meet for 'a small celebration' in the boardroom at nine. Saffy was touched and relieved. Marsh had been ignoring her since the White Feather pitch. Maybe this was a sign that she was going to be forgiven.

Marsh still had no idea about what had happened in the balloon. If she had, she would have fired her on the spot. But she wasn't going to find out. Nobody knew except Saffy and the balloon pilot. God, she had been sick on his *boots*. She should really get on to the PR company and get his number and call him to apologise and replace them or something.

There was a tray of champagne flutes and a plate of almond croissants on the boardroom table but nobody wanted to touch them till Marsh arrived. The word had spread and everyone congratulated Saffy except for Ant, who was playing Hangman on his iPhone. Even Simon seemed genuinely pleased. He kept saying 'well done!' as if she had passed an exam, which made her want to slap him. Vicky gave her a long hug that lasted even longer when Saffy's ring got tangled in her mohair cardigan.

Marsh arrived at nine exactly. She was wearing a black satin blouse with a pussycat bow, the skinniest jeans Saffy had ever seen and her signature five-inch heels. She always managed to make every other woman in the room look either over- or under-dressed. Her skin was flawless. Her bare, tanned arms were toned. Her hair was thrown up into one of those messy topknots that took about a hundred hairclips and half an hour to construct.

How early did you have to get up in the morning to look like that? Saffy wondered. How often did you have to work out? How many *Vogue*s and *Tatler*s and *Grazia*s did you have to consume? And where were you supposed to find the time to fit it all in?

'Mike,' Marsh snapped at the media manager, 'you're drooling!'

Mike hadn't been able to resist the croissants. He blushed and used a wet fingertip to transfer a couple of telltale flakes from his orange paisley tie to his tongue.

'Ciara, go back to reception. Somebody has to answer the phones.'

Ciara rolled her eyes and left, muttering something under her breath.

Marsh shook her head. 'Is that girl always that annoying or is she making a special effort today?' She picked up a champagne glass and there was a small stampede as everyone else did the same.

'This is a very special day,' she smiled, 'and I'd like to propose a toast . . .' All the heads swivelled towards Saffy. 'To Dermot Clancy who woke me up from my beauty sleep this morning to tell me that he loves the "Angels Are Everywhere" idea.' The heads swivelled back to Marsh. 'Komodo has retained White Feather.'

Mike let out a whoop.

Marsh held up her hand. 'I don't want to discuss the fiasco that nearly derailed Friday's pitch, and I'm not going to name names, but you know who you are. And it better not happen again.'

Saffy stared at the floor.

'Because if *anyone* in this room does anything to screw this up,' Marsh stared straight at Saffy, 'they will be shown the door and told to use it!'

'Well done, Saffy!' Vicky spoke up. 'The angel thing was all your idea.' Even Ant had a smile on his grumpy-baby face, though that might have just been indigestion.

'Marsh, can I just be proactive here?' Simon said. 'White Feather's due on air in July and I don't know if you've heard but Saffy's just got engaged. And I'm guessing that she's going to want to free up some time to plan her wedding. So I just want to pre-empt any potential resourcing issues from the get-go by offering to plug in on the client service side.'

He had known about the pitch win. That's why he had been so pleased when he heard she was engaged. Saffy had come up with a way to hold onto the White Feather account and now he was trying to take it back. Plug in? He could plug off!

'That's really thoughtful of you, Simon,' she said sweetly, 'but we're not planning to get married in the immediate future. And I have all the resources I need to handle this myself, thanks.'

Marsh put down her champagne glass. 'You'd better have.'

Lauren tipped maple syrup onto a plate piled with bacon and waffles. 'God,' she groaned, forking a hunk of dripping waffle into her mouth, 'it's a bloody relief to be back in a city where you can eat properly without someone reporting you to the food police.'

She was dressed, as always, in a shabby black trouser suit and shirt. Her hair was pinned into a bun that was already unravelling down the back of her neck. Appearances could, Greg thought, be receptive. Lauren was the most powerful agent in Ireland. If anyone could get him his break into Hollywood, she could. But he was going to have to do some grovelling first.

Lauren usually took him to dinner in Chapter One or Thornton's, so breakfast was a serious demotion, even if it was in The Clarence. Greg was just glad that Lauren wanted to see him at all after the Alanis Morissette incident and the fact that he'd gone against her instructions and proposed to Saffy.

When he texted her to tell her they were engaged he was expecting a meltdown. But she'd texted right back to say she'd be back from LA on Tuesday at seven a.m. and she'd see him on the way in from the airport. He was still waiting for the bollocking but it looked like it wasn't going to come.

'It's inspired,' she said now through a mouthful of bacon, 'absolutely inspired. A nice big glitzy celebrity wedding is exactly what we need to distract the media from your psychotic episode at *The Station*.'

Greg nodded several times and stirred honey into his yogurt. Saffy had role-played this meeting with him. He hadn't, obviously, mentioned the Alanis thing or the bit about Lauren telling him to wait for her to come running back to him, but he had mentioned the phone call to GOD and the fact that he was supposed to apologise to Roisin. Saffy had decided that the best course of action would involve saying very little and nodding a lot.

'I've talked to my moles,' Lauren said, as if she was reading his mind, 'and even if you had gone crawling back to GOD on all fours there was no way you were getting back onto *The Station*. Roisin's his niece. Fucking nepotism!'

Greg did some more nodding and tried not to stare at the trickle of maple syrup that was travelling past one of her moles and down her double chin towards her cleavage.

'That full fat?' Lauren waved her fork at his bowl.

He nodded.

'Jesus! Do I have to remind you that you are half the height of Liam Neeson? A few extra pounds go a long way when you're five foot seven. Don't make my job even more difficult than it already is, will you?'

Greg had to bite his tongue. He was five foot eight and a half. Half an inch taller than Robert Downey Junior *and* Sylvester Stallone. Two inches taller than Elijah Wood and—

'Colin Farrell,' Lauren chased a pool of syrup around her plate with a corner of waffle and posted it into her mouth, 'might be back in the picture.'

'What do you mean?' Greg was confused. 'What picture?'

'Is this early onset Alzheimer's? The Elmore Leonard picture? It's not confirmed but rumour is that if they can swing for a Maggie Gyllenhaal or a Cate Blanchett for the female lead, a major Irish actor is back onboard.'

Greg swallowed. 'But you said he dropped out. He can't just suddenly—'

'If it's Colin Farrell, Greg, he can do what he likes.'

Greg raked his scalp with his hands. This couldn't be happening. He had wanted this part before, but now that *The Station* was gone, he needed it. It was his only hope.

Lauren rolled her eyes. 'Oh, stop pulling your hair out. Let's think of this particular glass as half full, yeah? Whoever it is, he's changed his mind once. Which means there's a chance he'll change it again.' She belched.

Greg looked apologetically at Bono, who was having breakfast, alone, at a nearby table. The eyelid on his sore eye jumped and he had a horrible feeling that it looked as if he was winking because Bono frowned and looked away quickly.

'Anyway,' Lauren belched again, 'a delay will give me a couple of months to spin this wedding so we can get you a better deal.'

'But what am I supposed to do?' Greg felt dizzy and light-headed. He wondered if he was having a panic attack. 'I can't just sit around doing nothing.'

'You won't be doing nothing.' She wiped her hands on the tablecloth and wriggled into her jacket. 'You'll be planning the wedding of the year. Show-stopping venue. Lots of celebs. The sooner the better. June at the latest. I've managed to swing you an engagement feature in *ZIP* magazine. They'll be around to do a shoot, tomorrow. And do something about that eye before they take the snaps, will you? It nearly put me off my breakfast.'

'Listen, Lauren.' Greg tried not to sound as panicky as he felt. 'I'm a bit stuck for cash. *The Station* hasn't paid my salary into my account and I was wondering if we should sue them.'

'That's a great idea.' Lauren produced a cocktail stick and began to pick her teeth, 'if you never want to work in film or TV again. Look, just sit tight and I'll see if I can get you a walk-on in one of the English soaps. I think *Emmerdale* might be looking for a rapist.'

A rapist? Greg wanted to throttle her. But he remembered Saffy's advice and nodded again.

'Relax, Greg. You look like you've got a vibrator up your ass. The movie isn't cast yet. It might come back. And if it does, don't be on honeymoon in Borneo or the bloody Maldives, okay? Go for Mexico or the Caribbean. Somewhere that's a shuttle flight from LA.'

'Good thinking.' He attempted a smile. 'But that's what I pay you for, right?'

Lauren put her toothpick on his saucer. 'Right now, you're

paying me twenty per cent of nothing at all. So breakfast,' she stood up, 'is on you. Now I must go and say hello to Bono.'

The walls were papered in light blue silk and there was a bowl of lilies on the white marble mantelpiece. There was a grandfather clock and a crystal chandelier and an antique coffee table covered in magazines. It was all very *Homes & Gardens*, except for the smell of antiseptic and the people sitting waiting on the spindly antique chairs.

Jill checked her reflection in a gilt-framed mirror. She was wearing a little pink wraparound dress that she'd bought ten years ago; it still fit her perfectly. The receptionist had just admired it. Her skin was glowing. Her posture was fabulous. There was absolutely nothing wrong with her.

She took a seat. It looked as if she was the only person in the room who had come on her own. She hadn't told Len about her appointment. He would have been around in a flash with his bicycle panniers full of horrible herbal remedies and leaflets about reiki healers and ayurvedic diets. She had thought about telling Sadbh but they hadn't spoken since the day she had stormed back into her office and left Jill standing on the street.

Trying to pin her daughter down for lunch or supper had always been tricky but she had never treated her like that before. At first, she'd been devastated but when she'd had time to think it over, she had realised that maybe she shouldn't take it so personally.

Sadbh had been in shock, that was obvious. Jill couldn't blame her for over-reacting. She knew what it felt like to have someone walk out and take your future with them. She had experienced, at first hand, the misery of waking up every morning and realising that nothing would ever be the same again. The physical ache every time you saw a happy couple. The shame of breaking down, when you least expected it, in a crowded playground or a dentist's chair or a supermarket queue.

She had done everything she could to try to stop this happening to her daughter. She had told her, in a hundred different ways, that, until you marry a man, he can and will do pretty much anything he likes. But, of course, Sadbh hadn't listened.

Jill could have killed Greg for wasting six years of Sadbh's life but she couldn't really blame him. Her daughter had left a door open. All he had done was walk through it.

It broke her heart knowing what her daughter was going through and not being allowed to help. But this was something she wanted to go through alone. She'd made it pretty clear that she needed time to lick her wounds. And if time was what she wanted, that's what Jill had to give her.

She picked up a copy of *Vogue* and flicked through the glossy pages. All the models looked so *young*. When she had started out, the idea was to look like a woman, not a little girl.

She had been waiting for the bus to school in Bristol when someone touched her elbow. 'Are you a model?' It was an ordinary-looking, middle-aged man in a suit.

'A model what?' She was so unaware of her own looks that she genuinely didn't know what he meant.

Everyone in the bus queue laughed, including the man. The card he gave her had a black silhouette of what was supposed to be a deer but looked more like a Labrador with antlers. Some swirly pink letters spelled out 'Gazelles Modelling Agency'.

But Jill recognised it for what it really was. It was the ticket to London, Paris, New York and Tokyo. To all the places she would never see if she trained to be a teacher or a dental nurse, which was what her parents wanted.

She didn't tell them about the card. They were Seventh Day Adventists. Her mother had never worn any jewellery other than her wedding ring. Mini-skirts and make-up were banned. Her father turned the television off when *Top of the Pops* came on. Dancing was frowned upon and music that expressed 'foolish or trivial sentiments' was not allowed. She knew, without asking, that they thought that 'model' was just another word for 'prostitute'.

The woman at Gazelles was lukewarm. She needed to see some test shots before she would consider taking her on. Jill had no way of getting money to pay a photographer but she knew one person with a proper camera – Rob Reilly – who was married to her mother's best friend, Marie. Her parents tolerated Rob but she knew they didn't really approve of him – either because he was Irish or because he was a hairdresser, or because, even though he was her father's age, he dressed 'like a hippy', in jeans and an Afghan coat.

The next time he came to the house, Jill managed to get him on his own. She showed him the card and asked him if he would take some pictures for her. And that was her first mistake.

Rob arranged to take the shots in the hairdressing salon where he worked. Jill felt like a criminal telling her mother she was going to the library and using her lunch money to get the bus to the other side of Bristol. She was nervous but one of the junior stylists stayed late to do her hair and her make-up and she joked around while Rob was taking the shots, and that helped Jill get over her embarrassment.

Then, when she went back to pick up the prints she felt embarrassed all over again. The woman in the pictures he showed her wasn't the seventeen-year-old girl she saw in the mirror. She was a beautiful stranger with a mane of blonde hair, a heart-shaped face and a teasing smile.

Rob packed the shots away in a brown envelope and handed them over quickly and she realised that he was embarrassed, too, as if they revealed as much about him as they did about her. He wouldn't accept the ten pounds she had brought to pay him for the film. 'Ah, forget it,' he'd said. 'It's nothing.' And she had tried to. But it wasn't.

She stayed upstairs in her room when he came around to the house with Marie. But she thought about him all the time and, when someone else was taking her picture, she always imagined it was Rob.

Jill was too small for catwalk work but she had the perfect seventies look. She got a steady stream of fashion catalogue jobs through Gazelles and she forged absence notes for school to go to the shoots.

She didn't tell her friends about them and she hid what she was paid in the pocket of a cardigan at the back of her wardrobe. She never cashed any of the cheques. What she was doing wasn't about the money. It was about escape.

She loved leaving the stifling atmosphere of her parents' house and becoming, even for a few hours, the glossy, confident creature who emerged for the camera. It never occurred to her that her mother and father would see the pictures. Catalogues never made it into their house and it wasn't as if she was going to be asked to do a shoot for the Bible.

After six months, she rang Gazelles, as usual, on a Monday afternoon and was told that she had been picked for a magazine cover. Her heart leaped then sank. Her mother didn't buy *Women's Weekly* but that wasn't going to stop her seeing it at the newsagent's.

Jill decided that the only person she could talk to about it was Rob and that was her second mistake. She told herself she just wanted his advice but she went out and bought a short flowery dress and a pair of wedge sandals. She changed out of her uniform in the toilet after school and spent a long time putting on eyeliner and mascara the way she'd learned by watching the make-up artists. She waited across the street from Rob's salon until everyone else had left. Then she crossed the road, went in and made her third mistake.

Jill pulled another magazine from the glossy fan laid out on the coffee table. The models in the ads in *ZIP* were older. Movie stars of Jill's own age in ads for wrinkle creams and conditioners. All of them looked airbrushed to within an inch of their lives and none of them, Jill thought with satisfaction, looked any better than she did. She speed-read a piece about a newsreader and her shih-tzus and then turned the page and found herself looking straight at a picture of Sadbh.

The photograph in the paper after the break-up was an old one but this was recent. In it, Greg was carrying her daughter awkwardly in his arms as if she was a piece of dry-cleaning. He looked handsome, as always, though there was something odd about one of his eyes.

And maybe it was because she had just been thinking about him, and she hardly ever did, but Sadbh was the image of Rob. She looked so like him that it took Jill by surprise. She had his pale skin and his wide mouth and his eyes, brown from a distance, green up close. But it was what was on her ring finger that surprised Jill most.

EX-SOAP-STAR GREG TO WED SHY SWEETHEART

On Friday, tearful viewers will tune in to bid a fond farewell to hunky fireman Mac Malone, who will perish in a hospital blaze saving a sight-impaired premature baby. But actor Greg Gleeson has never looked happier.

Walking away from Ireland's favourite soap has freed him up to do something he admits he should have done long ago – pop the question to long-term sweetheart Sadbh Martin.

Throwing open the doors of their interior-designed, loft-style penthouse on Charlotte Quay, the star and his fiancée spoke openly about the thrilling details of their whirlwind engagement and Gleeson's plans for the future.

Looking at the loved-up couple it's hard to believe that they separated just a few weeks back amid rumours that their relationship was on the rocks.

'We broke up on Valentine's Day,' admits Greg. 'I thought I wasn't ready to commit. But Saffy was really understanding.'

'I told him there was no pressure,' murmurs softly spoken Sadbh, who sports a shy smile and a dazzling 2-carat princess-cut solitaire.

Gleeson moved out of their apartment and took a few weeks out to do some soul searching.

'I realised that my relationship was not the problem,' Gleeson says in his trademark husky voice. 'The problem was that I had outgrown The Station and I needed to move on.'

Once he'd made the decision to quit the soap, everything else fell into place.

'I just walked off the set and told my agent, "I'm ready for Hollywood. Bring it on!" Then I asked Saffy to come for a romantic stroll in the rain and the rest is history.'

There were four more pages of pictures and text but Jill couldn't look at any of them. She had spent the last few weeks worrying about her daughter. Hoping she was getting over her heartbreak. Wishing she was allowed to comfort her. And all the time Sadbh had been celebrating her engagement.

She felt a sudden, sharp pain, like a contraction. She had given up so much for her daughter. She had given up *everything*: her home, her family, her modelling career. She had moved to another country. She had made a life and tried to fit into it. Being a single parent was hard and lonely and thankless, but she had done her best. She had never let another man get too close in case he hurt them the way Rob had when he left. And this is how she was being repaid – by having to read about her daughter's life in newspapers and magazines.

The receptionist came to the door. 'Lynn Corbett for Dr Kenny?' A thin, white-faced woman rose unsteadily to her feet with the help of a younger woman and an older man.

She crossed the room painfully slowly, the man holding her steady and the younger woman walking beside her, whispering encouragement. 'That's it, Mum; that's brilliant. There you go, nearly there.'

Lynn Corbett was probably the same age as Jill, though she looked ten or even fifteen years older. But watching her, Jill felt so jealous that she had to turn away. Everything *she* had done, every step *she* had taken, she had taken on her own. There had never been anybody there to support her.

12

Jess was at the kitchen table working on the laptop when Conor got back from school. Her cardigan had a missing button. He leaned over and slipped his hand in through the gap.

'I hate those little bastards,' he said. 'I mean the students, not your breasts.' He kissed the top of her head. She was using one of his socks as a scrunchie. Half of her hair had escaped and she looked like a Renaissance angel.

She kept typing. 'Could you look after the terrible twins? I've got a deadline and it's screaming.'

'*Time to bin your thongs*,' he read over her shoulder, '*and shake your booty in sexy shorties from Figleaves.*'

He hated that she had to write this crappy advertorial. She had been turning into a brilliant features writer when the paper folded. But you had to be a schmoozer to get decent freelance stuff and Jess was too honest to do the sucking-up that was required.

He made Luke and Lizzie beans on toast and ran their bath. They still liked sharing but one of these days, he knew, they wouldn't. Soon they'd start growing apart from one another and from him. He caught himself hurrying so he could grab an extra half-hour to work on the book and stopped himself. There were only a finite number of times that the twins would squabble about who got the tap end and who could stay under the water for longest and pester him to turn their hair into foamy Mohican spikes with shampoo. Conor wanted to make the most of them.

Afterwards, he helped them to put on their pyjamas and left them in the living room making 'Missing Hamster' posters. They were sure that someone would recognise Brendan and bring him back. Lizzie's hamster looked more like a sausage dog and Luke's was wearing sunglasses and riding a skateboard. Conor thought it was probably a long shot.

He washed the dishes and tidied around Jess, clearing the clutter and lifting her elbows so he could wipe down the table.

He was about to bin a pile of junk mail when he found the letter stuck between a supermarket leaflet and a flyer from a local gym. It was addressed to him.

Douglas, Kemp & Troy
Literary Agency
11 Winnet Street
London W1D

Dear Conor,
As you noted in your letter, it is not our policy at Douglas, Kemp & Troy to accept unsolicited work. You are not the first aspiring author to have ignored this rule.

Over the years, we have received manuscripts in birdcages, in violin cases, wrapped in banana leaves and, once, delivered by hand (claw?) by a man in a chicken costume. Your strategy, however, was a first.

Packing the first instalment of a novel about the chaos of life with young children in an envelope covered in jam and what appears to be real hamster hair struck a chord with my assistant Juniper, who is the mother of Sam (4) and the owner of two gerbils whose names escape me.

Juniper decided to take a quick look at Doubles or Quits. *When she had read all the pages you sent, she passed them on to me and, though I don't want to get your hopes up, I really enjoyed it.*

However, I would like to read more of the book before making a decision to share it with a publisher.

Conor felt strange, as if the lino floor was tilting and he might slide off.

You mentioned, in your letter, that you have another 60k words to write before you complete the book. Could you contact Juniper by phone or email and let her know when you might be in a position to email some more chapters to us?
Kind regards to you and to Brendan,
Becky Kemp

He sat down and handed the letter to Jess. She scanned it.
'Shit!! I forgot to tell you, your book got involved with the

breakfast things. I thought I'd cleaned it up before I sent it. I'm sorry!'

'Don't be!' He wanted to laugh or cry, he just wasn't sure which. 'If it wasn't for the jam, it would have gone straight on to the slush pile and they'd never have read it. You're amazing!'

'No, you're amazing! Well done! Now can I read what you've written so far?'

Conor shook his head. He didn't mind what some stranger thought of it but he wanted Jess to love it.

'Bastard! You never used to have secrets from me!' She jumped up and began rummaging in the freezer compartment of the fridge. 'We should celebrate. I think there's some antique vodka in here somewhere.'

Conor was staring at the letter. 'I never thought I'd get a chance like this. I don't even want to think about it but a book deal would change everything, Jess.'

'Hey!' She slapped him gently with a frosty hand and pointed at the peeling lino, the lopsided cupboards and the wonky Buy & Sell table. 'I don't want to change everything. I *like* everything.'

'Come here.' He pulled her down into his lap. 'Forget the vodka,' he said. 'I can think of a better way to celebrate.'

Saffy checked the living room. It looked perfect. All Greg's things were back where they'd been before she packed them away, except for the sculpture of the bottom. She had told him how insecure it made her feel and he'd kissed her and told her she had a far nicer bottom and put the sculpture in the bin.

She picked up her glass, took it out to the kitchen and put it in the dishwasher. Then she cleaned her fingerprints off the dishwasher with a kitchen wipe and put that in the bin. The apartment had just been contract cleaned again. There was another press photographer due in the morning. She hoped this was the last one. She wanted the world to go away now so she could have her fiancé to herself.

Her fiancé was sitting at the sofa in the kitchen with his laptop. She kissed the top of his head.

'Greg, I'm getting a bit worried. I've called my mother five times this week, and left messages, but she hasn't called me back.'

'Maybe she's away,'

'Maybe.' But a trip away was usually an excuse for Jill to sneak in an unscheduled phone call to discuss whether she should pack a bikini or a one-piece and to moan about how flying dehydrated her skin and to remind Saffy that if Kevin Costner died while she was away, he was not to be cremated. Kevin Costner was her cat. Her mother had always named her cats after movie stars. Mel Gibson and Michael Douglas were buried in her tiny back garden under rose bushes.

Saffy sighed. 'I'll try again later. I don't want to have to tell her we're engaged on an answering machine. I suppose she'll want to meet up and celebrate. I was thinking of asking her around for lunch with Len.'

Greg raised an eyebrow. 'Can we have him fumigated first? Anything could be living in that beard, Babe.' He opened an email, scanned it and grinned. 'But I don't think you should wait till later. I think you should call her right now and ask her if she's free on May thirteenth.'

'Why?'

'Because that's when we're getting married.' He turned his laptop around so she could see the screen. 'And this is where we're doing it.'

Greg had been starting to panic about finding the right venue. Lauren had been pretty clear that it had to be a summer wedding but everywhere he'd tried was booked solid. Woodglen was the last venue on his A list and he hadn't been hopeful. But they'd just emailed him to say they had one day free in May. Apparently some people were superstitious about getting married on Friday the thirteenth.

Woodglen was amazing. It had a heart-shaped lake. It had been voted one of the '10 most romantic places in the British Isles' by Condé Nast. There was a dinky little church about half a mile away. Greg didn't normally do the God thing, but in this case, he'd make an exception. A church topped a register office for photo ops. The light was way better.

But the best thing about Woodglen was that it hadn't already been used for a celebrity wedding. Posh and Becks had done Lutrellstown. Castle Leslie had that bad Paul and Heather karma and at least one of the Corrs had done Dromoland Castle. How many Corrs were there? Greg tried to remember, turning to Saffy to kiss her. And were they still cool enough to make the guest list?

Saffy did the maths during the kiss. May 13 was less than eight weeks away. But the more she thought about it, the more she realised it made sense. June and July would be a write-off with White Feather TV production. And if Greg got the Elmore Leonard movie he could be in the States shooting for months.

She didn't want to wait another whole year to get married. The only problem was that she had stuck her neck out with Marsh and said she didn't need Simon's help. Which meant she was going to be working ten hours a day and she wouldn't be able to take any time off to organise a wedding. But Greg had already thought of that.

'Babe, I've got nothing to do. I'm just sitting round twizzling my thumbs here. I've already found the venue. I can do all the planning. Hey, it's just a big party. Right?'

She was amazed. 'Are you sure? You'd do that? It's a lot of work.'

'Sure I'm sure, Babe.' He grinned. 'All you have to do is show up in a white dress and say, "I do." '

'It's all happening so fast,' Saffy told her mother. They were sitting upstairs in Bewley's having coffee. Jill had claimed she was too busy to meet for lunch. 'But Greg keeps saying that a wedding is just a big party really.'

'He's right,' Jill said with a small smile. 'I don't know what the fuss is about.'

Saffy swallowed a mouthful of scalding cappuccino. *The fuss?* Had her mother had a personality transplant? She had seemed pleased on the phone when Saffy finally got hold of her and told her the news. And that was weird.

After six years of heavy hints and significant looks and reminders that Saffy wasn't getting any younger, Jill wasn't supposed to be *pleased*. She was supposed to be ecstatic. She was supposed to be brainstorming colour themes and scribbling down the names of dress designers and pulling out articles on oxygen facials and eyebrow threading and French manicures. And Saffy was supposed to be beating her away with a big stick.

Instead she found herself having to chatter to fill the silence while Jill looked out of the window at the crowds on Grafton Street.

'Mum, are you still annoyed about that day when you called into Komodo?' Saffy finally asked. 'I'm sorry if I was a bit frosty but it was a bad time for me and . . .'

Jill shook her head. 'It's fine, really. Forget about it. *I* have. I'm just a bit distracted. Work has been very hectic lately.'

Saffy tried and failed to imagine a sudden run on Louis XIV horseshoe chairs in the quiet antique shop on Francis Street where her mother worked.

'Right, well, I'd better get the bill so you can get back.' She waved at the waitress. She didn't know what game Jill was playing but she wasn't going to give her the satisfaction of playing along.

'We're driving down to look at the hotel on Saturday week,' she said coolly. 'You're welcome to come if you can fit it in.'

Her mother stood up. 'I'll see what I can do.'

'Guys, wait till you see this place.' Greg turned around to grin at Conor and Jess. 'I'm telling you, it's the god's bollocks.'

'Greg!' Saffy grabbed his leg. He turned back and jammed on the brakes just before they ran into a herd of cattle filing towards them on the narrow country lane.

Greg grabbed Saffy's hand and waved her ring at them out the window. 'Hey, girls! Any Beyoncé fans out there?' He began to sing 'All the single ladies!' He was way off key.

'It's the *dog's* bollocks, Greg.' Saffy shook her head. 'And those cows aren't ladies. They're bullocks.'

'Biology was never his strong point,' Conor laughed.

'Or music,' Jess said, 'apparently.'

*

Jess and Saffy went outside for a tour of the walled garden. Conor and Greg followed the manageress of Woodglen up the wide marble staircase and along a sun-splashed corridor. She had an unbelievably pert bottom and, at some point, she had swallowed a brochure and possibly a website, too.

'The upper floors of the hotel are an oasis of tranquillity. Those seeking romance and seclusion will find it in twenty-four sumptuous and luxuriously appointed rooms overlooking acres of magnificent rolling parkland, providing unparalleled vistas of natural beauty.'

She trotted ahead twitching her hips inside her tight pink skirt, treating them to an unparalleled vista of natural beauty of her own but Greg wasn't interested. Tanya was the first woman he'd let under his radar for six years and look how that had turned out. She was still sending him texts. If this went on, he'd have to change his number.

Conor hadn't even noticed. He was too busy looking around him. At the deep padded window seats piled with velvet cushions and the polished flagstone floors and the faded silk rugs. This was the kind of place he'd always wanted to take Jess. He didn't buy lottery tickets but inhaling the expensive scent of roses and sweet wood smoke, he thought maybe he might start.

The manageress opened a panelled door. 'This is the jewel in the Woodglen crown: our serenely private and sensually elegant honeymoon suite, the quintessential embodiment of contemporary romance.' She stood back and let them pass into the room.

Muslin curtains floated in front of the half-open window. A pale carpet had the words of a W.B. Yeats poem woven onto it. In front of the four-poster bed, there was a claw-footed bath, big enough for two.

Conor imagined getting into that bath and having sex with Jess and then taking her to sleep in the huge white bed and waking up and getting back into it again.

'Not bad,' Greg was saying, 'for four hundred euro a night.'

The mention of money woke Conor from his daydream. He hated to bring this up but if Jess found out that he'd used their credit card to buy Saffy's ring, she would never have sex with him again.

'Listen, Greg, talking of money, I know I owe you five grand from way back but—'

'That was a gift, man. I wish you'd stop going on about it.'

'Well, okay, but I'm wondering did the garage guy give you any idea of when he's going to pay for the car. Because I really need to get that ten grand you spent on the ring back into my credit card account.'

Greg opened the gilded armoire and looked at himself in the mirror. The swelling in his eye was finally going down but it was still a little bit pink and twitchy. He hoped that would clear up before the wedding. He needed to look seriously hot in the photographs.

'The garage won't pay me till they sell it on.' He wished they'd get on with it. He needed to give Saffy the fifteen grand he owed her and pay for his half of the wedding and the mortgage and find some over to give to Conor. He'd have to get a calculator out at some point and do the maths.

'Right.' Conor felt sick at the thought of what would happen if Jess opened the next Visa statement, but what could he do? He was just going to have to intercept it before she got to it.

Greg's phone beeped and he turned away to check his messages. It was a text. Another one.

UPON RECEIVING THIS TEXT YOU MUST SEND IT TO 1 PERSON YOU LIKE, 1 PERSON YOU HATE, 1 PERSON YOU LOVE, AND 1 PERSON YOU WANT TO SCREW. NOW THINK ABOUT WHY I SENT IT TO YOU! TBird ☺

'The Magnolia Ballroom is a timelessly elegant function room, with a capacity for up to two hundred and fifty seated guests.' The manageress clicked across the polished parquet floor. 'It is undoubtedly Ireland's most charming and prestigious nuptial setting.'

'Isn't this a bit big for us?' Saffy whispered to Greg as they all trailed after her like sheep. 'I thought we wanted something a bit more intimate.'

'You don't have *time* to think, Babe.' Greg tucked her hair behind her ears. 'That's why you're leaving it all to me. No interfering, that's the deal, remember?'

He was right, she didn't have time to think and they did have a deal. She was just going to have to bite her tongue and let him get on with it. But *two hundred and fifty guests*? Did they even know two hundred and fifty people? And what was it going to cost? She felt dizzy just thinking about it.

She left the others listening to the manageress rabbiting on about wine and slipped out through the French doors. The sky opened, as if it had been waiting for her specially. She stood on the veranda and watched some peacocks poking around the fountain in the downpour. In six weeks, she would be standing out there on the lawn in a wedding dress. It was hard to believe.

'Christ, that woman can talk for Ireland.' Conor had followed her out. 'Are you okay?'

'I'm fine. I just . . . I don't know, Conor. I'm wondering if it's all a bit over the top.'

'Come on,' he said. 'It's kind of amazing. And you're only going to do this once. You might as well give them bread and circuses,' he waved at the gardens, 'and peacocks and topiary in the shape of chess pieces and a fountain that looks as if it was designed by a distant relative of Bernini. One of the O'Berninis of Roscommon, possibly.'

Saffy laughed.

'Oh, and 2002 Les Clos Chablis,' Conor said reverently. 'Which is *so much more* than a wine.'

'It is?'

'It is the benchmark of excellence by which all other Grand Cru Chablis are measured. That's what the woman said.'

'She wants our guests to drink a benchmark?'

'I suppose if you have an ass like that, it's hard to resist the urge to talk out of it.'

Conor always cheered her up. It amazed her when people thought Jess was out of his league. He was such a lovely guy. Warm and kind and strong and solid. Except he wasn't, she realised looking at him closely, looking quite as solid as usual.

'Is everything alright, Conor?'

'What? Yeah I'm just absolutely shattered. I'm getting up at the crack of dawn to try to get a few hours of writing in before school. There's an agent in London who might be interested in my book and I'm supposed to get the next chunk over to her by the middle of May.'

'That's brilliant!'

'Try telling that to Jess. She thinks I'm crazy and she's probably right, but I have to give it my best shot. When I'm sixty and I'm standing in front of a class of cyberyobs teaching *The Complete Works of Katie Price*, I want to be able to look back and think: At least I tried.'

'When can we read it?'

'Not till it's finished. I haven't even shown it to Jess yet. I just want it to be right, you know?' He stared out at the rain. 'I should probably tell Greg that I'm writing it, though. Maybe I'll tell him after he gets this movie.'

Saffy sighed. 'He will get the movie, won't he, Conor? He wants it so badly and I'm not sure how he'll cope if he doesn't.'

'Come on.' Conor smiled. 'He's Greg Gleeson. Greg Gleeson always gets what he wants.'

'Okay, guys.' Greg came back through the swing doors that led to the hotel kitchen. 'I've made the final menu tweaks and I think we're nearly there.'

The others were sitting at a table by the window. Jess was losing the will to live. They had been at Woodglen for four hours and it felt like for ever. She'd managed to shut up while that horrible little manageress went on and on. How much more of this did she have to take?

Greg read from his notes. 'Starters: choice of Aubergine, Basil and Parmesan crème brulée or Oysters baked in a brioche with a Shellfish Veloute. Mains: Loin of Tuna seared—'

'Fish don't have legs.' Conor put his head in his hands. 'You have to have legs to have loins.'

'What's a *veloute*?' Jess groaned.

'I'm sorry, Greg,' Saffy said quietly, 'I know I said I wouldn't interfere but we're absolutely not having shellfish.' The word 'oyster' brought back that night with Doug. And that was the last thing she wanted to remember on her wedding day.

Conor and Jess followed Saffy and Greg out to the car park.

'God! I thought that little manageress was going to stick her tongue down Greg's throat.' Jess shook her head. 'Did you see the way she was shaking her ass at him?'

Conor took her hand. 'Mmm. This is a beautiful place, though, don't you think?'

Jess shaded her eyes and looked back at the house. 'Yeah, I suppose. But why do they need all this?'

'It's their big day.' Conor shrugged. Jess pulled her hand away. 'Days aren't big, Conor. Wars are big. Third-world debt is big. The only big thing about a wedding like this is the bill.'

'I'm sorry. I just think it's nice, that's all.'

'You think it's nice?' she said sarcastically. '*Nice?* You think it's *nice* to spend a fortune on a wedding in a recession? You think it's *nice* that our consumer-driven society has turned love and commitment into a multi-billion-euro industry that preys on idiots who don't know any better?'

Conor stuck his hands in his pockets. 'Well, there's no chance of them preying on you, is there, Jess? There's only one person here who wants to get married, so I guess that makes me the idiot. Right?'

She turned her face away quickly, as if he'd slapped her. His neck prickled with sweat. What was happening here? What was wrong with him?

'God! Jess! I'm so sorry.' He put his arms around her and pulled her close and kissed her hair. 'I don't know what came over me. I'm a shellfish veloute.'

Saffy was hurrying up the stairs to the work in progress meeting when her phone rang again.

'Hell . . . ow!' Her ring kept snagging in her hair and yesterday she'd had to Sellotape it to her finger so she could type her emails.

It was Greg. 'Babe, I've been looking at the picture in the *Indo*, again, and I think my eye looks really weird.'

The make-up artist hadn't shown up before the last (*oh please*, Saffy thought, *let it have been the last*) interview about the engagement. Saffy had done her best to hide the slight puffiness around Greg's right eye with her concealer but he was right, he did look a bit bug-eyed.

'You look gorgeous. Everyone here was just saying how good you look.'

Everyone wasn't. Everyone was jostling past her into the boardroom to lay claim to the raspberry muffins from the Queen of Tarts. There were never enough to go around. This was Marsh's trick to get people to show up on time for the weekly WIP meeting. If you were late, you got to sit there hungry while everyone else gorged themselves.

'Really?' Greg said. 'Like who?'

'Well, like Vicky and Ciara,' Saffy lied, 'and . . .' She spotted Ant on his way out of the door, which was a disaster. She needed him at this meeting. 'Ant!' she hissed. He didn't bother turning around.

'Ant said I looked gorgeous?' Greg sounded doubtful.

'Well . . . no . . . that's not what he said *exactly* . . .'

'Well, what *did* he say? Dude's a weirdo but he's an art director so I respect his opinion.'

Marsh made a wind-it-up gesture at her through the glass wall of the boardroom. She had been apoplectic when Saffy had gone to her to ask for time off for the wedding and the honeymoon. Saffy had to promise to put in the eighty hours she'd miss before she went.

'Um . . . he told Vicky, who told me that you looked . . .' Saffy tried to think herself into Ant's small, round bald head, 'like an airbrushed media whore.'

'But the pictures aren't airbrushed.' Greg sounded pleased.

'I know,' Saffy said. 'That's what I told him. I love you, Greg! Got to go.'

The weeks were flying past at a speed that would have made Saffy feel scared if she had a chance to slow down and feel anything other than exhausted. She couldn't believe it was already the beginning of April. She was keeping her promise to Marsh and working late every day and most weekends but she still had to bring her laptop home most nights to catch up on emails and read research reports and write PowerPoint presentations.

She felt terrible about how little time she was spending with Greg but he was being really sweet about it. He seemed happy to order in sushi or Thai and watch a DVD or work on the wedding plans. He had actual spreadsheets. Lots of them. She wasn't supposed to look but occasionally she peeked over his shoulder, and it all looked like a military operation. She was blown away by how much work he was putting into everything.

There were guest lists and checklists for table settings and church readings and links to photo references for florists and locations for the stills photographer and the videographer. There was a call sheet thing with contact numbers for journalists and ring designers and catering managers and string quartets and limo drivers. There was a DJ's playlist and an interactive diagram of a seating plan.

He had asked her to mail him her address book a few weeks back and flashed some plain but very tasteful wedding invitations past her before he sent them out. And, once he'd woken her up at four a.m. to tell her he'd decided to scrap the whole wedding gift idea and ask guests to make a donation to a donkey sanctuary instead but he refused to let her get involved in the details.

'All you have to do,' he kept saying, 'is turn up . . .' And she knew the rest: . . . *in a white dress and say, 'I do'*

'Okay.' Ciara shook her head in astonishment. 'Now I'm seriously considering calling in the bridal police. You're getting married in five weeks and you haven't had a single facial?'

'Look at her skin,' Vicky said. 'It's perfect. She doesn't even have pores. She doesn't need facials. Let's move on to the next question. "Your pre-wedding regime consists of: a) a raw food diet and daily yoga; b) a 'no carb' diet and three weekly workouts, or c) teeth whitening, hairstyle test-runs and weekly spa trips."'

Saffy poured the last of her crisps into the palm of her hand and tipped them into her mouth. She was supposed to be revising a really complicated media schedule for NoQ, the retail outlet in

Cork. She should have stayed at her desk. The minute she had come into the kitchen Vicky and Ciara had pounced on her and forced her to do this stupid bridal quiz and it was beginning to make her feel panicky. They were staring at her now, waiting for her answer.

'Pre-wedding regime? Um. Well, I haven't gotten round to it yet but when I do it will be B. Or maybe A.'

Vicky looked worried but she ticked a box anyway. 'Right. Question five. "The lingerie you'll wear under your dress is: a) sexy and extravagant; b) practical and supportive, or c) simple and elegant."'

Saffy stood up. 'Is there a D? As in non-existent?'

'You're going commando?' Ciara was impressed. 'I had you down for one of those shoulder-to-knee Spanx jobbies.'

'No. Of course I'm not going commando.' Saffy squeezed some Quix onto her hands and held them under the tap to try to get rid of the crisp smell. Tayto Cheese & Onion was turning into her signature scent. She couldn't remember the last time her lunch hadn't come out of a little foil bag. 'I just don't have the underwear, yet. I have to get the dress first.'

She didn't need to turn around to see the horrified expressions on their faces. She knew this was awful and just saying it out loud made her feel hysterical. But how was she supposed to buy a dress when she was at her desk from seven in the morning till eight every evening? You could pick up the ingredients for a four-course meal in the middle of the night but nobody seemed to have invented a twenty-four-hour bridalwear shop yet.

13

Greg had fallen asleep on the sofa in the middle of playing 'Island of the Dead' on the Xbox. Killing zombies was probably fun if you were an accountant or a quantity surveyor or something but when you were used to playing Mac Malone every other day it sucked.

The fires on *The Station* had been real and Greg used to get an incredible adrenalin rush every time he put one out. He still couldn't believe that he would never get to put on Mac's uniform and do it again.

He hadn't been able to watch the episode where he was killed off. Seeing something like that could really mess with your head. But he couldn't avoid the freaky fallout from the whole thing.

People had been leaving bunches of petrol station flowers and candles outside the entrance to the apartment block since the night it aired and fans kept coming up to him on the street and crying or, worse, acting like they were surprised that *he* was still alive. It was really creeping him out.

And on top of all this he had to deal with the huge hole that Mac Malone had left in *his* life. He missed learning his lines and having his make-up done. He missed working out every day and having to avoid carbs. He even missed having to set his alarm clock for five a.m. to get to the studio by six. He was tired of being a slacker.

He had meant it when he told Saffy that he would organise the wedding but the truth was that Vivienne, the manageress of Woodglen, had taken over the whole thing. He had given her the guest list but she was organising pretty much everything else. She sent him updated spreadsheets every other day but all he really had to do was approve her choices.

'This is your first wedding, isn't it, Mr Gleeson?' she'd said when he'd called her to arrange a meeting. He admitted it was.

'Well, it's my three hundred and twenty-third. And it is possibly the most high-profile nuptial event I will ever organise. My career depends on it and I want everything to be absolutely perfect. You've already made the really important decisions and I'm sure you have better things to do with your time than choosing table linen and cake knives. So why don't you leave everything in my capable hands?'

He didn't actually have better things to do but he didn't want to say that. And *his* career depended on it too. So he decided to let her get on with it.

He wandered into the kitchen and stared into the fridge and ate some hummus out of a tub with his finger. He went into the office and took out his weights then put them away again. He lay on the llama-skin rug in the living room and looked through his DVD collection but there was nothing he wanted to watch. The fact was, most of the stuff coming out of Hollywood was crap.

He wished Conor wasn't at school so they could sit around and brainstorm some screenplay ideas. Though, to be honest, Conor's ideas were pretty half-assed. They always involved too much reality. People didn't have to pay nine euro to watch ninety minutes of real life. They could just stand outside the cinema and look around.

He sat up and grabbed the laptop. He didn't need Conor for this. He could do this himself.

'ZOMBIES,' he typed, 'invade Dublin. A HEROIC FIRE-FIGHTER saves the day.' Brilliant. He should have gone solo years ago.

'TEENAGERS,' he typed, 'are stalked by a SURREAL KILLER—'

His phone beeped. It was another text from Tanya. This was the third one today. It was a blurry photo of her boobs with the caption: 34 C WHAT UR MISSIN? X TBIRD.

He'd shown some of the texts to Conor when they went to pick up their suits at Brown Thomas. They'd had an hour to kill because his had to be taken out a bit and Conor's had to be taken in. After three pints, Greg had spilled about the night in the Davison, which was fine because he really needed to get it off his chest. But then he'd had to listen to Conor banging on about how he should come clean with Saffy.

Come clean? Was he out of his mind? Telling Saffy would just be selfish. It would break her heart. She might even start to have second thoughts about the wedding. He'd managed to nip the whole thing in the butt and promised Conor that he'd delete all of the texts. And he had. All except the one where she was wearing this short little . . . damn! He was getting distracted.

He picked up his laptop again and began to type. 'A NYMPHOMANIAC becomes obsessed with A HAND-SOME ACTOR.'

Nah. He deleted it. That was just too scary.

Conor switched off the alarm clock and lay with his eyes closed, feeling the warm, smooth length of Jess's leg against his. He dipped his chin a little so he could inhale the sweet, sleepy scent of her. Then he forced himself to sit up, pushing his fingers into his eyes to stop them from closing again.

He had a hard-on. This was not good timing. He'd been at his makeshift desk till one last night and Jess had been asleep when he came to bed. Right now, he would have given anything to wake her up and make sleepy love.

But that was the whole point. If he could do this, if he could just keep going, if he could get this book finished and off to Becky Kemp, there was a possibility that maybe, just maybe, it would be published and that he could, at some point, give up teaching and write for a living. He wouldn't have to drag himself out of bed at five a.m. He'd have the time and energy to have sex with Jess every morning if he felt like it. Which he would.

He sat on his wonky swivel chair taking scalding sips of strong coffee and willing his brain to fire up. It should have been easier to write now that someone was interested in the book, especially someone from a decent agency like Douglas, Kemp & Troy, but for some reason it wasn't.

He felt as if Becky Kemp was looking over his shoulder. He had checked her out on the agency website. Her black-and-white profile picture showed an earnest, preppy woman in her thirties with long hair and glasses. He wished he hadn't looked at it because now he saw every sentence he wrote through her cool critical eyes and this was seriously slowing him down.

He had stupidly told her assistant Juniper that he'd complete the next 30,000 words of *Doubles or Quits* by the third week in May. It was nearly the middle of April now and he was way behind. He'd doubled and then trebled the hours he was putting in but it didn't seem to make a difference.

He was distracted at school and the kids had picked up on it and gone into overdrive. Yesterday, while he was writing an e.e. cummings poem on the blackboard, someone had drawn a penis on his satchel in black marker and signed it 'b.f. cuming'. There wasn't any point in reporting it to Mr Quigley, the headmaster. It was *his* job to keep discipline in the classroom. He was the one who would get into trouble.

And then there was Greg. He really wished he hadn't gone for a drink with Greg after the suit fitting. If he hadn't, he wouldn't have seen those tacky MMS messages from the make-up artist at *The Station*. And he wouldn't know that Greg had slept with her.

What was he supposed to do with this information? Saffy was his friend; he really felt that she had the right to know about this. But Greg was his friend, too, and he'd made Conor promise that he wouldn't tell anyone, especially not Jess.

He was kind of relieved in a way. Jess had been really on edge lately, which was understandable. She hated him working early in the morning and late at night. And she hadn't forgiven him for falling asleep at the cinema on the twins' seventh birthday, though Luke and Lizzie had thought it was hilarious. They had made snoring noises at him all through their birthday tea and he had played along, pretending to doze off to keep them amused but Jess hadn't even cracked a smile. Conor hated himself for making her unhappy but it made him even more determined to give this his best shot. If the book got published, if it really ended up on the shelves, she'd know that it had all been worthwhile. She might even be proud of him.

Nervous Dermot was living up to his nickname. So far he had rejected six of Ant and Vicky's TV scripts. Saffy's inbox was permanently hopping with nagging emails from Marsh and it was hard not to take Ant's posters personally.

Not when they said things like: *The answer is: it's your fucking fault. Now what was the question?* And: *How can I miss you when you won't go away?*

Even Vicky, who was always so understanding about re-briefs, was starting to look at Saffy like Bambi.

'I hope you can sell this,' she said when Saffy dropped by to pick up the latest script and storyboard on her way to meeting Dermot, 'because I've bought Ant all the Smints a man can eat and agreed to tidy up my half of the office. I could offer him sex but we both know he'd turn me down. I'm running out of ways to get him to keep working on this.'

Saffy hoped she could sell it too. And she hoped she could sell it in under an hour. She had managed to block out three hours at lunchtime. There was only time to go into one bridal shop but she had made an appointment at the best one in Dublin and she was going to come out with a dress. Because if she didn't, there wouldn't be a wedding.

Jess could think of several horrible things she'd prefer to do than go shopping for a wedding dress. Eat Conor's spagausages, for example. Collect spiders for Lizzie's show-and-tell. Comb Luke's hair for lice. Clean out Brendan's cage. Clean it out and put it away in the attic. Because at this stage, it looked like Brendan, as Greg might say, had scuttled off this mortal coil.

She dabbed at a strange, crusty stain on the front of a black jersey dress she'd bought for a funeral years ago. The mark wouldn't come off but she had to wear something presentable for Saffy's sake so it would have to do.

She was opening the front door to leave when the phone rang. It was Miles, the editor of *Looks*.

'Jess, darling.' Miles wasn't gay or posh, but he pretended to be both. 'Have you got anything *in particular* planned for this afternoon? Because I'm thinking of coming over to scratch your eyes out.'

'Great. I'll put the kettle on,' Jess said pleasantly. Having her eyes scratched out sounded tempting compared to a couple of hours in bridalwear.

'I'm looking at your copy for our Summer Splash section. Is

this meant to be a joke? You've written nothing, *nothing*, about Chanel Hydramax, and they're taking a double-page spread. Your have misspelled the name of that sweet French couple at Divine Cupcakes and *this* is how you propose to tempt our readers into Brazilian Babes Waxing Salon.'

His voice, already on the high side, shot up an octave. 'I Scream. You Scream. We all scream for ice cream. But not as loudly as we scream for a squeaky-clean, summertime bikini line. It's no pain, no gain at Brazilian Babes. Red-hot wax whips unsightly hair out by the roots. At sixty-five euro a session, the Barbie-doll bare-all is the ultimate rip-off.'

'Okay, I'll write it again, Miles.' Jess sighed. He might be high-maintenance but he was her only real client and he paid some of the bills.

'Yes, you will. And you'll have it on my desk in one hour. And not a second later. Because I am in no mood.'

Jess swore silently. Saffy would be on her way to the shop by now. 'I can do it, Miles, but I can't do it in an hour. I can have it for you by four.'

'If that's the best you can do,' Miles sneered, 'don't bother your behind. And while we're on the subject of your behind, consider yourself out on it.'

'On what?'

'Your ass, darling. You're fired.'

Saffy was late so Jess had to brave Blossom Bridal Atelier alone. She perched on a stupid slippery white satin and gilt sofa and helped herself to a glass of champagne from a bucket full of ice and feathers. She needed it. Her hands were shaking. Miles was just having one of his hissy fits. He'd come around. He always did.

The good news was that Saffy had persuaded Nervous Dermot to put the latest Angel script into research. Consumers would love it and Marsh would be happy because he'd signed off on another ten thousand euro for focus groups.

The bad news was that it had taken her two hours. And Marsh had texted her to tell her to join a three o'clock meeting on

Avondale. Which left her ninety minutes to buy her wedding dress.

'I'm sorry I'm late.' She kissed Jess. 'You look gorgeous. I like the dress. Is that champagne?' She poured a glass. 'Any sign of my mother?'

Jess ignored the disapproving glance of a hovering assistant in a baby-pink uniform and held out her glass too. She needed another drink after what had just happened. 'Looks like she's a no-show.'

Saffy switched on her phone and checked her texts. 'I just don't get it, Jess. I've tried to involve her but she's not interested. She didn't come down to Woodglen. We invited her and Len over to lunch last weekend and she cancelled the day before. And look at this!'

She held her phone out so Jess could read it: SORRY CAN'T MAKE IT. RUN OFF FEET. GOOD LUCK WITH DRESS.

She shook her head in disbelief. 'Seriously! This is not normal. I've only seen her once since we got engaged. What is going on with her?'

'I was thinking about that.' Jess picked a feather out of her glass. 'Maybe she's finding the whole wedding thing difficult.'

'Come on. This is what she's always wanted.'

'Yes I know, but I'm sure Greg's inviting a busload of Gleesons and Jill hasn't seen her family since before you were born. It'll just be her and Len. She probably never thought about that.'

Jess was right. Her mother had given her a list of half a dozen people to invite to the wedding but none of them were relatives. Jill had never seen her parents or her brother again after she moved to Dublin. Saffy was so used to the fact that it was just the two of them that it didn't seem strange to her, but it was.

'And maybe the fact that you're finally getting married is making her feel bad,' Jess went on, 'because she never did. Why didn't she, by the way? She's still young and I'm sure she's had lots of chances.'

Saffy settled back on the uncomfortable little sofa. She couldn't remember the last time she'd sat down with a glass of wine and had a proper conversation. It felt good. She leaned over to pick up the champagne bottle. 'I don't know. I've often wondered about that—'

The assistant swooped, moving the ice bucket out of reach. 'Which one of you ladies,' she said firmly, 'is Sally Martin?'

Amanda Wakeley. Vera Wang. Maria Grachvogel. They would have wept into their frilly hankies if they had seen their dresses on Saffy. Everything made her look like a cake in a car crash. Her hair frizzed up with static and her ring kept snagging in the delicate lace and tulle.

'Here, take this,' she took the ring off and handed it to Jess, 'or I'll have to hand it over to pay for the damage.' She ducked back into the dressing room.

Jess slid it onto her finger. It really was horrendous, she thought. It looked like something out of a Christmas cracker. And it had probably cost a fortune.

Saffy passed a dress out through the curtain. 'I'm not even going to try this one on. I'm not spending five grand on a dress. Even Greg would think that was over the top.'

Five grand? Jess didn't even want to touch it. She dropped it on the back of a chair quickly and asked the curtain the question she hadn't wanted to ask to Saffy's face. 'How much is the wedding going to cost?'

'I don't know yet. But I've had to borrow twenty thousand, so far, and Greg's selling his car for thirty-something. I don't think there'll be much change. But it's an investment in Greg's career. You kind of have to have a big wedding if you're in show business.'

Jess swallowed. Fifty. Thousand. Euro. That was obscene. That was five years' rent. Greg and Saffy had lost the plot. Why was she the only one who could see it? Conor just shrugged when she brought it up.

Since the letter from the agent in London, Conor had been weird, sort of jumpy and distant. She had overheard him talking to some assistant at the agency in London. He had sounded like somebody she didn't really know.

He had committed to writing another big chunk of the book. Jess didn't want to rain on his parade, but there was no guarantee that they'd take him on at all. He could be doing all this for nothing. And he was doing it at all hours of the day and night, which meant that she hardly saw him.

It was nearly a week since they had last had sex. And last night he'd asked her if he could move his desk and computer up to their bedroom. He said he was finding it hard to concentrate in the hall because it was so cramped and because the kids were playing Snap on the stairs and they were disturbing him.

'You find Luke and Lizzie *disturbing*?' she'd teased him. 'I'm sorry . . . who are you? And what have you done with Conor?'

And he must have realised, on some level, how unreasonable he was being because he dropped the subject and went back to writing in the hall.

Saffy came out of the fitting room in a Catherine Walker dress. 'What do you think?'

What Jess thought, for a horrible Julia Roberts chick-flick moment, was that she was going to cry. The dress was just a long, asymmetrical column of shimmering silk but it skimmed over Saffy's hips, clung to her narrow waist and brought out the faint hint of colour in her cheeks and the green in her eyes. She looked pale and delicate and absolutely beautiful.

'Turn around.' Saffy turned and Jess took her hair down out of her pony-tail, letting it fall onto her bare shoulders in feathery waves.

'You know how much I hate all this wedding crap,' Jess said. 'But this is the dress.'

Saffy looked at herself in the mirror. 'Are you supposed to pick your wedding dress in forty-five minutes? Isn't that bad luck or something?'

'Not if it you spend the next forty-five minutes having a salmon sandwich and a glass of Guinness in Neary's.'

'What about a veil?' Saffy asked.

'Are you a seventeen-year-old Italian virgin?' Jess asked.

Saffy laughed. 'Okay. No veil. But you're going to need a bridesmaid's dress . . .'

Jess had been dreading this. 'Please don't do this to me, Saffy. Greg's already given Conor some truly horrific little outfits for Luke and Lizzie. Don't make me wear a peach taffeta concoction. I'm begging you.'

'Okay. But you have to promise that you'll wear an actual dress and shoes with heels and that you won't buy them in Primark and that you'll let me pay for them.'

'I promise.'

'And that you'll have your hair and make-up done and—'

Jess steered her back into the fitting room. 'Don't push it.' She turned to the girl at the cash desk. 'My friend wants to take this dress . . .'

The girl tucked her hair extensions behind her ears and fluttered her eyelash extensions. 'You mean she'd like to *order* it.'

'No. I mean she'd like to *take* it.'

'It's a sample. It's not for sale. It has to be ordered.' The girl tapped her nail extensions on the glass counter.

'How long will it take to come in if we order it now?'

'Three months. At least.' She tried to take the dress but Jess wasn't letting go of it. She was getting out of this bridal hellhole and she was taking the dress with her.

'She needs it in *three* weeks,' Jess said.

'Well, I'm sorry,' the girl shrugged, 'but we need it too. We can't sell an order unless we have a sample on the floor.'

'Couldn't you make an exception?'

'I'm afraid not.'

'Not even if the bride is going to be *Mrs Greg Gleeson*?'

'I don't have time for the whole *shoe* thing. I'm just going to order a pair of Gina flip-flops online.' Saffy tried to wave down a cab. 'I know they'll fit and I won't be taller than Greg so . . . no! No! No! No!'

She shoved the dress bag into Jess's arms and dashed out into the street in front of a motorcycle courier. He swerved to avoid her and drove off swearing.

'Saffy!' Jess couldn't run after her. Not with the dress bag.

'Saffy!' A tall, tanned, guy with messy fair hair was shouting after her too.

Saffy disappeared around a corner on the other side of the road.

'Bloody hell! Where's the fire?' the guy said to Jess. He was Australian.

Jess shook her head. 'I don't know.'

'I'm Doug.' He held out a huge, tanned hand. It had a scattering of tiny white scars and one of those stupid Kabbalah threads around the wrist. She shook it.

'I'm Jess.' Did she know him? Was he someone from Saffy's office?

He gave her a lazy smile. 'Saffy and I spent the night together a couple of weeks back. *Obviously* she didn't enjoy it too much or she wouldn't be so keen to get decapitated to avoid me. And *obviously* it's not my day because I see you're already taken.'

'What?' Jess was confused. *Saffy had spent the night with this guy?*

Doug misunderstood her. He pointed at Saffy's ring, which Jess still had on her finger. 'Two,' he pointed at the wedding dress bag, 'plus two usually equals four. When's the big day?'

Jess snorted. 'Never . . .' she began. Then she stopped herself. She didn't approve of Saffy spending the night with some random Australian but that didn't mean she was going to tell him her business.

'. . . never thought I'd do this but it's in three weeks.'

'Well, tell your fiancé from me he's one lucky guy. And do me a favour, will you? When you catch up with Saffy, tell her Dublin's a small town. I'll catch her later.'

Saffy was sitting at the bar in Neary's. She had ordered two salmon sandwiches and two glasses of Guinness and she had drunk most of both.

'I'm sorry I ran off like that. That was David,' she said. 'He's a nightmare client and I'm trying to avoid him because—'

'His name is *Doug*.' Jess dumped the dress bag on a stool and glared at her. 'And he said he slept with you.'

Saffy put her head in her hands.

'It's not how it sounds, Jess. He threatened to cut up my credit card at a client lunch and he blackmailed me into going out for a ridiculous meal. And he dragged me all over Dublin and made me eat fast food and oysters and got me completely pissed. And then he bullied me into going back to his horrible apartment in Temple Bar to eat a soufflé and then, I don't know . . .'

'You don't know what?'

Saffy shook her head. 'I don't know what happened,' she whispered. 'I can't remember.'

Jess stared at her. 'You blacked out! And you had a one-night stand! Saffy! You're about to get married.'

'It happened when Greg and I weren't together. And I don't know if anything *did* happen. One minute he was making the soufflé and the next minute I woke up in his bed. I know I *ate* the soufflé because—' She had a sudden flashback to the balloon pilot's boots, spattered with tiny orange and brown flecks. 'Well, it doesn't matter how I know. But the rest is a total blank. Look, I kind of lost the plot when Greg moved out. But I'm fine, honestly. I just don't want to talk about it. Don't make me, okay?'

'But—'

'Please.' Saffy began to cry.

Jess wanted to shake her but instead she took out a tissue and handed it to her and told her to blow her nose. That's what you did when you had children. That's what you did when other people were out getting drunk and eating soufflés and oysters and sleeping with complete strangers. You looked after people.

Saffy was trying to think sexy thoughts but other thoughts kept interrupting. Unsexy thoughts about what would happen if she ran into Doug when she was with Greg. And whether or not she'd remembered to send the Avondale TV scripts to Copy Clearance. And how she was going to manage to sneak out of the office tomorrow to have her eyebrows tinted without Marsh, who saw *everything*, noticing that she'd had them done. And why Greg had suddenly become so weirdly athletic in bed.

Sex had always been good. She had always put a lot of work into making it good. Greg was happy to lie back and let her be in charge but, since they got back together, he had started to get more involved. This was not a bad thing except that he seemed to be in perpetual motion. He flipped her onto her back now, jabbing his elbow briefly but painfully into what she thought might be her liver and then kneeling on her right hand in what seemed to be an attempt to climb onto her face.

She wanted to please him, she really did, but she was exhausted and she had to be up in six hours. 'Um, Greg, what are we doing here?'

He grinned down at her wickedly. 'Anything you like, Babe. You want to tie me up?'

He looked incredibly sexy, like an Athena poster, except for the fact that she could see up his nose. He pinned her arms down, playfully.

'How about I tie *you* up? Or . . .' He reached for his mobile. 'We could take some sexy pictures of one another.'

Pictures. God. No. Not pictures. Not when she hadn't had eight hours straight sleep for a month. She wriggled free.

'Maybe we could do that some other time? Like the weekend? I'm sorry. It's just that I'm so tired I can barely move. We could do something, you know, less adventurous if you like.'

He rolled over and got out of bed.

'Greg, I'm so sorry. I don't mean to ruin the mood. It's just all the pressure at work. We have the rest of our lives to have mind-blowing sex. And we will. I promise.'

He leaned down and patted her hair. 'Chillax, Babe. Course we will.'

He put on his dressing gown and went to the bathroom. Saffy sat up and turned on the bedside light. She had hurt his feelings. She'd find a way to make it up to him when she wasn't so damned tired. She opened her laptop to check if she'd sent the Avondale schedule, but it wasn't hers it was Greg's. And when he came back, she was sitting up in bed reading his guest-list spreadsheet.

'Greg, I see you've, um, invited Bono to our wedding.'

'Yep.' Greg took the laptop and closed it. 'Dude hasn't confirmed yet but he made the cut.'

He'd invited all the Irish A-listers, including everyone at *The Station*, even that jerk Damo Doyle. The guy was a wolf in cheap clothing but if this was going to be the wedding of the year, Greg needed every celebrity he could get. So far only about half of the guests were confirmed. But there were still two weeks to go. He'd leave it a few days and then get Vivienne to call their people and get them to pull the finger out. 'Greg, I know I've met

Bono a couple of times, but I'm not sure I really *know* him,' Saffy said carefully. 'Or Andrea Corr or Cillian Murphy or Colm Meaney.'

Greg fished his mobile out of the pocket of his dressing gown and put it on the bedside table. When had he started taking his mobile with him to the bathroom? Saffy wondered.

'Of course you know Colm Meaney,' he said. 'You've seen *Deep Space Nine*, haven't you?'

Jess jumped as if she'd been electrocuted and slammed her foot into the headboard, stubbing her toe. 'Ow! What was that?'

Conor lifted his head. 'I was just licking the back of your knee. I thought you liked that.'

'I do, but not when you use teeth.'

'Sorry.' He hauled himself up to her end of the bed.

She ran her hand up his thigh. 'Hey, come back down here. We're not finished, are we?' Apparently they were. He pulled away so he didn't have to see the confusion and hurt in her face.

What was wrong with them? It was as if they'd forgotten the steps of a dance they'd done a thousand times, and it was weirdly embarrassing. Part of him wanted to try again but he didn't want to risk it.

'I'm sorry. How about if I just hold you for a while?' He put his arm around her. He could feel her body crackling with tension under his hand.

'Sure.' Jess lay on her back and stared at the familiar crack on the ceiling above the bed. It usually reminded her of an angel's wing but she was used to seeing it in a delicious post-orgasm haze of oxytocin. Now, in the cold light of sexual frustration, it looked more like a metaphor for their relationship.

Conor had been tired before. They'd both been tired. They'd hardly slept for the first two years after the twins were born but sex had been great. Sex had always been great.

But you couldn't have sex with somebody who wasn't there. Jess couldn't connect with him, no matter how she tried. It had been days since they had a proper conversation. She had a frightening thought. If this was what he was like now, when he didn't even have a contract, what would he be like if he was published?

She had always been so sure of him. She'd never even thought about the possibility of losing him to another woman. But now she was beginning to think that she was already losing him, along with the life that she loved, to a *book*. It scared her. This book, which she wasn't even allowed to read, was already taking Conor away from her for hours every day. But if he got what he wanted, if it was published, it would take him even further. To London. To meet new people who would make her feel uncomfortable. To parties where she would never fit in.

Conor stroked her back. 'What's going through that lovely head of yours, Jess? Come on, I know there's something you're not telling me. You've been on edge all week. What is it?'

There were so many things she hadn't told him. She took a deep breath and picked the easiest one.

'Okay,' she said defensively. 'Well, for a start, Miles freaked out and fired me.'

Conor squeezed her. 'Miles is an idiot. And you know what? He's done you a favour. This is a chance for you to set up some meetings with the *Irish Times* and the *Indo* and get some regular features or even a column . . . You're way too good to write that advertorial shit.'

'I know.' He could feel her beginning to relax. 'You're right. And there's something else, Conor.' Maybe it would bother her less, she reasoned, if she told somebody else. 'Saffy would kill me if she knew I was telling you this but she cheated on Greg.'

Conor pulled back so he could see her face. 'You're kidding?'

'We were out shopping for the dress – the wedding dress, I mean – and we bumped into this guy on the street.'

'What guy?'

'Doug something. Aussie. Arrogant. She had a one-night stand with him while Greg was living in that hotel.'

'Jess.' Conor shook his head. 'This is so messed up.'

'You have no idea. She blacked out, Conor! She doesn't even remember it.'

'That's not what I meant.' He had sworn to Greg that he

wouldn't tell Jess about the make-up girl but he had to tell her now. 'What's messed up is . . . Greg slept with someone too.'

Jess's eyes widened. 'What?'

'It was some nineteen-year-old who works on *The Station*. She's been sexting him.'

Jess looked at him blankly.

'Sexting him. You know, sending him porno texts. All the kids are doing it. He showed me some of them.'

'What were they like?'

'Pictures of her body and sexy messages, you know.'

Jess didn't know, but what she *did* know was she didn't like the idea of Conor looking at pictures of some naked nineteen-year-old.

'This is all wrong, Jess.'

'I know.'

For some reason, Conor felt closer to her than he had for weeks. He stroked her hair.

'I feel kind of dirty knowing about all this when they don't.'

She smiled up at him and ran a finger down over his shoulder and circled his nipple. 'You do? How dirty?'

'I'm serious. Do you think we should do something?'

She wriggled so that he could slide his leg between hers. 'We are doing something,' she murmured into his neck. 'This is something, isn't it?'

14

Greg had gone out to do something mysterious involving wedding rings, and Saffy was supposed to be working through her emails. Instead, she sneaked onto his laptop to take another look at his wedding spreadsheets. Everything seemed under control, down to the last detail. He'd even booked a hairdresser and a make-up artist, which was really thoughtful because no bride was ever going to need them as much as she did. She looked the way she felt. Completely burned out.

A file with the readings for the church was open and she scanned one quickly:

> *My Beloved is like a gazelle, like a young stag.*
> *See where he stands behind our wall.*
> *He looks in at the window, he peers through the lettuce.*

Neither of them was remotely like a gazelle, and she was pretty sure it was supposed to be 'lattice' not 'lettuce', but she wasn't supposed to interfere.

She closed the laptop. She had a couple of details to sort out herself. Like finding something old, something new, something borrowed and something blue.

Her dress was new. She had a sapphire on a silver chain to cover the 'blue' part. She'd borrow a hairclip or something from Jess. That just left 'old'. If her father was still alive, he'd be seventy-three now. That counted as old, didn't it?

Missing having a father was something she thought she'd grow out of but there was always a gap there, a space that nobody else could fill. Most of the time, it was just a dull ache that she had learned to live with but, at weddings, it changed into a sharp jab around the time that the father of the bride stood, tapped his glass and said, 'I'd like, if I may, to say a few words about my beautiful daughter . . .'

Without realising it, Saffy had stored away every father-of-the-bride speech she'd ever heard. There was the dad who had listed the names of every stuffed toy his daughter had ever owned. The one who used to lift his four-year-old every night so she could touch the four corners of the ceiling before going to sleep. The one who remembered walking down Grafton Street with his fifteen-year-old and suddenly realising, when he saw every head turn, that his little girl had grown up. The one who stunned a roomful of guests when he announced, 'Fiona is not my daughter,' then waited for a full sixty seconds before going on, 'she's my best friend.'

The shy fathers, the mutterers and stammerers, were the ones that got to her most. The ones whose voices cracked, who clutched their speeches in their shaking hands and fought back tears when they told the groom that he was the luckiest man in the world.

The door opened. It was the luckiest man in the world.

'Hey! You still working? Only one more day to go.' Greg grinned.

'Yep!' She grinned back. Tomorrow was her last day at work. She was going down to Woodglen on Thursday with Jess and the wedding was on Friday. There hadn't been time to organise a stag or a hen party and that was fine by Saffy. She'd always hated them.

Greg took her hand and pulled her to her feet and led her over to the sofa and they lay down face to face. This was the face she was going to look at for the rest of her life and she knew she would never get tired of it. She was almost sorry that they weren't going to have children. It seemed like a crime against genetics not to pass on those eyes and that mouth and those cheekbones to another person.

'I've got a surprise, Babe,' Greg said softly. 'I've just booked dinner at Halo tomorrow night. We haven't had much of a chance to hang out together with all your work stuff. I thought we'd try to catch some romantic you-and-me time before the madness begins.'

Her heart began to thump. 'Does it have to begin, Greg? Can't we just sneak away and do this in a register office? Or on the beach in Antigua? We don't need hundreds of people. We can say our vows to one another without anyone around.'

He stroked her hair. 'Babe, if that's what you want, just say the word.'

He looked so sexy and so kind and so *brown*. She sniffed him. There was a faint smell of coconut underneath his Creed aftershave. She wondered if he'd had a spray tan.

'Come on, get off the fence, Saffy.' Marsh rolled her eyes. 'We're all getting splinters in our butts watching you sit on it.'

Saffy had put off the decision on the director for the Avondale TV ads till the day before she finished up. It was down to two options. She had promised Ant and Vicky that she'd fight for a young English director they'd found. He had put together a really brilliant treatment and he was obviously keen. The Irish guy was way cheaper but his show reel was old and tired, and she knew from talking to him that he didn't get the 'cheesy' concept.

But there was fifty grand difference in price so it was never going to be an easy sell to Marsh.

'Well, I've brought the English guy down as low as he'll go,' she said carefully, 'but I know he'll deliver really high production values. And this isn't just an ad for Avondale. It's an ad for Komodo, too. With the right director, this idea has award-winner written all over it.'

'Yeah, but at what price?' Simon's hair was gelled up into annoying little spikes and his tie was the exact same annoying shade as his big blue eyes. Everything about Simon was annoying, especially the fact that he was getting to take over on the Avondale account while she was on honeymoon.

'Em . . . converted from sterling the price would be €239,876.71,' Mike said, thinking that this was an actual question. 'But that's before VAT . . .'

'Slam dunk.' Simon mimed shooting a hoop. 'The Irish guy is coming in at €189,000. If we go with him, we can add that fifty thou onto our mark-up.'

'Let's make this interesting.' Marsh crossed her legs, flashing a couple of inches of perfectly toned, tanned thigh below the hem of her nude Stella McCartney dress. 'Let's add a little spice to the pot. Let's say that if we go with the Irish production company and the lovely Simon here works his ass off to get them to deliver equally high production values, then everyone round this table could be looking at a nice five-grand bonus.'

Mike and Simon looked at Saffy. She looked down at the two budget sheets on the table in front of her but she wasn't seeing them, she was seeing the balance on the honeymoon in Antigua. Greg had texted her earlier to ask her if she'd pay it at lunchtime. It came to €4,960.

The poster on the door of the office said: *Jesus loves you, but he won't respect you in the morning.*

Vicky was looking at pictures of Venice, online.

'Are you going to Italy?' Saffy asked.

'No, I was just . . .' she closed her browser '. . . researching something.'

'Tell the suit the truth.' Ant jabbed a pencil into his Alessi pencil sharpener. 'Tell it you were snooping round the hotel where your shitty *boyfriend* is taking his *wife*.'

Vicky swivelled around. 'Shut up, Ant! Josh is taking Little Lindsay to Venice for her birthday and his *ex*-wife is going because of Lindsay's asthma. It's very damp in Venice. But they'll have separate rooms.'

'Yeah, right.' Ant tested the point of his sharpened pencil on the pad of his index finger. It left a small, grey mark. It looked like it hurt. Saffy took a breath. There was no easy way to say this.

'Listen, guys, I'm afraid I've got some bad news. I've just come out of a meeting on Avondale TV and I've been outvoted. I'm afraid the Irish director's going to be shooting the ad. I'm off tomorrow but Simon's going to set up a meeting with the production company on Thursday.'

The flush started at the top of Ant's shaved skull and moved down past his angry little eyes to his pointy chin. It flowed down his neck and disappeared under his black Banksy T-shirt. He let out a sort of mangled snort and threw the pencil sharpener on the floor. Pencil shavings spilled out onto the carpet. Saffy had never seen anything other than Ant's shoes on his half of the floor before. It was kind of shocking.

He opened his drawer and upended a plastic tray of grey paper clips, then grabbed a fistful of bulldog clips and hurled them at the wall.

'Ant! Calm down.' Vicky sighed. 'It's not the end of the world. The English director was amazing. But I'm sure we can get something just as good out of this other guy. We'll just have to babysit him a bit. And we still have the White Feather TV coming up, we'll hold out for someone really brilliant for that, right, Saffy?'

'Right.'

Ant picked up his waste-paper basket. It was empty except for a Smint box. He took it out, placed it carefully on his desk smashed it with his fist.

'You'd better go,' Vicky whispered.

'I'm sorry,' Saffy said, 'I feel terrible.'

'It's okay.' Vicky squeezed her arm. 'It's not your fault. We know you fought as hard as you could.'

Saffy had thought that her last day at work would be easier and she had planned to sneak off and have her hair done before lunch and then squeeze in a two-hour session of beauty treatments.

But at the last minute Marsh dragged her into an agency credentials presentation for a new client and she had to cancel the hairdresser. Greg had booked hair and make-up people for the wedding. She'd just have to ask them to do their best with her split ends.

The presentation ran into lunch and she had to swing by the travel agent on her way to the salon so she was forty minutes late for her Bridal Preen and Pamper treatment.

She had been looking forward to lying down and relaxing and letting go for a couple of hours. If there was new-age music and a scented candle thrown in, she had been planning to doze off. She was so tired she thought she might even sleep through the bikini wax.

The beauty therapist was sitting in reception, snapping her gum and her magazine. She rolled her eyes when Saffy apologised.

The treatment room was cold. It was scented with Pot Noodle from the salon kitchen where the other therapists were having their lunch. 'I, um, have to be back in the office in an hour and a bit,' Saffy said. 'So we're going to have to be pretty quick, I'm afraid.'

'I can do you a mini-mani, a half leg and a bikini.' The girl handed her a tiny towel. 'Or I can do an eyebrow shape, eyelash tint and mini-pedi.'

'I'm getting married in two days,' Saffy stammered. 'I need everything.'

The beautician snorted. 'Well, you should have thought of that before you showed up late. Now do you want me to heat this wax or not?'

Greg took extra care getting ready for dinner with Saffy. He picked out a new white Prada shirt, a black velvet Paul Smith jacket, black skinny jeans and black All-Stars for that rock 'n' roll edge. He took a long, hard look at himself in the mirror.

He hadn't worked out since he'd left *The Station* but his six-pack didn't seem to have noticed and the swelling in his eye had finally gone. Overall, he thought, Saffy was getting a pretty good package.

He was glad he'd decided not to have some kind of big, blokey stag. Going out for a romantic dinner with Saffy was much more his speed. Apart from Conor, he didn't have many mates. Guys were threatened by him, they always had been. And right now, he was glad that he was sitting on his bed putting on a pair of antique Chanel cufflinks, not kneeling beside it praying that a bunch of drunken nutters wouldn't strip him naked and chain him to a bus stop.

Saffy shut down her computer. She had written detailed contact reports for every job she was handling. She had sent lists of instructions to Vicky and Simon and Mike. She'd set up an automated mail to say she'd be back on 30 May.

It was too late to go back to the apartment to change but she'd brought a cream Reiss dress to wear to dinner with Greg. She closed her blinds, slipped into it and changed her shoes. She turned out her light and closed the door. She stood there smiling for a few moments. The next time she opened it, she'd be Mrs Gleeson.

Suddenly all the lights went on and there was a huge cheer from above her.

'Surprise!'

Leaning over the railing of the mezzanine, raining down rose petal confetti on her head, were Marsh, Vicky, Ciara, the girls from accounts, most of her female clients, Jess and her *mother*. She was surprised. She was so surprised that her mouth opened and a couple of dried petals fell in.

The boardroom had been turned into a private dining room. There were candles and bowls of white roses everywhere. All the place settings had been customised with black-and-white pictures of Saffy as a baby, as a toddler and as a teenager.

Vicky must have done these, Saffy realised, and she must have asked her mother for the originals. She tried to catch Jill's eye but two waiters, stripped to the waist, were bearing down on her. One handed her a flute of champagne. The other one held out a tray of erotic canapés. Saffy took the least offensive one, which looked like a tiny and scarily realistic pair of buttocks.

Marsh, in a white Gucci sheath slashed to the navel, grinned at Saffy. 'Take one good hard last look at *this*.' She put her arm around one of the waiters and gave his nipple a playful tweak. 'This is what you'll be giving up when you promise to love, honour and obey.'

Everyone in Dublin seemed to be crammed into the Fitzmaurice Cocktail Bar and they were all looking at Greg. He wished Saffy would hurry up. He'd already been asked to pose for two pictures and sign three autographs and some very drunk girls at a table behind him kept singing fire-related songs in his general direction. 'Smoke On The Water', 'Ring Of Fire', 'Great Balls Of Fire', 'This Fire' . . . It was beginning to wind him up.

'Where are you, Babe?' he said when Saffy called. 'I'm on my second Martini. And it's shit. We're never going to be taken seriously as a first-world country while we're still making third-world cocktails.'

'Greg, I can't come.'

'They're bad but they're not *that* bad. I think it's probably something to do with the ice.' He waved away a red-haired girl with an overbite who was hovering. 'I've ordered you a Bellini. It's pretty much impossible to screw up a Bellini.'

'What I meant is, I'm not going to be able to have dinner with you. I can't. Marsh has organised a surprise hen party for me at the agency. Everyone is here: the girls from the office, Jess, my clients, my *mother*!'

'Well, stay for a half an hour. I've booked the table for eight but I'm sure they'll hold it. Paul Dunn from the *Mail* is going to come by to take some snaps. I've picked up the wedding rings from the jeweller's to show you and—'

'I'm sorry,' she whispered. He could hear shrieking and giggling in the background. 'I'm so, so sorry. But I can't just leave.'

Greg felt winded, as if he'd been punched hard in the chest. Saffy had been working late every night since he'd proposed. And at the weekends. He'd barely seen her and, when he did, she could hardly keep her eyes open. He hadn't given her a hard time. All he'd asked for was one bloody evening. But when another offer came along, she'd jumped sheep.

'Listen, Greg, I love you. I love you so much. And I'd give anything to be with you right now. But if I leave, Marsh will flip out. She's really gone overboard with this. There's outside catering and half-naked waiters and a chocolate fountain—'

'What? Wait a second. Which half?' Greg interrupted. 'Which half is naked?'

He put his phone back in his pocket. The red-haired woman swooped. 'Excuse me, weren't you Mac Malone? Before he died?' He shook his head tiredly. A few months ago, he'd been Mac Malone, the fifth Most Eligible Man in Ireland. Now he was the has-been who had been fired from *The Station*, the loser who'd nearly made it to Hollywood, the saddo whose fiancé had stood him up to party with half-naked—'

His phone vibrated. It was Saffy. She'd changed her mind. Only it wasn't. It was an MMS. A shot of the back of a handsome guy in a black velvet jacket sitting on a barstool with his head in his hands.

'I C U. DO U C ME ?'

It was weird, Saffy thought, to see people from all the separate parts of her life talking to one another. Jess was showing Ciara pictures of Luke and Lizzie. Vicky was telling her mother about Little Lindsay's allergies. Jill was wearing a dramatic black-and-white geometric print dress that made her look a bit washed out. Saffy had tried to get Jill on her own but she kept slipping away and now they were seated at opposite ends of the table.

Marsh was surrounded by a circle of female clients who had that studious look women always got when they had a chance to look at her up close. She was so perfectly put together that you couldn't help looking really hard to see if you could find a flaw – a wrinkle or a bulge or a hair that was growing out of, or better still into, the wrong place. But there wasn't one. Not one that Saffy had ever found anyway.

She was telling them the story of her life. Saffy had heard it several times. How she'd gone to America on a green card with a hundred and twenty pounds, a couple of bikinis and a set of heated rollers and come back with ten years' experience on Madison Avenue, a divorce and enough money to set up her own agency.

'After I got away from the horrible Wall Street WASP,' she was saying, 'I had to let my hair down a bit so I moved into a loft on the Lower East Side. Let's just say I was Samantha from *Sex and the City* before there was a *Sex and the City*.

'And you never had kids?' Lucy, one of the NoQ girls, asked.

'You can't have kids and sex.'

Jess looked up. 'Excuse me! Yes, you can! I have twins. And I'm very happy with my sex life, thanks.'

Marsh narrowed her eyes. 'Really? Tell me, did you do labour or a Caesarean?'

'I had an emergency Caesarean. What's that got to do with it?'

'From what my male friends tell me,' Marsh laughed: 'everything.'

Jess wasn't laughing. 'Do you have any idea how sexist that sounds?'

'Do you have any idea what happens to your vajayjay after

you've pushed eight and a half pounds of infant through it?' Marsh shot back.

'My *what*?' Jess had to raise her voice to be heard over Ali's hooting.

'Everything changes after you have a baby,' Saffy's mother said sadly. 'Everything changes and nothing is ever the same again.'

It was a shrine. There was no other word for it. It was like something out of the *Blair Wish Project*. Greg swallowed hard. His saliva had the sharp, chemical burn of whatever Tanya had given him to snort earlier.

He sat down at the end of the bed, closed his eyes and listened to her clattering around downstairs, where she'd gone to find lemons and salt and glasses. Then he opened them again and looked around the room at the flower fairy lights trailed across the small mantelpiece. At the traffic cone, painted pink, perched on top of the wardrobe. At the bed with its pink spread and its pile of purple fun-fur cushions. He looked back at the alcove, hoping that maybe he'd imagined it but he hadn't. It was definitely a shrine.

The wall was papered with a swirling collage of his face and his words: photographs of Mac Malone in uniform, pictures of Greg cut from magazines, continuity Polaroids from *The Station*, snippets of Mac's dialogue torn from scripts.

If you fall, I'll be there to catch you and *Forever is just another word for tomorrow* and *The last thing you should let go of is your dreams.*

The miniature Aveda bottles Tanya had taken from the Davison were lined up in a neat row on the shelf along with a couple of buttons from Mac's uniform and a flask of Silver Mountain Water, Greg's favourite aftershave. This was scary. This girl was a nut job.

He had known that hanging out with Tanya wasn't a good idea but he had been gutted when Saffy had blown him out. He had spent so much time on his own in the apartment over the last few weeks. The thought of another night in staring at the walls was just too much.

They'd drunk half a dozen Martinis in the Fitzmaurice and then Tanya had taken him down to the car park and they had snorted whatever it was off the roof of a Nissan Micra. Then she'd said she had a bottle of tequila back at her place. It was only eleven o'clock and Saffy probably wouldn't be back for hours and a couple of slammers had seemed like a good idea.

Now that he'd seen the shrine, it did not seem like a good idea any more. Suddenly, it seemed like a very, very bad idea. He found his jacket in a ball in the corner where he'd tossed it and sneaked down the stairs. The TV was on in the living room. He waited for a bit of noisy applause to open the front door then he slipped out, closing it softly behind him.

Ali from Avondale was trying to tie a knot in a cherry stem with her tongue. The girls from NoQ were cheering her on.

Marsh dipped a strawberry in the chocolate fountain and let it harden for a moment, then she turned to Saffy. 'You're sure you're not making a mistake?'

'I'm sure.' Saffy smiled.

'I wouldn't get married again if you paid me.' Marsh nibbled the strawberry delicately. 'Not unless we're talking seven figures. I've got my career. I've got my freedom. I've got a hot, young guy ready to jump whenever I click my fingers, but I don't have to watch him cutting his toenails or eating his Bran Flakes.'

Ciara was convinced that Marsh was having an affair with Simon. And if she was right, this was very bad news for Saffy because she knew Simon would take any opportunity he could to shaft *her*, too.

'Once you're married, you'll realise that marriage is like a town under siege.' Marsh licked the chocolate daintily off her finger. 'Everyone on the outside wants to get in and everyone on the inside wants to get out.'

'Mmmm.' Saffy was trying to make eye contact with her mother but Jill was pretending not to see her. Saffy was going to have to corner her soon and ask her what her problem was. She wasn't going to let this kind of childish behaviour ruin her wedding.

'But,' Marsh said, 'I hope it works out for you. I really do.

And I hope you come back from Antigua relaxed, refreshed and ready to catch up with Simon. Because he's going to have a two-week lead.'

She stretched languorously and looked down to where Ali was slobbering over her tenth cherry. 'Bring me a one of those, would you?' She fluttered her eyelashes at the waiter.

And when he did she popped it in her mouth, moved it around for a half a minute and then pulled out the stem. It was tied into a perfect knot.

'Now there's something they don't teach you at Harvard Business School,' she said with a flirty smile.

Marsh presented Saffy with a pink leather Agent Provocateur spanking paddle. The NoQ girls gave her a book on Indian Cookery called *The Korma Sutra*. Ali gave her edible underwear. Ciara gave her a chocolate body-painting kit. Vicky gave her a book of love poems by W.B. Yeats. Jess, who had never been to a hen party and didn't know she was supposed to bring a present, gave her an ironic look and raised her glass.

Her mother had slipped away before Saffy had a chance to talk to her but she had left a package with one of the waiters. Saffy opened it nervously. The idea of Jill at large in Ann Summers was not a pleasant one.

It was a small, silver-framed photograph of a man in an Afghan coat and jeans with a lit cigarette in his hand. He was tall, with straight, shoulder-length black hair and he was looking at the camera with a half-smile and an inquisitive look, one eyebrow a fraction higher than the other. Saffy knew that look. She was guessing that it was on her own face right now.

♥ *15* ♥

People said that your wedding day was happiest day of your life. And, Saffy realised, stepping into the huge claw-footed bath in the honeymoon suite, they might be right. She felt wonderful, light-hearted and clear-headed. She couldn't wait to look into Greg's eyes and say, 'I do.'

He had stayed in Dublin and she had driven down with Jess and the twins the previous evening. Luke and Lizzie had played I Spy all the way but it was a very weird version of I Spy where you were allowed to spy things like 'air' and 'wind' and even 'stuff'. She had told Jess she had a headache and eaten dinner in the suite, and then slept ten hours straight in the huge, four-poster bed.

Now she lay in the warm, lemon-and-grapefruit-scented water and watched sunshine puddling on the carpet near the half-open window. It was a drowsy, golden morning. A girl with a wicker basket was picking flowers in the walled garden. The fountain was glittering. The lawn was glitzy with dew. It was going to be a perfect day.

Jess had already changed into the simple blue sundress she'd bought the morning before. The hairdresser, Daisy, had let her hair dry into natural rippling waves, then ruined the whole effect by spraying it with about a can and a half of Elnett. Now she was weaving tiny blue flowers into the crown.

'Do I have to have these?' Jess grumbled. 'I feel like Alice in bloody Wonderland.'

Saffy was sitting at the dressing table in a robe with her hair in huge Velcro rollers. Troy, the make-up artist, was priming her skin. He glanced over at Jess. 'Oh shut up! You look fabulous and you know it.'

The twins burst in. Lizzie was wearing a communion dress she'd bought at a car boot sale. The white lace was grubby and the hem had come down. Luke was wearing the bottom half of his pyjamas. His stomach was streaked with something red and sticky that Jess hoped was jam.

'Relax,' she said when she saw Saffy's face. 'I'll get them into their proper clothes just before the church.'

'Is there a chicken in that bucket?' Luke ran over and began to pull the decorative feathers out of the champagne cooler. Lizzie folded her arms and scowled at Saffy through her thick glasses. Her hair sprang out around her head like a dark, spiky halo.

'She looks nice, doesn't she?' Troy said. If she did, Lizzie wasn't saying so. 'What's her problem?' He patted blusher onto Saffy's cheeks.

'Unrequited love,' Jess said. 'She has a thing for the groom.'

'Can I come in?' Saffy's mother walked straight past her daughter and headed for the champagne bucket. She filled her glass and wandered over to the window. Then, as if it was an afterthought, she came back and gave Saffy a quick peck on the cheek.

'I don't want to ruin your make-up.' She stepped away as Saffy was standing up for a proper hug.

She had rejected the traditional mother-of-the-bride pastels look and gone for the full Jackie O. She was dressed in a black and cream suit and her blonde hair was swept back behind a wide cream hair band. She was wearing dark sunglasses. Indoors. There was something show-stealing about the whole thing, a 'look-at-me-ness' that set Saffy's teeth on edge.

Her mother wandered around the room restlessly, picking things up and putting them down. Saffy saw her touch the silver-framed photograph of her father on the dressing table and, for a moment, felt bad that she hadn't thought to bring one of her too. Then she pushed the feeling away. Her mother had always told her that she hadn't kept a single photograph of her father. And now, after more than thirty years, she had found one. Saffy didn't know whether to be touched or annoyed. She was still hurt that Jill hadn't wanted to be involved in any way in the wedding and now, when she finally decided to show up, she expected to be the centre of attention. But it didn't work like that. Not today. This is *my* day, she thought. It's not about her, it's about *me*.

'Did you get my text asking you to tell Len to wear a suit, Mum?' she asked. Greg had been worried that he might show up in a jumper and Jesus sandals.

'Len's not coming.' Jill drained her glass. She took off her sunglasses. Her eyes were red and ringed with running mascara. She began to cry. 'We broke up.'

Troy hurried over with a tissue. Jess refilled Jill's glass and sat her on the side of the bed. Saffy suddenly felt very tired. She'd been wrong. It *was* about Jill. It was always about Jill.

'Oh come on, Mum. There are plenty more frogs in the sea.' It sounded like something Greg would say.

'I'm not crying because of Len. I'm crying because I have something on my breast.'

Saffy looked down at her mother's chest, half expecting to see a stain, a spill, a dusting of pressed powder. Something ordinary and everyday. Something that would come off with Vanish.

'It's just a little lump.' Jill was shredding the tissue. 'I had one a few weeks ago and I went to a specialist and they did a biopsy but it was benign. But now I have another one. I was going to go back but I wanted to wait until after the wedding in case . . . in case . . . you know . . .'

Saffy stared at her. This was why Jill was looking so gaunt. Why she'd been avoiding her. Why she hadn't wanted to get involved in the wedding.

'But why didn't you tell me, Mum?'

'I didn't want to ruin your big day.'

Conor watched Greg's face film over with sweat as a sip of tea went down.

'Maybe we need to get you to a doctor.'

They had already stopped at a petrol station and a pub so Greg could be sick. The limo driver, Derek, had said that peppermint tea and toast might settle his stomach so now they were in a café on Baggot Street.

'It's not a problem, man,' Greg mumbled. 'I'll be fine.'

But it was a problem. It was exactly the kind of problem you'd set for a second-year maths test. Conor shifted uncomfortably inside his Dolce & Gabbana three-button tux and tried to solve it.

A vomiting man needs to travel to a church to attend his wedding. The church is forty-eight kilometres away. The wedding is in two hours and fifty-three minutes. The man needs to visit the toilet every fifteen minutes. If the driver has to stop the car for ten minutes every time the man visits the toilet, will the man get to the wedding on time?

Greg huddled down in the leather booth, waiting for the spasm to pass. The place was packed with pensioners eating scrambled eggs and reading the *Irish Times*. The last thing he wanted was to be recognised by one of these old dears. Though, frankly, from what he'd seen in the bathroom mirror, that wasn't likely. His skin was grey and spongy-looking. His hair was stuck to his head with sweat. His eyes were horribly bloodshot. He barely recognised himself.

What was going on? He'd been fine when he got home from Tanya's the night before last. Saffy was still at her hen party. He'd drunk some vodka to take the edge off whatever he'd snorted and gone straight to bed.

He had dreamed he was naked in an underground car park with his agent, Lauren. 'You're going to be huge,' she had whispered seductively. 'You're going to be bigger than Bono.' He'd started to tell her that he was *already* bigger than Bono and Larry Mullen but she backed him up against a cobwebby wall and began to grind against him. Weirdly, it was so arousing that he woke up and, before he knew it, he had rolled over onto Saffy and they were having sex. Really amazing sex, as a matter of fact.

He'd felt a bit rough next morning but he thought it would pass. Saffy had been incredibly apologetic after deserting him for the hen party and they had a chilled afternoon together packing for their honeymoon. She was spending the night down in Woodglen and, after she'd left he settled down with a couple of Sapporo's to watch *Kill Bill*. Then slowly at first, then with a force that made Uma Thurman look like Mary fucking Poppins, the hangover had kicked in.

He had spent the whole night in the bathroom hugging the

toilet. He couldn't believe that there was anything left in his stomach but a few minutes ago, in the Gents' in O'Brien's Bar he had produced a perfect, undigested pasta shell in a puddle of day-glo yellow bile. He hadn't had pasta for *two days*.

He picked up a piece of toast. If he could just keep something down, he'd be okay. All he needed to do was get through the next couple of hours, get through the wedding, get the ring on Saffy's finger and then he could—

'Shit!' He put the toast down and patted his pockets. 'We have to go back to the apartment.'

'What?' Conor stared at him. Was he out of his mind?

'It's the rings, man. I forgot the wedding rings. They're in a blue box in the inside pocket of my black velvet jacket. It'll only take a minute.'

It took twenty-five. Conor turned out the pocket of every jacket in the walk-in wardrobe and went through every drawer and crawled under the bed and stuck his hand down the back of the sofa.

Derek was polishing the bonnet of the Jag with a tissue when he got back. He shook his head sadly and pointed at his watch. 'You see this? *This* is what happens,' he said, 'when you plan a wedding for Friday the thirteenth.'

Greg was curled up in a foetal position on the back seat with a damp serviette on his forehead.

Conor got in beside him. 'I couldn't find them.'

Greg groaned.

'Look, it doesn't matter, Greg. We'll just borrow some at the church.'

'No! I just remembered something. I think know where they are.' It had come back to him in a horrible flash. He had taken his jacket off and tossed it on the floor at Tanya's place. The rings, two-and-half grand's worth of hand-engraved Tiffany platinum, were in her room somewhere. And he had to get them back.

Greg dictated a text to Tanya asking for her address and saying he needed to see her for five minutes. Conor sent it. They sat in silence and, after a couple of minutes, she texted back.

'Thirty years . . .' Derek muttered darkly, breaking the traffic lights at Trinity College. 'Eight hundred and forty-seven weddings and I've never been late for one.'

Greg closed his eyes and hung onto Conor, who hung onto the headrest as they shot up the Quays, hung a screeching left at High Street and headed, at about twice the speed limit, towards the Liberties.

The Jag mounted the kerb on a redbrick terrace on Cork Street and Conor helped Greg out.

Some kids in hoodies were hanging around the corner. 'Hey, it's Mac,' one of them yelled at Greg. 'You're supposed to be dead!'

Greg was expecting Tanya but, instead, the door was opened by a stocky man in his fifties in a vest and jeans.

'Sorry, I was looking for Tanya,' Greg stuttered. 'I'm—'

'I know who you bleedin' are,' the man said. 'And I'm Tanya's bleedin' dad.'

The small living room was crammed with people. Tanya, in Hello Kitty pyjamas that matched her purple-tipped fringe, was sitting on one sofa, crying noisily, while a younger girl in matching yellow pyjamas comforted her.

The other sofa was taken up by a large woman in her seventies wearing a sweatshirt with a picture of a kitten wearing a glittery crown and a tall, skinny boy with dyed black hair and full Marilyn Manson make-up who was eating Kentucky Fried Chicken.

'I'm sorry, Greg,' Tanya sniffed. 'My dad wanted to know why you were calling around and I got really upset and I ended up telling him, you know, like, everything.'

Greg swallowed a chunk of something he hoped was panic. Jesus! What did she mean by *everything*?

Tanya's dad sank heavily into the only free chair. He indicated a wobbly-looking glass coffee table and Greg and Conor perched on it.

'This is my sister Kerry,' Tanya sniffed. 'And that's my nan and my brother Eoghan.' She took in their suits. 'You look nice,' she said. 'You look like you're going to a wedding.'

Greg attempted a smile. 'My mate Conor here is getting

175

married this afternoon and I'm his best man so it's my job to get him to the church on time.'

What? Conor looked at Greg. What did he mean *he* was getting married? Had he gone mad?

Tanya's nan smiled at Conor. 'Aaah! I love a wedding,' she said. 'It brings out the best in everyone, doesn't it?'

Everyone, apparently, except Tanya's dad. 'Tanya tells us *you're* getting married, too.' He stared at his knuckles and then at Greg's face, as if pairing them in his head. 'She says it's been all over the papers. Is that true?'

'Well, I um . . . uh . . .' Greg's lips were moving but the words were trapped in his throat. He forced his aching brain to think. 'I was . . . er . . . involved with someone, yeah? But it all ended a few days ago. That's why I was in The Clarence the other night. I was drowning my sorrows.'

Tanya beamed but her dad wasn't looking happy.

'If you *were involved with someone*, maybe you'd tell me why you've been chasing after Tan?'

'I wouldn't call it chasing, man.'

'What would you call it,' Tanya's dad folded his huge arms, 'when you lured my daughter to a bleedin' hotel and spent the night with her and then dumped her?'

Everyone looked at Greg expectantly except Tanya, who dropped her head, demurely, and looked at the floor.

'It's no way to treat a innocent young girl,' Tanya's nan said after a long silence, 'in fairness.'

Innocent? Tanya was a drug-crazed nympho. Greg thought about taking out his phone and finding some of the porno texts she'd sent but he'd deleted them all. All except one, and he couldn't show that to her *nan*.

'Don't take this the wrong way, dude, but I don't think Tanya is as bloody innocent as you think.'

The brother put down a half-eaten chicken wing and wiped his mouth on the sleeve of his Fields of the Nephilim sweatshirt. 'Swear in front of my nan again,' he said in a surprisingly deep voice, 'and I'll tear your fucking legs off.'

Tanya's dad shook his head. 'I'll handle this, son. How old are you, Greg? Thirty-three? Thirty-four?'

Greg nodded. He must really look like shit. He was thirty-five but he usually passed for late twenties.

'That's fifteen years older than my daughter. When you were having your first pint, Tan was sucking on a dummy. You could vote before she was potty-trained. You finished school before she even started.'

He had a point, Conor thought. In fact, he had several.

Tanya started to sniffle again. 'Dad, I keep telling you I don't, like, care about the age thing,' she whimpered. 'When you love somebody, age doesn't, like, matter.'

'Yeah, Dad.' Her sister nodded. 'Look at Michael Douglas and Catherine Zeta-Jones.'

The colour drained from Greg's face. He put his hand over his mouth and made a dash upstairs for the bathroom.

'I'm a reasonable man,' Tanya's dad said to Conor. 'But nobody, no matter how famous they are, is going to take advantage of my daughter and get away with it.'

The brother clicked his skull and crossbones rings and sucked his teeth noisily but not noisily enough to cover the sound of Greg retching in the toilet upstairs.

Greg opened the bathroom door. It touched Conor to see how like his own bathroom it was: the damp towels on the floor; the clutter of toppled shampoo bottles and toothpaste tubes on the window sill; the pink razor with a hood of grey foam on the side of the sink.

Greg put the lid down and sat on the toilet. He looked queasy but determined. 'We've got to get out of here,' he whispered. 'You've got to help me.'

'Why?' Conor said. 'You just lied to that guy about whose wedding you're going to. And you lied to me. You told me you were deleting all the texts from this girl and now you tell me you were in her house, in her *bedroom*, two days before your *wedding*? What were you doing, Greg?'

'Nothing. I swear on my life! I was only here for ten minutes. Look . . .' He rummaged in his pocket. 'I got the rings.' He opened his hand and held out a pale blue Tiffany box. He had managed to sneak into Tanya's room and retrieve it from under a chair. 'But you have to help to get me out of here before Marilyn Manson down there tears me limp from limp.'

'Yeah? And how am I supposed to do that?'

'By acting,' Greg said grimly. 'Just take your cue from me.'

Greg had sent Conor to get Tanya and she had come out to the hall with her sister. They were both beaming.

'Your friend says you want me to, like, go to his wedding with you?'

'Yeah,' Greg said. 'That's why I came around to see you. I wanted to ask you to be my plus one.'

It was a very risky strategy but, if Conor delivered his next line and Tanya bought it, they were out of here.

'But-you-have-to-be-ready-in-five-minutes,' Conor said woodenly, 'because-we-are-running-very-late.'

The sister burst out laughing. 'Five minutes? It would take Tanya, like, five *hours* to do her make-up and decide what to wear. And then we'd have to dye her fringe to match.'

Tanya smiled wistfully. 'There's no way I'd be, like, even changed in five minutes. Maybe I could come to the afters.'

'There aren't any afters,' Greg said quickly.

'Oh well.' She turned to Conor. 'It was really nice of you to ask me. I hope you have, like, a lovely day. 'And thanks for calling around.' She put her arms around Greg. 'I was, like, really freaked out after you disappeared the other night. I thought we had a good time.'

'I'm sorry.' Greg patted her hair mechanically. It smelled of some sweet, fruity shampoo that was so horrible, he had to breathe through his mouth. 'I've just been so messed up since Mac was killed off. I've been doing all this weird shit lately. I think I might have post-dramatic shock syndrome.'

'What?' She blinked at him. 'Oh post-*traumatic* shock syndrome. Like Frank in the episode where he couldn't save those schoolgirls.'

Greg nodded. 'Listen, I'll call you okay? We can go out for a couple of drinks or to a club or something.'

She nodded.

'Say goodbye to your family for me.'

'Okay!' She lifted her face for a kiss then slipped her tongue into his mouth. His gut clenched but he had to act like he had feelings for her. He kissed her back.

It was only when Tanya had closed the front door behind them that Greg and Conor realised that her brother was standing waiting for them in the street.

'I saw the pictures you took of my sister on her phone,' he said to Greg, 'and I just wanted to give you this.' Then he punched him in the bad eye, hard.

Greg lay on the back seat with a bag of frozen sweetcorn over his eye. The petrol station had been out of peas.

Conor took a deep breath. 'You're going to have to postpone the wedding.'

'What about the reporters and the TV crews?' Greg said. 'They have other gigs. They're not going to wait around for hours.'

'I'm not talking *hours*,' Conor said quietly. 'I'm talking indefinitely. You need to come clean with Saffy about what happened with that girl.' And, he thought, Saffy needed to come clean with Greg about her one-night stand. They couldn't get married with all this stuff swept under the carpet.

'Man, you must be joking. That little psycho Tanya has already done enough damage. She stalked me and drugged me and nearly had me hospitalised. I'm not going to let her ruin the most important day of Saffy's life. Forget it.'

Conor shrugged. 'Well, I'm not going to let you go through with this unless you tell her what happened. And, if you don't, I will.'

Greg glared at him out of the eye that wasn't obscured by the sweetcorn. 'You wouldn't do that!'

Conor glared right back. 'Watch me!'

Saffy looked at her reflection in the gleaming window of the Rolls-Royce. She wasn't going to cry. Her make-up had taken two hours.

Jess pulled the last few flowers out of her hair. 'Saffy, try not

179

to get too upset about it. It's just a little lump and it's probably benign. She said the last one was.'

'But she's waited six weeks to have it biopsied, Jess, six weeks. Six weeks could mean the difference between life and . . .' She gulped the word back down.

'I don't understand.' Lizzie tugged at Saffy's hem with her grubby fingers. 'A little lump of what?'

The wedding date and location were supposed to be a secret but some of Greg's fans had obviously found out. They were waiting at the church. They started cheering when they saw the Rolls and Saffy pushed her fears about Jill to the back of her mind. This was her wedding day. It was finally happening. And it was supposed to be the happiest day of her life.

The driver got out but, before he could come around to open her door, a very tall, handsome, blonde guy came running down the path, which had been decorated with rows of ribboned bay trees. It was Damo Doyle, Saffy realised. The guy from BoyzRus. He had a quick word with the driver.

Jess rolled down the window. 'What's going on?'

'Ladies.' Damo flashed a very white smile into the back of the Rolls. He was wearing a white tux with a white shirt and tie.

Lizzie undid her seat belt and clambered forward to get a better look at him.

He ruffled her hair. 'Listen, the groom's not here yet. So, I've just asked this dude to take you on a scenic tour of the village and come back in ten.'

'Greg's not here?' Saffy said. 'He was supposed to be here forty-five minutes ago.'

'He's late.' Jess took Saffy's hand and held it tight. 'That's all. Greg is always late.'

'Can I have your autograph?' Lizzie asked Damo.

'Only if you give me her number.' Damo grinned at Jess.

'087 9812767,' Lizzie said immediately.

The Rolls pulled out and drove through the village. They passed a Jack Russell dog trotting along the pavement and a woman with a stroller and a man up a ladder cleaning windows, and about twenty pubs. One of them had a clock. It was half past three.

'Something's happened.' Saffy's voice was squeaky with panic. 'I have a bad feeling. Call Conor!'

'You know I can never find my mobile,' Jess said. 'Did you bring yours?'

Saffy patted down her wedding dress. 'What do you think?' She stared out of the window and bit her lip.

'We need to borrow your phone,' Jess told the driver.

He gave her a lairy look in the rear view. 'Is it a local call?'

'No,' Jess said, 'I'm calling the speaking clock in Argentina.'

'Listen, love, don't take that tone with me. I'm looking at a significant loss of earnings if this wedding doesn't go ahead. I don't want to incur any added costs at this point . . .'

'What do you mean if it doesn't go ahead?' Saffy said.

'Give me your phone!' Jess snapped. 'Now!'

Conor had his mobile switched off. But that didn't mean anything. He was always forgetting to charge it.

'What's Greg's number?'

'I don't know!' Saffy was breathing shallowly. 'It's on speed dial on all my phones. It's o87 something . . .'

The driver slowed down as they drew level with the church again. Damo was signing autographs. He shook his big blonde head and gave them the thumbs-down and the Rolls speeded up again. The woman with the stroller was gone. The Jack Russell was peeing on the bottom of the window cleaner's ladder. The clock on the pub said twenty to four.

'Maybe there's been an accident,' Saffy said quietly, 'a car crash.'

You've been jilted, a nasty little voice in her head told her. *You've been dumped at the altar and the whole country is watching and it's what you deserve because you blacked out and had a one-night stand with a stranger.* But Greg didn't know about Doug. Unless . . .

She turned and looked at Jess. 'Jess, did you tell Conor that I spent the night with that Australian guy?'

'What? No!' Jess lied. But she could feel her face begin to burn.

Saffy stared at her. 'Oh my God. You did tell him. How could you?'

Jess nodded miserably. 'But he would *never* tell Greg. He can keep a secret.' That was another lie. Conor had told *her* that Greg had a fling, hadn't he?

Saffy bit her thumb so hard that tears sprang into her eyes. It didn't matter if she cried now. It didn't matter if she ruined her make-up. Greg wasn't coming. He wasn't going to marry her.

'Can you turn this car around?' she said to the driver. 'Take me back to Dublin, please.'

'I'll need you to sign something,' the driver said, 'to confirm that I will be paid in full for—'

Lizzie started to wail. 'I want Daddy!' Her voice increased in volume until it qualified as a full-blown roar. 'Da . . . ddy!'

'Shhhh!' Jess said.

'Daddy!' Lizzie was pointing out of the window. 'Daddy!' And there was Conor with Greg, standing in front of the church.

Jess and Lizzie got out of the Rolls and Greg climbed in. 'Drive us round the village for ten, will you?' he asked the driver.

'Sweet, suffering Jesus.' He put his foot on the accelerator. 'Not again.'

There was a roar from the crowd and, this time, the photographers pressed against the windows, pushing one another out of the way to get the best shot.

'You're not supposed to see me in my dress before the church,' Saffy babbled. 'It's bad luck.' She had never seen Greg look so grim. His face was gaunt. His eyes were red, as if he'd been crying. She had done this to him. It was her fault.

'I won't look at you.' He turned his head and looked out the window. He didn't want to see her face when he told her about Tanya anyway.

'My mother might have cancer, Greg. She found a lump on her breast a few weeks ago. She was supposed to go for a biopsy but she cancelled it.'

'Oh, Saffy . . . I'm sorry.' Greg's mother was dead but he had his father and his two brothers. He was about to see them for the first time in nearly a year. He didn't like them much but at least they were out there somewhere. All Saffy had was Jill. He

182

squeezed her hand. 'Listen, we need to talk. I think maybe we need to call this wedding off . . .'

No! Saffy couldn't let him do this. She just couldn't.

'No! You listen! I know you're devastated, Greg; I'm devastated too. But what happened doesn't matter. It doesn't change how I feel about you. We're not perfect. We're both going to make mistakes. All that matters is that we can forgive each other, isn't it?'

He turned around and blinked at her in disbelief. She knew! Then it clicked. Conor must have told Jess about Tanya and she had told Saffy. But she wasn't angry. She was pale but she was looking at him as though she had never loved him more. She knew what had happened. And she forgave him.

'You're sure that this *thing* . . .' No, that wasn't specific enough. He swallowed hard and said the word, 'This *fling* hasn't changed the way you feel about me?' Saffy squeezed his hand so hard he almost yelped. 'It wasn't a fling, Greg; it was just a one-night stand. It didn't mean anything.'

'And you still want to marry me?'

'Yes,' Saffy managed to gasp as the spire of the church appeared through the trees. 'I do.'

16

Jesus, Greg thought, as the priest droned on about the Lord God making woman out of a rib of something, *that was close*! Jesus smirked down at him from the stained-glass window behind the altar. He was standing on a ball of snakes in a brown dress balancing a fat baby on his hand. If anyone other than the Lord God tried that, someone would call in Social Services.

Saffy's body knelt and stood, her hands lit candles, her voice spoke the responses, but her mind was darting around like a hyperactive butterfly. Was Greg really going to go through with this? Had he really forgiven her? There was still time for him to walk away. And then there wasn't. Nearly two hundred people were on their feet clapping and Greg was tipping her over and giving her a Hollywood kiss. She floated back down the aisle in a daze and then stood outside the church with her *husband* under a shower of confetti.

She let herself be hugged and kissed by an endless line of people she didn't know and by a handful of people she did and then they were in the back of the Rolls with the photographer snapping away from the passenger seat.

They stopped to take pictures on a humpbacked bridge and on the shore of a lake and then the car dropped them back to Woodglen and they had group shots taken: inside the hotel, on the lawn by the fountain, in the formal garden, in the walled garden, in the rose garden. While the guests stood around on the lawn drinking sixty bottles of champagne and eating 1,500 canapés, Saffy and Greg posed with Jill and then with Jess and Conor, with Greg's family, with various celebrities and alone.

Saffy was relieved that there wasn't time to talk. They were too busy following the photographer's directions. They kissed passionately and Greg carried Saffy backwards and forwards through a crumbling stone arch in a variety of positions including a very uncomfortable fireman's lift. Then they did it all over again for the wedding videographer and the TV crew then for the press photographers. Then Greg agreed to answer some quick questions from the assembled journalists.

Yes, this was the happiest day of his life. *No*, he didn't miss playing Mac Malone. And *sorry*, he couldn't confirm or deny whether he'd be dropping into LA for a screen test during his honeymoon.

Saffy stood beside him smiling so hard she thought she was beginning to get repetitive strain injury in her cheeks.

'What happened to your eye, Greg?' one of the journalists called as they were finishing up. There was, Saffy realised, a faint purple bruise on his cheekbone . . .

'It's my wife's fault.' He grinned and gave her a quick squeeze. 'What can I say? She's a knockout.'

Greg was still so nauseous he couldn't even drink a glass of water. He was getting a black eye. Colm Meaney was a no-show. So were the Corrs, GOD, Bono, Cillian Murphy and Johnny Logan. Lauren had texted to say she wasn't going to make it. The cast of *The Station* were ignoring him. That asshole Damo Doyle was trying to steal the show. And there was a fleck of something that was probably sick on the front of his D&G dress shirt.

But, he thought, looking down from the top table at hundreds of heads bent over hundreds of plates of Spring Lamb and Tuna Loins, it could have been a whole lot worse. He might not be sitting here at all.

He had dodged a bullock. Tanya was a nut job. She had very nearly ruined everything but she couldn't harm him any more. Saffy knew what had happened and she wanted him anyway. Any other woman would have left him at the altar, looking like an idiot. Conor was right. She was really something. He should have married her long ago.

He put his arm around her. She smiled and kissed him. Her breath had a fishy whiff and his stomach flipped a bit but he kissed her right back. That was how much he loved her at this moment.

Saffy let herself sink into her first, proper married kiss. Her heart expanded so much she thought it might burst through her

La Perla underwired basque and right out of her dress. She had really thought, when she found out Greg knew about Doug, that he was going to leave her at the altar. But she had underestimated him, this amazing man who was, she tested the word out in her head, her *husband*.

I am the luckiest woman in the world, she told him with her eyes. *Yes*, his eyes said back, *you are*.

If she found out that Conor had been unfaithful to her, Jess thought, she'd kill herself and then kill him. Though possibly it would be more sensible to do it the other way round. Either way, she'd kill them both. But Saffy and Greg were acting as if it didn't matter. They'd spent the day giving one another little loved-up looks. She just didn't understand it.

Conor didn't understand it either. The scene in Tanya's house had really got under his skin. Her brother was way out of line but her father was right: Greg had taken advantage of his daughter and he had taken advantage of Saffy, too. But Tanya had bought his lies and Saffy had forgiven him. Greg was getting away with it again, like he always did.

Vicky was standing in front of the mirror rubbing bright red lipstick off her teeth with a piece of loo roll. She was wearing a matching red vintage chiffon dress with a torn hem.

'Oh, Saffy. You look *so* gorgeous,' she slurred. 'Like Snow White played by Nigella Lawson.'

'Right. If Nigella was a 34A,' Saffy laughed.

Vicky lunged at Saffy and drew her into a clumsy hug then hiked herself up to sit on the rim of the sink.

'Look at me. I'm drunk and I'm swearing and you are cool and beautiful and serene. As always. Do a twirl.' She waved a full champagne glass and Saffy stepped out of the line of fire and twirled obediently.

'How's the Komodo table? I'm sorry I haven't had a chance to come over to say hello. I haven't had a chance to breathe. Is everyone having a good time?'

'Well . . . Ant has brought an *awful* woman. And I know I'm ancient but she is about a thousand years old. And every time he tries to say anything to me, she keeps interrupting.' She lit a cigarette.

'There's a smoke alarm!' Saffy pointed to the ceiling about the sink.

Vicky handed her the cigarette, took a condom out of her bag, opened it with her teeth, climbed up onto the basin and stretched it over the alarm.

'I might as well put it to some use,' she said with a sigh. She clambered back down again.

'Simon's too busy staring down the front of Marsh's dress to talk to his plus one and she's fabulous! She runs a waxing salon and she's been telling me about all the guys who go to her for this thing called "Escape the Ape", including, wait for it, Mike!'

Saffy tried to imagine the middle-aged Komodo media manager in his Santa socks having his butt waxed, and then she stopped herself. It just wasn't right.

'Marsh didn't bring a date and she's not wearing any knickers and she's being horrible to Mike's wife and . . .' Vicky smiled sadly '. . . Josh didn't come. He had to drive Little Lindsay down to Waterford to test-drive a horse.'

'Oh, Vicky, I'm sorry,' Saffy said.

'I suppose it's just how dads are with their little girls, isn't it?'

'I suppose so,' Saffy said. But how would she know?

Greg was waiting for her in the corridor near the double doors that led to the ballroom.

'Hey, Mrs Gleeson,' he called, 'I was looking for you. I was afraid you were going to miss our first dance.'

He put his arms around her. It was the first time they'd been completely alone since their talk in the Rolls and Saffy had been kind of dreading it but it was fine. It was all going to be fine.

'I'm so glad we did this,' he said softly.

'Me too.' She knew Greg would probably want to know the details about the Doug thing but at least it was out in the open now. This was a new page. They could start all over again.

'Thank you,' Greg said into her ear. 'Thank you for being so understanding about Tanya.'

'Tanya who?' Saffy murmured.

'Tanya is the name of the girl from *The Station*, you know, my little fling.'

Through the closed doors, Saffy could hear the DJ's voice. 'Ladies and gentlemen, the bride and groom will now take to the floor for their first dance.'

'What little fling?'

Part Two

♡

17

Saffy was lying under a palm tree on a Caribbean beach. A coconut landed with a thump on her sun-lounger. She turned her head and felt the tickle of the hairy shell against her cheek. The coconut began to push itself into her face and she opened her eyes and found herself staring straight into Kevin Costner's bottom.

She pushed him off the bed and he lay where he fell, in a fat furry heap, glaring at her and purring. She closed her eyes again and ground her face into the pillow, trying to force her way back into the dream.

I am lying on an icing-sugar-white sand beach, she told herself. *In a minute I'll get up and stroll back through a tropical garden to the honeymoon villa at the Amerkand Hotel and slip into the private plunge pool with Greg and—*

It was no use. She wasn't in Antigua. She was in her old bedroom in her mother's house. Weak, Irish sunlight was fighting its way through the pink curtains her mother had chosen for her when she was eleven years old.

She turned onto her side and stared at a poster of Monet's *Water Lilies* that was so faded that all the blues and lavenders had turned to dreary shades of grey. Tears leaked down her face and onto the lacy front of the nightdress she had borrowed from her mother. From downstairs, she could hear the clatter of dishes and the trapped-wasp voices of two women on the radio talking about hysterectomies.

There was a tap on the door and Jill bustled in wearing a scarlet Japanese silk kimono. She put a tray on the bedside table and tugged down on one the corner of the duvet sharply, as if she was inflating a life jacket.

'Wake up and smell the fifty per cent decaf,' she said briskly. 'The world looks better after a decent cup of coffee.'

Everything her mother had said since the wedding sounded like a bumper sticker. Saffy turned her back on the plate of slimy scrambled egg and charred toast on the tray. 'Please, Mum, can you just go away and take the cat with you?'

'Sadbh, it's been two days. You can't just lie there going over everything again and again. It's not healthy.'

But, as a matter of fact she could. Lying there going over everything again and again was all she could do.

She had no idea how she had done it but she had managed to walk into the ballroom and dance the first dance with Greg. They had turned slowly at the centre of a huge circle of swaying, smiling guests, to 'Too Good To Be True', the Lauryn Hill version.

This had always been *their* song. But now it was horribly accurate. Greg really was too good to be true. But she *could* take her eyes off him. They had only been married for seven hours and she never wanted to see him again.

When the dance finally ended, and everyone was clapping and cheering, she sneaked out of the ballroom and up the stairs to the honeymoon suite and locked herself into the bathroom.

She curled up on the marble tiles and put her arms around herself and cried. Her make-up dissolved in snotty trickles that ran down her neck onto the front of her silk dress. Strands of her blow-dried hair stuck to her wet cheeks.

Which one was Tanya? The skinny continuity girl who was always flicking her hair? The American actress who played the psychiatrist who had treated Mac for insomnia? The script editor with the dirty laugh?

She had imagined them in bed with Greg one by one, then all together, greedy for pain, as if there might be a point where she felt so bad that she wouldn't be able to feel any more.

After a while, over the sounds of her own wailing, she heard Greg banging on the bathroom door.

'Saffy, let me in, please; let me explain.'

She plugged her ears with her fingers. An occasional, muffled word got through: 'Sorry . . . please . . . nympho . . . love.'

She stood up unsteadily, her fingers still in her ears.

Greg was still talking. 'Bottom . . .' she could make out through her fingers. 'Heart . . . please . . . awful . . . sorry.'

She hobbled over to the mirror. Her hair was tangled and

damp and her dress was crumpled. A red pressure mark from the floor ran, like a scar, along one cheek. Her mascara had dissolved into inky streaks, like strange tribal markings.

When she took her fingers out of her ears to turn the tap on, he was in mid-sentence: '. . . not because I didn't love you. It was because I was so lonely without you. In a weird way, Babe, the fact that I slept with her really proves how much I actually love you . . .' She had intended to wash her face before she opened the door but she turned the tap off again. She wanted Greg to see her like this. She wanted him to see what he had done to her.

He was sprawled on a raspberry velvet armchair hugging a bottle of champagne to his chest. In his tuxedo, with this bow tie loosened, he looked like an ad for something expensive. Even the deepening bruise under his eye was attractive, something the make-up department might add to rough him up a little bit. Seeing him look so good when she looked so awful crushed her.

'How old is she, Greg?' she said flatly. 'What does she look like? How many times?'

He tried to grab her arm. 'You've got to believe me. It didn't mean anything. It meant less than nothing. I swear.'

'Just answer me.' She pushed past him to the luggage rack and pulled down the suitcase she had packed for the honeymoon. She opened it and found a pair of jeans and a T-shirt.

Greg put his hands over his face. 'Nineteen, I think. Kelly Osborne. And it only happened once, Babe. Just one time. It was in the Davison after we broke up. I was off my head – you can ask Lauren.'

'You told Lauren? You told your agent that you'd slept with somebody and you didn't tell me?' She yanked her ruined wedding dress over her head, threw it on the floor and pulled off her lacy basque and her stupid white hold-up stockings.

'Who else, Greg? Who else knows?'

'Conor. And Jess, I think. That's all. It was a mistake. One mistake. But it'll never happen again, I swear!'

Jess knew and she hadn't said anything. Saffy wasn't sure how much more of this she could listen to. She began to drag on her clothes.

'Saff, listen to me, please. I didn't even know what I was doing; I was completely out of it.'

Like she had been, Saffy thought, when she'd ended up in bed with Doug. Greg must have seen her expression soften. He put the champagne bottle down and approached her slowly, sideways, as if she was an unexploded bomb or a very nervous horse.

'This girl's unhinged, Babe. I should have seen it from the gecko. She slipped me these tablets for a headache but they were ecstasy. Then she practically raped me. She has a shrine to me in her bedroom, with pictures and candles and all this weird voodoo shit.'

Saffy was stuffing carefully folded clothes into a beach bag. She froze. 'How do you know?'

'How do I know she practically raped me? Well, I have a kind of hazy memory where she tied me to the bed with—'

'No, Greg. How do you know she has a shrine to you in her room if this happened just one time in the Davison?'

Greg swallowed. 'I did go to her place once, well twice counting this morning, but we only had sex once. I swear!'

'This morning? You were with her on the morning of our wedding!'

She hiked the beach bag onto her shoulder. 'You're unbelievable, you know that? You're just unbelievable.'

'Where are you going?' Greg said miserably. 'You can't just walk out and leave me here with nearly two hundred guests.' And four journalists, he thought. And one of them was from *OK!*

'Come to Antigua with me. We can sort this out, Babe. I know we can. It's like you said this afternoon. We're not perfect. We're both going to make mistakes. All that matters is that we can forgive each other.'

She shook her head. 'It's over, Greg.'

'But what about the honeymoon?'

'Take Tanya with you. And if she's busy I'm sure you'll find another nineteen-year-old to keep you company.'

The huge wooden door slammed behind her. Saffy ran down the service stairway, her heart hammering so hard that she thought it was Greg's footsteps behind her.

Some guests were smoking on the marble steps at the front of the hotel. Music was drifting out from the ballroom. 'Baby I Love You' by the Ramones. Saffy heard someone singing along. It sounded like Vicky.

She slipped past unnoticed and half-ran to where her car was parked. Jess was supposed to drive it back to Dublin next day so the key was in the ignition. It wasn't until she was nearly in Dun Laoghaire, with tears still pouring down her face, that she remembered that her key to the apartment was back at the hotel. But she couldn't go back. She was never going back.

'How you doing down there, dude?' Greg leaned over the liquid edge of the private plunge pool and sloshed some rum and pineapple onto the marble tiles. The ant, which was easily an inch long, turned towards the little lake of alcohol, combed the air with its antennae thoughtfully for a few seconds, then plunged his head straight in. It was his third cocktail and he was pretty unsteady on all six of his legs.

Greg waved his glass. 'Cheers, big ears,' he said. Did ants, he wondered blurrily, have ears? This was the kind of thing Saff would know. She was one of those amazing people who knew facts about pretty much everything. He sighed, lay back and looked up at the sky.

The upside-down constellations were fading and the horizon behind the line of coconut palms was getting light. Dublin was nine hours behind. He wondered what she was doing right now. He wanted to phone her. He wanted to phone her all the time but he was too scared. What if she meant what she said in Woodglen? What if it really was over?

He drained his drink. That was bullshit. Of course it wasn't over. They were married now. Nobody broke up on their wedding night. Except for Britney Spears, obviously. Even Eddie Murphy had made it to two weeks.

He still had no idea why Saffy had suddenly flipped like that. He had been over and over it in his head. She'd been so understanding when he had told her about the fling in the Rolls. He'd given her the option of calling the wedding off and she'd turned it down. Then when he'd asked her if she was sure she wanted to go through with it, she'd practically jumped into his arms.

So why had she thrown an epi up in the honeymoon suite? Maybe it had taken a few hours to sink in. Or maybe she was having some kind of hormonal thing, like Mia on *The Station* back in 2006.

He reached out and grabbed the rum bottle and poured himself another glass, remembering to splash some onto the tiles for the ant. He didn't bother with the pineapple juice. It was too far away.

Mia had turned out to have an ectopic pregnancy. Maybe Saffy was pregnant. It would certainly explain the mood swings. Or maybe it was just the world's worst ever case of PMT.

Whatever it was, he hoped it would be over when he got back. And he hoped that none of the papers would get hold of the fact that she wasn't on honeymoon with him because Lauren would freak if they did. He'd been too paranoid even to leave the honeymoon villa just in case. It was lonely here, night after night, getting pissed with an ant – it might not even be the same ant every night. It was quite hard to tell them apart. They all looked the same.

He leaned over to have a look. 'Hey, man, ready for a top-up?' The ant was staggering away from the sticky pool of rum with his head hung low. A warm, scented breeze rustled the thatch on the roof of the villa. Through the open door, Greg could see the huge white four-poster bed scattered with wilting rose petals. Maybe, Greg he thought, it was time both of them called it a night.

Saffy was in the kitchen, wrapped in a grubby sheet, eating Ambrosia Creamed Rice out of the tin with a fork when Jill came in, wearing a red pea coat and matching slingbacks.

'Hi, Mum,' she muttered. 'I was just going to take this upstairs.'

Her mother gave her a plaintive look. She was the kind of person who set a tray to drink a cup of coffee in the living room.

'Okay. Fine. I'll eat it down here if you like. Here, I'll put it in a bowl.' Saffy shuffled over to the cupboard in her sheet.

'You have to get dressed,' Jill said.

'I don't.' Saffy scraped the ricey gloop out with her fork. 'Don't ask me. Don't make me. Please.'

'You have to get dressed,' Jill said in a shaky voice, 'because I need you to take me to the hospital. I called a taxi but it never came and I've taken a Valium so I can't drive myself.'

Saffy turned around. 'Oh my God! Your biopsy! Why didn't you say?'

Her mother must have put her jeans and T-shirt in the wash and the only other clothes Saffy had were the light summer things she had packed for her honeymoon. She pulled on a white Ghost sundress and found a pair of gold flip-flops she'd thought she'd be wearing on a Caribbean beach. She caught sight of herself in the hall as she grabbed her car keys: her hair was greasy, her arms and legs were pasty white, her dark-framed glasses were wrong with the floaty summer outfit. She looked ridiculous.

But when she stepped outside the house, there was real heat in the sun and the air was charged with the smell of lilac and cut grass. The seasons had changed in the four days since the wedding. It was summer.

She put the roof of the Audi down and was relieved that it was too noisy to talk on the drive to the hospital. She didn't know what to say.

The radiographer positioned her mother's breast against a glass plate beneath a huge camera. She manoeuvred another plate down onto the trapped breast to compress it. It was horrible, Saffy thought. Like some sort of medieval torture.

'It feels a bit cold, doesn't it?' the radiographer said kindly. 'But you've been through this before. It will be over before you know it. I love your coat, by the way. Where did you get it?'

'It's M and S.' Jill was clenching her bottom lip but her voice was shaking. 'From last year's Autograph Spring Collection.'

The last time Saffy had seen Jill without her clothes on was ten years ago on a fortnight's holiday in Tenerife. One of her mother's friends had pulled out of the planned trip at the last minute and Jill had emotionally blackmailed Saffy into going along instead.

She had spent the entire two weeks fully dressed, sitting in the shade, listening to *Jagged Little Pill* on her mini-disc player and pretending she didn't know Jill, who lounged by the pool, soaking up admiring glances in candy-coloured bikinis and matching sun hats.

Jill had been in her early forties then but she'd had the body of a thirty-year-old. Now her breasts, still full and firm in clothes, sagged thinly against her bony ribcage and her stomach was slightly pouched over the waistband of her red skirt. It was awful to see her exposed like this.

She was glad when the radiographer asked her to step behind the glass screen and turned the lights out. She stood in the dark with her mother's coat and blouse and bra over her arm, listening to the hum of the machine and Jill's shallow gasps as she let out her breath between X-rays.

She looked past Mr Kenny's beaky profile at the wonky grey and black blur of her mother's breast on the computer screen. The consultant was in his sixties with a full head of that silvery hair that women's magazines always call 'distinguished'. He was wearing a yellow bow tie and a very expensive suit and far too much Silver Mountain Water by Creed. It was Greg's favourite aftershave and it made Saffy miss not Greg, but herself. The simple, uncomplicated person she had been just a few months ago. Before the headwreck of the break-up and heartbreak of the wedding and the shadow of her mother's lump. Her old life was like a foreign country now and no matter how much she wanted to, she could never go back.

'The abnormality we biopsied a few weeks ago was benign,' Mr Kenny told her while Jill was being prepped by his nurse, 'and this is probably another false alarm. Nothing to worry about, though she should have come in when she first noticed it. We're just going to put a needle in and take a few cells. She might be uncomfortable afterwards. You're her sister?'

For once, the mistake didn't raise Saffy's hackles. 'I'm her daughter.'

'So you'll be around to look after her for a few days after she gets home?'

She nodded. 'I'm staying with her at the moment but it's only temporary.' The minute Greg landed back in the country she had decided to get him to move out of the apartment so she could move back in and then put it on the market.

'Let's just take this one day at a time,' Mr Kenny said, 'shall we?'

Conor crouched on the stairs and held a towel over the printer to muffle the sound of its arthritic shudders while it spat out the next 30,000 words of *Doubles or Quits*.

He still had to proofread the draft. He could do that between classes, stay up late to do the corrections tonight and email it to Becky Kemp's assistant in the morning. But it was done. Somehow, despite the train wreck of Greg and Saffy's wedding day and the chill of Jess's disapproval and the bottomless pit of his own self-doubt, he had managed to do it.

He had been up all night and he was too wired to go back to bed. He wanted to mark the moment in some way but Jess and the twins were still fast asleep and it was too early to wake them. He pulled on a sweatshirt, found his trainers and, closing the door quietly behind him, went out onto the quiet street. It wasn't quite light and there were only a few cars around. He made his way down to the beach and walked out along the strand for a while, swinging his arms to ease the knot in his shoulders from a night spent at the keyboard.

It was going to be a beautiful morning. There was a small white, Howth-shaped cloud hovering over Howth and, as the sky got lighter, the smoke from the striped towers of the Pigeon House turned from grey to gold.

He cut up to the Martello Tower to walk back along Strand Road and, when he came to the petrol station, he thought of the perfect way to celebrate. The forecourt was still lit and the doors were locked.

'I'd like a cigar,' he told the sleepy-looking Russian guy behind the service window, 'and a box of matches.'

The guy brought them back. 'You have baby?'

'No.' Conor slid a five-euro note into the metal tray. 'I just finished writing a big chunk of my novel.'

'Tolstoy!' The guy grinned, pointing the cigar at him. 'Dostoevsky! Stephen King!'

When Conor came out of the staffroom, Graham Turvey was doubled up on the floor outside the science lab. His nose and chin were bloody and he was whimpering to himself. Conor put his satchel on the window sill and helped the boy to his feet. He scanned the corridor.

'What happened, Graham?'

'Nothing.' A thin red stream was trickling from his nose. 'I f . . . f . . . fell, that's all.' He wiped it on the sleeve of his jumper.

Conor felt around in his trouser pocket for a tissue but, of course, he didn't have one.

'Mr Fatty's having a wank!' someone up the corridor shouted.

'Come on. If you tell me who did this,' Conor put his arm around Turvey's shoulder, 'I can do something about it.'

Graham flinched and shrugged his arm off but the boys had noticed and there was a volley of whistles and catcalls.

'It's Turkey and Fatty in *Brokeback Mountain*,' Conor heard someone else yell, 'the sequel.'

Saffy didn't want to talk about the wedding and her mother didn't want to talk about the tests. And somehow they managed to avoid one another almost completely for the next few days, which was quite a feat in a two-bedroomed semi-d.

Mr Kenny had told Jill to rest but she said she felt fine. She got up early and went to work at the antique shop and then came home and made something to eat and went upstairs to bed with a tray.

Saffy slept during the days and got up at night to watch TV, trying to anaesthetise herself with late-night reruns of *Friends* and *Frasier* and modules from the Open University and hours of *Big Brother Live*.

Her mother left plates of food in the fridge and she ate them at odd hours or passed them on to Kevin Costner. Once, at about three a.m., she was standing in the dark in the kitchen eating a chicken leg when Jill came downstairs to let the cat in. She closed the back door and left, turning the light out again and Saffy felt a wave of gratitude. For the first time in as long as she could remember, her mother wasn't trying to pry or probe. She was just letting her be.

Jill had dressed in a jaunty cream summer suit with a matching bag and shoes, as if she had stopped off to pick up her test results on the way to a garden party or the races. Saffy perched beside her on a matching antique chair in Mr Kenny's second-floor office while he glanced at the file.

The biopsy had revealed a stage-one invasive lobular carcinoma.

'What it comes down to,' Mr Kenny said, after he had given them a few moments to take this in, 'is choice.' He was wearing another bow tie, black with red polka dots. 'You can opt for a lumpectomy or a mastectomy.' He made them both sound like preferences. Like fish or chicken, still or sparkling, black or white.

'Either way, we'll follow up with a course of chemotherapy and possibly radiation. I have to tell you that if you keep your breast, there's a twelve per cent chance that the cancer will come back.'

Saffy was afraid to look at her mother. She reached over and tried to take her hand but Jill was holding tightly onto her handbag, as if it was a floatation device and she would sink without it.

'I have some women who say, "Twelve per cent risk is too much. I'd rather just get my breast removed." I have other women who say, "Hey, I've got an eighty-eight per cent chance my cancer won't come back. I'm keeping my breast. If the cancer comes back, I'll have it removed later." The survival rate is the same.' Mr Kenny clicked his Mont Blanc pen. 'So it's a matter of what you're most comfortable with. Whatever your preference, I'd like to operate sooner rather than later. I have a cancellation on Monday.'

Hey. Comfortable. Saffy gripped the arms of her chair. *Preference.* These were strange words to use when you were talking about cutting out a living part of someone's body. She held her breath. A bluebottle was bouncing off the glass of the sash window. Someone in the office next door was talking on the phone. Outside, above the velvety greens of a golf course, two jet trails were crossing in a perfectly blue sky.

After a while, Jill stood up and said, very quietly, 'I'd like you to take it off.' Then she walked unsteadily across the thick gold carpet to the door. Saffy stood up to follow her but Mr Kenny shook his head. 'Give her a minute. It's a lot to take in.'

He pushed a box of Kleenex across the desk and then he looked out of the window and watched two golfers, in pastel clothes, crossing the sunlit green.

'I have a question,' she said.

Mr Kenny sighed. 'Of course you do. It could be hereditary. It could have been caused by diet or alcohol or the pill or pesticides, or the water she drank or the bleach she used to dye her hair. There are studies to support all these and scores of other factors as possible causes. But the answer to why your mother has breast cancer is,' he closed the file, 'we just don't know.'

Saffy sent Jill up to bed and set a tray and made a pot of green tea. She had read somewhere that it was supposed to prevent cancer, though it was probably, she thought, mashing the tea bag with a spoon and watching the water changing colour, a little late for that.

Jill was in her ensuite bathroom. It was years since Saffy had been in her room and somewhere along the line it had been redecorated. The carpets were gone and the floorboards had been sanded and varnished. There was a faded, rose-coloured silk rug. The wardrobes with sliding doors had been replaced by a white French armoire. The bed was heaped with velvet pillows and there were scented candles on the dressing table. It wasn't a bedroom. It was what the tabloids would call a 'love nest'.

Jill had never been a woman's woman. She had acquaintances not friends, but for as long as Saffy could remember, there was always a boyfriend lurking in the background. They never stayed the night when she was still living at home. In fact, she never even saw most of them. They were a bunch of carnations in a vase on the kitchen table, a deep voice on the telephone, a car idling outside the house while Jill parked Saffy on the sofa with a babysitter. Where was Len? Saffy wondered, putting down the tray. Where were all the frogs now that Jill needed them?

'I'm just having a shower,' Jill called through the bathroom door. Her voice was muffled by the splash of water. She was crying, Saffy realised, but she didn't want Saffy to hear her. 'Could you go to the supermarket? There's nothing in for dinner.'

'Sure,' Saffy said. She stood looking at the door for a minute. 'I won't be long.'

She pushed a trolley around Superquinn like a sleepwalker, filling it with the healthiest foods she could find; anything she vaguely thought might have an anti-oxidant, anything green. Her hands were shaking as she packed the bags into her car.

On the way home, she pulled over at a pub in Dundrum. It was empty except for the barman and two old men who were watching *How To Look Good Naked* on the TV. She sat at the bar and drank two double brandies, which, she remembered, was what you were supposed to do after a shock. Then she went to the Ladies and locked herself in a cubicle and kneeled on the green, faintly pee-scented lino and threw every drop back up again.

A bunch of fifth-years were huddled by the bike shed. Conor glanced over and saw Lesley Duffy's ratty hair extensions and Wayne Cross's shaved head.

'Hiya, Mr F.' Wayne waved. The other hand was behind his back. A plume of cigarette smoke curled up over his shoulder.

'Put that out, Cross,' Conor said, 'or I'll report you.'

He was unlocking his bike when he heard Lesley's voice.

'*We both laugh*,' she said in a lisping, sing-song way, as if she was reading something, '*and then Susan tells me I'm funny.*'

Conor froze. This sounded familiar. Why did this sound familiar? He turned around and saw that Lesley was reading from a typed sheet of A4 paper. '*Then I say, "Funny as in ha-ha or funny as in peculiar?"*' she went on. '*Susan looks up into my eyes. "Funny as in funny, we've been on this date for three hours and you still haven't kissed me," she says.*'

She was reading from the draft of his book. This was the scene where Dan, the main character, goes out with Susan, a woman from his office. The bit where they are flirting in the restaurant before they go back to her place and—

Conor had printed out a copy to proof before he sent it off to Becky then mislaid it, he thought, around the house. Now he realised he must have put it down that day he was helping Turvey in the corridor and then forgotten to pick it up.

Wayne grabbed the page. '*Susan leans forward and smiles.*' Cross read like a child half his age, stumbling over the words. '*She's not wearing a bra and I try not to notice the outline of her nipples through her dress.* This is *hot*, Mr Fatty. Very hot.'

Wayne pressed the tip of his cigarette against the edge of the page and a lick of flame appeared. Lesley flung a handful of pages into the air. A gust of wind caught them and they went tumbling towards the football pitch.

There was a burst of laughter and a chorus of jeers as Conor pulled his bike out of the stand and put his head down and began to walk away.

'Your mother's out of recovery,' the nurse told Saffy. 'She's just had a shot of morphine so she's a bit addled. But she's doing fine. She's in the bed by the window.'

The curtain around the bed was drawn, and when Saffy pulled it back, her mother tried to sit up but sank back down again, her eyes darting around the small ward.

'Where's my daughter? Can you get my daughter?'

Saffy couldn't remember when she'd last seen her mother without make-up. She looked awful.

'I'm here.' Saffy put down her flowers and propped her mother up using some extra pillows. She sat down carefully on the end of the bed. 'How are you feeling?'

'Sore,' Jill moaned. 'Where's Rob? Has he seen the baby?'

Rob? Did she mean Saffy's father? Did she think she'd just had a baby, not a mastectomy?

'You're in the hospital, Mum,' Saffy said gently. 'You've just had the mastectomy, remember?'

Jill looked at her blankly.

Saffy took her hand. 'Mum! It's me, Sadbh!'

'Rob wants to call the baby, Sadbh,' Jill sighed, 'but I think it's a bit of a mouthful.' Her eyes clouded over and closed. She began to snore softly.

A nurse popped her head around the curtain. She saw Saffy's face. 'Don't worry. The confusion's completely natural. She'll be herself again in no time.'

Saffy swallowed. 'Should I go? I mean, am I disturbing her sitting here?'

The nurse came over and smoothed down the sheet.

'Absolutely not. It makes a huge difference having someone there. It's the people who have nobody to look after them who take longer to recover. I see it every day.'

Later, lying in her uncomfortable single bed, listening to Kevin Costner mewing and scratching at her door, Saffy turned this over and over in her head.

Till today, Jill's operation had seemed like an end in itself. But it was just the beginning. It was going to take her mother weeks to get over the mastectomy and then there would be chemo and maybe even radiation.

Greg would be back from Antigua in a week and she would be due back in Komodo. She had decided that she should move straight back into the apartment but she couldn't walk out and leave her mother to fend for herself after she came out of hospital. It just wasn't an option; she was going to have to stay at home for a couple of weeks at least. Somehow, she was going to have to juggle work and Jill and – she let the idea in for the first time – getting a divorce.

She got up and let the cat into the room and eventually she fell asleep with her arms around Kevin Costner.

Saffy had cleared away the scented candles and the pretty pink Moroccan jewellery dish and the bud vase and now her mother's elegant bedside table was covered in medical clutter. Pill bottles. Prescriptions. Tissues. Gauze. Baby wipes. Disinfectant. Jill was propped up against the pillows, half asleep, a thermometer drooping from her lips like an unlit cigarette.

Saffy unfolded the instructions and found the section on emptying the drain.

Check that you have all the items you will need. Clean rubber gloves. Clean collection cup to measure drainage. Bowl of warm water, soap, washcloth and hand towel. Notebook to write down fluid amounts and information.

One end of the drainage tube snaked up under Jill's dressing. The other end was attached to a rubber bulb the size of a lemon. Saffy pulled on the only rubber gloves she'd been able to find in the kitchen, candy pink with leopard-skin cuffs.

Unpin the drain from the patient's clothing.

She unpinned the tube from her mother's pyjama top. She had stopped off at Dunne's Stores to buy the pyjamas on the way to the hospital. Jill had a drawer full of flirty nighties but she didn't have anything that buttoned down the front.

'This might hurt a bit, Mum. I'll try to be gentle okay?'

Jill watched her with round, blue, spaced-out eyes.

Remove the plug from drainage spout. Tip bulb upside down to drain contents.

Saffy held her breath as the fluid trickled into the collection cup. She squeezed the tube tightly to remove all the air and put the plug back into the spout.

Write down amount, colour and odour of fluid.

It had all seemed manageable, at first. When Saffy got to the hospital the evening before, her mother was dressed and ready to leave. She was even wearing lipstick, though most of it seemed to be on her teeth. She was groggy but Saffy managed to get her in and out of the car, upstairs and into bed without any problems.

What she hadn't planned for, but what Mr Kenny had warned her about, was the tiredness. Not Jill's, which at least had a cause, but her own. After she had settled Jill she went downstairs and threw away the gauze and rinsed out the cup and the tube and disinfected them. She told her feet to take her to the fridge to get out some chicken and start making soup for dinner but her feet weren't listening. They walked her upstairs and into her bedroom and over to her bed. She sighed and lay down, just for ten minutes.

Saffy dreamed that she ran over a swan. She sat in her car, afraid to turn around and look at the bird. It was lying injured in the road making an awful, hoarse screaming sound. She woke up with a jolt of relief. Then her skin goosebumped. Why was it dark? And, if the swan wasn't real, why could she still hear it?

Jill was half out of bed when Saffy got to her. 'I can't breathe. There's something lying on me. Please. Get it off! Please.' She began to scream.

'Mum, it's okay.' Saffy freed her arm and tried to get her settled again. But it wasn't okay. Her pyjamas were drenched with sweat. Her eyes were unfocused and wild. Saffy found the number of the ward and, after what seemed like a year, the staff nurse came on the line.

'We need an ambulance.' She had to raise her voice to be heard over Jill. 'My mother needs to come back in.'

'When did you last give her a painkiller?' The nurse was calm.

'Not since this afternoon.' She looked at the clock on Jill's bedside table. She had changed her mother's dressing at five and then gone for a rest. It was eleven. She must have been asleep for six hours.

'Give her two codeine now and prop her up with pillows. That will take the pressure off her wound. And if she's not feeling better in half an hour, call me back.'

Her mother wouldn't let go of Saffy's hand, but she managed, with her free hand, to get her to swallow two codeine and to manoeuvre her into a sitting position. Even after the drugs began to work, after the gasping sobs finally stopped and she drifted into sleep, Jill held on. And Saffy, whose left leg was numb and whose arm was beginning to cramp, let her.

Jess tried Saffy again. Her phone was still switched off. She went into the living room, pushed some magazines and papers to one side, lay down on the sofa and turned on the TV. She flicked through the channels. A presenter in a low-cut dress was interviewing a pre-op transvestite on TV3. On RTE a blonde presenter who looked like a post-op transvestite was interviewing a hairdresser about hair extensions. For once, Jess wished they had cable.

Saffy was freezing her out. Jess hadn't seen her since the wedding. She had been angry with her for telling Conor about her one-night stand. But that was nothing compared to how angry she was when she found out that Jess had known about Greg's fling. She was still speaking to her, technically, but only in monosyllables.

'Yes,' her mother was doing okay. 'No,' the second biopsy report wasn't back yet. 'No,' she hadn't heard from Greg. 'No,' she hadn't had time to figure out what she was going to do next. 'No,' she didn't need anything. 'Yes,' she would call if she did.

Jess took it because she knew that she deserved it. She wasn't sure she'd even say 'yes' and 'no' to Saffy if it had been the other way around. Not that she would ever be unfaithful to Conor or that he would ever cheat on her, unless you counted cheating on her with a book.

He had sent off the next instalment to the agent a few days ago and she'd thought that maybe he'd take a break but he was back at his desk the following morning. She had woken up and reached for him but he wasn't there. She lay awake for a long time, listening to the clatter of his keyboard and the creak of his chair, willing him to come back up and climb in beside her. But he didn't.

She flicked through the other channels irritably. *Judge Judy. A Place in the Sun.* A Japanese cartoon. An ad with a shouty man flogging oven cleaner. *Teletubbies.* Oh God, please, not Tinky Winky and La La.

She felt sleepy. She had gone back to bed for an hour after Conor and the twins left for school this morning. And all she'd done since then was read the paper. She should really get up and wash the breakfast things. She should shower and phone some editors to try to set up some meetings and then she should just get on her bike and cycle out to Saffy's mum's house.

She turned off the TV and settled back into the cushions,

pushing the wrapper from a packet of Fig Rolls she'd eaten for lunch onto the floor. There would be plenty of time for all that later, after she'd had a little rest.

Saffy didn't want to go back to work but she had no choice. She'd had to haggle with Marsh to get time off for the wedding and the honeymoon. She knew the kind of reaction she'd get if she asked for more time. And she needed her job. She had to pay back the loan for the wedding.

She hated having to leave her mother on her own. It was just a week since the operation and Jill was coming back to herself, slowly. She could get to the bathroom on her own but Saffy still had to do everything else: shower her, dress her, undress her, take her temperature, and cajole her into eating. It was like a surreal role reversal where Jill had become the child and she had become the mother.

'Thank you,' Jill said when Saffy buttoned her into a fresh pair of pyjamas. 'Thank you,' when she sprayed perfume on her wrist. 'Thank you,' when she combed her hair. For the first few days, they were the only words she said and she said them so meekly, so gratefully, that Saffy felt guilty. Because if things had been different, if they had turned out the way she wanted them to, she wouldn't be here to thank at all.

'I'll leave you a tray and I'll come back at lunchtime,' she told her mother now, putting her head around the door. She was wearing the least beachy outfit from her honeymoon wardrobe, a short navy dress with white buttons.

'You look nice! I'll be fine.' Jill was propped up on the pillows reading a book. 'I'm feeling much better today, really.'

'If you need anything I want you to call me? Okay? Promise?'

Jill tried not to smile. Saffy had spent her life avoiding her calls.

'I promise.'

Saffy had gorilla hands. The palms were an even, shiny brown and the backs were a horrible stained pine colour with a few albino patches around her wrists. If she was trying to fool anyone into thinking she'd been on honeymoon, she thought, once she was out in daylight, Fake Bake was not the answer.

Ciara grinned when she saw her. 'You haven't been in the sun at all, you naughty girl.'

Game over, Saffy thought. And she hadn't even made it past reception.

'That's fake tan! You spent the whole two weeks locked in your hotel room, didn't you?'

'Well . . .' Saffy began.

The phone rang and Ciara turned away to answer it.

She had got away with it. And it was just as easy with the rest of her colleagues. She didn't have to lie at all.

'The Caribbean's overrated, isn't it?' Simon leaned over to swipe an almond croissant as they sat down for the work in progress meeting.

'Depends on where you go,' Saffy answered truthfully.

Mike, who was an amateur entomologist, asked if she'd seen any tarantulas in Antigua and she said she had never seen a tarantula, which was also true.

Ant didn't ask her anything. He just looked right through her.

Marsh took off her tiny antique Rolex and put it by her coffee cup and gave her a tight little smile. 'I hope you had lots and lots of delicious honeymoon sex, because you won't have much time for it over the next few months.'

'Define lots,' Saffy said.

Vicky was late and so all she got a chance to do was mouth, *I want to see the pictures.*

It was a relief to be sucked back into the daily drama of Komodo. The Avondale shoot had not gone very well and the bargain-basement director had made a mess of the product sequence. The client was demanding a reshoot.

Top-line research on White Feather looked positive and the next step was for Saffy to meet with Nervous Dermot and the researcher to get sign-off on a final script.

Ant and Vicky had come up with a poster campaign for NoQ, the retail outlet village. Simon flashed the boards with a cocky grin, as if he'd written and art-directed them himself.

> Stella McCartney
> Mugs
> My Little Pony
> NoQ. For fashion, homeware and toys.

And:

> Giorgio Armani
> Perfumes
> Marc Jacobs
> Pants
> NoQ. For cosmetics, gifts, fashion and menswear

There was even a Christmas version:

> Santa
> Irons
> Barbies
> Knickers
> NoQ. For Christmas.

'What you're seeing here is the third round of creative,' Simon said smugly. 'There was no way I could present Ant's first ideas.'

Ant turned to Vicky. 'Did you know,' he said, for some reason looking at Saffy, not Simon, 'that you can have someone's legs broken for three hundred and fifty euros?'

Vicky cornered Saffy after the meeting, 'If you tell me all about Antigua, I'll make you tea and drool. Deal?'

'If you give me one of those.' Saffy pointed at the pack of Marlboro Lights in the pocket of Vicky's sequinned drawstring bag.

'I didn't know you smoked.'

'Neither did I.'

The tiny patio was surrounded by high walls on all sides. There were two rusting cast-iron chairs and some withered potted plants that were used as ashtrays. Saffy hadn't smoked for years, and then, only once or twice. The nicotine flew into her nerve endings like a swarm of bees. Her fingers and toes fizzed. Her hair felt dizzy.

'Honeymoon me,' Vicky said. 'I want every last detail. Leave nothing out. Was it unbelievable?'

Saffy took another puff of her cigarette and nodded.

'Before you get started, I'd better warn you.' Vicky blew a wonky smoke ring. 'Simon has been an absolute arse. He told us about the bonus thing you all agreed when you picked the Irish director for Avondale. Ant's livid.'

'Vicky, I'm sorry. I shouldn't have agreed to it. I feel terrible.'

'It doesn't matter. I guessed you were broke with the wedding. Don't worry about Ant. He'll get over it when the White Feather script gets the green light. But that's not all Slimy Simon's been up to. He's having an affair with Marsh.'

'No!'

'Ant forgot his iPod when he left on Friday and he called back in on his way home from his qigong and he heard noises from her office. He thought it was a burglar so he went up to check. The door was closed but he said she was squeaking. Like a chipmunk.'

'Oh God. They were doing it *in her office*?' Saffy pictured them thrashing around on Marsh's beautiful grey velvet sofa.

'Making the beast with two backs. Horrible, isn't it? You'd better watch out, Saffy. Simon wants to step into Marsh's shoes as much as you do, and they're a lot closer if he's already in her pants.'

Vicky was right. Saffy waited for the paranoia to kick in but it didn't. She already had too many things to worry about.

'Anyway, enough of their sordid little fling.' Vicky stuck her cigarette butt in the pot plant. 'Come on, take pity on me. I'm probably never going to have a honeymoon of my own, at least let me enjoy yours vicariously.'

Saffy stared at the ground. 'I didn't go,' she said. 'It didn't happen.'

'So you just hid out in your apartment for two weeks? Good for you! I was worried that you'd be too tired to enjoy it anyway.'

Saffy shook her head. 'Greg went on his own. We broke up. I found out he'd cheated on me. He told me on the night of the wedding.'

Vicky stared at her in disbelief.

'I've spent the last two weeks living with my mother, looking after her. She had to have an emergency mastectomy last Monday.'

'Oh my God, Saffy!' Vicky put her arm around her. 'You poor, poor thing. What a nightmare. Is your mother going to be okay?'

'I think so. I hope so.'

'I can't believe Greg did that to you and then went on honeymoon on his own. You must feel terrible.'

'I'm just numb really.' It was true.

'I'm sure he didn't mean to hurt you, Saffy. Maybe you'll take him back.' Vicky stroked her arm. 'If he's really, really sorry . . .'

Saffy shook her head. 'No. I won't. I can't.'

Vicky lit another two cigarettes and gave her one. 'Well, maybe it's part of some great celestial plan. Everything in the universe happens for a reason.'

'You're right.' Saffy held the smoke in her lungs until they hurt. 'Everything in the universe happens for a reason and sometimes that reason is that life is shit.'

At the luggage carousel, Greg was surrounded by a hen party wearing T-shirts with slogans that read: *Lisa's Last Lash*. He held his breath while they told him how devastated they were about Mac and then he signed some autographs, trying not to inhale their collective hum of Red Bull and cigarettes.

When he walked towards the automatic doors that opened onto the Arrivals hall, he saw a cluster of photographers waiting by the barriers. *Shit!* They would expect to see him with Saffy. If the papers got wind of the fact that he'd been on honeymoon on his own, he'd look like a complete muppet.

He doubled back. He couldn't ask Airport Security to smuggle him out. That would just draw attention to the fact that he was on his own. He was going to have hide in the toilet till they left.

The traffic on the M50 was backed up all the way to Cherry-wood. Saffy lit a cigarette and did the maths. She had thirty-five minutes to get home, make her mother some lunch and get back to the office for a NoQ meeting. She pulled out into the hard shoulder, churning up a satisfying spray of gravel. After a few exhilarating seconds, she saw the blue flashing light in her mirror.

The motorcycle Garda swaggered up to the car. 'There a fire, somewhere?'

She could see her own face, tiny and distorted, in the lenses of his mirrored sunglasses. A smell of warm leather rose from his trousers.

'It's my mother.'

'Your mother's on fire?'

She shook her head. 'No, Garda.'

'But I see you're smoking. This a company car?'

'Yes.'

'Are you aware that, under the Public Health Tobacco Act, 2002, Section 47, it is illegal to smoke in any workplace, *including* a motorised vehicle?'

This was ridiculous. 'Look.' Saffy dropped the cigarette out the window. 'No cigarette. Happy?'

He glared down at the smouldering butt that had landed on the toe of one of his huge boots. If he was happy, he was hiding it well. He lifted his foot and ground the butt under his heel.

'Are you aware that it is *also* illegal to overtake on the hard shoulder?'

'Yes, of course I am. Look, I'm sorry but my mother had a mastectomy and she's on her own and I have to get home to give her medication. When I saw the traffic, I just sort of panicked.'

He hesitated, and then her phone rang. It was on the passenger seat. They both watched as a picture of Greg appeared on the screen. 'You have a hands-free set for that?'

She did but it was locked in the apartment and she didn't have the key.

He flipped his notebook open, and shook his head. 'I didn't think so.'

When Greg called again she was at the kitchen sink spinning salad leaves for her mother's lunch.

'Hey, what's up?'

What's up, Saffy thought, *is that you slept with another woman. You cheated on me and you lied to me and you married me under false pretences. And I never want to see you again.*

But what she said was, 'I have nothing to say to you, Greg. Don't call me again.'

'Hang on one second.' He sounded desperate. 'Please.'

One second passed and then another one. Saffy looked out of the kitchen window. Her mother's elderly neighbours, Mr and Mrs O'Keefe, were lying in matching deckchairs in their garden, holding hands. What did you have to do to keep love alive after years and years? What was the trick?

'Conor told me about Jill's operation,' Greg said. 'How is she?'

'What do you care?'

'Babe, that's harsh. I'm just trying to have a normal conversation here.'

'Why would I want to have a normal conversation with you, Greg? Just give me one reason why I would want to do that?'

'Well, because I'd like to help. I could come over and keep your mother company. I could read to her. I could feed Kevin Spacey.'

'The cat is called Kevin *Costner*, and I don't want your help.'

So,' his voice was careful, 'you're going to stay with Jill then, until she gets better?'

'Obviously.'

'And when will that be?'

'I have no idea.'

'I'm just wondering when you're going to move back in? Are we talking weeks or months?'

'We're talking never.'

'Never say never, Babe. I know I messed up big time but we're married. The whole point of being married is that you work things out and—'

'I need to pick up some things from the apartment. Can you leave my key under the weeping fig by the lift? And can you not be there tomorrow evening?'

'Please, Saff, don't give up on us.' His voice was shaking.

'Let's just take a break. Three months, that's all I'm asking. We don't have to see each other, we don't have to talk. And at the end of it, if you still want out then I'll accept that, okay?'

It wasn't okay. It was absolutely *not okay*. But if this one little lie got him off the phone, if it stopped him from calling or trying to see her, then she was prepared to tell it.

'Okay.'

Her mother's pathology report had come back. The cancer had travelled to two lymph nodes.

'It's nothing to be frightened of, Jill,' Mr Kenny said after the nurse had removed the drain and taken out the stitches.

He was wearing a scarlet polka-dot bow tie today. Maybe he was a clown in his spare time, Saffy thought. Maybe, at the end of a day spent telling people that they were sick or dying, he needed to put on a red nose and make someone laugh.

He tapped the file and smiled. 'We'll start you off with a course of chemo and then move you on to radiation in six or seven weeks.'

'Will I lose my hair?' Jill was sitting in the same chair she'd sat in a few weeks back. She was wearing the same cream trouser suit but she had been too wobbly to wear high heels, so she was wearing trainers. She looked like a different person. The operation had changed her. For the first time ever, Saffy thought, she looked *her age*.

'If you do lose it,' Mr Kenny said, 'it will grow back. But you're going to need a lot of TLC. No work. No lifting or carrying. Your arm is healing but we don't want to risk an infection in the lymph nodes. So I want you to let your daughter look after everything. Which is what she's here for, right?'

Saffy nodded. *Right*.

18

Conor read the letter a second time, folded it up and put it in his pocket. Then he took it out, unfolded it, and read it again.

Douglas, Kemp & Troy
Literary Agency
11 Winnet Street
London W 1D

Dear Conor,
Thank you for sending in the next instalment of Doubles or Quits *to Juniper. I have some minor comments but, based on what I have read so far, I would be delighted to represent you. I enclose two copies of our standard client contract. Please read it carefully and, if you are happy, return one to me.*

Normally, at this point, I would set up a face-to-face meeting either in Dublin or in London, but there is a window of opportunity here that puts us both under a bit of time pressure.

I have a publisher in mind for the novel but I would need to be showing him a complete manuscript before the end of August. So far, you have sent us roughly two-thirds of your book and my understanding is that you still have 30k words to write. Would it be possible for you to complete the manuscript before the end of July?

I can then meet you in mid-August to take you through my editing notes and we can aim to get the book into shape to give to the publisher by the end of the month.

We at Douglas, Kemp & Troy are delighted to be adding you to our list of authors and we are very much looking forward to working with you.

Best regards,
Becky Kemp
Literary Agent

P.S. Regards to Brendan who deserves if not a dedication, then a 'thank you' for bringing the book to our attention!

AUDIO:

Music track up and under throughout. Indie version of 'Heaven Must Be Missing An Angel'.

VIDEO:

We open on a crowded urban street shot in black and white. A male angel has just fallen to earth. He's lying, his wings pinned beneath him. An elderly lady steps over him. We see a close-up of a man's shoes as they tramp past his head. We realise that they can't see him. He is visible only to us.

The angel struggles to his feet. He is naked except for a loincloth. The camera pans up his body, taking in his muscled thighs, and his taut abs. It moves up to linger on his handsome face.

We cut to our angel walking past a bus stop. A beautiful but sad girl is waiting in the queue. He stands behind her and puts his wings around her. She can't see him but it's as if she can feel the comfort of the angelic embrace. She sighs happily.

Now we see our angel walking past a row of terraced houses. It's raining. We notice an attractive woman looking out of an upstairs window, crying. Magically, our angel appears behind her. As he holds her, the rain stops and the sun comes out. As the angel disappears, the woman smiles.

We see a series of shots of our invisible angel comforting women in different situations. A surgeon in an operating theatre. A girl having a row with her boyfriend. A model on a catwalk. Each time, his invisible touch lifts their mood.

Now we see him walking along a deserted beach towards a hot-air balloon.

The film changes from black and white to colour as we see the angel in the basket of the hot-air balloon.

As he gets closer, we see that the balloon is shaped like the White Feather logo.

We cut to a shot of our angel in the balloon. Then the camera follows the path of feather as it floats up through the air.

218

Saffy attached the script to the email and copied it to the agency, the client and the three production companies that Ant and Vicky wanted to quote. Nervous Dermot had finally stopped nibbling scripts and approved one.

The two waiters in black suits exchanged a look and then, in unison, lifted the silver domes off the plates. Jess looked at hers. In the centre of the vast china plate was a tiny apostrophe of fish balanced precariously on small pile of leaves. Off to one side were four French beans, a miniature carrot and the smallest potato she'd ever seen.

She would have preferred to be at own kitchen table, eating a bowl of pasta, and still wasn't sure what they were doing here, but if taking her to lunch at Restaurant Patrick Guilbaud was Conor's way of making up for spending so much time working on the book, she was happy to go along with it.

She cut a corner off the tiny potato and put it in her mouth. It wasn't good. It was *incredible*.

'What do you think they do to make a potato taste like that? Sprinkle it with crack cocaine?'

Conor grinned. It was lovely to hear her making a joke, lovely to just sit here in this beautiful room and have a chance to look at her. To really look at her. To have time to notice the hollow of her throat and her delicate collarbones and the navy line around the pale blue of her irises and the way her dress clung to those amazing curves.

He had no idea how much the meal was going to cost. But another couple of hundred euros wasn't going to make any difference to the already enormous Visa card balance. Greg still hadn't paid him for Saffy's ring. Conor wished he'd hurry up. He'd had one statement already and the interest was mounting.

'Hey, I have an idea.' Jess was feeling light and deliciously giddy. 'Let's call the babysitter and tell her we can't be back till six and go to a movie. No, wait. Wait! Let's go to Whelan's and drink Guinness and do the crossword.'

'You're on!' Conor grinned. 'But I'm probably a bit rusty.'

'You were always pretty rusty.' She took his hand and smiled.

'That was amazing,' she said. 'I'm sure it wasn't worth whatever astronomical price they're going to charge for it but it was absolutely amazing.'

'There's more,' Conor said.

She groaned. 'I can't fit in any more. I need to leave some room for the Guinness.'

'It's not edible or drinkable.'

'I think you mean *potable*,' Jess said. 'I can see I'm going to be doing most of this crossword.'

'It's news,' Conor said.

'Good or bad?'

'It's all good.' He held onto his secret for another few seconds, touching her fingertips, one by one, with his thumb. 'It's about the book. I got another letter from the agency. Becky Kemp wants to take me on. She's given me till the middle of August to deliver the full manuscript. Then I'll probably have to do some edits and then she wants to show it to a publisher.'

Jess closed her eyes for a moment and when she opened them again all the fizz and giggle she'd felt was gone and all that was left was a tight, scratchy feeling behind her eyes that felt like the beginning of a hangover. All this – the food, the wine, the way Conor had been looking at her – wasn't about *her*. It was about his *book*.

She shook her head. 'So, basically, you've brought me here to tell me that you're going to be chained to your desk all summer?' And when she looked over his shoulder, she thought, he would open a new document so that she couldn't see what he was writing.

'Well, yeah, I will have to put in a lot of time. It's a tight deadline and I'll have to get stuck in but I won't be working all the time.'

'Okay.' Her voice was small and thin. 'Can we go home now?'

'Come on; don't go away from me like that. Be happy for me.

Please. This was always my dream. You know that. We talked about all this before the twins were born.'

'Did we?' She'd had dreams too. About living on a houseboat. Moving to New Zealand. Taking a year off and backpacking around the world. But, once they stopped being a couple and started being a family, she didn't need those dreams any more.

Now listening to Lizzie laughing because Conor had tickled her awake, watching him cutting the edges off every one of Luke's sandwiches because he hated the crusts, schooching into one bunk beside the twins while Conor told them a story and did all the different voices, *this* was her dream. She was living it. And until a few months ago, she had thought it was his dream, too.

'Jess, we agreed that I'd teach for a couple of years but that at some point I'd try to give it up and earn a living as a writer.'

'You're going to give up *teaching*?' She couldn't believe this. Teaching was what paid their rent and most of their bills.

'Well, not immediately, but if this works out, maybe I could scale back. Resign from St Peter's. Do more sub-work and grinds. Free up more time to write. Look, we can talk about all of this when I finish the book.'

Jess stared down at her glass. This time last year the bloody book didn't even exist. Now their lives revolved around it. And after this one, there would be another one. And another one. And nothing would ever be the same again.

A waiter came and placed a plate of petits fours on the table in front of them: a tiny square of marshmallow, a lacy brandy snap, a trio of miniature macaroons, a boat-shaped pastry carrying a single raspberry. As Jess stared at them, they dissolved into one wobbly pastel-coloured blur.

She spoke so quietly that Conor had to lean forward to hear her.

'I'm glad about your book. I really am. But every time you sit down at your desk, you turn your back on me and Luke and Lizzie. You don't even realise it but that's what you're doing. And I'm sorry but I can't stand it any more. So will you do something for me? Will you find somewhere else to finish it?'

Saffy had left a tray outside her mother's bedroom door before she'd gone to work. All Bran, yogurt, a muffin, a flask of green tea and a glass of prune juice. Jill was going to lose weight once she started chemo and Saffy was trying to get her to put on a few pounds before it began. She had left two codeine in a pill bottle with a note: *Take one at eight and one at twelve. Back at one to fix lunch. S*

When she opened the bedroom door there were splashes of purple prune juice everywhere – on the bed, the carpet, the wallpaper, even on the ceiling. Jill was propped up uncomfortably in bed, her face was white. 'The cat ate my yogurt,' she said. 'And then I dropped the prune juice. I'm sorry.'

'You didn't take your painkillers on an empty stomach?'

'I didn't take them at all. I couldn't find them.'

'Kevin Costner!' they said together.

Saffy fell on her knees and looked under the bed. She checked behind the wardrobe.

'We have to find him,' Jill said, 'and pump his stomach!'

'I've got a meeting at three, I don't have time to pump a cat's stomach.' Saffy pulled out the dressing table. 'You'll have to do it.'

'I'm too *weak* to pump his stomach!'

'Well, he'll have to pump it himself.'

One minute, they were glaring at one another, the next, they were laughing so hard that Saffy collapsed on the bed.

'Stop,' Jill gasped, 'please stop! You're shaking the bed. My stitches!'

The curtain twitched. Saffy lunged at it and pulled it back. Kevin Costner was crouched by the skirting board, the codeine bottle, still unopened, between his paws. He looked up at her and began to purr.

Conor was early, so he sat outside a café on South William Street and ordered a coffee. It was the hottest day of the year and way too warm to drink coffee but he couldn't bear to descend into the dank, windowless pool hall just yet.

It was the first day of the school holidays and he should have been relieved. The last few weeks at Saint Peter's had been a living hell. Bits of his draft (the dirty bits, of course) had been photocopied and passed around school. Even the first-years were treating him like a joke.

'*Oh, Dan,*' they'd moan when he was writing on the board. '*Oh, Susan.*'

Unfortunately, the joke was far from over. Tomorrow was his first day at the academy where he taught exam revision courses during the summer break and some of the students from St Peter's would be in his classes. It would be a whole new world of humiliation but he'd just have to get on with it. He didn't have any choice.

He was beginning to think that the whole book thing was a big mistake and if he hadn't signed the contract and promised to deliver the next instalment, he'd have given it up. It had already caused so much trouble between him and Jess and at the rate he was going, he seriously doubted that he was going to be able to meet the August deadline. He hadn't written at home since Jess had asked him not to. He was looking around for cheap office space but he hadn't found anything remotely affordable.

In the meantime, he was putting in a few hours at the library every day but it wasn't working out. He was used to doing most of his work early in the morning or late at night; that was when he had his best ideas. It was hell lying in bed, awake, while they rattled through his head, knowing that he would have forgotten them all by the time he got up.

Every other night, when he couldn't sleep, he'd get up, sneak out of the house and cycle along the deserted Rock Road to Sandycove. He'd scribble in his notebook for a while and then dive into the black, cold water and swim for twenty minutes. When he got out, he would feel numb. Numb was about as good as it got these days.

'Hello!'

He shaded his eyes. It was a girl in a very short black-and-white dress wearing huge sunglasses. For a second, he thought it was one of his students, and then he saw that her dark fringe was dyed white to match her dress.

'You're Greg Gleeson's friend, aren't you? Except you've been working out. You look different.'

It was Tanya. Shit!

'So how was your *wedding*?' she said sarcastically. 'And did you enjoy, like, lying, to my entire family? My nan was, like, devastated. She thought you were nice.'

'Listen, I'm sorry about that.'

Tanya put her hand out, palm facing him, index finger raised. It was that 'don't mess with me' Oprah/Jerry Springer gesture that all the girls used these days.

'Ask me do I care? Go on! Ask me do I, like, *care*?'

'Um . . . do you, like, care?' Conor scanned the street. If Greg showed up this could turn nasty.

Tanya smiled bitterly. 'No,' she said, 'I don't. To be honest, you did me a big favour. And if you see him, you can tell your *little* friend Greg Gleeson that I've gone right off him.'

'Right,' Conor said. 'I'll pass that on.' He had to get rid of her. Greg was already half an hour late. He'd be here any minute.

'Well, I'll see you . . .'

'Yeah.' Tanya gave a little snort of laughter and shot him a look of pure contempt. 'You'll see me, all right. If you read the right papers, you'll see quite a *lot* of me, actually.'

It was hot as hell down in the pool hall. Their cues were slippery in their hands, it was like playing underwater. After a while they just gave up and sat at the bar. Greg had spent two weeks in Antigua on his own, and now that he had someone to talk to, he couldn't stop.

Conor half-listened while he went over and over the wedding and the break-up and the honeymoon and the job in LA, but his mind was elsewhere. Where and how was he going to finish writing the book?

'. . . she needs some time out, which is cool, you know, with her mother being sick. I think she kind of freaked out when Jill told her she might have cancer and that's why she overreacted to the whole Tanya thing. You think that's possible?'

'Sure,' Conor said. What he really thought was that two people who could lie to one another like that didn't belong together. Of course, Greg didn't *know* about Saffy's one night stand yet, but it would come out. The truth usually did.

Which reminded him: it was time to tell the truth about the book.

'Listen, there's something I need to tell you.'

'What? I'm not going bald, am I?' Greg craned to see the back of his head in the murky mirror behind the bar. 'I think all this stress might be giving me alopecia.'

Greg's eye was twitching, and while Conor told him about the novel, he tore a beer mat into a hundred tiny pieces. 'Douglas, Kemp and & Troy, right? Have you signed yet? Because if you haven't I can talk to Lauren about lining you up with one of the big guns like Curtis Brown or A.P. Watt.'

'Thanks, but I've already sent the contract back.'

Greg waved his bottle at the barmaid. She put her book down, sighed and walked incredibly slowly to the fridge.

'So what's it called then, the great Irish novel? And when can I see it?'

'I'm not showing it to anyone until it's done. Not even Jess. And it's not the great Irish novel,' Conor said sheepishly. 'It's pretty lightweight really.' Why was he running himself down? Why did he always feel the need to make little of himself with Greg? 'It's called *Doubles or Quits*.'

'Well, there's your problem right there.' Greg slapped his palm on the bar.

There wasn't a problem, Conor thought; or there hadn't been until now.

'Mistake number one: a lousy title. I get where you're going with the 'doubles' thing. The guy, Dan, the main character has twins, you said that, right?'

Conor nodded.

'And I can see some housewife buying *Doubles or Quits* in the supermarket,' Greg said. 'But I can't see some cool dude reading it on the Dart. You've got to have something with more impact. That's it! That's your title: *Double Impact*!'

Conor took a last mouthful of his Diet Coke. It was warm and flat. 'Like your favourite Jean-Claude Van Damme movie?'

'Just shows, great minds think alike. Look, leave it with me, okay? I've got a lot of time on my hands. I'll come up with a shit-hot title. Now, what about your pitch line?'

'What?'

'Jesus, you've read about a million books on screen writing. A pitch line is a snappy sum-up of your storyline. It's the *hook*.'

'I know what a pitch line is,' Conor said, 'but I don't need a hook. I told you, the agent already has a publisher who might be interested—'

'Mistake number two.' Greg rolled his eyes. 'Never, ever listen to your agent.'

'You're going to make a shitload of money from this book,' Greg said while Conor unlocked his bike. 'I have a sick sense.'

'Listen, about money,' Conor said carefully, 'I know this is a bad time but—'

'Man, I'm sorry but the garage still hasn't paid up.' This wasn't true. Greg still had about eight grand left over from selling his car and Saffy was still paying her half of the mortgage but he had to pay his half and he had to live.

'I could ask Saffy to give the ring back.'

'Look, I don't want to put pressure on you and I know I owe you, it's just that I'm way overdrawn on the card and the interest is piling up.'

'I'll cover that,' Greg said, 'just keep a note of it and I'll pay it later, okay? Or, hang on, you could write it off against my time. I can be a consultant on your book, you know, like a story editor—'

'No.' Conor had to be firm now or the whole thing would get out of control. 'Thanks for the offer but this is something I have to do on my own.'

Greg's face fell. 'Just trying to help out, man.'

'There is something you can do to help.' Conor suddenly had an idea. 'You know the study at your place? Can I use it?'

'For what?'

'Jess doesn't want me to write at home any more. I could rent your study and work there and we could write it off against the interest.'

Greg thought about his huge, empty apartment. He was rattling around in it without Saffy. It would be kind of cool to have Conor around. It would be like old times.

19

Jill lay back in the big, grey leather reclining chair and looked at a bad reproduction of *The Sunflowers* while an Indian nurse injected a bright red drug into the port line Mr Kenny had implanted in her chest.

'I call this stuff the red devil,' the woman in the next chair said with a smile. She was hooked up to an IV pole, too. She was young, probably about the same age as Saffy, definitely too young to have cancer, and she was almost completely bald. She didn't, Jill noticed, even have eyebrows.

She opened her book and made a noncommittal 'hmmm'. The sight of that shiny pink scalp with its few wisps of hair made her feel queasy.

'Is this your first time?' The woman shifted around to face her. Jill nodded and kept reading.

'Well, it's nice to meet you.' The woman put out her hand. 'I'm non-Hodgkin's lymphoma, stage two,' she said. 'But you can call me Linda.'

She leaned over and tweaked Jill's IV line. 'You've got to keep your sense of humour, don't you?'

Saffy scanned the magazines and papers in the waiting room but she felt too anxious to read. Then a word in one of the tabloid headlines caught her eye. The word was 'Tanya's'. The other three words in the headline were: 'Teenage', 'Saucy' and 'Romps'.

There were two pictures. One of was of a pouting Kelly Osborne look-alike with pink-tipped hair dressed in a black lace teddy and a pair of patent boots. The other was of Greg in a tuxedo with Saffy standing beside him wearing a happy smile and that beautiful cream wedding dress.

A very tanned and very naked old man heaved himself out of the water and climbed up the steps to the knot of nudists by the bathing hut, dripping water on the flapping pages of Saffy's newspaper as he passed.

She had driven down to Killiney after she'd dropped Jill home and walked over the railway bridge down to the sea. She couldn't go back to work – not until she had read the article so many times that it couldn't hurt her any more. Soon she would know it off by heart.

Randy Greg sipped JD from my belly button . . . Little did fellow cast members know that beneath his uniform, hunky Greg was wearing Tanya's stockings . . . I tied Greg to the bed using the cords from our dressing gowns . . . Love-rat Gleeson exchanged a series of steamy texts with busty Tanya and stopped off on his way to his wedding for a last, torrid tryst.

Saffy felt a wet hand on her shoulder and looked up. It was the elderly swimmer, who was smiling down at her and offering her a metal cup.

'Here,' he said. 'Drink this.'

It was scalding-hot black coffee with a shot of something fiery in it.

'Metaxa,' he said. 'The cheap stuff. Cures hypothermia and stops your eyes watering.'

He squatted down beside her and stared out at the sea. Two grey-haired men were bobbing around near the rocks.

'Pascal's scored,' one of them shouted at them.

The other one roared, 'Go on, ya good thing.'

'Don't mind those old shites.' Pascal rummaged in a plastic Spar bag and produced a packet of Ginger Nuts. 'I'm gay.'

Saffy took a deep breath and pushed open the door to the boardroom. 'I'm sorry I'm late.'

She smiled at Nervous Dermot and slipped into a chair between Marsh and Vicky. Simon was on his feet and in the middle of speaking. He shot the cuffs of his Thomas Pink shirt and windmilled his arms.

'So, instead of the empty beach in the last shot, as the angel rises up in the balloon, hundreds of smiling women appear.'

What? Saffy couldn't believe her ears. What had happened to the lovely script Nervous Dermot had approved. And who had come up with this?

'They're young, beautiful, carefree. And,' Simon nodded his head, 'they're all wearing *white*, which shows their confidence and trust in White Feather. They're waving gratefully at the angel. Some of them might even be giving him the thumbs-up.'

The *thumbs-up*? This was tacky beyond belief. Why had this idiot been allowed to mess around with the script?

Saffy looked around the table but nobody met her eye. Ant and Vicky had their heads bent over the script. Marsh was scribbling something. Mike was munching his way through a plate of Lemon Puffs. Nervous Dermot was nibbling his knuckles.

'There seems to be some—' Saffy began.

Marsh jabbed her in the ribcage with an elbow and slid her a note which read: *Shut up. Get out. And be in my office in ten.*

'It's my account, Marsh. You know it's mine,' Saffy said, but she knew what was coming. She had stayed down by the sea talking to Pascal for nearly an hour. She had completely lost track of time.

'*Your* account! *Your* account?' Marsh snapped. 'You sound like a whiny little girl. And you're not going to get anywhere in this agency acting like one. White Feather is Komodo's account! And if you think you can show up thirty-one and a half minutes late for a meeting and then expect to run the show, you can think again.'

'I was with my mother, Marsh. She was having her first chemo session.'

'Really, Saffy? Was she having it in the pub? Because you stink of brandy!'

'I'm sorry, Marsh. Today has just been the worst day of my life. I've been trying to keep it quiet but Greg and I broke up after the wedding. He cheated on me with this awful nineteen-year-old and she sold her story to the tabloids and—'

Marsh put her hair carefully behind her ears and then put her hands over them. 'It's not my problem that your personal life is a train wreck. It's not my problem that your mother is sick. But when Dermot shows up in a panic demanding last-minute changes to the script and you're AWOL that *is* my problem. And I'm not going to sit around waiting for you to show up to solve it. Is that *clear*?'

Saffy nodded. 'It won't happen again.'

'It better not.' Marsh looked down at her diary. 'Now, don't you have a contact report to write or do I have to ask *Simon* to do that for you, too?'

It was pouring with rain. The hems of Saffy's trousers were soaked. Her suede sandals were ruined. She should have been sitting in her warm, dry office reviewing the casting brief for this afternoon's White Feather meeting. Instead she was spending lunchtime helping her mother to choose a wig.

'I don't *need* a wig,' Jill had insisted. She was up and around now. Her energy was coming back and she looked more like herself. 'I've lost one breast; I have no *intention* of losing my hair as well. It's mind over matter.'

But when the shower had blocked a few days ago, Saffy had found a clump of blonde hair, streaked with fine silver threads, wrapped around the filter.

She stood behind her mother now and watched as a woman fitted Jill into hairpieces with names that sounded more like *Playboy* centrefolds: Brandi, Carla, Amber, Crystal.

'This is the Fifi.' The woman tucked Jill's hair in with a metal comb. 'It's one hundred per cent human hair. It's hand-tied, with a velvet neck band.'

Jill lifted her head and heavy blonde hair fell around her shoulders. Saffy caught her breath. For a moment, she travelled through time, back to her mother's bedroom in the second flat or was it the third? The one with the bay window.

She was small, so small that her feet didn't touch the floor when she sat on the bed and watched Jill letting her hair down like Rapunzel. A sheet of shimmering gold that fell past her shoulders. A hundred strokes, every morning and every evening. Sometimes Jill would let Saffy brush it for her.

'This just looks ridiculous,' Jill said. 'It's way too young.

Sadbh?' Her mother's voice jolted her back from the past. 'Sadbh?'

She forced herself to smile at her mother's reflection, at her new face framed by her old hair. 'Maybe, just a bit.'

'Why don't we just go back and order the Crystal?' Saffy said after they had left the shop. 'It's just like your own hair. You could put it away in case you ever need it.'

'I still *have* my own hair.' Jill opened her umbrella, and handed it to Saffy, who was taller, to hold.

'So *far*. But you've only had two sessions of chemo. You have to think ahead.'

Saffy had spent the previous few nights Googling the side effects of Jill's drugs: nausea, diarrhoea, vomiting, mouth sores, infections, fatigue, anaemia. Hair loss was going to be the least of her mother's worries.

But Jill was in complete denial and it wasn't just about the chemo. She had refused to tell anyone about her diagnosis. She was ignoring calls from the few friends she had. She wouldn't let Saffy get in touch with Len and she'd made her call her boss at the antique shop and tell him that she had shingles and would be off for a couple of months.

'I've been reading the forums, Mum. Everyone says you improve your chances of recovery if you're honest. You need to be more *open* about the cancer,' Saffy said now.

'Well, you're not being open about what's happening between you and Greg. I read the papers, you know.'

Saffy flinched.

'I'm sorry.' Jill sighed. 'I know you don't want to talk about it and I don't blame you. It's horrible, Sadbh, just horrible. I won't bring it up again. Now, can we please talk about something other than my *fucking* illness?'

Jill swore so seldom that it made Saffy laugh.

'Like what?' she shot back. 'The fucking *weather*?'

Jill went to the bathroom while Saffy ordered two mint teas and two lemon pancakes and squeezed through the lunchtime crowd looking for somewhere to sit. There was a guy eating alone at a table for four.

'Is this free?'

'Sure.' He looked familiar and, as she sat down, too late, she realised why. It was the balloon pilot, Joe. She had tried to forget that awful morning in the field in Wicklow but now it all came back in a clammy wave of shame. She had tried to talk him into dressing in wings and a loincloth for six hundred euro. Then she had thrown up on his boots. She glanced down. Oh, God. He was still wearing the boots. And they still had tiny orange flecks of . . . of sick on them.

He saw her looking down. 'Have you lost something?'

'Um, no,' she said.

He looked at her blankly and then she saw a flicker of recognition in his cool blue eyes.

'You're Sally, right? From that advertising agency?'

She wanted to get up and run away but the restaurant was too crowded. It would take ages. She was going to do the right thing.

'Yes, I'm Sally. And I'm *so* glad I bumped into you.' She took out her wallet. 'I owe you a new pair of boots.'

He looked at her the way he'd looked at her when she'd offered him six hundred euro. It wasn't a good look.

'Sorry?'

'I, you know, ruined your boots.'

He shrugged. 'Forget it, really,' he said. 'I have.'

'Please.' She took out a hundred-euro note and put it on the table. 'Throw them away and get a new pair. I'd feel so much better.'

He smiled that sardonic smile she remembered. 'I *did* throw them away. This *is* a new pair.'

'But, there are little bits of—'

He shook his head. 'Paint. It's just paint. I'm a decorator.'

'Please,' she pushed the money towards him, 'take this anyway. I'd feel so much better if you did. If it's not enough, I can write a cheque.'

He stood up. She had forgotten how tall he was.

'That won't be necessary.'

233

'Well, if there's ever anything I can do, just let me know. Anything. Really.'

God that sounded all wrong, as if she was offering him sexual favours or something. She blushed.

'Hello.' Jill arrived at the table. 'Have we met?'

'I'm Joe,' he said. 'I was just leaving.'

'I'm Jill. I have cancer. I don't normally tell total strangers but my daughter says I have to be more open about it.'

Jill cut her pancake into tiny pieces but didn't eat any of them. She sipped her herbal tea and read *Marie Claire* while Saffy checked her emails on her BlackBerry.

'Look,' she tried one last time, 'I don't have to be back in the office for half an hour.' She had told Marsh she was doing a store check for White Feather. 'Why don't we go back to the shop and order the wig?'

'Why don't we go to Karen Millen so I can buy a little top? That would cheer me up.'

It was like bargaining with a child. 'I'll come to Karen Millen with you to buy a little top,' Saffy said, '*if* you order the wig first.'

Jill wasn't listening; she was looking out the window. 'What's wrong with your friend?'

The balloon pilot, Joe, had left five minutes ago but he was still outside, running back and forth in the pouring rain, trying to wave down a taxi.

'He's not my friend. I've only met him twice.'

'Well.' Jill raised her eyebrows. 'I think you're about to meet him again.'

Joe pushed his way past the queue and arrived at the table, dripping wet and out of breath.

'Sally!' He looked frantic.

'It's Saffy.' Jill said, 'Actually, it's Sadbh.'

'You said if there was anything you could do . . . well, there is! I need a lift. I don't have my van and I can't find a taxi. I have to get to my son's school. He's been hurt.'

'I'm sorry, I'd love to help, but I have to do something with my mother and then I'm due back at work.'

'Go,' Jill said. 'Go on. We can do the wig thing another time. I can take a taxi home.'

'Thank you!' Joe said.

'I know what you're doing,' Saffy said to Jill, shoving her BlackBerry into her bag, 'and I think you're being really childish.'

'You were childish for years.' Jill looked like Kevin Costner when he got a whiff of catnip. 'It's *my turn*!'

'Please, Mum, just Karen Millen, okay? You're still recovering. Don't stay out too long, promise?'

'Now why does that sound so familiar?' Jill said.

Joe didn't speak except to give Saffy curt directions and to curse the traffic, which was heavier than usual.

'Have you called your wife?' Saffy said at one point.

'My wife is not around.'

If you were this rude to her, Saffy felt like saying, *I'm not surprised.*

She double-parked outside the school gate and kept her engine running while Joe ran across a flooded playground towards a collection of dreary prefabs. She checked her BlackBerry. There was nothing urgent but she needed to get back to the office. Her store check alibi was good for another half-hour max. When she looked up, she saw Joe running back through the rain, carrying a boy in a school blazer with blood on his face.

Shit, Saffy thought. *My upholstery.*

Joe mistook her horrified look for concern. 'It's okay,' he said, 'nothing's broken. We won't have to go to A & E. I just need to get the little guy home.'

The boy, who looked about nine, buried his face in Joe's chest and began to cry, whether from the pain or from the humiliation of being called 'little' and being carried like a baby, Saffy couldn't tell.

She looked at Joe, standing in the downpour with blood soaking into his already soaking shirt.

'Get in.'

'Are you sure? We can get the bus.'

'I'm sure,' she said grimly, though she wasn't.

'You okay up there, Liam?' Joe had somehow folded his six foot three frame into the tiny rear seat so his son could sit in the front.

Liam wiped his nose with his sleeve. 'I'm f . . . fine.'

He didn't look fine to Saffy. He had already transferred what looked like several pints of blood from his nostrils onto her cream leather seats. The collar of his navy blazer was torn and he was beginning to get a black eye.

'What happened?' Joe said.

Liam fiddled with the cigarette lighter, pulling it out and pushing it back in again. 'Jack Williams called me a Yank, and rubbed my fa . . . ha . . . ha . . . ha . . . ce in the dirt.'

His what *in the dirt?* Saffy mouthed at Joe in the rear-view mirror.

His face, Joe mouthed back.

'I broke my glasses.' Liam began to sniffle, adding snot to the already impressive output of tears. He dug into the pocket of his grey shorts and pulled out a pair of glasses. They had snapped in half, neatly, at the bridge.

Joe took them. 'Tell you what, when we get back we'll get out the tool kit and see what we have to fix them.'

He had a different voice for speaking to his son, slower and deeper. It seemed to do the trick and Liam's sobbing faded to an occasional hiccup. Unfortunately, Saffy noticed, it didn't have any effect on the bleeding. They took a turn off the Dundrum Road into a maze of grey, pebble-dashed council houses.

'Left,' Joe said, leaning forward, 'left again. Now pull over there, behind the white van.'

Saffy hoped Joe's house wasn't the one with the Subaru up on breezeblocks or the one with the Alsatian tied to the gate with a length of orange nylon rope. She leaned over and opened the passenger door for the boy, then got out and lifted the seat so Joe could clamber out of the back.

'Listen, thanks,' he said in the same voice he'd used to talk to his son. 'You didn't have to do that.'

The boy was already running in the gate of a garden with, Saffy was glad to see, no dogs or scrap metal.

'Poor little guy, he's—' Joe stopped. 'He's completely ruined your seats! Hang on!'

He let Liam into the house then he came back out again and opened the passenger door. He began to swipe at the bloodstains with a threadbare blue towel.

'It's okay,' Saffy said. 'I'll have it valeted.'

He pulled out his wallet. 'Will you let me pay for that?' He caught her eye. 'No, I don't suppose you will.'

'Let's call it quits.' She changed into first gear, but he stayed where he was.

'My boots cost eighty euro, but the valet's going to cost a hell of a lot more than that.'

'Yeah, but I get the moral high ground for free.' Saffy smiled.

'Look, why don't you come on a balloon ride tomorrow evening?'

'After the last time? I don't think so.'

'You'll love it. I promise you. You can bring your husband.'

'I'm not married,' Saffy said. Well, technically she *was* married, but not in the real sense. 'Anyway, thanks for the offer but—'

'Well, bring your boyfriend, then.'

She shook her head.

'Mother? Wait, she's ill, isn't she? Just you, then. You work in Komodo, on Molesworth Street, right? I'll swing by tomorrow, around six. I've checked the forecast, it's going to be good.'

And before she had time to reply, he was sprinting back into the house.

Jess jabbed at the rock-hard spaghetti that was glued to the bottom of the saucepan. Luke had refused to eat the hot dogs she'd made for tea.

'I like dogs,' he said, 'but I don't want to eat them.'

'How long is it since Brendan went to Missing?' Lizzie asked.

The spaghetti was supposed to be in strands, but Jess had overcooked it and then the water ran dry and it had turned into a sort of *rope*.

'About a week,' she lied.

'Mum, am I gay?' Luke asked. 'Jake Murphy said I was.'

'I have no idea.' Jess turned the saucepan upside down. The spaghetti stayed put. God, where was Conor? Why did she have to do everything herself? 'We'll have to wait and see.'

Lizzie was combing the mane of her unicorn with her fork. 'I want to be gay. We're twins. It's not fair if he's gay and I'm not!'

'Oh stop it, Lizzie.' Jess threw the saucepan, pasta and all, into the pedal bin and opened the fridge. 'I'm warning you.'

There was nothing in there she could put in a sandwich except a liquifying lettuce and some ancient cheese. It was a very smelly Brie and Luke was the pickiest child alive but it was all she had to give him.

'If you're gay, you can't marry Mummy,' Lizzie said spitefully.

'I can marry Daddy instead,' Luke shot back.

'I don't care. I'm marrying Damo Doyle. I've decided.'

'What is it with this family and marriage?' Jess grumbled. She tore a piece of the Brie off and jammed it into a hot dog roll. 'Nobody is marrying anybody. Here, Luke, try this.'

Luke looked at the wonky sandwich suspiciously then he took a tiny nibble, chewed it thoughtfully and swallowed.

'It tastes of dirt,' he said, 'but in a good way.' He took another bite.

'Well, I don't know if you're gay,' Jess ruffled his hair, 'but you might be French.'

Conor stood under the pathetic trickle of water with his eyes squeezed closed, his hand on autopilot. When he came, he felt better for about thirty seconds and then he just felt dirty.

He found a towel that wasn't too damp and wrapped it around his waist. He cleared a patch in the steamed-up mirror. When had he turned into a saddo who tossed off at seven thirty a.m. while the most beautiful woman on the planet was lying in his bed in the next room?

And when, he thought, looking at his reflection, had he lost all this weight? He wasn't used to seeing muscles and bones, his body had been a soft blur for as long as he could remember.

He was still a long way from being thin, but he was heading that way. Even his face looked different. He just wasn't interested in food any more; he was too worried about the book.

Greg was lying on the sofa smoking, drinking Tiger beer and watching *Countdown*, with the volume so loud that, even though the apartment was huge and the study door was closed, Conor couldn't hear himself think. He got exactly thirty-seven words written in the first 115 minutes of his two-hour session. He had promised Jess he'd get home so they could all spend the evening together so he left it at that. But when he got back home, he found a note to say she'd taken the twins to the Botanic Gardens.

He stood at the window and gripped the edge of the sink. Why hadn't she texted him? He could have spent this time writing. Why was she being such a *bitch*? He caught his breath. He couldn't believe he'd just thought that. He wasn't just losing weight. He was losing the plot. He was turning into someone who didn't have time for his kids and resented his best friend and got pissed off with the woman he loved over nothing.

He could hear the sound of birdsong from the garden. The sky was gauzy blue and streaked with bands of pink and gold towards the horizon. A tiny fingernail of moon seemed to be caught in the branches of the neighbours' chestnut tree. This was his life. This was his home. So why did he feel like a stranger?

♥ *20* ♥

A white van was double-parked across the street from Komodo. Joe was in the driver's seat. The Meatloaf guy Saffy remembered from the day of the angel shoot was sitting beside him eating pistachio nuts.

He leaned back and slid the door open so she could climb in the back. Joe met her eye in the rear-view mirror. 'Saffy, this is Roger.'

'Just call me Meatloaf,' Roger said. 'Everyone does. No idea why. But it's better than Roger. Don't you just *hate* parents who give their kids dorky names?'

Saffy nodded. She did. She had been dreading having to make conversation with Joe but, in the end, she didn't have to. Meatloaf talked to him non-stop in what might as well have been Urdu about pyrometers and altimeters and rates of climb. She rolled down the window and sat back and tuned them out, enjoyed the feeling of the breeze on her face and the simple pleasure of leaving the city on a gorgeous summer evening. When they turned off the N11 at Rathnew, the road narrowed and they drove through long, cool, green corridors of trees. Saffy couldn't remember the last time she'd been out in the country; then, as they came to a familiar-looking village, she remembered horribly clearly.

She tapped Meatloaf on the shoulder. 'Where are we going, exactly?'

'Hotel about two miles away. Woodglen. Posh. Big wedding venue. You ever been there?'

'There are two things you need to remember about ballooning,' Joe explained as they walked towards the huge white hot-air balloon tethered in the middle of the lawn. 'You don't know where you're going and you don't know where you'll land.'

Saffy nodded dumbly. There was the wooden footbridge where she'd thrown her bouquet. There, on the first floor, was the open window of the honeymoon suite. There was the rose garden where she had posed with Greg for the press.

'Joe, stop!' Meatloaf said. 'Look at her face! You're scaring the crap out of her.'

Saffy heard a familiar voice and there was Vivienne the Woodglen manageress, appearing around the corner of the walled garden. She marched towards them, trailed by a couple. The woman was looking annoyed. Her boyfriend was looking at Vivienne's bottom.

'Our prestigious Diamond Package includes a range of sophisticated champagne cocktails served prior to the reception,' Vivienne parroted. 'Guests can mingle around the opulent marble fountain and avail of a *mélange* of finger food served by our courteous staff.'

She nodded at Meatlof and Saffy turned away before she recognised her and buried her face in Joe's chest.

'Are you okay?' Joe stopped in his tracks.

'Bit scared,' Saffy mumbled. He smelled of clean washing and leather.

'Don't be.' He tried to prise her off but she clung to him like a koala to a eucalyptus branch. 'Really. Only seven people have died ballooning in the last five years in the US.'

'Wow!' Meatloaf said. 'I'm sure she feels a whole lot better, now. I know I do.'

'As night falls,' Saffy heard Vivienne's voice receding, 'Woodglen's manicured lawn is illuminated by hundreds of flaming torches.'

'You don't have to go up if you don't want to,' Meatloaf said kindly. 'You can stay on the ground with the retrieve team.'

'No, I'm going up,' Saffy said. The thought of cutting adrift in what was basically a laundry basket attached to a huge tank of flammable gas wasn't remotely as terrifying as spending another minute on Woodglen's manicured lawn.

Ruth, the Lara Croft lookalike Saffy remembered from the White Feather balloon trip, was waiting by the balloon in a tight black jumpsuit. Meatloaf climbed in and she helped Saffy clamber in after him.

'Take it easy up there,' Joe said to Meatloaf, 'she had a bad experience last time.'

'Aren't you coming?' Saffy asked him.

He shook his head. 'No. Me and Ruth will follow you in the van. I mean it, Meatloaf.' Joe shaded his eyes. 'No stunt flying, okay?'

The wicker beneath Saffy's feet creaked and the balloon began to move. Meatloaf rolled his eyes and adjusted the fuel gauge. 'Yeah, yeah! We won't fly with scissors. And we won't smoke. But if she gets sick on *my* boots, I'm throwing her overboard, okay?'

Saffy blushed and turned to glare at Joe but she found herself looking down at the top of his head.

The balloon drifted up, slow as smoke, past the tops of a stand of feathery pines. Saffy stretched her hand out but there wasn't a breath of wind. They were gliding on an invisible air current. A sheepdog chased their shadow across a field where some boys were playing hurling. The sound of their shouts carried up, each individual voice clear as a bell.

Meatloaf was muttering into the radio, '562 feet. 7.8 knots.'

Ruth's voice came crackling back. 'Roger.'

'Shit! She *knows* I hate that,' Meatloaf said to Saffy, shaking his head. 'She does it to wind me up.'

He pointed down to the left and Saffy saw the white van, Dinky-small, driving along a winding lane behind a tiny tractor.

'We can see you guys down there,' he told the radio, 'so don't get up to any funny stuff.'

'Roger.'

He adjusted the flame and the balloon rose and changed direction, following the line of a valley. In the distance, behind the peaks of the Sugar Loaf, Saffy saw the hazy blue line of the sea.

She leaned out to intensify the feeling of floating. Behind her, Meatloaf fiddled with the flow of gas, humming something to himself.

'That's the British Airways ad track.' She turned to him with a smile.

' "The Flower Duet". It's from *Lakmé* – by Delibes.' He saw her face. 'Don't get me wrong, rock 'n' roll's my thing on the ground but opera works better up here. Now stop talking and enjoy the view.'

Saffy was already turning back to watch a village slip by below. A handful of rooftops, the winking disc of a paddling pool in a garden, the tiny figure of a woman shading her eyes to look up as she hung out her washing . . . and it was gone. They floated over a glittering snake of a line of cars crossing a bridge. She had been terrified the last time she'd been up in a balloon. She'd kept her eyes closed for the entire flight. But now she felt as if she couldn't open them wide enough. She couldn't believe that an hour had passed when Meatloaf tapped her shoulder and told her that they were going down.

As they lost altitude, the balloon seemed to be moving faster and faster and Saffy had the sickening feeling that the patchwork of green fields was flying up towards them. They skimmed a hedge and a flock of sheep scattered below them. Saffy remembered what Joe had told her and she bent her knees and held onto the wicker rim of the basket and then they were down, bumping along the ground a half a dozen times before they came to a standstill.

Meatloaf jumped out and grabbed the guy rope and Ruth and Joe came running across the field to tether the balloon.

Saffy felt dreamy and calm, but when Joe put his arms around her to help her to climb out, her body woke up with a jolt.

'Wow!' She looked up at him. 'Can we do that again, right away?'

'That's what all the girls say.' Meatloaf grinned. 'Right, Joe?'

Saffy sat in the passenger seat of the van beside Joe. Meatloaf and Ruth were in the back, bickering about Richard Branson.

'He's a twat. He has twatty hair and a twatty beard and a twatty airline.'

'Don't talk to me about twats, Roger,' Ruth sneered. 'In fact, don't talk to me *at all* till *you* circumnavigate the globe in your own balloon.'

The hedgerows flew past, scribbled with crimson fuchsia, the air smelled of wild honeysuckle and cut grass. Saffy was feeling giddy and light-hearted. It was probably some sort of altitude-related thing.

Joe pulled over at a pub in Stepaside and Meatloaf and Ruth got out and lifted Ruth's scooter out of the back of the van.

'Coming for a pint?' Meatloaf drummed his fingers on the roof. 'I'm not asking, I'm *begging*. Please don't leave me alone with her.' He leaned in through the passenger window. 'I'm scared.'

'I should probably get home,' Saffy said. 'I haven't eaten since lunch.'

'They do food,' Meatloaf said. 'Salted peanuts. Dry-roasted peanuts. There are two hundred and ten calories in a pint of Guinness.'

'You go, Joe.' Saffy opened her seat belt. 'I can call a cab.'

Joe leaned over and fastened her belt again. 'I'll take you home.'

He put his hands back on the wheel but Saffy could still feel the point of heat on her arm where his fingers had touched her.

'I will never, ever forgive you for this,' Meatloaf said to Joe. Then he slapped the roof of the van and as he turned away, he said something that might have been either 'see you soon' or 'get a room'.

Saffy tried to remember who had spoken last but she couldn't. Then both of them started to speak at once.

'You first,' Joe said.

'I was thinking, maybe we could stop and have dinner.' There wasn't really any rush, she'd told her mother she'd be working late and set a tray. She could heat up an M&S meal in the microwave.

'No.' Joe shook his head. 'I mean, I can't. I've got to let Liam's babysitter go at ten.'

Saffy backtracked as fast as she could. What was she thinking? Look how things had turned out the last time she'd had dinner with a strange man. 'I should get home anyway.'

'You could come home and eat with me,' Joe said, 'but I warn you, I'm a terrible cook.'

'You can't be that bad.'

'Try me. I'm pretty confident that the only thing you'll be able to eat is those words.'

Saffy waited in the tiny kitchen while Joe paid the babysitter. A Formica folding table and two chairs took up most of the floor space. A metal clotheshorse covered in drying towels took up the rest.

There was a Manchester United calendar on one bare wall and a yellow plastic piggy bank on the window sill. That was it. No piles of plastic toys, no stacks of books, no deflated footballs or frisbees, no cartoon fridge magnets, no paintings that were supposed to be but never actually looked anything like a robot or a little horsey.

A pair of slippers was parked by the fridge, as if someone small had opened the door and stepped inside. Each slipper was a Snoopy kennel. There was a raggedy Snoopy stuck on top of the left one, but the other Snoopy had gone.

'Liam's out cold.' Joe was standing in the doorway. He was so tall that his hair brushed the beam over his head. He was looking at her in a perplexed way, as if he was surprised to find her in his kitchen. 'Can I get you something to drink?'

'A glass of wine would be lovely.'

'I'm not sure I have any.' He opened the fridge. 'I don't drink. But I've got Ribena.' He pulled out a bottle. 'It's a 2008, I think that was a pretty good year.'

While Joe chopped onions and beat eggs, Saffy boiled water for potatoes and set the table. They moved around one another in the tiny room as if avoiding actual contact was some sort of obscure Olympic sport. She watched him out of the corner of her eye. His mouth was slightly crooked when he smiled. His hair fell into his eyes a lot and he had to push it back. He had nice hands. She had found a couple of gold candles in the cutlery drawer. They looked like they'd been left over from Christmas.

'Do you have any matches?'

Joe turned. 'You smoke?'

Saffy saw the look on his face and shook her head. She had only started a few weeks ago, and three or four a day didn't count, really, did it? 'No. I need a light for the candles . . .'

He lit one on a gas ring and handed it back, then poured a bowl of eggy stuff with chopped-up vegetables into a frying pan.

'So how did you get into flying?' Saffy sat at the table and stuck the candles onto saucers.

'It was a hobby.' Joe stirred the contents of the frying pan with a wooden spoon. 'I trained as a commercial pilot and a bunch of us bought a balloon – this was back in Chicago.'

'You lived in the States for long?'

'About fifteen years. I moved there in my twenties. Then two years ago, we – Liam and me – moved home.'

Saffy waited for him to go on but he didn't. 'Your marriage ended?' she said.

'In a way.' Joe turned the gas up and the eggy stuff began to sizzle. 'My wife died.'

'That's awful!' Saffy had presumed they were divorced.

'Shelley was killed in a car crash by a drunk driver. I was in Paris on a layover. It took eighteen hours to get back home to Liam. After that, I didn't want to fly planes any more. To be honest, my heart hadn't been in it since 9/11, and being so far away from my kid when he needed me, that was the final straw. So now I paint houses and the only thing I fly is balloons.'

'I'm sorry,' Saffy said.

'Don't be.' Joe's voice was sharp.

She bit her lip.

'Shit.' He turned around. His eyes were damp at the corners but that might have been the onions. 'I'm sorry. That was rude.' He clapped his hand to his forehead. 'Shit! Did I just say *shit*?'

Saffy held up three fingers.

'Three times?' He put the wooden spoon down, stuck his hands in his jeans pocket and dropped three fifty-cent coins in the piggy bank on the window sill.

'It's a swear pig. Liam's idea. His friend Gillian Coulter told him I had a potty mouth. If things work out the way he's hoping, Gillian Coulter will be my daughter-in-law some day, so I'm trying to cure the habit.'

The meal was easily the worst Saffy had ever tasted and that included a Nasi Goreng that had given her amoebic gastro-enteritis in Kuala Lumpur and a week-old tuna and pasta salad Greg had once given her without checking the Best Before date.

It wasn't an omelette and it wasn't scrambled eggs. It was slimy and rubbery, undercooked and burned. Saffy privately christened it 'omlegges'.

She pushed it around her plate and told Joe about her mother's cancer and then about her father and how he'd left when she was two.

'That's tough.' Joe forked a chunk of the omlegges into his mouth and frowned. 'Tough for you and tough for him, too. Leaving a child goes against every instinct you have.'

She had never thought that it might have been hard for her father to leave. It had never even occurred to her.

'Have you ever tried to find him?'

'No. He could have found me if he'd wanted. Dublin's small.' She tried to rearrange the food, trying to make it look partially eaten.

'His leaving like that,' Joe looked directly at her, 'that must have had quite an effect on your relationships with men.'

'Oh, well, you know, it was a long time ago.'

'I can see why it would be hard to trust anyone enough to get married or to have kids if that was your blueprint.'

'I was in a long-term relationship till pretty recently,' Saffy said carefully, 'but it didn't work out.'

She cut a piece of the omlegges and put it in her mouth. It was the texture of a trainer insole.

Somehow, she managed to get it down her throat.

'No kids?' He topped up her Ribena.

'No. I'd be a rotten mother. Your life just stops when you have a child. I've seen that happen to my mother. I don't want it to happen to me.'

'You've got it all wrong.' Joe shook his head so his hair fell into his eyes, and when he didn't push it out again, Saffy had to stop herself from leaning over to do it for him.

'Having a kid isn't the *end* of your life; it's the beginning of a whole other life. If it wasn't for Liam, I wouldn't be back in Ireland and I wouldn't have put every cent I own into buying a site in Wicklow and renting the cheapest house I could find so I can build a place of my own. I've done all those things to make his life better, but you know what? They've made my life better, too.'

'Don't you ever wonder where you'd be if you didn't have all that responsibility?'

Joe laughed. 'I know exactly where I'd be: in a bar in Chicago with a bunch of drunk air hostesses, wondering which one was going to let me take her home.'

Saffy had a sudden and very clear picture of this scene and she found she didn't like it.

'Look,' Joe said, 'there are things you can't do when you have a child, physically and mentally. So, you just don't. Like, there wouldn't be any point in me getting involved with someone who didn't, who couldn't, love Liam like I do. That probably rules out about ninety-nine per cent of the female population. I could see that as a limitation but I don't because what I get back from him is . . .' He stretched his arms out, as if he was measuring a huge fish, 'Way big. Making a child is the most amazing thing you'll ever do but here's the catch, you won't know that till you do it. Shit. By "do it", I mean *have a child*, I don't mean *do it* as in, you know, do it.'

He found another fifty-cent piece, leaned over and put it in the swear pig. And after the little clink, the kitchen was suddenly very quiet.

The bathroom was spotless and smelled of Jif. Glow-in-the-dark stars were stuck to the ceiling. Saffy thought she recognised the shape of Orion, the three stars for his belt with two stars above and below for his shoulders and his feet. While the loo was flushing, she open the bathroom cabinet. Joe's shaving things were lined up neatly on the shelf inside, along with bottles of shampoo and Calpol and cough mixture and mouthwash.

She stared into it for a while, unsure of what she was looking for, both relieved and disappointed that she didn't find it. She washed her hands and looked at herself in the mirror. She looked the same, but she felt strange. Her lips were tingling and there was a flutter in her stomach. She hoped that the omlegges hadn't given her salmonella.

They were washing and drying the dishes when they heard the car horn sound outside. It was Saffy's taxi. Joe had asked the driver not to ring the bell in case he woke Liam. She found her bag and her jacket and followed Joe out into the hall.

'Thank you. The balloon flight was incredible and dinner was . . .'

'Inedible?'

She laughed. 'Well, maybe cooking isn't your strong point but I'm sure you're good at other things.'

Joe hadn't switched the light on so she couldn't see his face. 'What about you? What are you good at?'

'Sorry?' Saffy said.

'Are you good at *this*?' Joe traced the line of her shoulder and her collarbone.

'How about this?' He leaned down and brushed her neck with his lips.

The taxi sounded its horn again.

Saffy pulled away. 'Look,' she said, 'you seem really nice, but I can't do this.'

'How about this?' He kissed her, very softly, on the mouth. She told herself not to kiss him back but she wasn't listening.

Then he was pinning her to the wall and she was opening the buttons of his shirt and he was sucking her fingers and she was biting his collarbone. He undid her bra and pushed her hands behind her back and held them there and moved his mouth down over her hot skin. She kicked off her shoes and Joe pulled up her T-shirt. His body pressed against her, warm skin against warm skin except for the cold metal buckle of his belt against her stomach.

There was sharp rap on the front door.

'Did you order a taxi?'

They both froze. They could see the cab driver's face, slightly distorted, as he peered through the bubbled glass, which meant, Saffy thought, he could almost certainly see them.

'What are you doing in there?'

Saffy didn't answer but what she was doing, apparently, was stepping out of her jeans.

There was a suitcase jammed behind the dressing table so the mirror wouldn't tilt properly. Jess could only see part of her body, a truncated torso in a twisted white suspender belt. She had to take it off, detach the stockings, put it on the right way and reattach the stockings again. God, who had time for all this? She put on the matching bra and tied the ribbon on the sides of the white lace thong. She had been tempted to buy the whole lot at Primark but she wasn't sure if cheap stuff would work so she had gone to BT instead. If it got their sex life back on track, it would be worth every cent.

Every cent of ninety euros. And that was without the stockings. At the cash desk, she panicked and threw in a bottle of perfume, bringing the bill to just over a hundred and fifty. That was nearly half a washing machine. A whole bike. New bunkbeds for the twins. She tried not to think about that as she ripped open the perfume packaging and sprayed some on her wrists. It had smelled good in the shop but now it just smelled of desperation.

Conor got Luke and Lizzie into their night things, wondering what he'd done wrong this time. Jess had locked herself into the bedroom and it didn't look like she was even going to bother to come out and kiss the kids goodnight.

He sat on the floor between their beds and read them their favourite bits of *Rover Saves Christmas* by Roddy Doyle. The twins didn't care that it was July. They loved it so much that it automatically fell open on their favourite bit, Chapter Six, which only had one sentence: '*I don't want to be Chapter Six.*'

Conor thumbed back to the beginning. '*It was Christmas Eve in Dublin and the sun was splitting the rocks. The lizards were wearing flip-flops and the cacti that line the city streets were gasping . . .*'

The story should have made him feel better but it didn't. The first photocopied pages of his book had turned up in his last class today. He had confiscated them but by Monday it would be all around the academy. He couldn't get that out of his mind. He thought about going for a cycle and a swim but he just didn't have the energy.

If his desk was still downstairs, he could have lost himself in his plot for a while but Jess had dismantled it and the alcove was already filling up with toys and shoes and Brendan's cage, which was empty except for a broken teapot and a pair of bicycle clips.

Jess arranged herself on the bed, trying to look casual. She had lit some candles, which was really stupid, because it was still bright outside. From this angle, she could see herself properly in the mirror, lying on the crumpled duvet. She looked ridiculous. She heard the soft click of the twins' door closing and she knew, suddenly, that she couldn't go through with this.

She grabbed Conor's dressing gown and pulled it on. She had managed to open her laptop, but not to switch it on, when he opened the door. She pretended to be typing so she didn't have to look up.

'The kids are asleep. What are you up to?'

'Working.' Jess kept her head bent over the keyboard.

'What's with the candles?' She'd forgotten to blow them out. She pretended to type, clicking her fingers over the keys randomly.

'Hmmm? Oh them. I'm writing a puff piece about a new range for the *Wicklow People*. They're pretty vile, aren't they?'

Conor drummed his fingers on the doorjamb. The room smelled exotic and sweet and kind of sexy to him actually but he didn't want to disagree with her.

She was lying face down on the bed. The thick towelling of her robe gave her cartoon curves. He wanted, more than anything, to walk over and slide it off, but he didn't know if he could. He'd had sex with other women that was just sex but with Jess, even the most cursory fuck had the potential to pull his heart out of hiding and pin it to his sleeve, and right now, another row would break it.

He sat on the edge of the bed. 'So how's the article going?' Jess froze. If the robe fell open, he'd see the underwear and the humiliation would be too much. She had to get him out of here. She stared at the screen.

'Not great. But I have to finish it tonight.'

He stood up. 'Well, if you're working, I might head back over to Greg's and try to do another couple of hours on the book. I've been a bit stuck but I had an idea when I was reading to the twins and I think I might be able to write my way out of it.'

'Right.' Jess's hair had fallen over her face so he couldn't see her expression but he didn't need to. She always looked irritated when he brought up the book.

He closed the door without looking back at the beautiful stranger on the bed. He didn't understand how it was possible to miss somebody who was only a few feet away. But he did.

Before Saffy was properly awake, she could feel the force of an unblinking gaze inches away from her face.

'Forget it, Kevin Costner,' she mumbled, 'I'm not getting up. Use the cat flap.'

She sank back into a delicious dream. Joe was carrying her upstairs and throwing her down on his bed, she was pulling him down to join her. Then she realised she wasn't dreaming, she was remembering, and she was still in Joe's bed.

She stretched and opened her eyes and found herself looking straight at the boy who had bled all over her car.

'Did you sleep over?' he asked immediately, as if he had been waiting to ask the question for some time.

Saffy's instinct was to deny this but all the evidence was against her. Her own clothes, for example, which she clearly remembered dropping in the hall and on the stairs, were folded neatly on a wooden chair in the small, tidy room. Joe was no-where to be seen. She decided to avoid the question altogether.

'Shouldn't you be in school?'

The boy – was it Ian or Leo? – was wearing a too-small Spiderman sweatshirt and a pair of red striped pyjama bottoms. His glasses had been fixed with silver gaffer tape. His hair was reddish not brown, but his eyes were the same cool blue as Joe's.

'It's Saturday.' *Saddaday*. Now that he wasn't stammering, he sounded American.

'Saturday! You know that that means?' She had to get him out of there so she could go to the bathroom. She badly needed to pee. 'That means there are great cartoons on TV.'

'Like what?'

She trawled her brain for the name of that stupid animation Greg had been watching at Conor and Jess's the morning after they broke up.

'Like *He-Man. Master of the Planet*.'

'It's *Master of the Universe* and my mom said it's sexist.'

Saffy remembered that his mother was dead but she didn't know what to say so she just said, 'Ummmm.'

'When you come for a sleepover,' he stared at her bare shoulders, 'you're supposed to bring pyjamas and a sleeping bag.'

Joe appeared at the door with a towel around his waist. He grinned at Saffy and she grinned right back. He was still damp from his shower. There was a lot to grin about.

'You two buddies yet?'

'Yes,' Saffy said.

'Nope.' The boy shook his head.

Joe grabbed him up and tickled him all over. 'It's Mr Grumpy!' The boy thrashed around and squealed. 'It's Mr Grumpy but hang on a second . . . he's laughing!'

'I was just telling . . .' *Leo? Liam?* Saffy didn't want to get it wrong '. . . *him* that I came for a sleepover.'

Joe flashed Saffy a grateful smile. 'Liam goes on lots of sleepovers, don't you?'

'Not with girls.'

Joe began to tickle him again. Saffy was horrified to find that she felt slightly jealous of all the attention Mr Grumpy was getting.

'Dad, stop!'

'If I let you go, you'll go straight downstairs and fix your cereal?'

'Yes!'

Joe released him and he broke away and ran to the door, breathless. They heard the thump of his feet on the stairs and the slam of a downstairs door. It was ridiculous, considering the things they had done together in the last few hours, but, now that they were alone, Saffy felt shy.

'Shit!' Joe leaned back and took Saffy's hand and covered his eyes with it. 'That wasn't supposed to happen. He usually sleeps late on Saturdays.'

'It's okay.' She desperately needed the bathroom but she was afraid that, if she went, he'd be dressed when she came back and then she would have to get dressed and all of this would be over.

'You think? God. I've never even introduced the little guy to a woman before. I guess it went pretty well, apart from the jealousy thing.'

How had he known that she felt jealous? Could he read her mind?

'I hope he wasn't rude. He's not used to sharing me.' Joe ran a finger over her wrist and up the inside of her arm. She shivered. He seemed to be finding erogenous zones she didn't even know she had.

'I guess I'd better go and get him dressed, and then I have to drop him to his swimming class and if you're not busy we could find something to do . . .'

He followed the line of his finger with his mouth, ending up at her earlobe. Saffy had plenty to do. She had to get back to her mother and sort out breakfast and do a supermarket shop and put on some washing. After that, she'd promised to take Jill for a drive down to the sea.

'I can't,' she said. 'I've got to go home.'

'You do? Right away? You don't even have ten minutes . . . ?'

She let him push her back down on onto the pillow.

'I have about seven.'

21

Marsh lowered her voice, peeping up through her lashes and let one hand hover a fraction of an inch above Harry Burke's thigh as she talked him through the reshot Avondale ad. The hand settled there when the lights went down in the edit suite. Saffy saw Ali notice it and bite her lip. She wondered if Simon had noticed it too. But he was too busy pretending that the reshoot wasn't his fault to notice anything else.

Saffy didn't need to watch the cut. She had sat through it with the editor a dozen times this morning. She had been at the studio since eight. She had stayed over at Joe's again and set her phone to wake her at five. Joe had woken up, too, and she'd let him pull her back into bed for fifteen minutes. Then she had driven home and showered and left a breakfast tray for her mother.

She was sleeping at Joe's every three or four nights. Mr Kenny's nurse said Jill was out of danger and would be fine on her own now but Saffy still felt guilty sneaking out and leaving her. Though Jill slept so soundly with the codeine that she didn't seem to notice that she was gone.

She closed her eyes in the cool, air-conditioned darkness and ran through an edit of her own. Joe opening the door of the shower cubicle and carrying her, soaking wet, back to bed. Joe sliding his hand up her thigh on a quiet country lane when they were following the balloon . . .

The lights went on and everyone looked at Harry, waiting for his response. Saffy could almost hear the collective clench of buttocks. He shook his head. 'It's not good.' Marsh's hand left his leg and travelled to her mouth to stifle a gulp. 'It's brilliant!' He grinned. 'Now, what's for lunch?'

Once, when Saffy was very small, someone had taken her to feed the ducks in St Stephen's Green. She couldn't be sure who it was but she didn't think it had been her mother. Jill dragged Saffy along to art galleries and cafés and shops; duck feeding wasn't really her thing.

The ducks, she remembered, swam together in a little cluster and all of them managed to get some crumbs. Except for one. His markings were different. He bobbed uncertainly at the edges, wanting to be part of the flock but never really fitting in. Mike reminded her of that duck. Mike in a blue nylon short-sleeved shirt and brown slacks and black reef shoes, which showcased his long, yellow toenails. Beside Simon in navy blue linen, Marsh in a tight black Alaia dress, Harry in Hugo Boss and Ali in her power suit, Mike just looked out of place.

Saffy got a nod from Gabriel Byrne, a finger waggle from Louis Walsh and a wave from Greg's agent – Lauren – who was having lunch with Damo Doyle. He grinned and gave her the peace sign.

'Celebrity friends. I'm impressed!' Harry looked at her with new respect.

'You're obviously a broadsheet reader, Harry,' Marsh said, fanning herself prettily with the menu, 'because if you read the tabloids you'd know that our Saffy is Mrs Greg Gleeson.'

'Well, actually I'm not—' Saffy began.

'My daughter is a big fan. Of Damo Doyle not Gleeson,' Harry said. 'Run over there and get me an autograph, will you?'

Saffy waited till Damo had gone to the bathroom and headed over to the table.

'Looking very happy,' Lauren raised an eyebrow, '*considering.*'

Her smoker's laugh made Saffy ache for a cigarette. She had been trying to cut them out. She'd stupidly lied to Joe about smoking and now felt she had to make the lie true.

'After what happened, I thought you'd be a total mess. Speaking of a total mess, how's your husband?'

'I don't know, Lauren. I haven't seen him in weeks.'

'I'm not surprised. I read about Greg's little shagfest. That's all I needed after his little episode at *The Station* and the wedding disaster. What's next? A spot of kiddie fiddling?' Lauren picked up a prawn and cracked the shell. 'There's a rumour going round that he's signed up with Venom to do *promo* work. If it's true, he's in breach of contract.' She sucked the meat out of the shell. 'And I will not be amused.'

Saffy wasn't here to talk about Greg. 'Can you ask Damo to sign an autograph for my client?'

'Sure, on condition that you think about taking Greg back. He only went off the rails after you guys broke up, sweetie. I can think of a hundred reasons why you changed your mind but change it back, please, for all our sakes.'

Jill couldn't sleep. For once, it wasn't the chemo-nausea that kept her kneeling at the toilet bowl shivering and retching most nights. It wasn't even the fear of dying that often woke her up, as real and frightening as a stranger in her room. What kept her awake was the fear of the mess she'd leave behind if she didn't make it. Sadbh was doing so much for her now. The least Jill could do was make things easy on her if the worst happened.

She had heard her daughter come back early, shower and then leave again. She had guessed that she had been spending a couple of nights a week with Greg, sneaking back in the morning to get changed for work.

She had mixed feelings about them getting back together. Greg had behaved unforgivably and then it was splashed all over the papers, which made it worse. But as Sadbh had said herself, you couldn't believe everything you read. Her daughter seemed to have forgiven him, and wasn't that the whole point of marriage? That guarantee that, no matter what happened, you stayed together. The promise that had sent Rob Reilly, who had sworn that he loved Jill, back to his wife?

If Sadbh moved back into the apartment with Greg, Jill would find a way to manage. She could get a live-in nurse or move into a nursing home. But she would miss her daughter. She had seen more of her in the last few weeks than she had seen in ten years. Having her around was the only silver lining in the dark cloud of the cancer. And she wanted to enjoy it for as long as she could. So she hadn't admitted that she knew Sadbh was staying out every other night. She had decided to simply ignore it. But there were things she couldn't ignore. Things she needed to sort out before it was too late.

Sadbh had covered the breakfast tray with cling film but Kevin Costner had nibbled his way through it and licked the butter off the croissants and left one long black hair, like a question mark, in the bottom of her cup. Jill wasn't hungry anyway. She pulled on a robe and sat on the stairs for a while, waiting to feel human. When that didn't happen, she went to the kitchen and made a pot of strong coffee. She wasn't supposed to have it but she forced herself to drink two cups, black. After about twenty minutes, she threw it all up again into the guest toilet but at least some of the caffeine had entered her bloodstream and she was finally awake.

She found a roll of bin bags and went back upstairs. Everything in her bedroom had been chosen because it was pretty or simple or luxurious. Her linen sheets, her antique chandelier, her hand-woven silk rug. Len had called it her temple, but Len had thought she was a goddess. He might change his mind if he saw her now.

She closed the velvet curtains and stood in front of the mirror. Her hair was starting to come out in clumps and her eyelashes were falling out too. Her lovely blue eyes looked pink-rimmed and rabbity without them. The weight she'd lost had come straight off her face, and her skin sagged beneath her cheekbones. She had cold sores on both sides of her mouth.

Since the operation, she had tried not to look at the wound at all. Now she undid her robe. Her chest was tender and her arm was still numb but the physical pain was nothing compared to the shock she felt looking at her body. She had been dreading losing her beauty slowly to age but she had never imagined that it would be torn away suddenly and violently, like this.

The skin was stretched tight across her ribcage where her left breast used to be, pulled together by a raised, livid scar, as if Mr Kenny had taken a marker and drawn a lumpy, red line between the woman she had been before and the woman she would be from now on.

She put the robe back on, opened the door of the armoire and began pulling out the clothes she would never wear again: a sheer white satin blouse, an off-the-shoulder sweater, a jersey top, an armful of wraparound dresses. Everything clingy or low cut went onto the pile; and that was almost everything she owned.

She tackled the chest of drawers, her T-shirts, her underwear, her silk slips and nightdresses. The idea of the woman in the mirror wearing her red polka-dot, halter-neck bikini or her rose-pink silk teddy would have been funny if it wasn't just so sad. She struggled to her feet and began stuffing everything into bin bags.

When she was finished, she was breathless and clammy with sweat. Her left arm, where Mr Kenny had removed her lymph nodes, was throbbing but she was angry enough now to do what she had been putting off till last.

She went out to the landing and pulled down the ladder that led to the attic. She found a torch and managed to haul herself up, rung by rung. She rested for a while then crawled into the narrow space, moving boxes and bags with her good arm until she found what she was looking for. She dragged the heavy brown suitcase to the attic trapdoor and stepped down onto the ladder, taking its weight on her shoulder. She wasn't strong enough to hold it and it slipped. One of the brass corners caught her as it fell, ripping her robe and raising a long scratch down the inside of her arm. The case landed with a thump on the floor and burst open, spilling old papers and photographs down the stairs.

'It doesn't look like a pig.' Luke frowned at the twisted knot of balloons.

'If you *imagine* it's a pig, it *is* a pig.' The balloon man switched on a grin that wrinkled his clown-paint but his eyes were not smiling.

'If I imagine *you're* a pig, are *you* a pig, too?' Lizzie asked.

Jess pulled the twins away before things turned nasty. She had always loved the World Music Festival. They had been coming to the park in Dun Laoghaire every summer since the twins were born. Somewhere in a box, or possibly, given the state of their attic, in a dusty casserole dish with a comb and a spent battery, there must be photographs of Luke and Lizzie in their papooses, then in their double buggy, then as plump toddlers, jiggling to Mexican mariachis and Japanese drummers.

But this year, she just couldn't get into it. The twins were acting up. It was overcast and muggy and the clashing jangle of music from every corner of the park was giving her a headache. Conor was buying chips. She could see him in the distance, waiting by the van. He looked bored and grumpy and even though she felt the same, she resented him for it.

She squinted at the programme, wishing, for the first time in her life, that she owned a pair of sunglasses.

3.15. Ultarak Stevens assaults the eardrums with a mind-blowing mash-up of ninja-surf and traditional music from Kazakhstan.
3.45. Debashish Nacharya enchants with his Shruti Stick, a 2-string creation inspired by the 22-note octave used in Indian music.

She sighed. It was going to be a long afternoon.

Saffy was waiting by the wooden stage where she'd arranged to meet Joe and Liam. Some dervishes were due to whirl there at three. She could see them through a gap in the curtain, chatting and eating Pringles and adjusting their ornate skirts.

She plucked nervously at her own skirt. Today would be the first time she'd seen Liam since that morning when she'd woken up at Joe's and he'd been standing there. It felt, bizarrely, like some kind of date. She had agonised over what to wear for ages. In the end, she'd gone out and bought a red fifties-style frock.

Looking around at the crowd who were mostly in shorts and T-shirts, she realised that, apart from the dervishes, she was the most overdressed person here. But at least, she reasoned, she was wearing more than she'd been wearing the first time she had met Liam.

Even though she'd stayed over at Joe's a couple of times a week, they always had made sure that she arrived after the boy had gone to bed and left long before he was awake. She didn't mind getting up early. She loved driving back to her mother's house through the sleepy suburbs, cutting across familiar tree-lined roads where all the houses still had their blinds drawn.

Ranelagh, Clonskeagh, Milltown. This was a side of Dublin she had been desperate to escape when she moved into her first apartment at twenty. Now it was strangely comforting to pass by her first school and the flat above the chemist her mother had rented for a year and the bus stop where her fifteen-year-old self had had her heart broken when she saw Eoghan Casey kissing Orlagh Kavanagh.

But a few nights ago, everything had changed. Joe had organised a babysitter for Liam and taken Saffy for a drive down to Brittas Bay. They had made love under a rug in the sand dunes, narrowly avoiding being discovered by a couple of kids chasing a runaway springer spaniel.

Afterwards they lay drowsing in the mellow evening sunshine. If Saffy had walked by, she wouldn't have recognised herself lying in the sand in her wrinkled Jaeger skirt and shirt with her shoes kicked off and her head in the lap of the lanky, dark-haired man in paint-spattered overalls.

'I'd like to meet your mother, sometime,' Joe had said, turning on his side to look at her. 'When the time is right. She seemed nice.'

'She is nice,' Saffy said.

She wouldn't have said it a few months ago, she thought, but her mother was different somehow. She had lost her breast and then she had lost her independence and now she was losing her looks. But she had been stoical and sweet and uncomplaining. And she was being unbelievably tactful. The old Jill would have bombarded Saffy about the fact that she was staying out nights. She guessed that Jill thought she was seeing Greg again and, for the moment, that suited her. She wasn't ready to tell anybody about Joe yet. It was too soon and too special.

'I think it's time for you and Liam to get to know one another properly,' Joe had said. 'You guys have a lot in common.'

'Like what?'

He tickled her lip with a blade of grass. 'You're both only children from one-parent families. You're both long-sighted. Neither of you will eat anything I cook. And I love you both. In different ways, obviously.'

He'd used the L word. Saffy would have fallen over if she wasn't already lying down.

Lizzie was crying because Jess wouldn't buy her a set of tom-toms. Luke had turned green after his chips. He said his tummy hurt and that the only cure was ice cream but Jess knew that if she gave him ice cream he'd get a headache. The ninja-surf was making her ears bleed. She tried not to let it all get to her but for some reason she wanted to cry. She looked around for Conor. He was standing a few feet away, lost in a daydream. He didn't even know she existed.

She felt a sudden and overwhelming wave of envy, and the awful thing was that the person she envied was herself. The Jess who'd stood right where she was standing a year ago, probably even wearing the same khaki dress and flip-flops. Her old self wouldn't have let all these little irritations wind her up to the point of tears. And, even if she had, the old Conor would have noticed that she was in trouble and put his arm around her and tucked her hair behind her ears and said something sweet or silly that would have had her smiling again in seconds.

She stared around, willing the tears back into her eyes and saw a couple wrapped around one another coming towards her through the crowd followed by a sweet, owlish-looking little boy wearing glasses.

The man was tall with a slightly crooked nose and dark, longish hair and heavy stubble. The woman had dark, shoulder-length hair and she was wearing a garish red dress and dark glasses but she looked strangely familiar. Jess stepped over and tugged Conor's elbow sharply.

'Conor,' she said. 'Isn't that . . . ?'

'Hmm?'

Just at that moment, the guy leaned down and cupped the woman's chin and she turned her face to kiss him. But when she turned back again Conor recognised her immediately. He grinned and called her over.

*

Saffy introduced the tall guy as Joe and the little boy with the glasses as his son, Liam. She and Conor were acting as if this was all perfectly normal but Jess wanted to scream.

What was happening? Why were the two people she was closest to turning into strangers? She felt as if she barely knew Conor lately and now she didn't recognise Saffy either. The Saffy she knew wouldn't get drunk and black out and have a one-night stand with a stranger. Or run out on her husband after a few hours. Or refuse to answer any of her calls and then suddenly show up, out of nowhere, with some random stranger who couldn't keep his hands off her. All the time Conor and Saffy were talking about the weather and the music, this dark-haired Owen Wilson look-alike was giving her a body search.

Saffy tried to silently telegraph an apology to Jess. She was sorry she hadn't told her about Joe but she hadn't told anyone – not her mother, not anyone at work. She knew that everyone would think she was just on the rebound from Greg but she wasn't. She didn't know exactly what it was yet but it was more than that. She hadn't imagined that she'd be caught like this, but even though she should have felt ashamed of herself she couldn't stop smiling.

And to Jess's annoyance, Conor was smiling right back.

'D'you guys want to grab a cold drink?' he said. 'The surf ninjas are just a warm-up for the Indian bloke. And I'm not sure how his Shruti Stick will go down on top of the hot dog I had earlier.'

Saffy looked at Joe shyly and they shared one of those annoying smiles. That smile that says, 'We can think of something better to do. And you probably don't have to think too hard to imagine what it is.'

'It's great to meet you guys,' Joe said, 'but maybe we'll take a rain check this time.'

22

The little fucker jumped out of a pile of pots in the sink, darted across the granite worktop, then, defying gravity, ran straight down the door of the integrated oven and disappeared beneath the Smeg fridge.

Greg's frying pan cracked down hard on the floor, missing the rat's tail by a hair's breadth and knocking a neat triangle of marble off the corner of a tile. He straightened up, picking what looked like a grain of wild rice off the sole of his bare foot. Rat crap. Great. That was all he needed – Weil's disease.

'I'll get you, you little shit!' he roared, beating on the fridge with the frying pan. 'You can run but you can't hide.'

He had a sudden mental snapshot of himself from the rat's perspective: a naked, bellowing man, brandishing a piece of Jamie Oliver cookware. It was a bit too close to *Tom and Jerry* for comfort.

He put the pan down, wrapped a tea towel around his waist and flicked on Sky News to show the rat he had more important things to think about. Then he flicked it off again because he did have more important things to think about. Like the letter he'd just opened from Lauren.

BlueSky Talent Agency
Dublin, Sydney, LA

Dear Mr Gleeson
Re: Your Contract with BlueSky Talent Agency

We refer to the contract between us dated 10 January 2002.
The terms of this document clearly state that you are exclusively employed through L.S. Personal Management.

May we remind you that undertaking work though any other agency represents a breach of this contract.

We understand that your profile is currently listed on the books of Venom Models, Inc. Unless your name is withdrawn from this

list within fourteen days, your contract with us will be terminated
without further notice to you and we will institute a claim for
damages, costs and interest as a result of this breach.

We look forward to hearing from you as a matter of urgency.
Yours faithfully,
Lauren Smith & Associates

Scribbled under her name was a hand-written message from Lauren: *One more strike and you're out!*

Greg balled up the letter and threw it at the fridge. Let Lauren sue him. As far as he was concerned, she stopped being his agent when she didn't stand up for him after his falling-out with *The Station*.

It had all been downhill since then. The humiliating breakfast where she'd ticked him off and made him grovel then swanned off to hobnob with Bono. The movie job in LA that had disappeared into thin air. The fact that she hadn't even bothered to show up for his wedding. And now she had stopped taking his calls.

Bloody right, he had signed up with Venom. He was down to the last few thousand of the money he'd made on the car and next month's mortgage payment was going to be a problem. What was he supposed to do? Starve?

He had bumped into Greta, one of Venom's bookers, a few weeks back. She'd been at the wedding and she just came up to him to say how fabulous it had been. They ended up going for drinks and sushi. She'd even paid the bill and she'd said she could get him loads of work.

She'd already sent him on a go-see for an underwear catalogue. To be honest, he could think of better things to do than being spritzed with baby oil and standing around in skimpy jocks in front of a fat businessman and a faggy PR, but if he got it, the gig would pay really well. Plus there was the Mark Wahlberg factor. Strutting round in jocks didn't seem to have done *his* career any harm.

A tiny, whiskered nose poked out from under fridge and then disappeared again. Greg smiled. If Ratty wanted to play a waiting game, that was fine with him. He had everything he needed for a stakeout. A little joint he'd rolled earlier, a carton of cold orange juice, the remote control and a draft of Conor's novel, which he'd 'borrowed' from the shelf in the study. Plus his trusty Jamie Oliver 12-inch non-stick. Ratty was going to the big hole in the sky. It was only a matter of time.

At the end of his last class, Conor handed back all the corrected essays on 'Canal Bank Walk' except for one.

Wayne Cross hadn't shown up for the first three weeks of the revision course but it turned out he'd been at Irish College and, when he got expelled, he'd appeared at the back of Conor's Leaving Cert Preparation class. Not that he did much except listen to his iPod and play Snake on his mobile phone.

'Whose essay is this, Cross?'

The boy leaned back in his chair, crossing his nicotine-stained fingers under his beefy neck. 'It's mine.'

'You didn't write this essay.'

A crease appeared under Wayne's shaved hairline and rippled down his forehead, gathering in a fleshy wave over his eyebrows. 'Are you calling me a liar?'

'Are you calling me stupid? First page, the one with your name on it?' Conor put it down on the desk. 'Black Bic. Rest of essay?' He flicked through the pages. 'Blue fountain pen.'

Wayne smirked. 'Me biro broke.'

'Right.' Conor picked up the essay again. 'Was that before or after you wrote: *Kavanagh begins this poem with the neologism "Leafy-with-Love", suggesting that the growth of plants and grasses on the banks of the canal have been nurtured with God's love.* What is a "neologism", Cross?'

Wayne scratched the tattoo of a scorpion below his left ear. 'That's for me to know and for you to find out.'

'Listen, Wayne, this is not school, okay? This is a course that your parents have *paid* for. Stealing someone else's work is pointless. You're here to practise for an exam, not to get an A for an essay.'

'Is that what I got? An A?' Wayne stood up.

He took the essay from Conor and stuffed it into the plastic

Centra bag he used instead of a schoolbag, then he stepped around the desk so they were nearly eye to eye.

'Fucking A, Mr Fatty! You've made my day.'

Conor couldn't believe it. It was five in the afternoon and Greg wasn't even dressed. He was sitting at the breakfast bar in the huge white kitchen holding a frying pan, and all he was wearing was a dirty tea towel.

'Man! You are never going to believe this!' His eyes were glassy. He was stoned again. 'We have rats.'

'I'm not surprised.' Conor opened the fridge. 'This place breaks every health and safety rule in the book.'

A pork steak wrapped in cling film that had been in there since he started using Greg's study was turning green. A trickle of yellow yolk was leaking out of a box of eggs. There was a pool of something pink and chunky leaking out from under the salad crisper.

Conor put a carton of milk and a bag of coffee on a shelf and closed the fridge door. He didn't mind buying occasional groceries but he drew the line at cleaning up. He wasn't a houseboy. He opened a net of mandarins and piled them in a bowl.

'Got anything to eat?' Greg picked one up and put it back again. 'Anything that isn't orange?' His towel slipped to one side, giving Conor a full-frontal of his crotch. It was shockingly hairless.

'Christ! What have you done to yourself?'

'Had to shave for that underwear catalogue casting,' Greg re-tied the tea towel. 'Trade secret: it gives you a better profile in your tight whites.'

Greg ordered a sixteen-inch Thick Crust Caribbean Deluxe pizza, a six-pack of Budweiser and something called 'Death by Tiffin' Mousse.

'So,' Conor peeled a mandarin, 'how did the casting go?'

Greg shrugged. 'Not sure if I'll take it.'

'They offered it to you there and then?'

'Not officially but they want me, I can tell.' He stood up and swaggered to the sink. There was a small but unmistakable roll of fat hanging over his tea towel. He straightened up, sucking his belly in. 'What's not to want?'

'Greg, what's *this* doing in here?' Conor pointed at the lever-arch folder under the frying pan. It was the working draft of his novel. 'Did you take that out of my study?'

Greg did a hammy double take. 'Your study? *Your* study? The last time I looked, it was *my* study and you were renting it.' He rinsed a wine glass and filled it with water.

'Did you read it?'

Greg nodded. 'Yeah. I didn't think it was a big deal. And you left it, you know, lying around.'

Christ. He hadn't shown a line of it to anyone except the agent. Conor looked out of the window, waiting for Greg to say something. Anything. A seagull landed on the balcony, shat, and then flew off. Greg sat down on the stool again. He picked up the remote control and began to channel hop, keeping the volume on mute.

Eventually, Conor cracked. 'So what did you think?'

'Of what?'

'My novel, Greg!'

'I didn't read it all. I just skimmed it. It's . . . you know . . .'

Conor reddened. 'No, I don't know. That's why I asked you.'

'Well, it's kind of heavy and I don't really buy the way the guy ends up looking after the kids. Would he just let his wife go off with another dude like that?'

Greg picked up a piece of mandarin skin and began to shred it.

'It would be better if the wife was murdered or went to prison. That would be less emasculating. And I think there should be just one kid, not two. Maybe a girl, a teenager, with all these beautiful friends. The really sexy one could come on to the guy but he ends up rejecting her. That way you can get in lots of sexy stuff and a moral.'

Conor shook his head. 'So what you're saying in a nutshell is that you think I should rewrite the whole book.'

'Hey, don't get defensive. It's more tweaking than rewriting. Look, I've nothing on this afternoon, I can give you a hand brainstorming or—'

The doorbell rang.

Greg pointed at his tea towel. 'Can you get that?'

'That's forty euro.' The pizza delivery guy peered over Conor's shoulder. 'Deadly gaff, head. Someone famous live here?'

Conor handed the money over. 'Yeah.' He was pissed off having to pay for Greg's takeaway again. He wasn't going to serve it up to him. He stood back and waved at the pizza guy and pointed at the kitchen. 'Colin Farrell. He's out but he's due back any minute. Why don't you wait?'

Conor's fingers flew over the keyboard. Whenever they slowed down, he pictured Wayne Cross's smirk or the smug look on Greg's face when he said this was *his* study or the way Jess flinched when he touched her lately.

He had been feeling miserable for weeks but now he was angry and anger was a feeling he could channel into his story. It was something he could write out of. He worked for three hours straight, finishing an important scene between his main character and his ex-wife then spending another hour re-ordering the scenes that led up to the climax.

When he was finished he sat back in his chair and let the world in again: the loud metallic babble from the TV, the smell of cooked pineapple and dope smoke, the voice of the pizza guy, who hadn't left, yelling at Greg from the bathroom where he was pissing like a horse.

'Hey, man, when's Colin going to show?'

Jess was sitting on the stairs squeezing Locktite onto a pair of bunny ears, which she was about to glue to a triangle of pink fun fur that was supposed to look like a bunny's head. The twins were having a fancy dress day at Summer Camp. Lizzie was going as an angel. Luke was going as a rabbit and he wanted to be a pink one.

'Rabbits are grey or brown, usually,' Jess had reminded him.

'I'm a special rabbit,' Luke announced. 'Called Daisy.'

'Maybe this is why they call it "Summer *Camp*"!' Conor had said, laughing.

But it was easy for him. He didn't have to make the eye patch or cut up a sheet for a ruffled shirt or go to Ann Summers for bunny ears. 'They're not for me,' she'd told the woman at the till.

'Course they're not, dear.' The woman had given her a coy smile. 'We've got a lovely black satin boyshort with a detachable tail if you're interested.'

Jess had looked around at the loved-up couples and giggling girls browsing Rampant Rabbits and rubber nurse's uniforms. Why was everyone so bloody obsessed with sex?

She and Conor had finally broken their three-week-long abstinence last night. And it had been, well, just all right. She bit her lip. No. That wasn't true. It had been terrible. She was beginning to understand all that new-age crap about sex being the continuation of a conversation. She and Conor didn't seem to have much to say to one another these days, in or out of bed.

The phone rang and she reached for it with one gluey hand, pressing the ears down onto the fun-fur head with the other.

'It's me!' It was Saffy – Saffy putting on a shiny-happy-person voice, as if this somehow made everything okay.

'Oh, hello,' Jess said coolly.

'Jess, I don't blame you for being annoyed with me. Look, I'm sorry I didn't tell you about Joe. I'm sorry you had to find out like that. I wanted to tell you but I didn't think you'd approve.'

'You're right. I don't.' Jess lifted her hand to see if the ears had stuck. They had. To her fingers. 'But hey, don't worry about it. Don't let what *I* think stop you sneaking around with some married guy.'

'He's not married,' Saffy said.

'Sorry. Sneaking round with some *divorced* guy. My mistake.'

'He's a widower.'

Jess tried to shake the ears off her fingers but they had bonded to her skin, possibly permanently. 'Well, that's convenient. Now if only Greg would jump out of a high building, you'd be free to marry *him*. I'll let him know the next time I see him.'

'Um . . . Jess, would you mind not mentioning Joe to Greg?'

Jess shook her head. 'I'm getting the strangest sense of déjà vu here, Saffy.'

'Or vice versa? I just want to do all this in my own time.'

'Have you even told this new guy that Greg exists?'

'Of course. He knows I've just finished a long relationship but he doesn't know I got married.'

Jess didn't trust herself to speak.

'Come on, Jess, it's not like we're really *married* married. We split up after about twenty minutes.'

Jess wedged the ears under her bare foot and jerked her hand. They came away leaving a sliver of her skin stuck to the pink fur. Her fingertip began to bleed.

'I'm sorry, Saffy, but it does count. You have to be separated for four years in this backward country before you can start divorce proceedings.'

'Oh my God, you're right. I never thought about that.' Saffy sounded genuinely shocked.

'What was I doing, Jess? Marrying Greg, I mean. It was never going to work. Being with Joe has made me realise that. There's this incredible emotional honesty between us.'

'Which would explain why you're *lying* to him about being married.' Jess knew she was being horrible to Saffy but she couldn't help it.

'Jess.' Saffy's voice had started to wobble. 'I completely understand that you're pissed off that I didn't tell you about Joe. I was really pissed off when you didn't tell me about Greg's fling. But can we call it quits? Life's too short, and you're my best friend.'

Jess pressed her finger onto the pink fun fur. She made one perfect crimson polka dot of blood then another.

'Am I, Saffy? I thought I was but I don't know what's happened to us in the last few months. I have no idea what's going on in your life and you have no idea what's going on in mine.'

'Well, tell me,' Saffy said. 'Tell me everything that's happening in your life. I'm here. I'm listening.'

Jess sighed. Saffy was right, life was short and she could certainly use a friend at the moment. She felt her anger drain away.

'All right, I will. But this is not a good time, Saffy. I'm in the middle of something here.'

'Well, let's meet soon. Okay?'

Jess sighed. 'Okay.'

'Oh, listen, I nearly forgot. I want to hire a movie for Joe's son. What's the best kids' movie ever? Something he won't have seen? I'm trying to worm my way into his affections. The little creep hates me.'

All the anger returned in double quantities. 'He's not a little creep; he's a little kid, Saffy. You're competing for his dad's attention. And from what I saw in Dun Laoghaire last Sunday, you're winning. Think about it. Think how awful that must feel to him.'

'I *will* think about it but right now I have to find a film and I have to find it in the next five minutes.'

Jess caught her breath. 'You're in the video shop *now*?'

'Yes! I'm on my way over to Joe's.'

'So you rang me to ask me for a film recommendation?'

'Well . . .' Saffy tried to backtrack. 'Obviously I wanted to talk to you about Joe and everything, too . . .'

Jess squeezed a dot of Locktite onto her finger to stop the bleeding. It stung like hell.

'I've got an idea,' she said. 'Why don't you get that movie you brought over for Luke and Lizzie?'

There was a long pause. 'I don't remember hiring a movie for Luke and Lizzie.' Saffy sounded confused.

'Really?' Jess said. 'That's probably because you didn't. Not once. Ever.' And she hung up.

Joe answered the door and kissed Saffy, long and hard, in full view of a man who was repairing a motorbike in the next garden and a woman in a tracksuit walking a Pomeranian. Then he pulled her into the house and took her shopping bags.

'Popcorn,' he said, looking inside. 'Maltesers. Coke. And . . . a DVD.'

'I thought we'd have a movie night, you, me and the little guy.'

'*A Fish Called Wanda*.' Joe opened the box. 'Haven't seen it. Hang on, it's a fifteen.'

'Are you sure?' Saffy hadn't thought to check. 'I saw it years ago. I don't remember it being violent or sexy or anything. It's by those Monty Python guys, so it's pretty surreal.'

'Good call. Liam loves surreal and he's got his friend Alex sleeping over. This'll make their day.'

Saffy curled up on the worn, brown, corduroy sofa and the two boys threw themselves onto the big beanbag that took up most of the tiny living-room floor. Joe was fiddling with some cables at the back of the old-fashioned TV.

'Okay.' He sat down on the sofa and put his arm around Saffy. 'We're ready to roll.'

Every time he touched her in some casual, absent-minded way, Saffy felt as if she was exactly in the right place. She had listened to her head for her whole life but it had finally stopped trying to figure everything out and, for the first time, she could really hear her heart.

'Helovesme, helovesme, helovesme, helovesme,' it was saying. 'Helovesme, helovesme, helovesme.'

The first 'fuck' came about ten minutes in. An ordinary 'fuck' would have been bad enough. This one was off the scale.

'Even if you were my brother,' Jamie Lee Curtis's character said to the character played by Kevin Kline, 'I'd still want to fuck you.'

Liam swivelled his head around and looked at Joe. His eyes, behind his gaffer-taped glasses, were popping.

'Dad,' he said uncertainly. 'She said the F word.'

'Duh,' Alex said. 'Everybody says it. It's just a *word*.'

'Wow!' Saffy cut in. 'Have you guys ever tried eating popcorn and a Malteser at the same time? It's like making chocolate Rice Krispies in your mouth!'

Joe clenched his jaw, trying not to laugh. 'Well, Saffy hired the movie so she gets to put fifty cents in your swear pig. Okay?'

Liam turned back to the TV.

'We have to turn it off!' Saffy whispered to Joe. 'I don't think it's suitable.'

'We can't,' he whispered back. 'That would make Liam look stupid. Anyway, how much worse can it get?'

Quite a lot, as it turned out.

Over the next ninety minutes, there were another twenty-two 'fucks', three 'dicks' and several 'assholes'. Saffy counted each

273

one, her face burning. She reckoned she owed the swear pig at least fifteen euro, though she might have to pay extra for the bit where the Kevin Kline character calls the John Cleese character a 'stuck-up, snot-nosed, English, giant-twerp scumbag, fuck-face, dickhead, asshole'. But what made her really squirm was that the character played by Michael Palin had a stutter, just like Liam had had the day he bled all over her car.

'This is way *cool*!' Alex shook his head. 'My dad never lets me watch fifteens.'

The boys were upstairs getting ready for bed. Saffy folded a twenty-euro note and stuffed it into the swear pig.

'You don't have to do that.' Joe came up behind her.

'It can go towards the therapy Liam's going to need in ten years.'

He put his arms around her waist and turned her to face him.

'Look on the bright side. You've quadrupled his street cred in front of the coolest kid in his class.'

'You're just being nice.' She buried her face in his chest. He smelled so good. Cool and clean, like wet gravel.

'You're the nice one.' Joe stroked her hair. 'He's an awkward kid. You're amazing to reach out to him like that. So don't feel bad, okay?'

Saffy remembered what she'd said to Jess about Liam being a 'little creep' and about worming her way into his affections and she didn't feel bad, she felt terrible.

She didn't mean to eavesdrop but the door of the Liam's bedroom was open.

'Why don't you have a TV or computer in your room?' Alex was saying. 'Are you poor?'

Liam's voice was small. 'I have a telescope.'

'Duh! A telescope?' Alex hooted. 'That's so geeky!'

Saffy stopped halfway up the stairs. Why didn't Liam tell him to stop? Why didn't he stand up for himself?

Alex's voice was muffled as he pulled something over his head.

'Was that your new mum getting all soppy on the couch with your dad?'

'No! She's just his fa . . . fa friend.'

'His fa . . . fa . . . fa . . . friend?' Alex mimicked him. 'You. pa . . . pa . . . pa . . . pompous, s . . . s . . . stuck-up, s . . . snot-nosed, *American*, giant-twerp—'

'Liam?' Saffy called. 'Can I talk to you for a second?'

Alex was dressed in a blue star-spangled velour Harry Potter dressing gown and matching pyjamas. Liam was wearing a faded T-shirt and tracksuit bottoms, a size too small, and the slippers with the missing Snoopy.

'Your dad needs you for something,' she told Liam. He scampered down the stairs. Alex leaned in the doorway with a half-smile, like a debonair midget.

Saffy remembered kids like Alex. The smug girls who never let her forget that she didn't have a father and that she lived in a flat instead of a house, who sucked up to her mother then made fun of her for her flashy clothes behind her back.

She wanted to slap Alex's handsome little face but she couldn't. Instead, she leaned down till their eyes were level.

'Alex, you know I'm a top international scientist, right?'

He shook his head, and that was fair enough. She hadn't known it herself till a second ago.

'Well, I'm involved in this secret research project that has just proved every time you're mean to someone, you produce extra saliva?' Saffy didn't know where this was coming from but she was enjoying it.

'And if you swallow too much of it, it reacts with your digestive juices and produces an acid that burns through the lining of your intestine. So you have to wear a nappy for the *rest of your life*.'

Alex's smile faded.

'Love the dressing gown by the way. It's very drag queen.' She clutched her throat and swallowed. 'Oops!'

Liam went back upstairs as Joe was putting on his jacket to go to the takeaway.

'Is everything okay up there? Liam came down for a hug.'

'Don't ask me. I'm worse with kids than you are with food, and that's saying something.'

'Hey! I haven't seen you slaving over a hot stove to make *me* a meal,' he said, 'and the idea of you *slaving* is kind of interesting.'

While he was gone, Saffy put on some music and lit two Diptyque candles. She'd been introducing little luxuries into the house. Joe didn't seem to notice that she'd changed his Dunne's Stores sheets for Egyptian cotton or swapped his old towels for extra-fluffy bath sheets but the Body Shop massage oil hadn't escaped his attention.

She kept it out of Liam's sight, on the shelf Joe had cleared for her in his wardrobe. She hadn't brought much over: cleanser, moisturiser, contact lens solution, perfume and a few changes of underwear.

Sometimes she wished she had access to the drawer full of Myla and Agent Provacateur lingerie she had back at the apartment but it wouldn't really matter what she wore because she never ended up wearing it for very long. Some people notice the wrapping paper; some people just want to get at the present.

She went out to the garden to sneak a cigarette before Joe came back. The sky was light, though it was ten o'clock and the paving slabs under her bare feet were still warm. She closed her eyes. Was this what it felt like to be happy?

It wasn't a rush. It felt slow and deep and almost ordinary. It was a glass-of-cold-water not a flute-of-champagne feeling, a sense of being in the right place at the right time, doing the right thing.

It was her turn to stand in the golden evening air, like millions of women since the beginning of time, and wait for her man to come back from the hunt or, in her case, from the Great Wall Chinese Takeaway.

She walked across the damp grass and picked a couple of passionflowers that were tumbling over the wall from a neighbour's garden. She could float them in a bowl with some nightlights. She held one in the palm of her hand. There was an outer circle of pale green petals then a whirl of feathery, blue filaments, then two rings, one of purple, one of gold, then green and three yellow stamens. She could never have imagined that something so beautiful could grow in a small, scruffy suburban garden.

'I scared you the other day, didn't I?' Joe licked the sauce from a spare rib off his finger. 'When I said I loved you? I should be treating you mean and keeping you keen. Isn't that how this dating thing works?'

Saffy laughed. 'Don't ask me. I haven't been on a date for six years.' The night with that awful Australian Kitchen Guy didn't count, did it?

'Because you were with the actor.' Joe nodded. 'Glen?'

'Greg,' Saffy mumbled through a mouthful of satay.

Joe finished one rib and took a second one.

'Right. Let's get the caveman bit over with.' He waved the rib over his head and beat his chest with his other hand.

'He's not bigger, stronger, richer, funnier or better in bed than me, is he?'

Saffy shook her head.

'Come on. I can take it.'

'Not bigger, not stronger, richer maybe, but probably not any more.'

It felt like bad karma to be talking about Greg here in Joe's kitchen. She felt as if he was sitting at the table watching them. It made her want another cigarette. She spooned hoisin sauce and shredded duck onto a pancake and rolled it up, fighting the urge to pick it up and inhale it.

'Well, he was certainly stupider,' Joe said, 'to have let you go. As the great nine-year-old philosopher, Alex would say: "Duh!" Didn't he ever offer to, what's the expression, "make an honest woman" of you?'

If there was ever a time to be an honest woman, this was it.

'Say, for the sake of argument, we were married,' she said, carefully, 'we would have split up anyway. Whether we were married or not doesn't really matter.'

Joe threw his head back and laughed.

'Only someone who *wasn't* married could think that,' he said. 'Believe me.'

Now Saffy felt as if Joe's wife, Shelley, was sitting at the table too.

Joe never spoke about her – it was obviously still too painful for him – and he didn't keep a single photograph of her in the house. Saffy imagined her as pretty and vivid and blonde, the kind of woman that always made her, with her pale skin and brown hair, feel faded and drab. She couldn't help thinking that Shelley had been the real thing. She was just the consolation prize.

'Hey!' Joe put down his chopsticks. 'I didn't mean to upset you.'

He pulled her onto his lap and tucked her hair behind her ears.

'Sometimes you look like a little girl,' he said. 'Did you know that?'

He kissed her forehead. 'I'm kissing you when you're thirty-two. And thirty,' he whispered between the kisses, 'and twenty-five. And twenty-three. And nineteen. I'm sending myself back in time, to kiss all the girls you've ever been. I'm kissing you when you were seventeen and,' he laughed, 'I think I'll stop kissing you at this point before it gets a bit strange.' He put his arms around her and squeezed her hard. 'But I'm *holding* you,' he said, 'when you were twelve. And nine. And seven. I'm holding you when you were five and three.'

'Kiss me when I'm thirty-three,' she said into his hair. 'Kiss me, now.'

23

Jess stared at her screen. It felt strange to be sitting down to work again. Lying to Conor about writing an article for the *Wicklow People* had given her the idea of really phoning the *Wicklow People* and, to her surprise, they had given her a commission.

She had gone from praising the merits of scatter cushions to writing about the exciting arrival of a new bin collection service based in Kilcoole. But at least she didn't have to deal with Miles and she was getting paid.

'Wicklow People. Draft 1,' she typed, '31 July.'

Her hands froze on the keyboard. *31 July*. It was exactly eight years since Jess had found out she was pregnant with the twins.

There were two kinds of guys who wanted to ask out a girl like Jess. The first kind wanted her because they thought she was a perfect piece of design. Like a Bang & Olufsen stereo or a Gaggia espresso machine or a Porsche Boxster. Once they realised she was flawed they usually got pretty angry, as if she'd pretended to be someone she wasn't.

The second kind put her on a pedestal. When they finally plucked up the courage to ask her out, they presumed she'd say 'no'. Then, when she did go out with them, they spent the whole time looking for proof that she thought she was out of their league. They were angry right from the start.

Conor was different. He saw past what one of her college friends had called her Miss-Sweden-dragged-through-a-hedge-backwards-looks to who she really was. He treated her like an ordinary person, which was all she wanted to be. He had been reaching for a condom, she remembered, that morning eight years ago. She told him sleepily that he didn't have to because her period was due but then she realised that she was wrong. Her period wasn't due, it was *overdue by four whole weeks*. She'd been late before but never this late.

After they'd showered, she'd made sandwiches and a flask of coffee and they'd walked over to St Stephen's Green. They stopped to buy the papers and, while Conor was in the shop, Jess slipped into the chemist next door and bought a pregnancy test.

Later on, when he was dozing on the grass, she took the metal cup from the flask into the public toilets and rinsed it carefully, then locked herself in a cubicle.

It was a hot afternoon and the toilet was full of children. Their high, sweet voices bounced off the concrete walls and marble floors as she waited for the kit to develop.

'Sean *pushed* me. He said it was on *mistak*e but it was on *purpose*.' 'Rufus is a *big* doggie.' 'Tracey took my ice cream.'

Jess was twenty-four years old. She had only been going out with Conor for two and a half months. She thought she might love him but she hadn't told him yet. She was taking things slowly.

When she opened her eyes, there were two strong blue lines on a white stick. One for Luke and one for Lizzie, though she didn't know that yet. Jess forgot about taking things slowly. She burst out of the cubicle and ran out of the cool, dank toilet into the sunshine to find Conor.

'Mummy!' a small girl with fuzzy plaits shouted as she ran past. 'The lady didn't wash her *handies*!'

Jess looked up from the sofa, where she was working. What appeared to be a huge bouquet of flowers with legs opened the gate and walked up the path. Conor had stopped giving Jess flowers years ago. She hated the whole girly charade of them. Flowers looked best growing in the ground not stuck in a vase. But the fact that he had remembered this day, this time, was a sign. These flowers were a reminder of how happy they'd been all those years ago and a promise that they'd be happy again.

'Thank you!' she whispered, long after the delivery girl had closed the gate and driven away. 'Thank you!'

The boy was lying half under a desk by the window. His body was jerking and, at first, Conor presumed he was having an epileptic fit and that the others were helping him. Then Wayne Cross raised his foot and stamped on his hand.

By the time Conor had crossed the room, Wayne had raised his foot again but before it could connect with Turvey's face, Conor made a lunge for his shoulder and pulled him away, knocking him sideways so he lost his footing and fell heavily against the desk.

It was Wayne Cross again. Bloody Wayne Cross. Turvey's hand was dirty and a bit squashed but it didn't look broken.

'Graham!' Conor tried to make eye contact but the boy wouldn't look at him. 'Are you okay? Do you need someone to look at that?'

Turvey stood up, grabbed his satchel and ran for the door.

'That was assault!' Conor heard Cross's deep voice behind him.

He turned. Wayne was sitting on the floor. His cheek was gashed where he had caught the corner of a desk on the way down. His shirt was already blotched red with blood but he was smirking up at the other students.

'That was assault. Mr Fatty went for me. You saw that, didn't you?'

Brenda Toner, the head of the academy, was standing by the open window in her office, smoking a roll-up.

She was a permanently flustered woman with long greying hair. 'Mr Kelly is escorting the "Cross-We-All-Have-to-Bear" to A & E.' Brenda flicked her ash out onto the window sill. 'God, that boy is repulsive.'

She was involved in amateur dramatics and she spoke in a theatrical way that made everything she said sound like a line from a play. She dropped her butt into a styrofoam cup and it made a small sizzle.

'We had a little tête-à-tête, the lovely Wayne and I. He informed me that he is going to press charges.'

'Take a pew,' she said, 'and tell me all.'

So he did, going back to the time he'd found Turvey with a bloody nose and adding in his suspicion that Cross had been bullying him into writing his essays. But he knew the rules. If a pupil was under eighteen, he could come at you with a baseball bat and, according to the Department of Education, all you could do was cover your head and face.

'Off the record.' Brenda's roll-up had gone out. 'I admire you for stepping in to save the lovely Graham, but if Cross does decide to press charges, we are all in a delicate situation.'

Conor let it sink in. Preventing Wayne from rearranging Turvey's features had ended his career at the academy. Three months of easy, well-paid work every summer gone. Just like that.

'I'm really sorry, Conor, but I'm going to have to suspend you until this gets sorted.'

He made himself nod. 'I understand.'

'Put it all down in a report for me,' she said quickly, 'don't leave anything out. I'll see what I can do. Will Turvey back you up?'

'No, they're both in my fifth-year class at St Peter's. If he did, Cross would probably kill him.'

'What will happen if the powers that be at St Peter's hear about this incident?'

Conor shook his head. 'I don't know but it won't be good.'

He had been teaching at St Peters for seven years but he was still on contract, which meant that he had to interview for his own job every year.

Five teachers had retired and been replaced but Conor had been passed over each time. They didn't seem keen to give him a permanent position and it wasn't hard to figure out why. St Peter's was a Catholic school. Conor was living with a woman who wasn't his wife and they had two children and the board of managers probably didn't approve.

But maybe there was more to it than that. He was a lousy teacher, anyway. Some people were born to it but he wasn't one of them. He'd only done his H.Dip to please his parents; he'd never intended to use it and went straight into journalism, instead.

Then, exactly eight years ago, he suddenly remembered, to the day, Jess had found out that she was pregnant. Three days later the *Irish Voice* had folded. And by the following spring, he was standing in front of a class of fifth-years who had hit on the same nickname he'd had when *he* was at school. Back then there hadn't been a 'Mr'; it was just plain 'Fatty'.

St Peter's was hell but it was a hell that Conor and Jess relied on to pay the mortgage.

There was a clamping van parked across the entrance to the car park next to the academy. It was after five and there was just one car left – a brand-new BMW. Sitting on the glassy, black bonnet was an enormous man in a clamper's uniform. He had a shaved head and a meaty forehead. It was obvious that he and Wayne had been swimming in the same gene pool.

'Mr Fahey?' He squinted up at Conor. 'Mick Cross. Wayne's dad.'

'Nice to meet you.' Conor gauged the distance to the corrugated iron shelter where he kept his bike.

'You seem like a nice bloke.' Mick Cross held up a hand. There was a very unrealistic tattoo of a tarantula near his elbow. 'It would be a shame to lose your fucking job because you hit a defenceless boy.'

Conor edged slowly towards the shelter. From behind his back, Wayne's dad produced his other hand. It was holding a tyre iron.

'Do you want me to make this go away?' He fluttered his fingers in an attempt to mimic birds taking flight. 'Three grand and Wayne won't press charges. Three grand and you still have your job. Let's call it an offer you can't refuse.'

Adrenalin flooded back into Conor's system.

'What did you get for Christmas?' he said over his shoulder. 'The boxed set of *The Sopranos*?'

Wayne's father brought the tyre iron down hard on the bonnet of the BMW.

'You like your car?'

'Yeah.' Conor was almost at the shelter now. 'I like my car. I like it a lot.'

He heard the smash of the tyre iron hitting one headlight. As he got to his bike, he heard the second one shatter.

When he turned around, Wayne's father was standing on a glittering carpet of splintered glass.

'You still like it?' He jabbed the air with the tyre iron.

'Yeah, I do. My car's a ninety-seven Fiat Punto,' Conor said, climbing onto his bike and forcing his shaking legs to pedal.

The ex-boxer who owned the nightclub next door was hurrying across the car park, followed by two very large security guards.

'The BMW belongs to him.'

Conor threw his satchel on the table, almost toppling a vase. The house was quiet and there was something weird about the kitchen but he didn't have time to work out what it was. He needed a drink. He searched the fridge, checking in the salad crisper where he sometimes kept a can or two of beer but there was nothing in there except a head of decomposing lettuce and half a Spanish onion.

He thought about going through the cupboards in case an unfinished bottle of wine had been stashed in there by mistake but they hardly ever had wine and when they did, they always finished it. Then he remembered the vodka. There was an ancient bottle somewhere in the freezer. He was sure of it.

He dug around and came up with a pizza that was out of date by nearly two years, a lone, battered cod fillet that had been welded to a rubber ice-cube tray and a half-eaten Magnum that Lizzie had started and never finished last summer. Frozen peas rained down on his shoes. But the bottle was there. It was still there.

It came out in a shower of powdery frost. There was an inch left in the bottom, just enough to put a small, soft distance between him and the shock of the fight and the fear of what Wayne's dad would do if he ever caught up with him. He put his hand out to grab a glass from the draining board. Most of their plates and pans and cutlery moved between the sink and the table, so the cupboard didn't usually come into the equation and, for the first time he could remember, the draining board was not just empty, but gleaming, as if it had been polished. Conor looked around.

The cooker was spotless. The heap of books and toys that lived under the table was gone. The clutter of CDs on the counter had been boxed and neatly arranged on the window sill. The floor, apart from the recent shower of frost and peas, was shining.

He closed his eyes and pressed the cold bottle to his forehead. Maybe he'd wake up and find that the whole day had just been a dream. Could you get smashed in a dream? There was only one way to find out.

He had knocked back most of the vodka when Jess appeared at the door with two M&S plastic bags.

'Hey.' She beamed at him. 'I've been to the Dundrum Shopping Centre. But I got out alive.'

'Hey,' he said back, like an echo. He tried to get his mouth to match her smile but all he could raise was a lip tremble.

'Lizzie and Luke are on a sleepover at Max's house.' She opened the fridge and began to unpack her bags. 'I thought I'd cook us something nice.' She looked at him over her shoulder. That smile, again. 'Thank you for the flowers.'

'The flowers?' He looked at the bouquet. It must have been there when he came in but he was so upset he hadn't even seen it.

'Thank you for remembering that it was eight years when . . .' she waved her hand at the spotless kitchen, 'when all this began.'

He shook his head. 'Look, I know it was eight years ago today that we found out about the twins but I don't know anything about the flowers.'

Her smile flickered on and off and on again, like a faulty fluorescent tube. She dug in her jeans pocket and pulled out a small white square and put it on the table.

He reached over and picked it up. It was a florist's card with a cartoon of a sheep with its hooves (did sheep have hooves?) over its eyes.

'Feelin' sheepish!' it said in bubbly yellow type over the mortified-looking animal. He turned it over. 'Sorry things haven't been great lately. Let's start all over again, from *today*. X'

'It's not from me.' He handed it back to her.

Jess felt an idiot. For spending four hours cleaning the kitchen. For buying Scottish smoked salmon fillets and fresh strawberries and crème fraiche. For imagining that Conor was sorry for anything.

The flowers were from Saffy, she suddenly realised. It must have been her way of trying to make up. Conor took a gulp from the vodka bottle.

'What are you *drinking*?'

He looked at the label. 'It's vodka. Very cheap, very old vodka.'

Jess slammed the frigde door closed.

'Is this what you do over at Greg's when you're supposed to be writing? Sit around and drink vodka?'

'There was an incident at the academy today,' Conor said carefully. He already sounded as if he was briefing a lawyer. 'And I've been suspended until further notice.'

Jess sat down heavily. 'Let me guess? You were drunk in class?'

Conor didn't expect her to sympathise, but she could at least wait until he had explained what had happened before she judged him.

'One of the kids was beating the crap out of another kid. I pulled him off before he did some permanent damage. He fell and cut his head.'

'Is he okay?' Jess's eyes widened.

What about me? Conor thought. *Why aren't you asking if I'm okay?*

'He'll need a few stitches but he's fine.'

'He needs *stitches*?'

Jess was probably seeing some eleven-year-old child, Conor thought, not a six-foot-something, shaven-headed meathead like Wayne Cross.

'There's something else. I'll probably lose my job in St Peter's because of this. In fact, I'll probably be banned from teaching altogether if there's a court case.'

Jess laughed but it wasn't a nice laugh. 'How convenient,' she said, 'how very convenient. You won't have to work so you can spend all your time on your book, right?'

Conor put the bottle down with a bang. He felt as if there wasn't room inside him for all the amount of blood that was racing around his veins. 'Is that what you think? You think I got suspended *on purpose*?'

'I don't know what to think. You hurt some poor kid. You manage to write off ninety per cent of our income. And your response is to get drunk.'

Conor stood up.

'No,' he said, 'that's not my response.'

Jess heard him climb the stairs. Over the thud of her own, pounding heart, she heard drawers opening and closing and the sound of a wardrobe door slamming then she heard his footsteps on the stairs again.

He stood at the kitchen door with a suitcase in one hand and a rucksack over one shoulder. He was practically living at Greg's place already. He might as well move in.

'This is my response,' he said.

24

It was a perfect evening for flying. Joe was on a commercial job, piloting a balloon in the shape of a pot of yogurt called Shanti. Saffy had helped him unpack it from the trailer and now Meatloaf and Ruth were laying it out on the grass. They were bickering, as usual.

'Take John Travolta,' Ruth was saying. 'He's rich. He's talented. And he has a 747 parked in his driveway.'

'He doesn't need a driveway.' Meatloaf was connecting the fuel system. 'You could land an Airbus A380 on that chin.'

Ruth laughed. 'Have you looked in the mirror lately?'

Possibly not, Saffy thought, looking at the tatty old Def Leppard T-shirt and the baggy khaki shorts that revealed Meatloaf's beefy but strangely hairless calves.

'I mean, you're thirty-five, right?' Ruth sat back on her heels. 'You're halfway through your life. What have you got to show for it?'

Meatloaf looked worried. 'Jesus! You think I'm only going to live to seventy?'

'That's right. Avoid the question!' Ruth smirked.

'I came fourth in the Irish Air Guitar finals in 2003.' Meatloaf stuck out his bottom lip in a rock 'n' roll scowl, bent his knees and began to play an imaginary instrument.

'That's pretty good.' Saffy smiled.

'Bite my ass, Michael "The Destroyer" Hoeffels.' Meatloaf threw his head back and roared. 'You are not worthy, Elvis "Fender-bender" Virgo.'

Ruth shook her head. 'You're wasting your time showing off for Saffy,' she said. 'It's me you should be trying to impress. She's already taken.' Saffy was going in the retrieval convoy with Liam, and she wasn't looking forward to it. He was standing a few feet away now, his back to her, his head bent over his GameBoy, studiously ignoring her attempts at conversation.

'Wow! Is that Pokémon you're playing?'

Silence.

'Hey! Have you ever played Nanosaur? I've got in on my laptop. You can have a game on the way back if you like.'

Nothing.

She had tried to make him like her but the harder she tried, the less he responded. She couldn't remember the last time he'd spoken to her or looked her in the eye.

Saffy sighed and counted her blessings. White Feather was ticking along. She wasn't in Marsh's bad books and, best of all, her mother was halfway through her course of chemo now. She had lost most of her hair and her appetite and she looked ten years older than her age and twenty years older than she'd looked before her mastectomy. But that, Mr Kenny had said, was to be expected. His nurse had given Saffy a batch of nutritional drinks with five hundred calories in each eggcup-sized helping and Jill was managing to keep those down. She was too weak to do much more than shower and dress herself and lie on the sofa all day in her dressing gown and a headscarf. Saffy had gone back to the shop and ordered the Crystal wig. It was in a box under the stairs but her mother wouldn't wear it and she didn't have the heart to make her.

She hadn't spoken to Jess since their row on the phone but she'd sent flowers, which, she thought, was pretty generous considering that Jess was the one who'd hung up on her. And then there was Joe, walking across the field towards her, grinning as if he had a winning lottery ticket and she was the prize. He looped a long, bare arm around her shoulders and she breathed in his earth smell and they stood, looking up at the giant, inflated yogurt pot. The endline was scrawled in blue across the logo: *I believe in Shanti.*

It was a blot on the landscape. And Saffy, who had encouraged Marsh to have the White Feather balloon customised, felt oddly guilty. The sky wasn't some giant hoarding where you could scrawl your endline for panty pads or dairy products. Some things should be sacred.

'I believe in Shanti,' Joe said under his breath. 'Fuck me!'

'Here? With all these people watching?'

He gave her pony-tail a firm tug. 'Don't tempt me,' he said. 'I'm just looking for an excuse not to go up in that eyesore.'

'Look on the bright side.' She smiled. 'You're the only person in Wicklow who won't have to look at it because you won't be able to see it from inside the basket.'

'Gondola, Saffy. It's called a *gondola*.'

The frantic, high-pitched music from Liam's GameBoy was hurting Saffy's brain so she opened the window but the smell of silage leaked into the car so she closed it again.

It was hard enough to follow the erratic course of the van in front as it tracked the path of Joe's balloon, without this soundtrack from hell.

'So, Liam,' she said through gritted teeth, 'what class are you in anyway?'

He didn't even bother to look up. He fiddled with the controls and, maybe it was just her imagination, but the music got louder and faster. Any minute now, her ears would start to bleed.

'When I was at school,' she babbled, 'I hated maths but I loved English. How about you? What subjects do *you* like?'

Not a flicker.

The van took a sudden left and Saffy overshot the turn. She reversed the TT, at speed, not caring that the brambles were catching, and probably scratching, her paintwork.

'So, how's that little bastard Alex these days?' She yanked the wheel round and pulled the car onto the narrow, muddy lane. 'Is he still treating you like shit?'

Liam's looked up from his game. She had his attention now.

'Yeah,' she said. 'I swore twice. The swear pig gets a euro. I heard Alex making fun of you the other night, you know. He's a nasty piece of work.'

Liam glared at her. 'He's my friend.'

'Your friend?' Saffy snapped. 'Bullshit. One euro fifty. Your friend? Give me a bloody break. Two euro. Alex is not your friend. He's a toxic little brat.'

The GameBoy was still going but Saffy had forgotten her headache.

'You think that you have to put up with friends like that

because you have an American accent or no mother or a bit of a stutter? That's crap. Two euro fifty. If you think like that you're just *asking* to be treated like crap. Three euro. If you don't fit in, do something about it.'

Liam did. He put one small, trembling hand on the handle of the passenger door. They were only travelling at about twenty kilometres an hour, but if he jumped, Saffy thought, he would kill himself. And Joe would never forgive her.

She pulled over. The van disappeared around the next bend, but she didn't care. She was suddenly desperate for Liam to understand.

'Imagine Alex, right? Now take away the floppy fringe and the funky T-shirt. Give him a ratty old sweatshirt and shorts that are too small and socks with leather sandals. What do you have?' Liam stared at his knees.

'A geek, that's what!' Saffy said. 'And kids pick on geeks. It's not fair but it's true. Here, try these.' Before he had time to stop her, she whipped off Liam's glasses and replaced them with her own.

'They probably make you feel a bit drunk, right? Because our eyes have different prescriptions.' She flipped down the sun visor so he could see himself in the vanity mirror. 'But you know what? They look really cool.'

She was telling the truth. It wasn't just the botched repair. Liam's glasses were way too big for his face. Her small, dark, rectangular frames brought out the blue in his eyes and made his carroty hair look almost blond.

'I'm not saying you should change who you are *inside*,' Saffy said, 'but sometimes, it's only when you change the outside that people *see* what's inside.'

She had lost him. She had kind of lost herself.

'My mom used to get me clothes and stuff I liked,' Liam said in a small voice, 'but everything's gotten broken or too small and now Dad buys it and he gets it wrong.'

He took off her glasses and folded them carefully and handed them back to her.

'Why don't you say something?' she said. 'Why don't you tell your dad what you want?'

Liam looked out of the window. He was searching for Joe's balloon in the sky.

'You worry about your dad, don't you?' she said quietly. She was guessing that he had seen Joe fall apart after his mother died and he was scared that, if he said the wrong thing, it would happen again.

Liam shrugged.

'But you know something, that's not your job.'

His eyes met hers briefly. They looked naked and vulnerable without his glasses. He looked like he might be about to cry.

'It's his job to worry about you, not the other way around, and it's your job to be as happy as you can, so he doesn't have to.'

She handed him his glasses and he put them back on.

'He'd do pretty much anything you asked him to, you know that? If you said you wanted to move back to the States, he'd put you on a plane,' she said. 'If you told him you really hated me, he'd never see me again. You're *the* most important person in the world to him and you always will be, okay?'

The giant yogurt pot appeared, briefly, between some trees off to the right. It was drifting down towards a patchwork of fields about a mile away. 'Now, can you turn the GameBoy off and help me find my way to wherever your dad's going to land that shag—' Saffy made a face. 'Oops. Does that count? Three euro.'

'Three euro fifty,' Liam said. She thought she saw the corners of his mouth begin to twitch.

Saffy started the engine again. 'I think you'd better spend it on a bigger swear pig.'

A few miles outside Blessington, Joe took his hand off Saffy's knee and put it on her arm.

'Stop for a second, will you?'

They were on a ribbon of road overlooking a lake. He shaded his eyes and pointed to a stand of old trees on the opposite shore. 'That's our house.'

Saffy looked but she couldn't see any kind of building.

'I bought the site when we came back from Chicago. Paid way too much for it and the planning permission came through in

March. We'll have to keep renting till we get the basic structure up, but it'll be worth the wait. The side of the house facing the lake's going to be pretty much all glass.'

'We're going to build a tree house,' Liam said. 'We've already picked the tree and I'm going to get a dog.'

'We thought you were asleep,' Joe laughed and leaned back to ruffle his son's hair.

The edges of everything were gilded with evening light. A flight of swallows turned in the sky above the trees. A small boat unzipped the glitter of the water.

'We go camping there sometimes,' Joe said. 'We bring a tent and light a fire and have a cook-out, like cowboys. Maybe you can come next time?'

'I don't know, sounds like a boy thing.' Saffy looked for Liam's eyes in the rear-view mirror.

He was looking out the window. 'There are cowgirls, too.'

Saffy sat on a grimy leatherette stool and waited for Jess and the twins to come back from the bar. She had promised to collect the kids and hand them over to Conor. She was still in shock after Jess's phone call. She couldn't believe that Conor had moved out. How had this happened? She remembered thinking that they seemed on edge the day she bumped into them at the World Music festival but how had they fallen apart *so fast*?

Dented barrels and crates of bottles were stacked along one wall. Wonky plastic tables had been set on a patch of gravel littered with cigarette butts. There was a strong smell of beer and the only garden bit was a wilted hanging basket with a chip wrapper caught in its rusty chain.

It was half-eleven on a Sunday morning and the place was deserted apart from two men furtively smoking a joint and a pit bull puppy joyfully licking its balls.

Jess came out carrying a tray of drinks, followed by the twins. Her hair was a wild blonde frizz and she had dark shadows under her eyes. She was wearing a grubby black cardigan over a brown sundress with a torn hem. She could, Saffy thought, be a bag lady. The hottest bag lady of all time, obviously, but it was worrying.

'I couldn't remember what you wanted.' Jess put the tray down. 'So I got you a wine.'

Saffy had asked for water but she didn't want to rock the boat. The boat, from what Jess had told her, was already pretty unsteady.

The twins hoovered up their Cokes in about ten seconds and went off to play with the puppy.

'I don't care about myself,' Jess filled her glass to the top, 'but I will never, ever forgive Conor for what he's done to Luke and Lizzie.'

It was three days since Conor had left. Three days of waiting for him to turn up on the doorstep and beg her to take him back. Three days of silence and managing the kids on her own without any idea of when he was coming back. Jess guessed that Conor was at Greg's but she had never run after a man and she wasn't about to start.

Then this morning, he'd sent a text: SORRY ABOUT SILENCE. NEED SPACE. WOULD LIKE TO SEE TWINS TODAY. DON'T WANT TO FIGHT AGAIN SO BEST IF WE DON'T MEET. CAN PICK L AND L UP FROM SAFFY'S MOTHER'S AT 2 AND DROP BACK AT 7. WILL BE IN TOUCH. C

Jess had read it over and over several times but there wasn't a single soft word, a hint of an apology (unless you counted 'sorry about silence', which she didn't), a clue about when he planned to come home.

Will be in touch. It sounded like something at the end of a letter from the bank. Her heart had clenched and tightened with anger. If he could be brief, she could be briefer.

OK J. she'd texted back, wondering where they could go when everything she had to say to him could be contained in three letters.

'What have you told them?' Saffy squeezed her hand. 'The kids, I mean?'

'I haven't told them anything. He's the one who left. He can tell them why he did it and then maybe they can tell me, because I have no idea.'

She took a gulp of her wine. It was warm and sour but she forced it down.

'He hit a *child*, Saffy. He attacked a defenceless boy. And then he just walked out.'

Saffy nodded distractedly. She was watching Lizzie and Luke out of the corner of her eye. They were posting crisps into the puppy's mouth. Was that hygienic? Was it safe? There was no way Joe would let Liam play with a pit bull. She forced herself to focus on Jess.

'Look, I don't know what happened at the academy but I do know that this is all some sort of a misunderstanding. Conor wouldn't leave you and the twins, Jess. He's crazy about you and nothing can change that.'

But, even as she said it, she wondered if something had already changed it. When she had called Conor to arrange handing the twins over later she'd had expected him to be upset but he sounded worryingly calm.

'What did he say when you were talking to him?' Jess's nails were bitten, Saffy noticed. When had she started biting her nails? 'Did he say anything about me?'

He hadn't, but Luke appeared at Saffy's elbow and saved her from having to say so.

'Excuse me,' he said politely, 'what time it is?'

'What time *is it*, Luke,' Jess corrected automatically.

Saffy looked at her watch. 'It's half eleven.'

He lowered his voice to a whisper. 'It's time for my poo.'

Jess waved him away. 'You can do it later, at Saffy's mum's house.'

'I can't go in strange houses.' Luke looked worried. 'It's weird and freaky.'

Saffy knew exactly what he meant.

'Oh God,' Jess sighed. 'Okay, you can go in the pub but you're too big to go in the Ladies and I can't take you into the Men's, so you'll have to go in there by yourself. Lizzie! You go too.'

The twins trotted off obediently.

'And wipe your bottoms properly,' Jess said over her shoulder.

And don't talk to strange men, Saffy wanted to call after them but there were two strange men in the beer garden and she didn't want to broadcast the fact that two young children were going to the toilet on their own.

Jess picked at a crust of something stuck to the table. She had thought that talking to Saffy would help but it hadn't. She had never known how to open up the way women did to one another. She had never needed to. And now that she did, she was afraid that if she said what she was thinking out loud, it would come true. She loved the life she had with Conor and the twins. It was ordinary and messy but it was real. She had thought he loved it too. But it wasn't enough for him. *They* weren't enough for him. He wanted money and success, and she knew what that did to people. It would change him. It already had.

'You should have seen him the other day, Saffy.' She bit her lip. 'You should have seen the blood on his shirt, from where he hit that poor kid.'

'Don't cry, Jess,' Saffy said softly. 'It'll be okay. I promise.' As the day heated up the beer garden was developing a damp, ratty smell that was turning her stomach.

'It won't be okay. How can it be okay? We're in deep shit, Saffy. The academy won't take him back and once this gets out, he'll be fired from St Peter's. I've earned three hundred euro in the last six weeks. How are we supposed to live?'

The pit bull puppy wandered across the gravel and pissed on the leg of their table, right by Jess's foot, but she didn't even seem to notice.

'Hey, gorgeous,' one of the joint-smoking men called softly, 'want to join us for a toke?'

Jess turned around. 'Do you mind? I'm having a conversation here.'

'Don't flatter yourself, love,' the man sniggered, 'I wasn't talking to you. I was talking to your friend.'

Jill came to the front door before Saffy had time to open it. She was wearing make-up and a long green dress and she had swapped her headscarf for the wig. The dress was awful, high-necked and frumpy. She had padded out the front and it looked all wrong. But it was nice to see her making an effort. She usually didn't get dressed at all unless she was going to chemo.

'You look great, Mum!' Saffy told her.

'I didn't want to scare the children,' Jill whispered.

'Hello, Lizzie,' she said to Luke, who was wearing a pink T-shirt.

'Everyone thinks he's a girl,' Lizzie said, 'but he doesn't mind.'

Lizzie wanted to stay in the kitchen and help Saffy make lunch. Conor wasn't due for an hour, so they had stopped at the Spar and Saffy had let the twins pick for themselves: orange squash, crisps, sliced bread, cheese and a packet of fairy cakes.

'Can I butter the bread?' Lizzie asked.

'Are you allowed to use a knife?'

'I'm seven,' Lizzie said contemptuously, 'and a bit.'

Outside, in the garden, Jill was putting sun block on Luke. When she was finished, she squeezed some into his hand and bent down so he could put it on her face.

'I'm finished now.' Lizzie had used almost all the butter on one slice of bread.

'That's perfect.' Saffy gave her the cakes. 'Should we put these on a plate?'

'Yes.' Lizzie wiped her buttery hands on her shirt. 'Is my dad really coming? Do you promise?'

'Cross my heart and hope to die.'

'If you go to Missing for a long time,' Lizzie dropped a fairy cake on the floor and picked it up and put it back on the plate, 'you can die. That's where Brendan went. He's our hamster. He's white with brown patches and a really soft tummy.'

Saffy wasn't sure what you were supposed to do when children talked about death but she made an interested 'hmmm' sound in case Lizzie had any more to say about it, which she did.

'I think maybe Daddy went to Missing to *find* him.' Lizzie blinked up at her. 'Do you think he died?'

Saffy shook her head. 'Of course he's not dead sweetheart. I was talking to him this morning.'

'Who?' Lizzie was piling all the cakes on one side of the plate. 'Daddy or Brendan?'

Saffy lay back in her deckchair. It was too hot to move. Bees were humming round her mother's roses. Somewhere in the distance, someone was mowing a lawn. Joe was going up in the balloon later and she hoped the weather would hold.

Lizzie was sitting in the other deckchair stroking Kevin Costner very vigorously. He didn't look as if he was enjoying it much. Jill was sitting on the grass, helping Luke to make a daisy chain.

'We met a dog called Fanny,' he was telling her. 'We gave him crisps. He weed on our mum's flip-flop.'

'I'm too hot in this thing.' Jill tugged at her wig, trying to settle it on her head.

'Take it off.' Saffy trailed her hand in the cool grass beneath the shadow of her chair.

'I can't.'

'I dare you.'

Jill waited a second then pulled the wig off. She was almost completely bald. She put it down on the grass.

Luke looked up at her in horror. 'You can't put that on the *long* daisies,' he told her. 'They'll get squashed and they're the best ones for the chain.'

'Oh, okay.' Jill moved the wig away.

'You'd better put some sunscreen on your head, Mum.' Saffy handed Jill the bottle. 'It's pretty hot.'

Lizzie jumped up and Kevin Costner took the opportunity to make a break for the apple tree.

'Luke did your face,' she said. 'It's my turn.'

'Thanks for this, Saffy.' Conor had lost more weight since Saffy had seen him last. He looked stressed but he also, she thought, looked great. 'Is it okay if I bring them back at half-six?'

They were standing on the front step. The twins were tearing around the lawn, chasing the O'Keefes' Yorkshire terrier.

'Of course. It's fine.' She touched his arm. 'But why don't you take them back home, instead? You need to talk to Jess. You guys need to sort this out.'

'I'm all talked out.' He shook his head. 'And I'm not ready to see her, not for a while anyway.'

'Don't do this to her, Conor. She loves you.'

He looked at her for long moment.

'Maybe, but she doesn't like me very much.'

'Come on, you don't really mean that.'

'I can see it in her eyes. Whatever I do she finds the worst possible motive for it. I try to write a book so I can do something I might be good at and provide for my family and I'm betraying her. I step in to stop a kid having the living crap beaten out of him and I'm the bad guy.'

He shook his head sadly.

'I don't know who she thinks I am, Saffy. But you know what? I don't like him very much either.'

25

Greg changed into his costume in the staff toilet. Greta at Venom had told him to bring trainers and that the supermarket in Dun Laoghaire would provide the rest. The rest turned out to be a celery outfit: a green body stocking, a ridged green tube with armholes that stretched from his neck to his knees and a tall, leafy headpiece with a cartoon face. He almost walked away. Then he reminded himself that Brad Pitt used to wear a chicken costume to promote a restaurant, and look at that dude now!

He had lucked out on the underwear catalogue and none of the other go-sees had come to anything. He was kind of relieved because Lauren's threatening letter had made him nervous. He'd told Greta that he would only take jobs where his face wasn't visible. He didn't want to burn his britches.

The other vegetables were gathered in the manager's office. There was a cute girl dressed as a tomato, a tall guy in a carrot outfit and woman with buck teeth in a purple padded body stocking who was meant to be an aubergine. They were probably getting fifteen euro an hour max but Greta had managed to swing modelling rate for him, even though this was a promo job: €63.49 an hour. Greg had done the maths on his iPhone. If he could stick this out for five days he'd cover half of his mortgage.

€507.92 a day for dressing like a vegetable? It was a no-brainer. *Vegetable. No-brainer.* Now that was funny. He should really think about writing a sitcom.

'Right, guys.' The manager was a bear of man in a badly cut suit. 'You know the drill. No swearing. No snacking. No smoking in costume. No fraternising with customers.'

He handed them each bundles of coupons.

'Hand these out to customers,' he was saying, 'but watch out for the pensioners. They're coupon sharks. The rule is strictly one per person.'

Greg examined a coupon. It had a picture of a face with

tomatoes for eyes and a banana mouth and some unrealistic-looking broccoli hair.

The Easy Way to Five-A-Day!

Eat a banana at breakfast.
Have carrots with lunch.
Snack on grapes, cucumber sticks or cherry tomatoes.
Tuck into broccoli with your dinner.
And enjoy an apple or an orange for dessert.

This coupon entitles you to €1 off €10 of fresh fruit and vegetables.

Greg turned the coupon over. The back was blank.

'Houston,' he said, his voice strange and echoey inside the hollow headpiece, 'we have a problem.'

'Sorry?' The manager didn't look sorry at all, he looked irritated. Greg hated when people did that. It was so passive aggressive.

He pointed at the coupon.

'Dude, the coupon name-checked carrots, tomatoes and cucumbers. But I'm celery, right? There's no mention of celery.'

'What a disaster,' the manager said, 'we've printed 500,000.'

The aubergine tittered.

'Plus,' Greg looked around, 'we're all vegetables. This is a fruit *and* veg promotion. Where's the fruit?'

The tomato put her hand up. 'Um, I'm a fruit, technically.'

'I think Zac Efron is kind of hot,' the carrot said. 'Does that make me a fruit?'

Greg spotted a woman in the confectionary aisle. Massive thighs. Double chins. Serious case of muffin top.

'Hey there, what's up?' His voice sounded different, nobody could see his face, making him anonymous. It was a strangely liberating experience. 'Did you know that celery is a negative calorie food?' He handed her a coupon. 'So the more you eat, the more weight you lose.'

He strode away, smiling inside his hollow head. A hack actor wouldn't bother with research. But a real pro, a De Niro or a

Nicholson, wouldn't rest till he'd found the celery's motivation. Till he'd answered the question, 'What makes celery tick?' He'd used his iPhone to Google some nutritional facts on a toilet break. When he hit the floor again, he wasn't just a bloke in a vegetable costume; he was a super food with the power to save humanity from obesity. His destiny was to roam the aisles, seeking out the bloated, the constipated and the overweight with their trolleys full of complex carbs and trans fats. Once he had cornered one or two, he had the hang of it and he was able to pick them off in rabbit succession.

'Celery is an excellent source of dietary fibre,' he told them. 'Celery contains compounds called pthalides that lower your blood pressure. Celery is the ultimate diet food.' By mid-afternoon the carrot had caught on and was copying his tactics. Greg overhead him telling two hefty teenager girls in Soups and Biscuits that carrots were the perfect low-calorie snack. He doubled back and waited for them in Frozen Foods. 'Listen, a carrot has thirty calories. A stalk of celery has just six. So the next time you want a low-cal snack, you can have five stalks of celery.' He held up a green, gloved hand.

'Or one carrot.' He held up the other hand and showed them one finger. It was *the* finger and it was for the benefit of the carrot who was watching from the other end of the aisle.

'You decide.'

Joe came up behind Saffy while she was bending down to pick a bottle of sesame oil. 'I'm saving that image for later,' he grabbed her waist, 'but only because there are children present.'

Liam appeared around the corner of the aisle with a huge box of Coco Pops, dumped it into Joe's trolley and trotted off again. He was wearing his new glasses and he'd had his hair cut so that it spiked up a little at the front. He looked like a different boy. Saffy and Joe had split up to do the shopping because it would take less time and because their lists had absolutely no crossover.

'What have we got here?' Joe looked down at Saffy's basket. 'Duck breasts. Champagne. Coconut milk. Double cream. Passion fruit? This is going to be quite a meal.'

Saffy smiled. 'That's the idea.'

'You need any spaghetti hoops or baked beans to go with all that?' He rummaged in his trolley. 'Hot dogs? Cheesy Dippers? Pop Tarts?'

Saffy looked at her list. 'I need ginger, cucumber and pak choi, and then I'm done. I'll meet you at the checkout.'

She was weighing a root of ginger when the celery cornered her. Saffy didn't like clowns or people in costumes. They made her feel slightly unhinged.

'I know we're not supposed to talk,' the celery said, 'but it's an emergency. I need to borrow Kevin Spacey.'

'Sorry?' She looked around for support but the only other customer was an ancient woman on a Zimmer frame inspecting melons.

'Kevin Spacey! I need to borrow Kevin Spacey. I've got a rat,' the celery went on, 'and the little fucker has to die.'

This was one of those *Candid Camera* things, she realised. 'Very funny,' she turned back to the scales, 'but I know how this works and I'm not going to sign a release form so you'll have to find someone else.'

'There's nothing funny about rats, Saffy,' the celery said. 'Have you ever Googled rats? Rats carry thirty-five diseases. The have sex up to twenty times a day. In eighteen months, two rats could become over a million.'

'Greg?' Saffy stared at the cartoon face on the front of the leafy head. 'Is that you?'

'Yes! Of course it's me and I need to borrow your mother's cat.'

'Kevin *Costner*.'

'Costner. Spacey. Bacon. I don't care which Kevin it is as long as it can kill.'

'Greg, why are you dressed like that?'

'Well, let's see. I lost my job. My wife left me. I'm stuck with paying half of a one-and-a-half-million-euro mortgage. And I'm trying to earn a living.'

He shuffled a little closer.

'What are you doing with those breasts?'

'What?'

'Those duck breasts.' He poked a green gloved hand into her

basket. 'And that champagne and that double cream and all that other aphrodisiac stuff.'

'A duck isn't an aphrodisiac,' Saffy said, playing for time.

The leafy head shook. 'We're supposed to be on a three-month break but you're seeing someone, aren't you?'

'I only agreed to that so you'd leave me alone, Greg. And don't talk to me about seeing people,' Saffy said. 'I read the tabloids. Been tied to any interesting bedposts lately?'

A small hand tugged the sleeve of her jacket. It was Liam and he was holding a bunch of bananas.

'Can you weigh these for me? I can't get the thing to work.'

She had forgotten about Liam. God! She had to get him out of here.

'Of course I can.' She tried to sound like a friendly stranger helping a child she didn't know.

Her heart was hammering as she stuck the price onto the bag and handed them back to him.

'There you go!' she said cheerfully. 'You can take them to the till now. You're sorted!' He looked at her, bewildered, then walked away slowly.

'Don't bullshit me, Saffy.' It was weird to hear an angry voice coming from inside the cartoon head. 'And don't try to change the subject. You knew about Tanya before we were married but we had an agreement, Saffy, and this,' he picked a passion fruit out of her basket and threw it at a display of turnips, 'is breaking all the rules.'

'Look, I'm not seeing anyone. I'm cooking a meal for my *mother*, okay?' she whispered. 'My mother who has cancer? I'm trying to cheer her up.'

Liam tugged her elbow. She scanned his face in panic. How long had he been there? And had he heard Greg saying the 'we were married' bit? 'We have to go now because *The Simpsons* starts at six.'

Saffy had to keep pretending she didn't know him. She didn't have any other choice. 'Well, you'd better run along then. Seriously. Because it's ten to six now.' She turned her back on him, willing him to go away.

'S . . . S . . . Saffy?' He only stuttered, Saffy had noticed, when he was tired or upset.

'Look, I'm very busy. I don't have time to talk to you, okay?'

He looked as if she'd slapped him as he turned and walked away.

'S . . . S . . . Saffy?' Greg leaned over so she could see his face through the gauze panel in the celery head. 'How does he know your name?'

Saffy didn't answer.

'Who are you seeing? How long has it been going on?'

Saffy put down her basket and walked away. After a few yards, she broke into a run. Greg tried to keep up, but his costume was tight and it hobbled him around the knees. He stopped and ripped open the green tube just as the manager came puffing up the aisle.

'My office now!' he barked, planting a hand on Greg's chest.

Greg tried to make a break for it but the manager was too quick. He pinned one of Greg's arms behind his back, the carrot came running up and took the other and they began marching him towards the back of the supermarket.

'Take your fucking hands off me!' Greg roared. 'Take your fucking hands off me now, you fuckers!'

'Well,' he heard one of the shelf-stackers say to another as they passed, 'now we know why they call them crudités.'

Saffy waited by Joe's van. Every cell in her body was telling her to keep running but she had to stay and she had to act as if everything was normal.

Greg had said something about them being married. She tried to remember if Liam had heard that part or if he'd heard Greg using her name.

Joe crossed the car park with Liam, pushing a trolley. He was laughing.

'There's a psycho in there dressed as a vegetable having a meltdown.' He slid back the door of the van. 'It's priceless.'

'I saw him.' Saffy was afraid to look down at Liam. 'He had a go at me earlier.' To her surprise, her voice was shaking.

Joe pushed the trolley away so he could put his arms around her. 'What did he do? Are you okay?'

'I'm fine. I just wanted to get away from him but I left all the stuff I'd picked out for dinner.'

Joe tipped her chin, tilting her face up so he could see her eyes.

'I think we've got enough sausages and beans and rocky road ice cream for three. What do you say, Liam?'

Liam didn't say anything.

Liam moved his food from one side of his plate to the other and then back again. He arranged everything into a puddle, rounding up stray beans with his fork. The sound of metal scraping on china made Saffy's teeth tingle.

'Liam!' Joe gave him a look. 'Don't play with your food.'

They had stopped at a deli on the way home and picked up some antipasti and she'd set out the vegetables, cheese, olives and Parma ham on a wooden chopping board with warm bread and a bowl of olive oil, but the atmosphere was so tense that Saffy couldn't swallow anything.

Liam speared a bean and put it in his mouth. He transferred it back onto the fork, stared at it for a while and then tried to balance it on top of a sausage. It fell off and rolled over towards Saffy's water glass.

Joe stopped chewing and stared at it. Saffy touched his knee under the table.

'This is nice,' she said. 'You finished, Liam?' Without waiting for an answer, Joe took his plate, scraped it into the bin and then dumped it into the sink.

Liam retrieved the bean from beside Saffy's glass and began kicking it with the foot of a red-and-black plastic action figure.

'Who's that?' Saffy asked him. 'Is he *Star Wars*?'

There was a long silence broken only by a bang, as Joe closed the fridge, some rattling as he rummaged in the cutlery drawer and a double clatter as he dumped two bowls of ice cream onto the table.

'You heard Saffy,' he said quietly. 'Answer the question.'

Liam mashed the bean with the action figure's foot.

'Liam?' There was a warning in Joe's voice.

'It's a Bionicle,' Liam said reluctantly.

'Come on,' said Joe. 'You can do better than that.'

'It's-a-Toa-Tahu,' Liam said mechanically. 'He-has-a-Kanohi-Hau. A-great-mask-of-shielding-and-a-fire-sword-that-can-melt-even-stone-he-merges-with-Pohatu-and-Onua-to-form-Toa-Kaita-Wairuha-one-of-the-Super-Toa.'

'Wow!' Saffy shook her head. 'How do you remember all that stuff?'

Liam scowled at the table. 'Can I have my ice cream?'

'Sure,' Joe said pleasantly, 'right after you apologise to Saffy for being so rude.'

'He doesn't have to, really. He hasn't done anything wrong. Here . . .' She pushed her bowl over to Liam. 'You can have mine.'

'No he can't.' Joe pulled the bowl back and leaned down so his head was level with Liam's.

'What's going on, little guy? You've been acting up since we were in the supermarket. It's not Saffy's fault that you missed the start of *The Simpsons*, and even if it was, it's not okay to freeze someone like that. If you have a problem spit it out, we'll deal with it. That's how we do things round here, remember?'

A wave of panic hit Saffy, followed by a wave of shame. She wanted to get Liam off the hook but that would mean telling Joe the whole truth about Greg and he'd find out that she had lied to him and she wasn't ready for that, not yet. It was too soon. It was too complicated.

'Saffy's waiting.' Joe drummed his fingers on the table.

She looked at Liam's small, upset face. 'Joe, please,' she said. 'Can we drop this?'

'Okay, you had your chance, Liam. Go to your room.'

Liam stood up slowly, scraping the legs of his chair on the tiled floor. He picked up the action figure.

'No!' Joe put his hand out. 'No toys, no books, no TV till you say sorry.'

'Joe,' Saffy said when he was gone. 'I think that was a bit harsh.'

Joe shook his head. 'He shouldn't treat you like that; you've been so sweet to him.'

She bit her lip.

'All the little things you did, like finding that place that cut his hair and helping him pick those glasses, they mean a lot to him and I just want him to show it, that's all.'

He stood up and began to run water into the sink.

Saffy followed him and put her arms around him from behind. She put her cheek against his back. She could feel the warmth of his skin through his T-shirt and the faint but steady hammer of his heart beneath her hand. She could stand like this for ever.

'Maybe you're right.' Joe put a sudsy hand up and stroked her face. 'Maybe I was too harsh.'

'I'll go and talk to him. I'll sort it out.'

Saffy went and found a bag she'd left in the bedroom and then tapped on Liam's door. After a while, she tapped again. She sat on the landing floor. The seventies carpet was pale green with a foreground pattern of wavy bright green lines. Being this close to it made her feel nauseous.

'Liam?'

Five minutes passed then another five.

'I don't blame you for not speaking to me. I won't blame you if you never speak to me again but I'd like to come in just so I can explain what happened, okay?'

Liam was lying face down on a Spiderman duvet which, given the tangled web of Saffy's life, seemed kind of apt.

'Look, I don't know what to say,' she said. That wasn't very inspiring but at least it was true. 'I was rude to you in front of my friend. I pretended I didn't know you. Maybe you think I did that because I'm ashamed of you but it's not that. I'm really proud of you.'

That was true, too. Liam had lost his mother, his friends, his home, and his whole life in Chicago. She couldn't imagine how much that must have hurt, how strong you had to be to get through all of that, aged nine.

'The person I'm ashamed of is *me*. I just panicked. The vegetable guy in the supermarket is someone I used to, um, go out with.'

That was partly true. If she was being one hundred per cent

truthful, she should explain that she'd been married to Greg, but what kind of person went around confiding the details of their screwed-up life to a little boy?

Liam propped himself up on one elbow.

'You dated the celery?'

He looked at her with Joe's eyes: long-lashed, cool blue with a darker blue line around the iris. It was unnerving.

'Yes, we went out for a long time. When I broke up with him, he asked me if we could take a few months to think things over, to decide whether to get back together or split up for good and I didn't really want that, but he was upset, so I said okay.'

Liam nodded, as if this went on every day at school.

'But then I met your dad,' Saffy went on, 'and I really, really liked him.' That was the truest thing of all.

'I should have told him – the celery guy – that I'd met someone else but I didn't and when I saw him in the supermarket, I was afraid that, if he saw me with your dad, he'd cause a scene. That's why I pretended not to know you. But it's no excuse and I'm really sorry.'

'It's okay.' Liam shrugged.

'These are a peace offering.' She'd bought them a few days before. She'd checked his shoe size first, to make sure the slippers would fit. They were in the shape of big black-and-white plush footballs with holes for his feet to slip into.

'Your Snoopy slippers are broken,' Saffy said. 'I was going to get you Harry Potter ones like Alex's but I thought these were cooler.'

Liam stuck his hands into the slippers, and walked them along the bed.

'Thanks! They're neat.' He put his arms out level with his shoulders. Saffy thought he was admiring the slippers then the penny dropped. She put her arms round him and gave him a quick hug. He smelled faintly sweet, like meringues.

'Did you tell Alex that you were a top international scientist?'

Saffy nodded. 'Kind of.'

'Did you tell my dad the celery used to be your boyfriend?'

'Not really.'

'You make up a lot of stuff.'

Saffy nodded again. 'I know.'

Joe had gone upstairs to make up with Liam. Saffy was running over some notes for a presentation on Monday and half-listening to him reading a story. She couldn't hear the words, but she loved listening to the soothing rhythm of his voice.

She had a foggy memory of falling asleep while someone read *Where the Wild Things Are*. She would have been too old for it to be her father, but it didn't seem like the kind of thing Jill would do. Maybe she was just imagining it.

Her father had lived with Saffy and Jill for two years before he walked out. Hundreds, thousands of moments she spent with him had been captured and recorded by her mind but she couldn't get at them. She could remember the lyrics of pretty much every Coldplay song but not a single word her father had ever said.

He had taken the only record of those moments with him when he walked away and then, apparently, he had erased them. She had never understood how he could do that and being around Joe and Liam made her understand it even less. How could he close the book before the story had really begun?

According to the magazines, the best sex happened in four-poster beds on weekends in country houses after a champagne dinner or a candlelit bath or both. It wasn't, as far as Saffy knew, supposed to happen under an Argos throw on a beanbag in a living room the size of a postage stamp with *Have I Got News For You* on in the background.

Joe groaned as Saffy wrapped her legs around him and pulled him in further.

She grazed his chest with her teeth and grabbed his hair and then all her nerve endings exploded in one hot firework of feeling.

'Hello.' Joe grinned down at her. Their wet bodies stuck together like Velcro. A drop of sweat fell off his chin onto her bottom lip. She licked it.

'I used to go out with a giraffe,' Paul Merton was saying. 'I used to take it to the pictures and that. You'd always get some bloke complaining that he couldn't see the screen.'

They both burst out laughing.

Sex with Greg had never been like this and, looking back, that was probably *her* fault. She knew that younger, more attractive women were coming on to Greg every day and sex had felt like a kind of test that she had to pass to keep him. She had never really relaxed. She had been too busy second-guessing what he wanted next, trying to find a position that didn't make her look too flat-chested. Once or twice she'd even found herself daydreaming about having implants. But she knew that, with her average face and her average body, they'd look ridiculous, like high heels on a little girl.

She didn't have time to worry about how she looked when she had sex with Joe. It just happened. Suddenly, urgently, erotically. The only problem was that it happened in a house with paper-thin walls and a small boy sleeping a few rooms away. So it had to happen pretty quietly.

Joe rolled over and nuzzled her neck. 'What are you thinking?'

Saffy laughed. '*I'm* supposed to ask *you* that.'

'Right.' He nodded and crossed his arms over his chest. He had little constellations of freckles on his shoulders. Sometimes Saffy had an uncontrollable urge to join them all up with a biro.

'And I'm supposed to say, "I'm thinking about you", when really I'm thinking about the Chicago Bears line-up for the game with the Miami Dolphins.'

'Exactly. Except you're not in America now so you'd probably be thinking about soccer not baseball.'

'It's football.' Joe shook his head. 'But I'm not thinking about the football. I'm wondering what you're thinking.'

'I was thinking about Liam. I was wondering if maybe you should put a picture of his mum up somewhere.'

Joe leaned forward and pulled the plug of the TV. The room was suddenly dark.

'He must be forgetting her, Joe. That's like losing her for a second time.'

She heard him gulping a drink from the glass she'd left on the table but she couldn't see him.

'You know, there wasn't a single photograph of my father in the house when I grew up. The first time I saw a picture of him was just before . . .' She had almost said 'my wedding'. She caught herself just in time. 'Well, it was just a few months ago.'

The photograph her mother had given her at her hen party was in a drawer in her office. She took it out and looked at it sometimes. But it was too late to really mean anything now. It was one tiny piece of a huge jigsaw that had been broken up years ago.

Saffy's eyes were beginning to adjust to the dark. Joe had his back to her.

'I know he was a rotten father,' she said. 'Some married guy who messed up my mother's life and then ran back to his wife, and I know he never wanted anything to do with me, but I would have given anything to have a picture of him when I was Liam's age.'

She reached out and touched his back. She could feel the strong, straight line of his spine under his warm skin. 'I used to think that I could walk past him in the street and not even recognise him.'

'Well, that's not going to happen with Liam and Shelley,' Joe said bitterly, 'is it?'

She sat up and put her arms around him. 'I know it would be hard for you. I understand why you can't look at pictures of her. They must bring it all back, the pain of losing her.'

Joe pushed her away and turned around. It was too dark to see his eyes but his mouth was set in a hard line. 'You don't *know* anything, Saffy.' The line broke as he laughed. 'You don't *understand* anything, believe me.'

Saffy wanted to pull the throw around her but they were lying on it.

'You want me to give Liam a picture of Shelley? How about this one? She was having an affair. One of many, apparently. The guy who was driving the car when she died was her latest little fuck buddy: a cabin steward, twenty-two years old. He was drunk out of his mind and high as Denver on coke. And so was she.'

Saffy had imagined Shelley so many times, she felt she knew her. She wasn't like this. She was perfect.

'They'd just had sex in the car, so forensics told me, anyway. I hope it was the best sex he ever had because he's in a wheelchair now. He's twenty-five years of age and he can't even take a crap on his own so I doubt if he'll ever have sex again.' He covered his eyes with his arm.

'I thought we were happy, Saffy. We had a life. We had Liam. It wasn't perfect but we were good friends. I thought we were good friends. If it had been a one-off thing maybe I . . . but she'd been doing this stuff for years. Everybody knew about it except me.'

'Get up,' Saffy said softly. 'Just for a second.'

She dragged the throw out from under them and she covered them both up. His skin was clammy and cold. She pressed her body along the length of his body.

'I had to quit my job.' He was shivering. 'I started to drink. I got into fights. Broke my nose. Didn't even bother getting it fixed. I was a mess. I couldn't look after Liam. I wasn't capable. I had to leave him with Shelley's parents for six months while I went into rehab.'

His voice was muffled. 'I nearly lost him, Saffy. I nearly lost everything.'

She held him as tightly as she could, till he heated up, and he finally stopped shaking. And, all the time she was holding him, she was lying on something small and hard that was digging into her hip. It was Liam's action figure, the one with the sword of fire that could cut through stone.

'. . . *legs*.'

Conor couldn't believe that this particular four-letter word was the final word in his book.

There was nothing left to write. The main character, Dan – who had been left to bring up his six-year-old twins when his wife, Lucy, walked out – had completed his journey.

He had started out as a hard-bitten, high-flying journalist who hardly ever saw his kids and ended up as a part-time, low-paid journalist and a full-time dad. Along the way he rushed his daughter to hospital with suspected meningitis, turned down his dream job in New York, cured his son of bed-wetting and made a piñata in the shape of the Easter bunny from scratch.

He had grappled with his work/life balance, his inability to cook anything that didn't come from in a packet from Donnybrook Fair and his complete ignorance of the basic rules of Kerplunk.

He had kissed three women and had sex with one but he was beginning to think that he was going to miss Lucy for the rest of his life. Then, in the last paragraph, there is a hint that he might be wrong. He is waiting outside the school for his kids when he sees a woman standing a few feet away.

She is dark-haired, pale-skinned, bare-armed. She has on a blue summer dress and flip-flops.

Brunettes aren't Dan's type. Blondes have always been his weakness and wherever she is, whoever she is with, Lucy is still the fairest of them all. But even as he spots Robin and Rose running down the steps towards him, something makes him turn to look at the dark-haired woman again.

She catches him looking at her and he drops his eyes down along her arms, down past her narrow waist and the curve of her hips to the hem of her dress. She has, he can't help noticing, the most amazing legs.

This couldn't be *it*. Maybe he should have Ben's eyes finish up somewhere else, but he wasn't going to end his book with the word *breasts*.

A broken espresso machine was dismantled and pieces strewn around the sunken sofa. The wires from Greg's PlayStation snaked across the floor. The whole apartment smelled dark and mushroomy, like a teenage boy's bedroom. Conor pulled back the white lacquered door of the concealed bookcase. It was pretty obvious which books were Saffy's and which were Greg's.

The last word of *We Need to Talk about Kevin* was 'clean'. *The Girl's Guide to Hunting and Fishing* finished with 'night'. *Rich Man, Poor Man* had 'remembered'. Even *Hot Chix – 20 Years of Sizzling Centrefolds* ended on 'dream'.

Any of these words, Conor thought, was better than 'legs', but he had to let it go. If he gave in to his demons, he'd end up unpicking the whole thing, word by word. He went back into the study before he could change his mind.

Dear Becky,

I'm sending you a full draft of Doubles or Quits. *It includes the 60k words I've already sent you plus the final 30k words (34,576 words to be exact!). I have managed to complete it two days before your deadline, much to my surprise and, I'm sure, yours.*

I hope it's not complete rubbish.

I have some sad news. Brendan has gone (according to my daughter Lizzie) 'to Missing'. I am hoping he has smuggled himself onto a plane and gone somewhere exotic, though hopefully not to South America, where he might end up on someone's plate.

All the very best,
Conor Fahey

He pressed Send. He had done it. He had finished a novel. Obviously, it was only the first draft and Becky might hate it, but, still, it was a huge achievement and there was nobody to share it with except a grubby seagull picking at a takeaway box that Greg had left on the balcony.

It had been six days since he'd last heard Jess's voice. He had seen her at the door of the house every other day when he picked the twins up and dropped them off but they hadn't spoken. Since he'd left, they only communicated by text.

I WILL PICK L AND L UP AT 4. OK? C

OK. J

IF UR TAKN TWINS 2 POOL, MAKE LUKE WEAR H2O WINGS. J

OK. C

A month ago, Conor couldn't have imagined a time when they didn't have anything to say to one another. Now they were reduced to swapping syllables.

It was tearing him apart, but he couldn't forget the look of contempt on Jess's face when he'd told her about the fight at the academy. He cycled back to the petrol station where he'd bought his celebration cigar when he'd finished the last chunk of the book. The Russian guy was still there.

'I've finished the book.' Conor grinned. 'I'm going to need another one of your cigars.'

The guy looked at him blankly.

'My book.' Conor mimed opening a book in the air. 'I was here a few months back? It was really early in the morning? You thought I'd just had a baby? I told you I was writing a novel. Remember?'

'What you want?'

'A cigar.' Conor mimed smoking.

'Four euro.' The Russian put one on the counter.

'Tolstoy?' Conor's grin was fading. 'Dostoevsky? Stephen King?'

'You want or not?' The guy scowled at him. 'People wait!'

Conor looked behind him. A couple of customers were queuing to pay for petrol.

'I'll take an evening paper.' He strolled over, as slowly as he could, to pick one up from the rack at the back of the shop.

'And some Rennies.' The Russian had to walk the length of the counter to get them. His neck, Conor saw, was getting red.

'No, not these ones.' He pushed them back across the counter.

'I want spearmint. And I'll need some razor blades.' The Russian had to get a key and open a cabinet to get them. 'And a pack of Marlboro Lights. No, make that Silk Cut.'

A few more people had joined the queue.

'And a box of matches. Wait. I've changed my mind. Give me a lighter instead.'

After Conor got outside, he hated himself for being such a shit. The Russian probably saw hundreds of customers every day, why would he remember the one time he'd served *him*? He stuffed the bag of things he didn't want or need into the basket of his bike, cycled to an off-licence, and bought himself a bottle of champagne. That was what you were supposed to do when you had something to celebrate? Wasn't it?

'Lean into the phone, Alyssa. Wrap your arms around him. Tilt your head back. That's good. Smile. And again.'

Greg – who was wearing a phone costume – and the blonde model – who was wearing a bikini – were posing under a huge banner that said: *Text in the City*.

He tried to remember her real name. Sharon? Karen? It certainly wasn't Alyssa. She had featured in an early episode of *The Station* as a pyromaniac novice who set fire to convents. As Mac Malone he had kissed her once before handing her over to the police and she had made it pretty clear that she would be willing to replay the scene off set.

She looked hotter in a bikini than she had in a habit. And given that Saffy had broken the rules of their agreement, there was nothing to stop him finding out how hot she'd look without it.

He couldn't wait to see the look on her face when he took off his big styrofoam head. She had absolutely no idea who he was. This was what he loved about these promotional gigs. When he was Greg Gleeson, he was public property, but dressed as the Nokia E95, he was the Invisible Man.

He thought he'd blown his chances of more promo work after the celery fiasco, but a few days later, the supermarket manager had called Greta. It turned out that the Five-A-Day coupons were numbered and the ones Greg had given out had been redeemed more than any of the others – seven times more. They wondered if he'd consider coming back.

You wouldn't catch a Billy Bob Thornton or a Toby Maguire giving them a second chance and, as far as Greg was concerned, they would be waiting for ever. But Greta had lined up lots of other promotional gigs. So far, he'd been a bottle of Bacardi Breezer, a giant Smint and a can of engine oil. It was performance art, really. Alyssa and the photographer went inside the O2 store on Grafton Street to do a few shots with the staff. Two guys in shell suits stopped to gawp at Greg in his mobile phone suit as he handed out flyers.

'There's a *number* of things I wouldn't do for money,' one said, 'and that's one of them.'

'Yep,' his mate said. 'That really is the end of the *line*.'

Greg folded his arms and tilted his black styrofoam head.

'Careful now,' the first one threw in. 'I think you're pushing his *buttons*.'

'Why don't you go screw yourself?' Greg said. 'Because, with a face like that, nobody else will.'

The taller guy jerked his chin. 'Who do you think you are, pal?'

Greg moved a little closer to a burly female Garda who was standing by the door of the shop.

'I'm a compact, feature-rich, 3G multimedia device that enables seamless networking between TVs, audio systems and PCs,' Greg said, 'but I'd say you'd have to rob a few more handbags before you can afford one.'

Conor hurried towards the scuffle. He had a cigar in one hand and a newspaper in the other and he was having trouble keeping the bike straight. He wasn't due to meet Greg for an hour but they needed to talk.

'It's okay.' He grabbed the shoulder of Greg's padded handset costume and pulled him away. 'He's with me. I've got him!'

He leaned his bike against the wall and frog-marched Greg around the corner.

'I wouldn't leave your bike there, man!' Greg straightened his foam head. 'Unless you want one of those guys to rob it.'

Conor shoved the paper at him. 'Have you seen this?'

Greg unfolded the tabloid. He peered through the letterbox-sized slit over his eyes. A picture of Mary Harney covered most of the front page.

'Man, tell me about it,' he said. 'What other country would have a health minister with a weight problem?'

'No! No! Not that!' Conor pointed at a headline below: *It's a Gay Day for Greg.*

Days after he tied the knot at his star-studded wedding, fans of former TV fire-fighter Mac Malone were gobsmacked to read about the love-rat's kinky romps with a busty teenager.

But Gleeson fans are in for an even bigger shock. The out-of-work soap star has moved a gay lover into his million-euro penthouse apartment . . .

Greg shook his head. 'Shit! Do you think it's only worth a million? The last valuation was one point six.'

Conor made a small strangled sound. 'Look!'

He jabbed the smouldering cigar at a tiny out-of-focus picture set into the text. It showed a man going into Greg's apartment building with a suitcase. Greg held the paper up to his phone head and peered at it.

'Is that you?' He tilted his phone head back so he could look at Conor. 'You look *thin*. Have you been working out?'

'Greg! This is a disaster!'

'So they think we're gay. Who cares?' Greg shrugged.

'*I* care, Greg.' Conor gripped the handles of his bike, his knuckles were white. 'I have a girlfriend and two children and I'm a schoolteacher and the last time I looked the education system in this country was run by a bunch of right-wing homophobes called the Catholic Church.'

The bits about having a girlfriend and being a teacher, Greg thought, weren't entirely accurate, but this probably wasn't the best time to point that out to Conor.

'Dude, are you drunk?'

'Maybe. I had champagne.'

Conor had been so freaked when he read the article that

he'd drunk the whole bottle, warm. Along with three bottles of Bacardi Breezer that Greg had left in the fridge.

'I finished the book,' he said sadly. 'The last word was "legs".'

'You know what we have to do?' Greg put his arm around Conor. 'We have to celebrate.'

Conor shrugged him off and glanced around nervously.

'I don't think you should touch me,' he said. 'There are photographers around.'

'Yeah, but I'm in disguise.' Greg slapped his hand on the number buttons on his chest. They lit up. 'Hey, that's so cool; I didn't know they did that.'

Conor couldn't remember when he'd been this drunk. In fact, he was having trouble remembering the last five minutes.

'What's the name of this bar?' He had to shout over the music. 'And what are the names of those girls we were talking to?'

'Spybar. Alyssa. Brittney. Allegedly,' Greg shouted over the music.

'I thought there were only two of them?'

The girls came back from the bathroom. They were both in their twenties. One was blonde, the other was dark. They had very long hair and very high shoes.

Even if Conor had been sober enough to talk he wouldn't have had any idea what to say to them. But Greg had plenty to say about the time he'd comforted Madonna on a hairy flight to New York and the time he'd hung out with Heath Ledger at Johnny Fox's and the time Kate Winslett had to take a bath in his hotel suite because she didn't have a plug for her tub.

If he could manage to make up stuff like this on the fly, Conor thought, how come Greg had such trouble coming up with an original idea for a screenplay.

'Is he for real?' Brittney, or was it Alyssa, leaned over. She smelled like orange blossom.

'Don't ask me,' Conor said. He'd been asking himself the same question for twenty-two years.

The music in the living room back at Greg's apartment was so loud that the windows were vibrating. It was the Fun Young

Criminals or the Fine Lovin' Cannibals. Conor wanted to ask Greg which but he was stretched out on the sunken sofa kissing the blonde girl. Conor suddenly remembered his bike. He had to find his bike. He remembered unlocking it outside the bar but it wasn't in the hall, where he usually left it.

He went to check in the kitchen but when he got there, he remembered he hadn't eaten since lunchtime. He was starving but all he could find was a few stale water biscuits and a jar of pickled ginger. He was on his second cracker when the dark-haired girl came in.

'Mmmm. Can I have some?'

She came over, opening her glossy mouth like a baby bird waiting to be fed. Conor broke off a corner of a cracker, stuck some ginger on the top and popped it in. He hoped she wasn't too hungry. There were only a couple of crackers left.

She chewed it carefully. 'It's weird but that's good. Weird combinations of food are great appetite suppressants, did you know that?'

He shook his head. If he had, he would have spent his teenage years eating liver and ice cream or pickles dipped in strawberry jam. She hiked herself up so she was sitting under a spotlight on the black granite worktop. Her short silvery dress seemed to be made of spangles of light.

Conor couldn't work her out. Not as a person, but mathematically. How could that narrow back support those huge breasts? And how did the head, with what must be several kilos of hair, balance on top of the tiny neck? She didn't look like a woman, she looked like a Disney character – Pocahontas or the Little Mermaid – with wide, glassy eyes and a huge mouth and a nose that was hardly there.

'I drink Fairy Liquid when I'm trying to lose weight.' She kicked off her high silver peep-toe shoes and raised her legs so her feet were flat against the Smeg fridge. 'I'm a model. What do you do?'

'I don't know.' Conor wished she would go away so he could finish his crackers. 'I used to be a teacher and I've just finished writing a novel.'

'Clever you!' She opened her small silver bag and took out a slim joint then lit it with a lighter in the shape of a shoe. 'What's it about?'

'It's about ninety-five thousand words long.' Conor heard the slur in his voice: *wordsh*.

She laughed a silvery little laugh to match her shoes and her bag and her dress. 'You're funny. You want a hit?' She held out the joint.

He leaned down, put his lips around it and inhaled. He held a cough in his lungs till it passed.

The blonde girl, wearing only her underwear, flashed past the kitchen door, followed by Greg, shirtless and whooping.

The dark-haired girl smiled at Conor again. She had a line of something sparkly and silver above her lashes.

'You're very pretty.' He took another hit of the joint. He wasn't flirting. This was an actual fact.

'Alyssa's way prettier.'

Brittney (she had to be Brittney if the other girl was Alyssa) tilted her head and shook her curtain of long dark hair so that it fell over one shoulder.

'What's my best feature?'

He looked down at her long polished legs. They were, he realised, trapping him between the fridge and the sink. But he didn't mind. There were worse places to be.

'Your hair,' he said.

'Oh, it's not real!' She wrinkled her tiny nose. 'It's just extensions. Pick something else.'

'It's hard,' Conor said and the word caught, like a cracker crumb, in his throat. He wasn't lying. He had an erection for the first time in weeks.

'Most people think,' Brittney smiled, 'that my best feature is my—'

Conor saw it at a fraction of a second before she did: the small pointy whiskered nose poking out of one silver peep-toe shoe.

'Rat!' Brittney shrieked, scrambling onto all fours on the worktop. 'Rat! Rat!'

Conor opened one eye. His skull felt as if it had been scoured out with wire wool. God, how much whisky had they drunk last night? And how late had they stayed up talking? His face was stuck to the seat of the cream leather sofa. Greg was curled up around his feet, bare-chested and snoring softly.

He heard a faint scratching and he smiled, though smiling with his hangover was extremely painful. He had no idea how Brendan had got from his cage in the twins' bedroom to Greg's penthouse but he had, and they had managed to trap him last night, using a frying pan and waste-paper basket. He vaguely remembered locking him inside the bookcase. It was just as well he had. The apartment door was wide open. The girls hadn't stopped to close it when they fled.

'I've always wanted trees.' Joe tugged his T-shirt over his head. 'When this house is built, I'm going to plant loads of them. Turkey oaks. Larches. Birches.'

'Mmmm.' Saffy looked at his arms. They were tanned and flecked with tiny spatters of pale blue paint.

Joe tossed his T-shirt on a chair. 'You look hot.'

She was lying on his bed in a black T-shirt bra and shorts, fanning herself with a builder's supply catalogue.

'In the muggy, humid, I'm-starting-to-believe-all-that-stuff-about-global-warming sense?'

Joe opened the buckle of his leather belt, pulled it through the loops of his jeans and dropped it on the floor.

'Nope. In the come-here-so-I-can-put-my-hands-all-over-you-you-sexy-woman sense.'

Saffy's phone rang. She checked the display. It was Jess. 'I'd better take this.'

Joe sighed and stretched out on the bed beside her. He licked a finger and put it on her thigh. He made a 'tsssss' sound, like a tiny sizzle.

Jess's voice was shaking. 'Saffy! Can you come over?'

'Are you okay? Are the twins okay?'

'The twins are fine. It's Conor.'

'What about him?' Saffy tried to wriggle away from Joe.

Jess swallowed hard, as if she was fighting down tears. 'Did you see his picture? In the paper?'

'The one of him moving in with—' Saffy stopped herself

before she said 'Greg'. 'I'm sure it's just a temporary thing, Jess. He probably just needs space.'

Joe grabbed Saffy's arms and held her down. He began kissing her collarbone very slowly. Her nerve endings fizzed and popped, like space dust.

'No, not that one,' Jess said. 'That was yesterday. This one was in today's paper. It's a picture of Conor and Greg in some club called Flybar.'

'Spybar?'

'He's all over some dark-haired girl, some model. I knew this would happen. I saw this coming. He's found someone else.'

Saffy squirmed away from Joe. 'Of course he hasn't found someone else. He was probably just talking to her and someone pointed the camera.'

'You're probably right. I'm probably just overreacting,' Jess gulped. 'And it sounds as if you're busy so I'm going to go.'

'I'll come over. I just have to, um, finish something but I could be there in an hour.' Joe shook his head. 'Maybe an hour and a half.'

'No. It's okay.' Jess sounded choked. 'I'll be fine. Call me tomorrow. I could meet you for lunch or something, maybe.'

'Not maybe, definitely,' Saffy said. 'I'll definitely call you and we'll definitely have lunch, okay?'

Joe was undoing her bra with one hand when her phone rang again. 'Sorry!' Saffy made an apologetic face. 'It's my mother. I'd better take it, just in case.'

'Sadbh, I'm sorry to disturb you and I know you're with Greg so I won't keep you,' Jill said.

Joe dropped her bra on the floor and hooked a thumb under the waistband of her shorts. 'Mum, can I call you back to talk about this. I'm at work . . .'

'Please! I'm not a fool. I know you're staying at the apartment every other night. You can stop pretending. Mr Kenny removed my breast, not my *mind*.'

Saffy glued the phone to her ear. Luckily Joe hadn't heard. He was too busy pulling her shorts off using his teeth.

'The thing is,' Jill was saying, 'I need a man to do a little job for me. I don't want to ask Mr O'Keefe, he's not supposed to drive with his cataracts. I was wondering if Greg could do it. If he's not too busy.'

Joe began to make slow circles around Saffy's belly button with his tongue.

'What is it?' she gasped. 'I'll ask him.' Whatever it was, she would do it herself then she would sit down and tell her mother about Joe. And tell Joe about Greg. And tell Greg about Joe. Everything was getting way too complicated.

'I need him to go to the charity shop and the tip for me. I have two big green bags of rubbish and an old suitcase for the tip and five black bags of clothes to go to the charity shop. He doesn't even have to call in. I know things are delicate between you. I've left everything round the side of the house, beside the bird table.'

'Mum, tell me you haven't been dragging heavy bags around,' Saffy said. 'You're not supposed to be lifting anything . . .'

Joe blew on her stomach. The sensation of cool air on warm wet skin was unbearable. She squealed.

'I'll, I'll have to call you back . . .' Saffy thought she heard Jill laugh as she hung up. She threw the phone down and grabbed Joe by the hair. 'How am I supposed to talk to my mother when you're doing that?'

The phone rang again. He passed it to her.

'I don't know,' he sighed. 'Why don't you show me . . . ?'

'Who's that?' Greg said. 'Your new boyfriend?'

'Listen, this is not a good time,' Saffy said evenly. 'Can I call you back?'

'No, you can't.'

She pointed at the phone and mouthed the words *work* and *five minutes*. Joe pointed at his crotch. *Erection*, he mouthed back. He held up three fingers. *Better make it three*. Saffy pulled on her robe and went out on to the landing, closing the door behind her.

'Sorry! Are you in bed with him or something?' Greg said pleasantly. 'Did I catch you in mid-shag?'

She padded down the stairs. 'Well, *I'm* not sorry,' she whispered. 'I met someone else, okay? I thought I'd never be able to trust anyone again after what you did but I was wrong.'

'After what *I* did?' Greg laughed. 'Yeah? Well, that's pretty funny coming from someone who spent the night with some Australian dude and conveniently forgot to mention it *before* or *after* she said "I do".'

Saffy went into the kitchen and closed the door behind her. 'What?'

'Your little secret's out. Conor got hammered last night and told me all about it.'

'Look, I spent the night with him but I don't know if we—'

'You lied to me. You made me crawl around that honeymoon suite begging you to forgive me when all the time you'd done the same thing yourself.'

'It's different, Greg. Women are always throwing themselves at you.'

'You're right, Saff. Think of all the women who've thrown themselves at me. Hundreds of them. Let's say a thousand. But I only ever cheated on you once. That's one in a thousand. And I was out of my head. How many guys have thrown themselves at you, Saff? How many times have you cheated? I'm betting it's closer to one in ten.'

It was more like one in five. 'You're right. All I can say is, I'm sorry,' she said quietly. But he had already hung up.

Saffy lay down beside Joe again. She was suddenly very tired. Even her teeth felt exhausted. He picked up the belt of her robe and gave it a tug. 'That's strange,' he said. 'Usually when I touch you, your phone rings.'

There was a tap on the door. Saffy jumped up, sat on the chair and opened the builder's supply catalogue. Liam came in and padded over to the bed, blinking sleepily. Saffy wasn't even sure he saw her. He wasn't wearing his glasses.

'I had a bad dream,' he said. 'And I heard v . . . voices.'

Joe lifted his arm and Liam climbed into bed and burrowed under the duvet. His eyes closed as his head touched the pillow. Joe looked at Saffy and smiled.

What can you do? he mouthed. Then he lifted his other arm and Saffy climbed in too.

*

Saffy had a horrible feeling that Nervous Dermot was getting cold feet. He was supposed to have signed off the script but he kept coming back with concerns. Wasn't it a bit seedy if the angel was bare-chested? Should they put him in clothes? Wouldn't a leprechaun be a bit friendlier than an angel, anyway, and more Irish, which would communicate the brand's heritage? And wasn't the whole thing a bit downbeat? What about having the women cheer when he showed up? And maybe sing and dance a bit?

He had approved the director's showreel a week ago and then decided that he couldn't fully commit till he'd met him in the flesh and insisted that the meeting take place at the White Feather headquarters in a bleak industrial estate in Tallaght.

The boardroom was tiny and cramped and shoehorned into a roof space above the factory floor. Saffy, Nervous Dermot and the director had to squeeze past boxes of White Feather to get to the table. And they all had to raise their voices to be heard over the hum of the machinery and the growl of forklift trucks from below.

Hiring a top New York director was Saffy's peace offering to Ant – a way of apologising for sticking him with the second-rate guy who'd shot the Avondale ad. Ben Rosen, an East Coast hippy, had arrived straight off the New York flight. He was grey and grizzled with a long, straggly pony-tail and a huge ego. He dropped so many names in the first ten minutes that Saffy started counting. 'When I worked with Martin Scorsese [3] . . . As I was just saying to Steven Soderbergh [9] . . . And then I got a call from my old buddy Al Pacino [11].'

She could hardly bear to look at Nervous Dermot, but when she did, she realised he was completely starstruck, like a teenage girl. She was expecting to have to fight him tooth and nail on every point but he just rolled over like a pussycat while Ben Rosen shot down his concerns one by one.

By the end of the meeting they had a shooting script that was pretty much identical to what Ant and Vicky had presented in the very first round of creative. Saffy emailed Ant and Vicky from her BlackBerry. Judging from the poster on Ant's door when she got back to the agency, Ant was delighted. And it looked as if Ant, in his Anty way, had forgiven her.

It said: *I take it back! Unscrew you!*

She stuck her head round the door. Vicky was sitting at her desk with her head in her hands. Saffy's first thought was that Demot had thrown another wobbler. She should have known the meeting was too good to be true.

'What happened?'

Vicky wiped her eyes on the black chiffon sleeve of her dress. 'Josh has gone back to his ex-wife,' she said. 'He moved out of the flat last night.'

'Oh no. I'm so sorry.'

'I didn't tell you,' Vicky's eyes had panda-rings of mascara, 'but he's been borrowing money from me. Nearly ten thousand euro. And I found out that he spent it on a boob job for that woman. And a down payment on a horse for Little Lindsay.'

Fresh tears trickled down her cheeks.

'I thought we were going to get married. I thought we were going to try to have a baby. I'm nearly forty, Saffy. By the time I meet someone else, if I meet someone else, it will be too late.'

Saffy pulled in on a clearway outside the charity shop on Camden Street. Sneaking the bags out of her mother's garden had only taken a few minutes, but the traffic had been bad on the way back from the tip. She was already ten minutes late for Jess. She popped the trunk, pulled out the last two bags and dragged one to the door of the shop. Then she ran back to get the other one.

A woman came hurrying out of the shop after her. 'I'm sorry, we don't take personal items.' She pointed to a hand-written sign in the window.

Under a smiley face, it said: **WE DO ACCEPT CLOTHING**

Under a frowning face, it said: **WE DO NOT ACCEPT BOOK'S, CARD'S, PHOTOGRAPH'S, ETC.**

What was it with charity shops and punctuation? Saffy wondered. Was somebody out there donating apostrophes?

'It *is* clothing!' She opened one of the bags. It was full of

328

papers. 'Shit!' She must have dumped the clothes at the tip and brought the tip bags here by mistake.

The woman recoiled. 'Pardon?'

'Sorry, I didn't mean to . . . sorry.'

The woman turned to go back into the shop. 'Honestly,' she said to a man browsing through a box of paperbacks, 'some people.'

As Saffy was heaving the second bag back into her boot, it snagged on the number plate and split open. A pile of old bank statements and letters and cards spilled out onto the road. She was tossing it all back into the boot when she saw her name on an envelope.

There was a PO box number instead of an address but her name was written clearly above it, neatly, in blue ink. Sadbh Martin. Nobody called her 'Sadbh' except Jill but it wasn't Jill's writing. There was a return address on the back. The letter had come from someone in Swansea. Saffy frowned. She didn't know anyone in Wales. She looked down at the pile on the ground and saw that she was standing on a postcard of a fluffy duckling. She picked it up and flipped it over.

There was her name again and the same PO box number and there was a message in the same handwriting.

13 October 1976

Hello Poppet!

Remember when we used to feed ducks on the pond in St Stephen's Green? This little fellow reminded me of the one you liked best! Happy 3rd birthday! Love, Dad

27

Dad.

The word hit Saffy behind the knees and she had to lean on the car to stay upright. She must have made a noise because the man who had been browsing through the books came over.

'Are you okay? Do you need to go into the shop to sit down?'

She shook her head.

'Here, let me give you a hand.' He picked up the letters and papers and stuffed them back into one of the bags. 'Where do you want these?' She pointed at the passenger seat. She didn't trust herself to speak.

She was shaking too much to drive far. At the canal on Mespil Road, she pulled over and parked. She upended the torn bag onto the passenger seat and snatched up the first envelope she found with her name on it. It had already been ripped open. There was another postcard inside with a cartoon of a frog sitting on a lily pad playing a guitar.

12 October 1982

Dear Sadbh,

I didn't know what you'd want for your ninth birthday. I thought about a Barbie. But maybe you already have a Barbie. Or maybe you hate Barbie.

He had been right, Saffy thought, on both counts. She had a Barbie *and* she hated it.

So I am sending you some money and you can choose whatever you like for your present.

She shook the envelope and a very old English twenty-pound note fell out.

I know it's a long time since we've seen each other, but I think of you every day. And I'll be thinking of you on your birthday and hoping that, when you blow out your candles, all your wishes come true. Love, Dad

Her breath was coming in shallow gulps. Outside, the world was still turning. A Labrador puppy was barking at a swan. A woman was sitting under a tree eating a sandwich. A teenage couple were standing on the lock gate, kissing.

Saffy turned back to the pile on the passenger seat and pulled out another envelope. The handwriting was different. A sheet of notepaper with three hundred-pound notes folded inside.

1 November 2003

Dear Sadbh,

It's been nearly a year since I was in touch but I was hoping to get back on the air before your thirtieth birthday and here I am. I didn't get a chance to buy you a card but I'm sending a few quid so you can buy yourself a present.

I know I'm not supposed to send you letters but I didn't want to tell you my news on a postcard. It didn't seem right. I'm sorry to tell you that my wife Marie died in her sleep on 30 September last year. It is never easy to let someone go but I keep reminding myself how happy she'd be, after twenty-eight years, to finally get out of that bloody wheelchair (pardon my French!).

Marie always wanted to meet you and I hoped it would happen sometime. I'm sure you would have liked her, everybody did. I haven't been an easy person to live with. I have had my share of depression and she probably thought

I had a lot of regrets about leaving you and your mother and she was probably right.

If she had to go then I'm glad that she went when she did because I had a stroke myself in June and I've been in hospital ever since. They finally let me out last week. I am nearly back to normal, though I have to use one of those Mrs-Brady-Old-Lady walking frames so I feel like a right old fart and I can't write properly yet so my friend Frank is writing this for me. He's loving it, the nosy old bugger!!!

I can't believe you are really thirty. Where did the time go?

Love, Dad

She opened another envelope. A cartoon angel with a glitter halo. A fifty-pound note.

12 December 1988

A Christmas angel for a Christmas angel. Happy 16th Christmas!

Love, Dad

And another one. A card with seven dancing poodles, a twenty-pound note and a photograph.

Happy 7th birthday Sadbh. Here's a photo of me with our terrier (the holy terror!) Ted. He's the same age as you. But that makes him forty-nine in dog years, two years older than me!

Ted was a terrier mix with eyebrows and a beard. He was jumping for a frisbee held by the same man who was in the photograph Jill had given her. The same lean, handsome face.

The same wide mouth, the same dark eyes. Her eyes. Her father.

Saffy's hands were shaking as she sifted through the papers. Most of them were just rubbish. Old bank statements and theatre programmes, train tickets and chequebooks, scribbled recipes and dog-eared prescriptions. She stuffed all of these back into one bag.

There was a sheaf of professional photographs from Jill's modelling days and a clear plastic envelope with a handful of magazine tears. She pushed them under her seat and stared at what was left . . . Fifty-eight envelopes and one small package. Her mother had hidden every single one.

The handwriting was the same on all of them except for one envelope and the package. The dots on the letter 'i' s high above the letters. The 't's crossed low. The tails on the 'y's and 'p's slanting almost horizontally to the left.

Twenty-eight Christmas cards. A reindeer silhouetted against a full moon. Two teddy bears pulling a cracker. A marble statue of an angel with snow on her wings. A Christmas stocking with a baby mouse poking its head out. A greyhound wearing antlers. A penguin in a Santa hat sliding down an ice floe. A grey squirrel in a patchwork pinafore wrapping a present. Santa riding on his sleigh above a roof that sparkled with frost; glitter from the roof cracked off and stuck to her fingertips. Book tokens and old bank notes, wafer-thin and flimsy as pressed flowers, slipped through her fingers.

Christmas 1978. Santa asked me to send this book token so your mum can buy you your favourite book. (It's not your favourite book yet but it will be soon!) It's called 'Where the Wild Things Are'. Happy Christmas, Poppet. Love, Dad

December 1992. Missing you this Christmas, and always. And wishing that we might meet soon and often. Love, Dad

14 December 1999. Happy Christmas and Happy
Millennium! Going up to London to see the fireworks from
Tower Bridge on 31 Dec. Our friends Frank and Susan are
coming to help with Marie. Couldn't manage on my own,
as I'm officially an old man. (Sixty-five this year. Bus Pass.
Old Age Pension. Hairy ears like you wouldn't believe.)
Love, Dad

Greg had taken Saffy to London for the Millennium. They'd had dinner in Soho House and walked down to the South Bank to watch the display. Her father could have been standing next to her in that crowd by the river, watching it, too.

Twenty-seven postcards with birthday messages. A Jack Russell curled up in a deckchair: *Have a cool birthday!* A green parrot with a red tail and 'Pardon my French' in a speech bubble: *Repeat after me: I will have the best birthday ever!* A cartoon rabbit on a space hopper: *Happy 5th birthday! So hop till you drop, Poppet!* Two sheep with handbags and high heels: *Happy birthday two ewe.*

Her favourite Gary Larson cartoon, the one with the cows on their hind legs and one cow shouting 'Car!': *I hope cows really do this! And I hope you have a wonderful birthday, Sadbh. I will be thinking of you at 8.45 on the evening of 17 October because that is the exact moment you were born fifteen years ago.*

A folded-up parchment certificate that said: 'Let it be known that the star located at RA 273.21034164 DEC 63.68550278 shall hereby be know as: Sadbh, in honour of: Sadbh Martin's 17th birthday. And a card with a single gold star that said: *You don't have to see your star every night to know it's out there somewhere. Have a lovely birthday!*

A detail of *The Water Lilies*. The same print she'd put on her bedroom wall when she was fifteen. It was still there. *Happy 21st Birthday. Forgive the lateness of the card. I had pneumonia for a month (serves me right! Those damned cigarettes!). Hope the enclosed is enough to get you to Paris to see this painting (and back!!)*

There were only two letters. The one she'd already read and another, longer one. She unfolded it carefully.

1 January 1992

Dear Sadbh,

I have been writing this letter in my head for years and I have to tell you, it didn't help! My waste-paper basket is full of attempts but I've made a deal with myself that I will send this version, no matter how it turns out.

After I left Dublin, the agreement was that I would send maintenance to your mother's bank till you were eighteen and she would pass on birthday and Christmas messages but the solicitor made it clear that I wasn't to write that anything that wouldn't fit on the back of a postcard, so I know there's a chance that you won't read this letter.

I know that your mother is still angry with me because the first payment after your eighteenth birthday last year was returned to my bank account in November. I was hoping I could help out with any university or gap-year plans but I won't push it except to say that if you ever need anything (no strings attached) please let me know.

I don't know what Jill has told you about me or why I left but I know there's something she didn't tell you because, to be honest, back then, I didn't know it myself.

I suppose you know that I was married when I met her and that my wife was a friend of her mother. Also that there was an age gap of twenty-three years between us. It doesn't look good on paper but all I can say is that that there is one person for you and if you find that person, you

335

can't fight it. Jill was that person for me. I loved your mother. I still do.

She wanted us to run off when she found out she was pregnant but I made her tell her parents. I didn't want her to lose her family but that's what happened in the end. Has she told you that her mother and father were Seventh Day Adventists? I don't know much about them except that they give the Catholics a run for their money. No drinking or music and the girls are supposed to save themselves for marriage. An eighteen-year-old girl having a baby with a married man was the end of the world for them and they put her out on the street. I don't think they ever got over it. There was a brother, Tony, but I lost track of him. I think he went to New Zealand.

I brought your mother to a counselling service and they talked to us about doing away with the pregnancy but she couldn't do that and neither could I so we left. We tried to get as far away as we could but that ended up being Dublin. I had worked there for a few months before I went to England, so I knew my way around. I had left the house to Marie and we had nothing, but we were happy. I thought we couldn't be happier, then you came along and I found out I was wrong. You were the most beautiful baby, Sadbh, and the image of my mother who died when I was fifteen, so we gave you her name.

It wasn't just the day you took your first step (23 January 1975!) or your first word ('tickle') when you were seven months old. Every day with you was a wonder. You used to lie in your pram outside the kitchen window of our *flat in Ranelagh, laughing to yourself. When we woke up in the morning, we'd hear you singing away in your cot.*

Then when you were nearly two, Marie was diagnosed with MS. It was quite far gone by the time they found it. Her parents were gone and her sister had five kids. There was nobody to look after her so she was going to have to go into one of those homes. We had been married for nineteen years. I didn't want to go back but I had to.

Jill took it very badly and I don't blame her. She said that if I left, I would never see her or you again. I thought she'd change her mind but I never heard from her again, except through the solicitor. I wanted to get in touch but I knew I'd done enough damage so I left her alone. I'm sorry if this letter reads like a list of excuses because, at the end of the day, there's no excuse for walking out on your family.

The thing I wanted to tell you, the thing I didn't know when I left, was how much I would regret it. Not a day goes by that I don't miss you, Sadbh. You're the first thing I think of when I wake up and the last thing I think of at night.

Love, Dad

Saffy had left the package till last. It had been torn open and some photographs, held together with a rubber band, had been pushed back inside.

There were half a dozen pictures of her father. There was his whole life, in fast-forward. One moment he was brown-haired, standing, smoking beside a stone lion. The next he was silver-haired and bearded, toasting the camera with a glass of red wine at a party. Then he was bald and hollow-cheeked, leaning on a walking frame in a sunny garden.

The other pictures were a series of black-and-white 10 x 8s of a dark-haired girl of about two. Each one cleverly caught a different expression: she was solemn, surprised, laughing, looking squarely at the camera with candid, trusting eyes. She might have forgotten all about it, but Saffy had loved her father once; she couldn't have looked at him like that if she hadn't.

There was something else in the package; one last card with a picture of a rainbow over a lake.

30.08.2005

91 Wilbur Road
Swansea
SA1 9RE

Dear Sadbh,

I am an old pal of your dad, Rob. I regret to tell you that your father passed away on 27 August 2005, after a bad stroke. I have been clearing out his home and, as I helped your father write his last letter to you, I thought of you when I found these pictures and knew he would want me to send them on to you.

With deepest sympathy,
Frank Fielding

Joe was grinning when he opened the door. 'I've been trying to get hold of you all afternoon! Liam's on a sleepover and we have the house to ourselves.' He saw her face. 'Saffy! What is it?'

'My father died.' She leaned against the pebble-dashed wall, pushing her fist into her mouth to squash her sobs, choking down mouthfuls of air.

'Today?'

'Nearly three years ago.'

Joe helped her inside then he picked her up and carried her up the narrow stairs and then he lay down beside her and pulled the covers over them. After a while, he went out to her car and brought in the cards and the letters. He spread them out on the duvet and Saffy read them all over again. And again.

'It's just so amazing.' Joe had brought her up a tray of tea and toast. It was nearly midnight and Saffy hadn't eaten since breakfast. 'The fact that your dad was trying to stay in touch with you all of those years.'

'It's so *sad*,' Saffy said. 'It's so *sad* to think of him *dying* thinking that I didn't want to see him.'

'You need to call your mother. You need to ask her why she never told you he wanted to see you.'

Saffy shook her head. Her mother had killed her father – maybe not with a knife or a gun, but with a lie. A long, complicated lie that she had told so convincingly and so *often*, that Saffy had never doubted it.

Your father knows where we are, Sadbh. If he wanted to see us, he would.

How could she do that? How could she have been so cruel to a child?

'There must be a reason why she didn't tell you about all this.'

If there was, Saffy didn't want to hear it. It was too late for excuses. There was nothing her mother could say that would make up for what she'd done.

'Do you want me to drive you over to her place now?'

'I don't want to see her, Joe. I don't want to go back there. Please, don't make me!'

He put his arms around her.

'Shhh. You don't have to go anywhere. You can stay here with me.'

Saffy dreamed that she was the only person on a huge ocean liner. She ran from deck to deck, through deserted dining rooms and ballrooms. She pulled open the doors of abandoned cabins. She searched the engine room and climbed up into the bridge but there was nobody there. Who was steering this ship and how was she supposed to stop it on her own?

'Wake up,' Joe was saying softly, 'you were having a bad dream.'

He stroked her hair and settled the duvet around her.

'Don't go anywhere, okay?' she whispered.

'I'm right here.'

After a moment she heard his voice again, close to her ear.

'Nobody teaches you to how be a parent, you know. You get it wrong. You get it wrong every day in a different way. You don't mean to but you do.'

'Are you telling me something about my mother or my father?'

'I don't know,' Joe said, 'probably both.'

S, JUST WONDERING IF YOU WILL BE HOME TO TAKE ME TO CHEMO AT TWO. IF NOT, DON'T WORRY, I CAN TAKE A TAXI, M X

Saffy deleted it. Then she sent one back: M, I JUST FOUND OUT THAT MY FATHER DIED ON AUGUST 27 NEARLY THREE YEARS AGO. WILL NOT BE BACK TODAY. WILL COME BY MON EVENING TO PACK UP MY THINGS. S

It had taken Saffy two hours to move out of the apartment she shared with Greg. It took her less than five minutes to clear her bedroom at her mother's house. She emptied the drawers into a suitcase, rolled up her clothes – still on their jangling hangers – and stuffed them in on top. Then she threw her shoes into a holdall and she was done. She picked up the case and carried it down the stairs.

Her mother hadn't appeared but when she brought her bags out on to the landing, Jill was standing in the doorway of her bedroom in a grubby pink dressing gown. She was wearing her wig and some badly applied lipstick but she looked exhausted and she smelled bad. For a moment, this almost softened Saffy's anger. Her mother had never smelled of anything except hairspray and Joy by Jean Patou.

Jill was twisting the belt of her dressing gown round and around her fingers. Her mouth was trembling. 'Sadbh, I never meant to . . .' Her voice was cracked and husky.

'Lie to me for thirty-one years?'

'I kept it. I kept it all to show you, but I never found the right time.'

Saffy came back upstairs and closed her bedroom door. 'The right time to what? Dump it at the tip so I would never know?' She picked up her holdall.

'You can't forgive him for walking out just because of a few birthday cards, Sadbh.'

'His wife had MS. He was trying to do the right thing.'

'The right thing would have been to stay with us, not go back to her! He turned his back on us.'

'That's a *lie*. You gave him an ultimatum and then you shut him out. When were you going to tell me he paid maintenance, Mum?'

Jill was holding the banister with one hand and clutching the empty side of her dressing gown with the other. She was pale and her breath was short. 'Please, can we talk about this? Can we just sit down and talk?'

She was deliberately playing pathetic, Saffy thought, and maybe if there had just been one letter, if there hadn't been that second one, from his friend, saying that her father had died, Saffy could have forgiven her. But her mother had read that final letter. She had known what it said all this time.

She had known it when she had finally given her that picture of her father in the silver frame before her wedding. And that, more than anything, was what slammed Saffy's heart closed. Her mother had held back so much and then, finally, when it was all over, she had thrown her that picture, that one little crumb.

The holdall slipped out of Saffy's arms and shoes spilled down the stairs. Kevin Costner, who was watching them from the hall below, dodged a stiletto and ran out through the front door. Saffy went downstairs, kicking stray shoes out of the way.

'We had *years* to talk about this, Mum. You've had three years to tell me he died. That was your decision and this is mine.'

She took the key off the ring and put it on the hall table then she pulled the door shut behind her. And, watched by Mrs O'Keefe, who was pretending to prune a rosebush, she ducked behind her mother's magnolia tree and was sick.

28

Lizzie and Luke were digging a hole near the deflated paddling pool. Out there, in the small, overgrown garden, they looked like the same kids they'd been before the summer, but they weren't.

Luke was barely eating and Lizzie had started to wet her bed again. They were upset when it was Conor's day to take them and upset when it wasn't, which meant, Jess thought, rinsing her cup under the tap, they had been upset every day since he left and today she was going to do something about it. Conor had texted earlier and asked if he could come over at two and she had cleared the afternoon. She was going to ask him to come back. They were going to sit down like adults and sort this out.

He was the one who had walked out. He had to see that his actions had consequences. But she had probably been too harsh when he had told her about breaking up the fight. Saffy was right: Conor wouldn't ever hurt someone on purpose, especially a child. And it wasn't the end of the world that he'd lost his job at the academy. There were other summer revision colleges. They'd manage.

She wasn't going to ask him to move back in right away but her parents had a holiday home in Kinsale and, now that Conor wasn't working at the academy, she thought maybe they'd bring the kids down for a week. They could spend time together. Try to work things out.

Jess looked at her reflection in the window. She looked the same as she always did. Same messy blonde hair, same too-big mouth, same blue-grey eyes. She was wearing an old grey cardigan that had lost most of its buttons and a pair of black leggings that had shrunk in the wash. She hadn't planned to change but suddenly she wanted to. It wasn't like before, with the stupid underwear. She just wanted him to see her at her best. She brought the kids in and parked them at the table with their lunch and ran upstairs to shower.

She found a clean T-shirt dress in the hot press, put on some perfume and combed her hair. She opened the wardrobe to get her sandals. One of Conor's sweatshirts was stuffed in behind the shoes. Jess shook it out. She had always loved how big Conor's clothes were. They made her feel safe. Had she ever told him that? She buried her face in the soft, grey cotton. There was a faint trace of his smell caught in the folds. Nobody smelled like Conor. He smelled of home to her. She missed him so much. She missed everything about him. Something crinkled in the pocket. She pulled it out. It was a bill for their joint Visa account. And it came to nearly twelve thousand euro.

'It's Brendan!' Lizzie came running into the kitchen where Jess was sitting at the table. 'It's Daddy and he has Brendan in a *box*!'

A moment later, Luke arrived holding Brendan's cage, his face blazing with excitement. Conor was behind him. He was holding a shoebox with a hole punched in the side. A tiny white nose poked out then disappeared again.

He smiled. 'Guess who I found? He made an appearance a few days ago but I wanted to save the surprise till I saw you.' He opened the box carefully and produced a hamster. 'It's Brendan.' Jess had to give him some credit; he'd managed to find an almost identical one.

Her voice was sharp. 'That's not Brendan,' she told the twins. 'Brendan is dead. Daddy has bought a hamster that looks like him, which is fine but it's not him.'

Their faces froze. Luke's bottom lip began to wobble.

'No, it really *is* Brendan,' Conor said. 'I don't know how he managed to get over to Greg and Saffy's but he did. He's been living wild in the kitchen. Greg thought he was a rat and tried to kill him with a frying pan.'

'I *hate* Greg,' Lizzie said.

'It is Brendan, Mum! It is.' Luke took the hamster from Conor. 'Look he has that little brown bit on his tummy.'

Lizzie made a grab for him and Brendan escaped and scampered out of the kitchen, the twins charged after him.

'Very smooth.' Jess looked at him with a hard little smile on her lovely mouth. 'Full marks for replacing the missing hamster.'

She put the Visa bill on the table.

'Let's hope you can do the same with this missing twelve and a half grand.'

'You bought an engagement ring for Saffy? You bought Saffy's *engagement* ring?'

'Of course I didn't buy her ring. Greg borrowed our card to buy it but he's going to pay me back.'

'Why? Why would you do something so stupid?'

'Because I owed it to him, Jess,' Conor said quietly. 'I borrowed some money from him about five years ago and I still owe it to him.'

'You *what*?'

Conor tried to find a way into her eyes but she wasn't letting him in. He wished she would cry. It would give him an excuse to put his arms around her. This wasn't how it was supposed to turn out. Finding Brendan on the same day he'd finished the book had seemed like a sign that everything was going to be okay. That now they could both go home to where they belonged, with Jess and the twins.

'Look, I'm sorry. We were broke. I should have told you, back then and I should have told you when he borrowed the credit card. I wish I had but it will be okay, I swear, Jess. He's going to pay me back.'

'How? He's unemployed,' Jess said, 'and you've lost your job at the academy. How are we going to save twelve grand on what you earn at St Peter's?'

Conor thought about not telling her but he had too. There had been enough lies for one day.

'I've had call from St Peter's. The board of managers had an emergency meeting. I've been suspended until after they do an investigation so I won't be starting back in September.'

She put her hand over her mouth. She looked like she might be about to cry but he couldn't put his arms around her now. The moment had passed.

'But, you'll get paid while you're suspended, right? They have to pay you till they decide what to do.'

'They would if I had a permanent position,' Conor said, 'which I don't.'

Jess wouldn't meet his eye. 'I can't take any more of this. I just can't. Can you please just go now? Luke! Lizzie!' she called the twins. 'Daddy's going to take you out now.'

Lizzie came back into the kitchen. 'Do we have to go? Can't we stay here and play with Brendan instead?'

'I told you,' Jess said in a small, hard voice, 'that's *not* Brendan! Brendan is gone and he's not coming back.'

Joe wrapped himself in a towel and sat beside Saffy on the rug. They watched Liam playing in the rock pool below.

'Does it bother you,' Joe said, 'that I can't have kids?'

Saffy shook her head. 'Honestly? No. I'm not really a children person. Except for Liam. And Lizzie and Luke. I'm getting quite fond of them but I've never wanted to have any of my own.' She looked at him. 'Does that bother you?'

He thought for a second. 'I don't know. Shelley was so sick when Liam was born and I felt I had to have the vasectomy. But now I'm wondering if I should have it reversed. I don't want to scare you *again*, but I think this is it, you and me. I could see it all for us, kids, marriage . . .'

Saffy's heart bumped down the length of her spine and then back up again.

'Sorry,' he laughed. 'I am completely freaking you out!'

'No! You're not. I'm not. It's just . . .' It was just that she had no idea when or how she was going to tell him that she was *already married*.

'Look.' He put his arm around her and squeezed her shoulder, 'Let's talk about this another time.'

She nodded. 'Okay.'

'How about we talk about it when I'm thirty-eight.'

'When's that?'

'Sunday. I promised I'd take Liam camping. I was hoping you'd come and maybe even take Monday off.'

'If I put in a day on Saturday, that should be fine.'

'Good. And listen, don't worry about what I said before. I'm probably rushing things.'

'No, you're not.' She leaned into him. His body was cool after his swim. She would find a way to tell him. He'd understand. Joe was the most understanding person she knew.

He tucked her hair behind her ears. 'It's just that I think there's one person for you and if you find that person, well, you know.'

Her father had said something like that in his letter: *There is one person for you and if you find that person, you can't fight it.*

'Yes,' she said, putting her face against his heart and smiling into his damp, salty skin. 'I know.'

29

Saffy hurried past Mike's office window – he was leaning back in his chair, poking at one of his ears with a paper clip – and ran straight into Simon.

'Saffy, can we catch five? I have some issues and concerns about Vicky that I've raised with Marsh and I'd like your input.'

'Not now, Simon,' Saffy said. She was on her way to meet Jess for lunch. Jess had waited for her for over an hour the day she found her father's cards and letter. She had been so annoyed that Saffy hadn't told her about them yet. She had some of them in her bag now, to show her.

Marsh was at the reception desk lecturing Ciara. 'You can chew gum on your own time. I really think the sound of you masticating does not send the right message out to our . . .' She noticed Saffy. 'Have you checked your mail in the last ten minutes?'

She hadn't.

'There's a small White Feather fire in your inbox. Don't even think of leaving the building until you put it out.'

Back at her desk, Saffy had only just sat down when Ant appeared at the door.

'Have you got a . . . minute?'

She swivelled in her chair to look at him. 'Ant, did you just *speak* to me?'

He shrugged and came in, closing the door behind him. Saffy waved at a free chair and he sat down and looked around. He had never set foot in her office before.

'You have no . . .' there was a long silence, 'gonks.'

'Sorry?'

'Or trolls or plushies or beanie babies.' Ant blinked rapidly. 'It's unusual. For a woman. Your office is impersonal. I like that.'

He stood up, took a packet of hand wipes out of his pocket,

wiped the chair down carefully, put the hand wipe in the waste-paper basket and sat down again.

'I need to talk to you about Vicky. She is having . . .' He looked up at the ceiling.

Thirty seconds ticked by on Saffy's watch.

'Problems. She's finding it hard to . . .'

Twenty-three seconds. Saffy leaned forward, willing him to finish.

'Cope. Work. Function. Manage,' Ant said finally.

'It's understandable, Ant. She's upset about Josh.'

Ant nodded. 'Yes! And she's taking . . .' He looked around frantically.

'It badly? I know.'

'She's taking Xanax. And anti-depressants,' Ant said. 'And drinking a lot of vodka.'

'That's not good,' Saffy said.

'That bastard. He stole her—'

'Money. I know. She told me. He spent it on plastic surgery and a horse.'

Ant's lower lip trembled. 'Self-esteem. Faith in human nature. Innocence.'

Oh my God, Saffy thought. *He's in love with her. Ant's in love with Vicky.*

Nervous Dermot's email was a long, rambling account of how Vicky had turned up drunk at a casting session, demanded wine instead of coffee, insisted that if the actors had to strip down to their underwear, everyone else should too, and finally passed out on the sofa.

It was signed: *. . . I remain very nervous, Dermot.*

Apologising was something Saffy had learned how to do from Marsh. The secret was to exaggerate the effect of any offence caused and to use the other person's name as often as possible.

Dear Dermot,
Thank you for taking the time and the trouble to share your issues and concerns following on from this morning's casting session. Reading between the lines of your email, I can see that your faith

in Komodo has been seriously compromised by this lamentable event.

Dermot, it is our responsibility, as your agency and as a trusted partner, not just to help you to achieve your business goals but to do so in a professional manner.

Vicky is under tremendous strain in her personal life but that is our concern not yours. I apologise, unreservedly, for her unforgivable behaviour.

I hope, Dermot, that you will accept my heartfelt apology and give us the opportunity to prove how much all of us here at Komodo value you as a client and a friend.

Yours,
Saffy Martin

After she had sent it, she wrote two briefs, queried a photographer's invoice and tweaked a radio script Vicky had written for Avondale Cheese. It was way over length and full of typos, which wasn't like Vicky at all. She tried to call Jess to apologise for missing lunch again but Jess wasn't picking up and she didn't blame her.

She was still at her desk at seven. Marsh popped her head around the door. She was fully made-up and wearing a pale green off-the-shoulder jersey dress that Saffy had seen in the window of Brown Thomas. She looked, if not like a million dollars, then like the €2,000 she must have had paid for it.

'Booty call!' Marsh wiggled her tiny behind suggestively. 'And I'm late. But I wanted to say well done on the email to Dermot. It struck just the right note. And I want you to put a date in your diary.'

'Sure.'

'I've put the word out for a new creative team. I'm seeing Tom and Aoife from Ogilvy at two-thirty on the seventeenth. I'd like you to sit in on the meeting with me.'

'Wow! They're good. I didn't know we were hiring.'

Marsh took a little pot of Chanel lip-gloss out of her Mulberry handbag. 'We're hiring and firing. Vicky is the only person who can keep that sociopath Ant in check and if she's losing it, we're better off without the pair of them.'

349

Saffy swallowed. If Vicky lost her job *and* Josh she really might go over the edge, and Ant, judging from their earlier conversation, might join her. 'Look, let me have a word with her, Marsh, I'm sure—'

'So am I.' Marsh dotted some lip-gloss on her bottom lip. 'Let's wait till we have the final cut of White Feather in the bag,' she smiled, 'and then make some cuts of our own.'

It was Saturday morning and Joe was pacing around the garden on the phone. Saffy put a plate over his scrambled eggs and poured herself a cup of coffee.

'That was an architect,' he said when he came back in. 'His decorator's let him down and he wants me to quote for a job today. It's a really big one but I don't think there's time to organise a sitter for Liam. Shit! I'm going to have call him back and take a rain check.'

'Go.' She handed him a coffee. 'Liam can come to the office with me. There won't be anyone around; he can play a video game or watch a DVD on my laptop.'

'Are you sure? I owe you.'

'You don't owe me,' Saffy said, 'but you owe the swear pig fifty cents.'

Liam packed his rucksack with books, his football slippers, two DVDs, his GameBoy, a peanut-butter sandwich, a carton of juice and two packets of cheese-and-onion crisps. He made her put in the second packet because he said that if he only had one, she'd eat half of it.

'I don't really like crisps,' Saffy said.

'You like other people's crisps.' Liam grinned and there was that flash of Joe again.

What if she changed her mind and Joe reversed his vasectomy and they had a son? What if he had something not just of Joe but of her father too? For the first time ever, Saffy got it. She understood the real reason why people had children. Because nobody really dies, not completely, as long as someone, somewhere, is still smiling or raising one eyebrow or shrugging a shoulder the way *they* used to.

*

Liam sat quietly in the meeting room beside Saffy's office and played Nanosaur on her laptop while she went through the White Feather pre-production schedule that had arrived by email the day before. The timeframe was ridiculously tight. According to the schedule, locations and casting had to be approved in two weeks; the ad would be shot in three and on air in four.

To do that with an Irish director would be tricky enough. But Ben Rosen was based in New York. If all this was going to happen, someone was going to have to stay on top of every last detail. That someone should have been Vicky but Vicky had gone AWOL. According to the schedule, Rosen was due to fly back to Dublin the following Tuesday for the Irish casting session. If she could persuade him to delay it for a few days, she'd have a chance to get Vicky back on the rails.

Saffy picked up the phone and dialled his cell phone. It was 7.30 in the morning in New York and it was the weekend. She hoped he was an early riser.

If Liam looked over his right shoulder, he could see the big steel reptile on the wall downstairs. It was cool, but it looked more like a monitor lizard than a komodo dragon to him. He had never been in a big office before. It was a bit weird with all the desks and chairs empty, as if there had been an earthquake or a plague or something or everyone had been beamed up onto an alien spaceship. And it was so quiet that the quietness made a sort of humming noise.

But any time the humming bothered him, he turned around and leaned sideways so he could see Saffy and that made him feel okay again. He couldn't see all of her through the open door of her office, just part of one leg and both feet. She had different shoes on today, black ones with a hole in the front for her toes.

She had so many shoes, it was hard to keep track. His mom had had lots of shoes, too. He wasn't sure how many because, before the accident, he'd been too young to count past twenty. But it had been way more than twenty anyway. He finished his carton of juice and immediately wanted to pee. Saffy was on the phone, but she'd shown him where the toilet was.

His football slippers made no sound on the carpet, which he would normally have liked, but that just made the humming sound even louder. There were glassed-in offices instead of walls. Sometimes the blinds were open and you could see there was nobody inside. But sometimes they were closed, so you wouldn't know if someone was inside looking out at you.

He had to push hard against the swing door to open it. It felt as if there was someone on the other side pushing back. He felt so scared that he wanted to run back to Saffy's office, but being scared made him want to pee even more so he couldn't. There was a shorter corridor on the other side and then a toilet. It had an outline of a girl on it, but he didn't care. The door opened with a little squeal and then hissed closed behind him.

He closed the door of the cubicle. His hands were shaking so badly that he couldn't open his zip. That was when he heard the moan. It was far away and then closer. It sounded like someone hurt. He froze. He heard it again, nearer this time and then he heard the little squeal of the door opening.

Liam just had time to climb onto the toilet so nobody could see his feet under the cubicle door before two people came crashing in.

'No.' It was a woman and she sounded scared. 'No! Don't! Please!'

The man coughed. 'I know what you want and I'm going to give it to you.' He coughed again. 'Sorry.'

Liam wanted to scream but if he screamed, they would know he was there. He pushed his fist into his mouth.

'In front of the mirror,' the woman was saying. She sounded a bit cross now. 'No, not there! Here! By the basin! Now say it!'

'Em . . . I'm going to rip your blouse off,' the man said in a tired voice.

'No! No!' The woman sounded really cross now. 'Don't *actually* rip it, you idiot! It's DKNY!'

One of Liam's football slippers lost its grip and he slipped and landed on the floor with a crash. Then the door of the cubicle was pushed in by an old man with his trousers around his ankles wearing Bart Simpson underpants. Behind him, an old woman with her skirt pulled up was leaning over the sink, looking over her shoulder at him.

'Who the *hell* is that?'

Saffy was just winning the argument with a sleepy and bad-tempered Ben Rosen when she heard the screaming. 'Liam!' She dropped the phone and raced down the corridor. 'Liam!'

He raced towards her, colliding with her legs.

'There's a man. K . . . k . . . killing a lady in the t . . . t . . . toilet.'

'Liam! Go back to my office!' Saffy said. 'Lock the door! Get my phone. Ring your dad. Don't open the door for anyone except your dad, have you got that?'

Mike was in one corner of the Ladies' fastening his trousers. Marsh was standing by the sink. Her lipstick was smeared and her blouse was buttoned up wrong. Her face was white with rage.

'Saffy! Are you responsible,' she hissed, 'for that horrible little tyke *sneaking* round *my* office?'

Saffy didn't get it. And then she did. The hot guy that Marsh had boasted about, the one she had on call whenever she wanted, wasn't Simon. It was *Mike*. Middle-aged, cartoon-socked, *married* Mike.

'Seeing Marsh and Mike like that has probably screwed up his entire adult sex life in one horrible go.' Saffy covered her face with her hands.

They had played a long game of Cluedo after she brought Liam home but all she could think about was *Marsh in the bathroom with the media manager*.

'Come on.' Joe pulled her hands away. 'It's not that bad. He probably didn't even notice what they were doing. Even if he did, he'll have forgotten it all tomorrow.'

'You think?'

'I think.' He dropped the pieces back into the box and folded the board.

Saffy covered her eyes with her hands. 'I think it might have screwed up *my* entire adult sex life. I wish I could wash my mind out with soap.'

'I like your mind dirty.' Joe laughed. 'But I think you're going to have to deal with some fallout over what happened today.'

'How do you mean?'

'Well, I've only met her once,' Joe said, 'on that balloon trip you put together for your client, but your boss is a tough cookie. Seeing what you saw gives you power over her. She's going to have a problem with that.'

Saffy had bought Joe a new pair of Caterpillar boots and a book of photographs of the earth from the air, a Nigel Slater cookery book and an iced cake from Marks and Spencer's. Liam had bought him a key ring in the shape of a silver tree and a mug that said, *Age only matters if you're a cheese.*

'This is way too much,' Joe said after they'd had a birthday tea of burnt sausages and crispy eggs cooked on a disposable barbeque. But he was grinning and he took off his old boots and put on the new ones and fixed his keys on the key ring and poured his Coke out of the can into the mug. Then it started to rain and they retreated inside the tent and ate birthday cake and watched the steadily increasing shower put their fire out.

'I think this has been my most perfect birthday ever,' Joe said.

'Except for birthdays with Mom, in Chicago.' Liam looked anxious.

Joe stole a piece of icing off his plate. 'You know what? Those were perfect, too.'

Saffy had never slept in a tent before and it didn't look as if she was ever going to sleep in this one. Her sleeping bag was twisted around her legs and she was afraid to move in case she woke Joe and Liam. She kept imagining that something with too many legs was crawling on her face. Rain pitter-pattered on the canvas wall by one ear and Liam's snores took care of the other one.

She was hot. She was hungry. She was itchy and, by the time she gave in and squirmed out of her sleeping bag and escaped from the tent, she was dying for a pee. Except, of course, there was no loo. She found a dripping tree and crouched under it, praying that there weren't any leeches in the damp grass and trying not to urinate on her own foot.

She couldn't find any tissues in her handbag but she knew there was a packet of hand wipes in the glove compartment of her car and when she got in it the seat was so warm and smooth and *dry* that she lay down for a minute and closed the door.

She was woken by tapping on the window. She screamed and, while the sound was still hanging in the air, she saw that it was only Joe.

She rolled down the window. 'I'm sorry!' she whispered. 'I just came out for a pee. I didn't mean to go to sleep.'

Something was wrong. She could tell from the way Joe was standing in the rain and from the way that he wouldn't look at her. He handed over her BlackBerry.

'There's a call for you.'

'Who is it?' She tried to find his eyes in the dark but he was already turning away.

'It's your husband,' he said, 'apparently.'

Greg had plenty of practice at breaking bad news. When he played Mac Malone he'd done it in pretty much every episode. But back then, he'd had a script and now all he could do was gabble.

'It's your mother, Saffy. She . . . Shit, I don't know if . . .'

Saffy gripped the roof of the car to stop herself falling over, forgetting that she was already sitting down.

'What? What about my mother, Greg?'

'She collapsed. That Catweazle dude, the boyfriend – Ben? Ken?'

'Len?'

'He went round to her house and found her. It's bad . . . I mean . . . it's not good. How fast can you get here? I mean . . . to the hospital. Vincent's?'

Saffy started the engine and switched on the lights. Dripping trees and bushes sprang out from the darkness. 'An hour. An hour and a half. Is she okay, Greg? Is she going to—'

Saffy held the word 'die' in her mouth, like a splinter of glass, but she couldn't spit it out.

'I don't know. An hour and a half? Saff, where are you? I thought you were supposed to be looking after her? Shit! Pigs! I'm not on hands-free. Got to go. Hurry, okay?'

Joe was standing a few feet away from the car with his back to her in the pouring rain. His feet were bare and muddy. His black trunks were soaked through. His hair was plastered to his head.

'I have to go back to . . .' Saffy started the engine. 'My mother is . . .'

'I know.' He wouldn't look at her. 'Your *husband* told me.'

The shower was right overhead. Huge, fat drops drummed on the roof of the car. He said something she couldn't hear.

'What?'

'Do you need me to drive you?'

'No. You stay here with Liam.' She wished he'd look at her or come closer to the car. 'Joe, I can explain everything.'

'There's nothing to explain.' His voice was flat. 'I've been lied to before. I know pretty much all there is to know about it.'

'I didn't lie,' Saffy told him. 'I swear to you, Joe. I'm married to him, technically but—'

'I don't want to know. Really. Go,' he said. 'Just go.'

Part Three

♡

♥ 30 ♥

The old, bald woman lying on the metal trolley couldn't be her mother but it was. Jill was unconscious. Her body bristled with wires. Tubes ran into her arm and out of her nose and disappeared under the blue blanket. One of her bare feet stuck out at the end of the trolley, the heel was dirty and the pink nail varnish was chipped. Saffy took off her sweater and covered it.

She sat down on a grubby green plastic chair and took her mother's hand. It was cool and lifeless, as if Jill had slipped out of it, like a glove. And it was wet. For a second, Saffy couldn't understand why. Then she realised she was crying.

Someone put a hand on her shoulder. She turned around and there, in a shapeless grey jumper, was her mother's old boyfriend, Len. She had only met him a couple of times but he gave her a quick hug. Then he handed her a perfectly ironed white hanky and told her what had happened.

Jill had called him five days ago. She had told him she had the flu and asked if he could bring some groceries over.

'I was supposed to leave the bag at the door; she said she didn't want me to catch it but I managed to see her for a minute. It didn't look like flu to me but I didn't want to push it because, well, because we hadn't been in touch for a few months.'

Saffy could only imagine how her mother must have looked to someone who hadn't seen her since she started chemo.

'She said she was okay but I was worried. So I tried ringing her a few times over the last few days,' Len went on, 'but she didn't call me back. Then, tonight, I was cycling home and I thought I'd go by the house. I rang the bell and then I had a look through the glass and I saw her lying on the floor of the hall so I called the ambulance.'

'I'm so glad you were there, Len,' Saffy said. What she didn't say was, *It should have been me.*

*

A very young doctor who looked as if he was about to fall over with tiredness told Saffy and Len that he was confident they would get Jill's pneumonia under control. The bad news was that an untreated infection in her lymph nodes had developed into sepsis and there was a chance that it would not respond to antibiotics and that could mean organ failure.

A beeper on his lapel flashed and he turned it off. His nails, Saffy saw, were bitten down to the quick.

'We're doing our best but it's complicated by the background issue,' he looked tiredly at the floor, as if he would like to lie down on it and go to sleep, 'of the cancer.'

Len stared at him and then at Saffy. 'What cancer? What do you mean?'

Saffy gave him back his hanky. He needed it more now.

'It's not ideal,' Mr Kenny said, 'but all we can do is play a waiting game.' He was wearing a pale green bow tie today. He tweaked it, and looked wistfully out of the window at the golf course.

A *game*? Saffy flinched. She wanted to say something but she was too muddled. She was in an anxious, sleep-deprived stupor. She had spent the night by her mother's bed, afraid even to go to the toilet in case something happened while she was gone.

Mr Kenny closed the file. 'I'm afraid we can't continue chemo until her current medical issues are resolved and that could take some time. The worry is that, by that point, the cancer will have metastasised.'

'Metawhat?' Greg cut in.

Mr Kenny sighed. 'Spread. To other parts of her body.'

'Right and how do you know if that's happening?'

Saffy was glad Greg was here to ask these questions. She couldn't have done this on her own.

Mr Kenny frowned. 'We do a CAT scan. But when a patient is immunocompromised, we usually wait—'

'Dude, I'm not a doctor, yeah? So I don't know what that means. But we don't want to wait.' He felt wide awake for the first time in months. He felt like Mac Malone. 'We'd like you to do the CAT scan, today.'

'This is not a television series, Mr Gleeson.' Mr Kenny shook his head. 'Hospitals run according to process.'

He looked at Saffy and the flicker of irritation in his eyes turned to a flicker of recognition. He recognised her, she realised, from the beach in Killiney, where she'd seen him with Pascal.

He swallowed. 'I suppose we could do one tomorrow morning.'

'And we can see you again, tomorrow afternoon? For the results?'

'You'd have to check with my . . .' He faltered. 'Tomorrow afternoon. At three.'

Greg had called Jess and she arrived with baby wipes and clean underwear and a tracksuit for Saffy. She washed and changed in the bathroom along the corridor from her mother's room.

'You need to eat something,' Jess said as she stuffed her old clothes into a bag. 'I'll get you coffee and sandwiches and bring them up to the ward? Okay?'

'Okay,' Saffy said meekly. 'And thanks for coming. Is Conor looking after the twins?'

Jess nodded. The twins were hundreds of miles away in Cork and Conor was a million miles away in London. But Saffy had enough on her mind without having to deal with her problems.

Conor had called on Wednesday evening while she was putting the twins to bed. She had snapped at Luke because he wouldn't eat any of his dinner. Lizzie was barely speaking to her because she wouldn't believe that the fake hamster was the real Brendan.

'What is it, Conor?' She had felt exhausted just hearing his voice. 'What is it *now*?'

'I'm just calling to ask you a favour. I need to go to London for a couple of weeks. I've just heard from the agent. I have to turn some editing around pretty quickly and she thinks it'll go better if I work on the book there.'

This wasn't strictly true. Becky Kemp had mailed Conor to ask him if there was any chance he could pop over to London to talk through the edits. But he was the one who had suggested that he stay there till they were done.

He needed some time to figure out what he was going to do next. He couldn't stand the idea of even another few days living at Greg's and he couldn't go home and he had nowhere else to go. And it was killing him seeing Luke and Lizzie trying to cope with being shuttled back and forth between himself and Jess. A couple of weeks off this emotional roller-coaster would do them good. And, if he was completely honest, it would do him good, too.

'I just want to check that it's okay with you.'

'Right. And do I have a choice?'

'Of course. If you can't do it, just say so. But the sooner I get the book done the sooner I might get a deal and earn some money. You were right about Greg. He's not in a position to pay me back for the ring and, like I said, it won't be for long. A few weeks at the most. Do you think you can manage?'

A few weeks, Jess thought. *Right.* She was going to have to handle things on her own for a few weeks. And then for the rest of her life.

'Yes. I can manage. Is there anything else, Conor? I'm in the middle of putting Luke and Lizzie to bed.'

But she couldn't manage. The idea of managing made her feel so frantic that she called her parents and asked them to pick up the twins on their way to Cork the following day, making up a lie about an urgent deadline. And, after she'd kissed Luke and Lizzie goodbye, she'd climbed the stairs and closed the curtains on the blaze of blue sky outside and got into bed, fully dressed. She planned to stay there for as long as it took to get over the fact that Conor, like the real Brendan, wasn't coming back.

'So what's going on with Saffy and this Joe dude?'

Greg was jabbing the button on the drinks dispenser repeatedly, like a child. The Coke was frothed into his cup in spurts. Jess fought the urge to grab his hand and do it herself.

'I don't know, Greg. And I don't think this is the time to ask her.'

They were in the hospital cafeteria. Jess was at the coffee

machine, tipping styrofoam cups of coffee into Luke's Batman flask. How many times had she watched Conor filling it with milk or juice? How had it never occurred to her that there would be a last time, a time when he wasn't there to do it any more?

'Dude was with him last night when I called her,' Greg said. 'He answered the phone at three in the morning.'

Jess screwed the lid back on the flask. 'What does it matter, Greg? You slept with some random teenager. Saffy slept with a total stranger. And now she's with someone else. It doesn't matter. It all falls into perspective when someone is going to die.'

'Jill's not going to die.' This time Greg got the voice just right: deep but not too gruff; steady, with an undercurrent of compassion. 'She's going to make it. We're all going to make it; we just have to be strong.'

He put his arms around her. He'd sometimes wondered what it would feel like to really hold Jess. Not in a pervy way. She was just so outrageously pretty that he had been curious. But now he was holding her it felt all wrong. She was much too tall. Her elbows were pointy, like coat hangers and her hair smelled of stale cake.

'What?' Jess pulled away and started to laugh. 'Oh, God!' She put down the flask and clutched her side. 'I'm sorry. You're just so funny. You're acting like the hero in some crappy made-for-TV drama.'

'Yeah?' Greg folded his arms and began to laugh, too. 'And you're acting like a bloody pre-Madonna. As usual.'

The IV bag drained through a tangle of pin-thin plastic tubing into the line in Jill's arm. After two hours and twenty-seven minutes it was just over half-empty and Saffy felt she would recognise every single drop if she ever saw it again, along with every detail of the tiny, overheated room.

The scuffed swing door; the battered steel locker; the plastic bin with the peeling yellow biohazard sticker on the lid. The small basin and the roll of hospital-issue green paper towel. The dark mirror of the window with its crooked grubby cream blind. The faded print of *The Gleaners* that hung, slightly crookedly, on the wall above the bed.

Jill had been unconscious for three days now. When Saffy couldn't stand to look at her mother's motionless body and her closed eyes and slack face and her limp arms, spotted with purple and green bruises from all the blood tests, she stared at the IV bag instead.

The softly spoken Lebanese doctor who did the seven a.m. round this morning had told her that if Jill didn't recover consciousness in the next week or so the next step would be to put a peg in her stomach for a feeding tube.

'This might be not necessary,' he said when he saw her face crumple; 'she might, of herself, turn this corner.'

But even if Jill turned this corner, there were other, darker corners. Even if she recovered from the pneumonia and the sepsis, there was still the cancer. Mr Kenny was not happy with the CAT scans. There was something that looked like a lesion on the bone. He wanted to do a marrow extraction as soon as Jill was strong enough.

The thought of what could be ahead terrified her. She wished Joe was here. He couldn't have done anything to stop what might happen, but if she could just put her head on his chest and listen to his heart beating and feel his arms around her, she knew she would be able to get through this.

Surely he would want to know how Jill was doing? Surely he'd be interested? Surely he'd appreciate a call? She found her phone and she stared at the small screen for a long time, trying to think of what to say. Then she put it back in her bag again.

When she had tried to explain why she hadn't told him she was married he had said, 'I don't want to know.' There was no loophole in those five words. No space for ambiguity. It was like Joe himself. Clear. Direct. Honest. She stared hard at the IV tube and watched a drop form and fatten and fall. He had meant what he said. And she couldn't blame him.

31

Sometimes Saffy managed to sleep for a few hours here and there, sitting upright in the armchair she had dragged in from the TV room. Everything solid she swallowed threatened to come back up again. She survived on coffee and cigarettes, smoked outside the main door of the hospital with old men in wheel-chairs and women in dressing gowns who dragged their IV stands behind them.

Jess came and sat with her during the day and Greg came every evening, bringing grapes that Jill couldn't eat and flowers that she couldn't smell and the latest Marian Keyes book, which, Saffy thought, with a lump the size of a fist in her throat, her mother might never read.

One night, when she came back from the loo, she heard his voice and she stood at the door for a while, watching him sitting in a moulded plastic chair by the bed holding up *OK!* magazine as if Jill could see it.

'Man, look at this. Anne Robinson's had a shedload more surgery: cheek implants, eyes, lip filler, veneers. She looks kind of foxy. I mean, she's no Dame Helen Mirren but in a certain light . . .' He turned a page.

'David Beckham has had another tattoo. I was thinking of one a few months back but scratch that. Dude's arm looks like the sleeve of some stretchy long-sleeved T-shirt from Primark.'

Saffy had never seen him so focused on anyone, except, of course, himself.

Len usually arrived an hour or so after Greg left. He had a key to Jill's house and he brought roses and sweet peas from her garden. Once he had arrived with a pair of cream fluffy mules. He had lined them up carefully under the bed, ready for a time when Jill might step into them.

Saffy usually went to the café for half an hour to give him time with her mother and, when she came back, he'd already have his jacket and his bicycle clips on and his eyes would be red. He'd give her an awkward hug before he left and, though this meant choking on a mouthful of jumper, she didn't mind.

She got to know the nurses. Pamela, the freckly blonde who always smelled of Red Bull and cigarettes and chatted to Jill while she switched her IV bags and took her blood pressure and adjusted her catheter. Harimi who hummed Indian songs while she changed her sheets. Rosa, from the Philippines, who rubbed Vaseline into her skin after her bed bath.

One night, Saffy went through Jill's toilet bag and took her chipped nail varnish off and cut her nails and rubbed her feet with peppermint cream. She remembered the oil she'd bought for Joe and the way he'd raise an eyebrow and grin when she offered to massage his back and then she was remembering other things. Ordinary things that she didn't even know she'd noticed.

The way he dried himself after a shower, towelling his hair first and then his legs and then his arms, then his body. The way he ate, like an American, with a fork and how his free hand made a loose fist on the table. The way he rubbed his eyebrows with his thumb and forefinger when he was tired. The way he slept on his back, with one arm behind his head and the other thrown across her.

She had lost him. And soon she would lose these tiny fragments of him, too. That was what life seemed to come down to, she was beginning to realise. Losing things. And even now, while her mother was still here, still alive, still breathing in spaced-out staccato sighs, Saffy was losing parts of her, too. The mental picture she had always had of her mother as young and strong and glamorous was being erased by the reality of the sick, vulnerable woman lying motionless in the bed. The assumption that Jill would always be around, pushing her buttons and overstepping her boundaries, was being overwritten by the fear that maybe she wouldn't.

Saffy patted Jill's feet dry with a paper towel and tucked them back under the covers. She kissed her mother on the cheek and turned out the light. Then she curled up in her chair and cried quietly, the way you learn to cry in hospitals.

*

Jess had called Komodo and filled Vicky in on what was happening.

Ciara and Vicky sent texts every day, sending her love and asking if she needed anything.

Ant sent a single MMS picture of his forehead which had *Kind Thoughts* written on it in biro.

An enormous ceramic pot of orchids arrived from Marsh, who also texted every day. Sometimes twice a day. Or more.

At the start, her texts were reassuring, or as reassuring as anything typed in block capitals could be. Marsh always wrote her texts in capitals.

BEST WISHES FOR MOTHER'S RECOVERY, EVERYONE AT
KOMODO WISHING YOU WELL. M

Then the tone began to change.

DON'T FEEL YOU HAVE TO RUSH BACK. TAKE YOUR
TIME. WILL A WEEK BE ENOUGH? M

HOW MUCH LONGER WILL YOU BE ABSENT? M

HOPE YOU CAN PICK UP MAILS AT HOSPITAL. COPYING
YOU IN ON ALL WHITE FEATHER WIP TO KEEP YOU IN
THE LOO. M

She had obviously meant to type 'loop'. Was this a Freudian slip?' The last time Saffy had seen her was the afternoon she'd been making out with Mike in the toilet at Komodo. Was Marsh insane? How could she imagine that she would pick up her emails at a time like this? She decided to ignore it.

The next one was even more outrageous.

WHITE FEATHER PRE-PRO TOMORROW AT 9. SIGN-OFF
ON LOCATIONS AND BUDGET. PLEASE ATTEND. 2
HOURS MAX. M.

Saffy had no intention of going but, after an hour staring at the IV bag and *The Gleaners*, she began to wonder if she could afford not to. She was on thin ice with Marsh after the Mike thing and she didn't want to make things worse.

She asked Greg to bring in a shirt and a trouser suit and shoes from the apartment and he offered to come in at seven and spend the morning with Jill. Saffy had already got used to washing in the ward bathroom but this time she had a proper shower and dry-shampooed her hair with a can that Pam, the red-haired nurse, lent her. She hadn't driven for nearly a week and she felt shaky and reckless as she slipped out into the rush-hour traffic, as if she was the one who had been sick and she still hadn't recovered.

The poster on Ant's door said: *Too many freaks. Not enough circuses.* Saffy had a feeling of dread. It was always like this with a big shoot. Everybody had an opinion and everybody intended to fight for it. Vicky had once observed that a seven-hundred-thousand-euro budget could bring out the raving egotist in His Holiness the Dalai Lama.

People were milling around the boardroom. Saffy was so used to dressing gowns and white coats that she felt as if she had arrived at a fancy dress party. There was Marsh as a femme fatale in a navy Roland Mouret dress. Grizzled Ben Rosen as a Hell's Angel in jeans and a leather biker jacket. Simon as a businessman in a suit that he had probably bought just for the occasion.

There was Ant who looked like a bad-tempered baby in black overalls. And Vicky, also in black, who looked like death. And Mike, in his slacks and short-sleeved shirt, who looked, as he always did, like an off-duty bus driver. He blushed so furiously when he met Saffy's eye that she thought his head was going to burst into flames.

She introduced herself to Dylan Rick, Ben's assistant, who looked like a tiny, Asian Clark Kent in a dark suit and glasses and a pair of diamond baguette earrings. And shook hands with Nervous Dermot, who looked spectacularly rabbity in a beige jumper and chinos. She had never seen him looking quite so twitchy.

'I heard about your mother,' he said. 'That must be very hard for you so soon after your father had his heart attack. How is he?'

'He died,' Saffy said quietly. Marsh did a double take but she didn't care. It was true. She didn't have the energy to tell another lie.

'I'm sorry.' He squeezed her hand. 'I'm so sorry for your loss.'

'Thank you, that means a lot,' Saffy said. And she meant it.

Saffy pretended to be listening to Dylan talking through the production agenda but she wasn't really there. Ninety per cent of her attention had travelled the two and a half miles back to the hospital and taken the lift up to her mother's ward and opened the door. And it was sitting by her bed now, willing her to wake up.

She missed it completely when Nervous Dermot dropped his bombshell. She only realised that something had happened when Vicky kicked her under the table.

'All I'm saying,' he was nibbling his thumbnail, 'is that you're going to have to look again.'

'Let's just be real here, Dermot.' Ben Rosen waded in with his alpha male drawl. 'We've had five casting sessions in all. Two in Dublin. Two in London. One in New York. We've seen around a hundred people—'

'That's my *point*!' Nervous Dermot insisted. 'We're not looking for a flipping *person*! We're looking for a *flipping* angel. And you haven't shown me one yet.'

There was a collective intake of breath. Nervous Dermot had never sworn before, so hearing him saying 'flipping' was just so wrong.

'Nervous Dermot is right,' Mike said.

Seven heads swivelled to his face. Seven pairs of eyes blinked in disbelief.

'What I mean is,' Mike said, 'you're *right* to be nervous, Dermot. Nobody we've seen here today has what it takes. For my money, there is only one man out there who is right for the White Feather angel.'

He examined a dark stain on his yellow tie. It was in the shape of Spain. Saffy wondered if his wife knew that he'd been having an affair. If the awful clothes, the grubby ties, the holey socks were some kind of revenge.

'It's the actor who played Mac Malone on *The Station*,' Mike went on. 'Greg Gleeson.'

Saffy couldn't believe what she was hearing.

'Greg Gleeson?' Ant grabbed Vicky's sleeve. 'Tell these ass-holes that Gleeson's too plastic and shiny and fake,' he hissed, 'and—'

'Wait a sec.' Rosen held up his hand. 'Who is this guy?'

Dylan Googled Greg and clicked on a shot and it filled the screen. He was standing in a field without his shirt on holding the reins of a horse. Greg didn't like horses normally but he was looking at this one as if he was in love with it.

'That's him!' Nervous Dermot's nose twitched in double time. He sat forward and pointed at the screen. 'That's our angel. If we can get him, I'm happy to go ahead. If not the shoot is off.'

In the pause that followed, three-quarters of a million invisible euros floated just out of reach in the air above the table. There wasn't time for another casting session. Even if there was, they had already spent their casting budget.

Ben and Dylan flashed one another a quick look and rolled over without a whimper.

'That guy definitely has *something*,' Dylan said.

'He's kinda camp.' Rosen rubbed his chin. 'But I'm confident we can rough him up a bit. I like him. Yeah, I really like him.'

'Good call, Dermot.' Simon wasn't going to pass up an opportunity to schmooze. 'He's bang on the money for the White Feather target market.'

Marsh put her arms over her head and stretched like a cat. There was a tiny shadow of stubble, Saffy noticed, in her armpit. 'People, we have our guy!'

Ant leaned over and began banging his forehead on the table.

Vicky cut in. 'What Ant is trying to say is that Greg's too closely associated to a character in a soap and he's a bit, sorry, Saffy, but he's really, really short.'

'We can trick the height thing.' Dylan frowned. 'But if he's tied into a soap we might have contract and fee issues.'

'His character was killed off a few months back,' Simon smirked. 'The guy's not doing anything except product promos.'

Ben Rosen nodded. 'Hell, what are we waiting for? Let's bring him in!' He turned to Marsh. 'Anyone got the name of his agent?'

Marsh smiled. 'I don't know the name of his *agent*, Ben.'

March fluttered a perfectly manicured hand at Saffy. 'But you're looking at his *wife*.'

For as long as he could remember, Conor had thought he was greedy and he had lived with the clammy shame that was the price tag for a second portion of dinner, a double helping of dessert or a couple of cold, half-eaten fish fingers from the twins' plates.

He thought his appetite was part of his DNA, like curly hair and freckles. But lately, he and food had developed a strange, new relationship. The spark had died. The passion was gone.

He walked past the hotel breakfast buffet with its huge stainless-steel vats of sausage and egg and bacon and fixed himself a bowl of fresh fruit and a cup of coffee. As he sat down at his table, he saw himself in a mirror on the wall opposite. It was ironic. He had never looked better but he had never felt worse.

When he had booked this trip to London, he thought he would use the time away to make a decision about his relationship with Jess. But, now that he was here, he was beginning to realise that he'd already made the decision.

He'd had fights with Jess before but he could never stay angry for long. He'd make the first move and she'd soften and come back to him. That was how it had always worked. But he couldn't do it. Not this time.

If it came down to a choice between being right and being happy – and all rows came down to that in the end – then they had had their last row, because this time, he would rather be right.

Becky Kemp was nothing like the picture on the Douglas, Kemp & Troy website. She still had the glasses, but the frames were flecked with the same muddy green as her eyes and her hair was more red than brown and she was incredibly shy.

'Hello. Well, it's great to finally . . .' She leaned over as if she was going to kiss his cheek and then changed her mind and stuck out her hand to shake his. And when he took it, it was clammy, which made him, for some reason, feel less awkward.

Her office was cramped and neat and book-lined, with just enough room for a desk and two chairs. She brought him a cup of coffee and then managed to spill most of it onto his leg.

'It's okay.' He mopped it up with the tissue she found for him. 'I've already had too much caffeine this morning. I've got the shakes.'

She smiled at him gratefully and they settled down to go through her feedback on *Doubles or Quits*.

'It looks like more work than it is,' she said apologetically a couple of times.

'No, this is good. This is great,' he told her, and he meant it. There was quite a bit of work to do but he could tell from her comments that she got the book. And whenever she picked up a plot inconsistency, she suggested a solution.

She talked rapidly and slightly breathlessly, and while she talked, she kept gathering her hair into a tight pony-tail with her hands, and then letting it go so that as she moved her head, it unravelled again in gleaming coppery strands.

'You can work here in the office,' she said when they had come to the end of her list. 'I mean . . . not *this* office but . . . my partner David's away so you could work in *his* office if you need to.'

Partner. Did she mean partner or *partner*? 'I'm staying at a hotel. I can work there.'

He had borrowed Greg's laptop and set it up on the desk in his room. There was a print shop around the corner if he needed it.

'As long as you're comfortable.'

'If you could see where I wrote the book,' Conor thought of the alcove under the stairs, of having to stash the swivel chair sideways after he'd finished, 'you might not say that.'

'Look . . . I . . .' She began twisting her hair again. 'I know there are no guarantees, Conor, but I have a really good feeling about you. I mean,' she let her hair go and made a tent of her slender, pale fingers, 'your *book*.'

She slid her notes across the desk to him. 'I'm sure you'll fly through the edits. Oh, God! I don't mean to put you under pressure. What I mean is, I'm sure you'll want to get through them quickly so you can get back to your wife and your kids.'

'Well, not really. I mean . . .' It was Conor's turn to stumble over his words. 'My . . . . . . my *partner* and I are not together any more. We . . .' What was the word? Even after he found it, he didn't know if he could really say it. It seemed so formal. So final. 'We separated. A few weeks ago.'

He bit his lip. What was he doing spilling his guts to this woman? They'd only just met. It was stupid this feeling he had that she knew him really well because she'd read his book.

'Oh dear. Oh, I'm sorry. I hope this isn't making things worse, I mean, I hope we haven't dragged you over here at a bad time.'

'No.' He met her eyes. This much he did know. 'This is a good time. This is what we all need, as a matter of fact.'

'Well.' Becky gathered her notes and found an envelope for them. 'I hope it works. I mean, I hope things work out for the best.'

Conor stood up. 'Me too.'

Conor's plan was to lock himself into his hotel room and spend every waking hour working his way through Becky's edits. He had managed to write for hours at a stretch back in Dublin, but editing was different. A small change in one chapter could have a knock-on effect in the next six.

He had to hold so much information in his head that his brain started to melt if he didn't have a break every couple of hours.

His hotel was in Soho and, when he needed to clear his head, he would take a walk across to Hyde Park or stroll over to Covent Garden through Chinatown, where the air crackled with the smell of burning chillies and the shops sold fruits and vegetables he'd never seen before. He studied the cardboard, hand-written signs above the baskets. Was a rambutan hairy all the way through, he wondered. Did a durian fruit taste as bad as it smelled?

He started skipping the hotel breakfast and bringing his note-book to Patisserie Valerie every morning to plan his day. And when the Latvian waitress with the Meryl Streep cheekbones asked him if he was a writer, he told her he was a teacher before he remembered that this wasn't true. Not any more.

Wasn't this what writers did? Sit in cafés and take long walks to straighten out the characters in their heads? All he needed to complete the cliché was a freezing garret. Which was probably what he was going to have when he got back to Dublin. He couldn't stay at Greg's any longer and he couldn't move back in with Jess and the twins.

Becky had been straight with him. There was no guarantee that he'd get a deal. But whatever happened, he was never going to set foot in a school again. He would clean toilets or stack shelves before he'd stand in front of a room full of teenagers again. It was over now. He wasn't going back.

Jess had only called him once, to tell him that Saffy's mother had been taken to hospital. The conversation had lasted less than a minute and Conor was glad about that. He had been lonely before, but never as lonely as he was talking to the woman he loved as if she was a stranger. She'd told him it was better if he didn't talk to the twins in case it upset them and he hadn't pushed it, though he had wanted to hear their voices so badly it hurt.

He had ordered flowers to be sent to Saffy's mum at the hospital. Standing in the shop, inhaling the pepper and sherbet smell of the roses, it crossed his mind to send a bouquet to Jess but he had no idea what he would say.

'I'm sorry?' The truth was he was sad but he wasn't sorry. 'I love you?' He did love her but loving her wasn't enough any more. And simply saying it again wasn't going to change that.

Jess had never liked cut flowers anyway. She always said she preferred them when they were stuck in the ground.

Becky called every day to see if he had any questions about her edits. Conor looked forward to talking to her. It was easier on the phone. When her hair and her fluttering hands weren't part of the equation, he found he held up his end of the conversation quite nicely.

A couple of times she asked, hesitantly, if he was okay and he guessed that she was checking to see if he was moping in his room, missing his family, so he made up some Irish friends who lived in London and told her he saw them every day or two.

But one evening, when he was sitting at a window table in a

Vietnamese restaurant on Frith Street, she passed by and, before he knew what he was doing, he knocked on the window. She waved and walked by but a few minutes later she sent a text: WANT COMPANY?

He texted back: SURE. And in just a few moments, she walked into the restaurant and did that flustered I'm-going-to-kiss-you-on-the-cheek-oh-hang-on-I'm-not-I'm-going-to-shake-your-hand thing, and then she sat down opposite him. She was wearing a cream skirt and T-shirt and she had a pale green bracelet on one arm, thin and delicate as a grass stalk with a single daisy on the clasp. She looked fresh and cool, as if she'd just come in from a walk in a garden. He was glad he'd showered and changed into a clean shirt before he came out. She put on a pair of dark-rimmed glasses and opened the menu and then shut it again, knocking over his water glass.

'I'll just have what you're having,' she said when he'd mopped up the water, using both their napkins. 'It's too hot to think and it's all lovely in here anyway.'

She asked for a beer and Conor decided to have one too, though he didn't usually have a drink till he'd finished work and he still had a few hours of edits to do after dinner. The dish they ordered turned out to be a do-it-yourself job. There were rice pancakes and bunches of herbs and matchsticks of carrot and bowls of dipping sauce, and assembling everything kept Conor and Becky distracted till the first beer kicked in and, by time they had both finished their second, neither of them was nervous any more. Becky talked about a film she'd seen and a walking holiday she was planning to take in Greece.

She took a pencil and an envelope out of her bag and drew the outline of Crete for him.

'We'll be walking from Chora Sfakion to Paleochora. It's mostly goat paths and they're pretty treacherous,' she doodled a goat's head with curly horns, 'but it's a bit of a cheat really because we won't have to carry our luggage. Someone will drive it on to wherever we're staying the next night. I can't wait.'

There was a small stalk of coriander caught in her hair. Conor wondered whether or not to mention it. His mother had always said that a man should tell a woman if her skirt was caught up in her knickers. He had often picked crumbs out of Jess's hair but he wasn't clear on the rules where strangers and coriander were involved.

'And do and your *partner* do much walking here in England? Or just on holiday?' Conor asked.

'Oh, I don't have a partner.' She blushed, her freckles fading then reappearing as the colour in her cheeks died away. 'I mean, not in that way. I used to be married for a while. But I'm not any more. I'm going with a friend. She's very girly. It's going to be a bit of a struggle getting her out of high heels and into walking boots actually.'

They had another beer and then another. The restaurant had filled up around them and Conor felt buoyed up by the wave of chatter. It was nice to be out of his hotel room. It was nice to be talking to someone.

Becky asked if he had pictures of the twins and he flipped open his wallet. She put her glasses back on to look at them.

'Photos of kids are what a man carries in his wallet,' she quoted, 'where his money used to be.'

'Except I didn't have any.' Conor laughed. 'Money, I mean. God! I'm sorry, that sounds awful. As if I'm trying to guilt you into getting me a deal.'

She began doing that thing with her hair again. 'No, I don't think that. Honestly. But as you're so desperate,' she smiled, 'I'll do my best for *Doubles or Quits*.'

He laughed. 'Well, that's good news because I am officially unemployed and possibly unemployable as a teacher. There was a situation with one of the kids at the academy where I was teaching exam revision courses.'

'Oh!' Her eyes widened and he realised she might be wondering if he was some sort of a paedophile.

'No,' he said. 'It was nothing like *that*.'

He told her about Graham Turvey and the fight he'd broken up and about Wayne Cross's dad trying to blackmail him and about getting suspended from St Peter's.

She shook her head when he was finished. 'I can't believe the way they treated you. You did absolutely the right thing, Conor. You had no other option.'

'You think?'

'Of course!' She shuddered. 'You'll never know what would have happened to that boy if you hadn't stepped in. He could have been seriously hurt.'

Conor paid the bill while Becky was in the Ladies. Outside, the air was warm and soupy. Crowds of people were milling around outside pubs and restaurants. Conor suddenly realised it was Friday night. He didn't feel like going back to the hotel. He had been lonely, he realised. He just hadn't realised how lonely he'd been. He wondered whether he should suggest going for another drink.

'I'd better let you get back to work,' she said before he had a chance to say anything.

She leaned over and gave him a quick hug then walked away. It was only when she got as far as the corner that he saw that her skirt *was* caught up in her knickers.

It felt like about fifty people were squeezed into the tiny casting suite to watch Greg stripped down to his AussieBum trunks, try-ing to charm the pants off Nervous Dermot and Ben Rosen.

'Can you turn around, Reg?' Ben Rosen said. Greg did a slow 360.

'I dunno, I'm not hundred per cent sure about the ass.' Rosen turned to Dylan. 'You're the expert. Whaddya think?'

Greg was sweating under the lights. He wished Saffy was here for moral support but she was at the hospital.

Dylan folded his arms. 'It's a sizeable butt, you know, with those little legs and all. But he'll be wearing a loincloth and we can always do a bit of CGI on it afterwards.'

'No, you can't. Don't touch it,' Nervous Dermot said rever-ently. 'It's perfect. Everything about him is perfect. If I was a woman and I imagined an angel, he would look *exactly* like that.'

One of the night nurses found Saffy stretched out asleep on a bench in the nurses' kitchen and shook her awake.

'This is ridiculous. It might be weeks before your mother

comes round. You have to pace yourself. Go home and get a decent night's sleep.'

Saffy called a cab and went back to Jill's house. The garden had been taken over by weeds and Kevin Costner, who had got used to being fed by Mrs O'Keefe, hissed at her as if she was a stranger. It was nine days since she'd slept in a proper bed and she fell into a light, anxious sleep. She was too scared to let go. What if her mother woke up alone and frightened in her dark hospital room or, worse, what if she died while Saffy wasn't there? What if her presence by the bed every night was the thing that was keeping her mother alive?

'You sound exhausted, Saffy,' Jess said, when she rang. 'Go back to sleep. You need it. I'll drop in for a couple of hours and sit with Jill.'

When Saffy woke up again it was nearly twelve. She showered and dressed quickly, stumbling over Kevin Costner, who had suddenly decided that he was pleased to see her and was winding himself around her legs.

At the hospital she was too impatient to wait for the lift. She took the stairs, holding her breath as much as she could. The worst of the hospital smell gathered in the stairwell. For some reason, it seemed especially bad today, a fug of urine and boiled vegetables and the sharp, dark scent of rotting geraniums that she was beginning to realise was the smell of dying people.

She took a short cut through the orthopaedic ward, passing by a line of old people who were being made to exercise after their hip operations. Through the open doors of the shared wards she saw huddled figures in beds, two teenage girls in neck braces sitting back to back sharing an iPod, a nurse spoon-feeding a man with a cast on each arm.

Then she turned the corner and saw Jess and Greg standing at the end of the corridor that led to her mother's ward. Her breath caught. Something had happened. She knew she shouldn't have left her mother on her own!

She broke into a run but, as as she overtook the lunch trolley, she was met with an unexpected waft of boiled meat and burned toast and scrambled eggs and her stomach did a somersault and she had to dive off the corridor and through the open door of a toilet cubicle. She kneeled on the damp floor by the bowl and threw up the cup of coffee she'd drunk in the car.

'Saffy?' Jess was at the door.

'What is it? What happened? Is she okay?'

'I was just about to text you. Your mum's come round. She's awake! She's not making any sense but they say not to worry about that. It'll take time for her speech to come back properly.'

Jill was propped up into a lopsided sitting position. Her eyes were unfocused but they were open and that was all that mattered.

'Pieces of my face keep touching pieces of my face.' She blinked at Saffy. 'Why am I crying?'

Saffy wiped her eyes and sat down on the edge of the bed. Her knees were weak and she felt dizzy and she realised that part of her had thought that Jill was never coming back.

'Don't try to talk, Mum. You've been asleep for a few days. You need to take things slowly.'

Pamela brought in a tray with a plate with a stainless-steel cover. 'I heard Sleeping Beauty was awake. Some solid food would be an idea but I think we should keep her away from the knives till she gets her mind back.' She gave Greg a flirty look. 'Maybe Mac Malone here would like to feed her?'

Greg lifted the cover. 'Corned beef and cabbage.' He made a face. 'I thought that went out with the harp.'

'The ark, Greg.' Jess rolled her eyes.

The smell of cabbage caught at the back of Saffy's throat and she had to stand up, open the window and take a few breaths of fresh air.

When she turned around, Jill's eyes were closed.

Jess saw Saffy's face. 'It's okay. She's just tired, I think. She ate a spoonful of cabbage and . . .'

Saffy winced. 'Can you not talk about food for a minute?'

Greg stood up. 'I've got to go. I just dropped in to bring Jess a coffee. It's brilliant about Jill, Saff. And if you hear anything, anything at all, about the White Feather casting, call me, okay?'

Saffy took her mother's hand. It was lighter now than it had been when she was unconscious. She could feel the life in it, close to the surface of her skin.

'Saffy, you've been feeling sick a couple of times lately, right?' Jess was staring at her.

'What? Yeah. A couple of times. It's probably the stress and the vomiting bug. There's always one ward in here that's closed down because of it.'

'When was your last period?'

'I don't know. A few weeks ago, I think. It'll be in my diary in my bag.'

Her periods were always erratic but she always kept a note of Day 1. Jess pulled it out of her bag and flipped back through the pages. The last red circle Saffy had made was on 1 May. Today was 14 August.

'I probably forgot to mark it in. My cycle always goes out of synch when I'm— Jess!' The air left her lungs as if she'd been punched in the chest. 'You don't think . . . ?'

'Well, if you haven't had a period since May . . .'

'I must have had one.' Saffy grabbed the diary and began to rifle through it.

'Two,' Jess said. 'If the last one was on May the first, you should have had two. Maybe even three.'

When Jess came back with the pregnancy kit Saffy took it to the toilet up the corridor. It still smelled of her vomit. She peed on the stick and hurried back to her mother's room.

She stared at it for a long time, long after the two blue lines appeared.

Jess held her hand and squeezed it. 'You'd better tell Joe about this,' she said.

'It isn't Joe's, Jess.' Saffy felt as if the room was shrinking or she was expanding or both. 'Joe had a vasectomy.'

'God! It's not that Australian guy . . . ?'

Saffy shook her head. 'That was in February.'

'Well then, it must be Greg's. When did you last have sex with Greg?'

'I don't know, May sometime. But we used a condom. We always use a condom . . .' She stopped. 'Except for this one time. The night of the hen party. I was half asleep. Shit. Do you think . . . ?' She stared at Jess miserably.

Jess did the maths in her head. 'I think you're just over three months' pregnant.'

'I'm pregnant?' Jill's opened her eyes and smiled at them. 'Congratulations.'

32

'I think you're probably spot-on about the conception date.' The doctor in the walk-in clinic peeled off her latex gloves and sat down at her desk again. 'You're about thirteen weeks on.'

It *was* Greg's baby. It wasn't the doctor's fault but Saffy hated her anyway. She hated her immaculate coat and her blonde pony-tail and her tanned legs and her perfect little feet in her strappy beige sandals.

Saffy swung her own feet down off the examination table. They were half a size bigger and nothing fit except her flip-flops. She started to get dressed.

'There's a great new gynaecologist at the Rotunda. He's just back from the States. I can refer you to him or you could think about Holles Street.'

'I'm not sure that'll be necessary.'

The doctor didn't turn around. 'Right. So you don't want a referral to a maternity hospital, then?'

'I don't think so.' Saffy tried to fasten the zip of her skirt but the waistband wouldn't close. She'd been living in stretchy tracksuits at the hospital. She hadn't realised that nothing fit properly any more, except for the adjective 'fat'.

She pulled her T-shirt down over the gappy zip and opened her bag to find her purse. 'Look, I know you can't talk to me about this so it's okay. I did a test but I just wanted to be absolutely sure.'

The doctor turned around and looked at her kindly, which just made Saffy feel even worse. 'Do you have options? Is the father involved?'

'We're separated.'

'What about doing it on your own with his support?'

'I don't think so,' Saffy snapped. 'My mother was a single parent. It's not exactly a walk in the park, you know.'

'Yeah, I do.' She smiled. 'But it has its upsides.'

Saffy followed her eyes to some snapshots pinned to the

corkboard over her desk. A blonde girl blowing out four candles on a birthday cake, asleep with her arm around a teddy bear, standing on tiptoe in a snowy garden.

'As you can see,' the doctor said, 'the father is not in the picture. So I know what you're going through. And if you decide to go ahead with your pregnancy, you know where I am. Oh, and don't worry about feeling like you hate everyone. It's a hormonal thing.'

Saffy was going to take Greg to the pub across the road to break the news, but Len hadn't arrived and she didn't want to leave Jill on her own. So she told him in the tiny hospital room, while they were sitting on either side of the bed with her mother asleep between them, like a lumpy wall.

She closed her eyes so she didn't have to see Greg's mouth open to let out whatever tactless thing he was going to say. She kept it simple.

'I'm pregnant, Greg. It happened on the hen night. It's your baby. But you don't have to do anything, okay? I'll deal with it.'

He didn't say anything and, when she opened her eyes, he was staring at her in that Jesusy way again. 'You can do this, Babe.'

He said it as if he was telling her she could rewire a plug or change a printer cartridge.

'Are you giving me permission to have an abortion, Greg? Because I don't *need*—'

'No, I'm not. I'm not talking about an abortion. I'm saying you can have this kid. You're ready for it. You just don't know it, that's all.'

'I don't want a baby, Greg. You know I've never wanted a baby.'

This wasn't strictly true. For a fraction of a second, when she thought it might be Joe's, before she remembered that it couldn't be, the closed door in her heart had opened but it had shut again.

'Come on, Saff. You're over a third of the way there already. The worst part is probably over. Except for the birth, obviously. But they give you lots of drugs for that.'

God, he was so naïve. 'A child doesn't take up nine months of your life, Greg. A child takes up eighteen years, minimum.'

Or more, she thought. She was thirty-three and still living in her mother's house.

'And it's definitely mine?' Greg narrowed his eyes. 'Not that Australian dude who—'

'No!'

'What about the other guy? The one who answered the phone the night your mum collapsed?'

Saffy shook her head. 'God, Greg, do you have to make me sound like such a slut? No. It's not Joe's.'

'But you haven't done a DNA test or anything?'

'He can't have children, Greg, okay?'

'What about that little ginger that was hassling you in the supermarket? I saw the three of you in the car park through the window of the manager's office and—'

'He had Liam years ago and then he had a vasectomy.'

'Is that a fact? The dude shoots blanks.' He looked pleased.

'Look, I don't even know why we're talking about this. It's yours, okay?'

Jill stirred. They waited until she had settled down again.

Greg lowered his voice to a whisper. 'I believe you, I just think it's pretty amazing. That was probably the only time we've ever had unprotected sex, except that weekend in Ibiza when we were in the swimming pool after everyone went to bed and you—'

'Stop!' she whispered. 'I don't want to go there.'

He shrugged. 'That's cool. I just think that it seems like fate, you know, to get pregnant from just that one time. Maybe this baby is like that band, you know? Destiny's Child.'

She put her head in her hands. Only Greg, she thought, could move a conversation from a termination to Beyoncé.

'Think about it, Saff,' he was saying now. 'We made a little baby!'

She hated it when people said 'little baby'. 'Little' as opposed to *what*? 'Huge'?

'Greg, I'm on my own. I'm broke. My mother is ill. I have an incredibly stressful job . . .'

'You're not on your own, Babe,' he said. 'I'm here.' He reached across the hump of her mother's knees and took her hand. It was strange seeing their hands together again. 'Look, it's

384

your call, but if this happened six months ago I would have been here for you. And all I'm saying is, I'm still here and I'm not going anywhere.'

She avoided his eyes and looked out of the window. A man with a post-stroke shuffle was crossing the car park with a nurse.

'But it didn't happen six months ago . . .'

'I know. I fucked up. You fucked up,' he said quietly.

She waited for him to decline the rest of the verb. *He fucked up. She fucked up. We fucked up.*

'But we have something we didn't have six months ago, Babe. We're married. We could do this together, Saffy. We could have this baby!'

She stared out at the man in the car park below, standing, docile as a well-trained dog, while the nurse chatted on her mobile phone.

'I'm confused, Greg. Do you want us to be a couple again? Is that what you're saying?'

'Yeah,' he grinned, 'it is. Look, you don't have to decide right away. You can move back into the apartment and I can look after you and we can take the whole married thing one day at a time. Then, when the baby comes, we can look after it together. You can keep working, I can stay at home, between jobs . . .'

Saffy shook her head. 'What jobs? You haven't worked for months.'

He grinned. 'I got the White Feather gig. Lauren hasn't signed yet but she's pushed them to twenty-five grand.'

'You're joking! That would completely wipe out the agency mark-up.'

'Yeah, but if they don't have me on board, that will completely wipe out the ad.'

She must have dozed off after Greg left because she dreamed that she was in Killiney with her mother. They had been for a swim and they were sitting on the rocks in the sun, drying off. Her mother had the long blonde hair she'd had when Saffy was a little girl but she was wearing her hospital gown and she had an IV line and an oxygen mask.

Pascal and Mr Kenny swam past and waved. Jill waved back

and then she turned to Saffy. 'What are you going to do?' Her voice was muffled by the mask.

Saffy looked down and saw she was naked and very pregnant, as if she might be going to give birth any minute. 'I don't know.'

Her mother stood up and wrung out her hair. 'Well, don't do anything I wouldn't do!' She pulled out the IV line, took off the oxygen mask and dived into the water.

Saffy woke up with a start. Her mother was sitting up in the bed, looking at her.

'Who will look after me when I'm gone?' she said. Then she shook her head in frustration.

Saffy took her hand. 'It's okay, I think I know what you mean. You mean who will look after *me* when *you're* gone.' Everything her mother said was still coming out backwards, but she was aware of it now and the nurses said that was a good sign.

'You must have thought,' Saffy said quietly, 'of having an abortion. You must have wished sometimes that I hadn't happened.'

Her mother frowned. 'They tried to make you get rid of me, but you wouldn't let them.'

She shook her head again as if she was trying to shake the words loose so they would come out in the right order.

'I'm the best thing that ever happened to you, Sadbh.'

'I know you are, Mum. Don't get upset. Why don't you have a rest?'

Jill lay down again, exhausted. Saffy watched her sleep for a while and then she remembered the photographs. She opened her bag and took out the picture Jill had given her of her dad and a second picture that she'd taken off the mantelpiece in her mother's living room. It was a photograph of Jill and Saffy taken in a beach restaurant on that last holiday in Tenerife.

They were standing with their backs to the sea. Her mother was wearing a pink bikini and a matching-lipstick-smile and she had her arm around Saffy's waist. Saffy was wearing white jeans and a long-sleeved blue T-shirt and she wasn't smiling but she wasn't scowling either. In fact, she was leaning very slightly towards her mother, so that their heads were almost touching. It was a lovely picture. After Jill got better, she might ask if she could borrow it to get a copy.

She put the two frames on the window sill, close together so that it was almost as if the three of them were in the same picture. Her father, in his forties and handsome, smoking his cigarette. Her mother, tanned and beautiful and, magically, the same age as he was. And Saffy between them, awkward, but prettier than she had known back then. They were a family. They had always been a family, even if she hadn't known it.

It was only much later, when Saffy was standing by the machine, trying to find money to pay for her parking ticket, that she realised what her mother had been trying to tell her.

She had said, 'I'm the best thing that ever happened to you.' But she was trying to say, '*You're* the best thing that ever happened to *me*.'

Simon smirked at Saffy as she passed his office. 'Wrong time, wrong place,' he said. 'The wardrobe session is in the Four Seasons and it started ten minutes ago.'

She hadn't realised there was a meeting. She had only dropped into the agency to pick up her laptop so she'd have it for the White Feather shoot. There was no question of her not going. Marsh had made that very clear.

'What wardrobe session?'

'I know you've stopped writing contact reports but I didn't realise you'd stopped reading them. The model maker flew in from London this morning with the wings. No pun intended.'

'Shit!' Saffy ran back out to reception. 'Ciara,' she said, 'call me a cab. No! Forget it! I'll just catch one on the street.'

'What the hell are you doing here?' Marsh leaned over the mezzanine. 'Dermot just called. He's having issues with the wings.'

'I'm just on my way over now,' Saffy said. 'I'm due back to the hospital but I can drop by for half an hour.'

Marsh folded her arms. In her khaki shirt-dress, she looked scarily military, as if she was just waiting for someone to hand her a gun so she could shoot something. 'Really? Well, don't bother. You obviously have better things to do. Simon can go.

But if you *could* spare a couple of minutes, I'd like a chat in my office.'

'Of course.' Saffy climbed the metal stairs wearily. Now that she knew she was pregnant, she felt pregnant. She had to stop herself from putting her hand on the small of her back and sticking her stomach out.

A few objects, carefully selected for their beauty, were arranged on Marsh's huge, empty desk: a pink peony blossom in a tiny white vase, a red crocodile-skin Hermes organiser, a white china cup and saucer. Each one, Saffy knew, had been chosen to say something about Marsh herself. *I'm pretty. I'm organised. I'm precious.* It must be exhausting, she thought, being so self-obsessed. Where did Marsh get the energy?

'I'm not happy,' Marsh said, and her tone was so conversational that, for a moment, Saffy thought she was going to confide in her. As if this was a girly chat that was long overdue. Then she noticed her eyes. They were glacial.

'And I'm not the only one. Several members of the team have started to question your commitment to Komodo.'

'Well, obviously, I've had to spend time at the hospital lately and—'

'Oh please! I'm running a business here not a counselling service. You're paid a fantastic salary to do a fantastic job and, frankly, the only thing you are doing fantastically well is fucking up.'

'Marsh, I *am* doing my job. The ad is cast. The budget is signed off. The shoot is on track.' Blood rushed to Saffy's head. Blood that was coursing with hormones, lots and lots of hormones.

'I came to the pre-production meeting when my mother was in a coma and you're questioning my commitment?'

Marsh's tiny nostrils flared, very slightly. 'I. Beg. Your. Pardon?'

'Well, you can't have it. And neither can Simon, who is the only other person in this company who would say I'm slacking off. I'm doing my best. Stop being such a bitch and give me a break.'

Marsh nodded her head so hard Saffy thought she might snap her little neck. 'Fine. Have a break. And make it permanent.'

Saffy's heart thumped around in her chest as if it was looking for an escape route. Marsh had her exactly where she wanted her. This had been a set-up all along. She couldn't let this happen. 'Please, Marsh—' she began.

'Save it,' Marsh said, 'you're fired.'

'You're firing me? Ten days after I caught you and Mike having sex in the office toilet. That's quite a coincidence.'

'Are you trying to blackmail me?'

'You can't fire me without three warnings.'

Marsh leaned back in her chair. She was smiling. 'You've had three verbal warnings, Saffy, about your appalling punctuality. There are witnesses. That's all that's required by law.'

Saffy smiled right back. 'I get it! You're firing me because I'm pregnant!'

Marsh's eyes snapped open. 'I didn't know you were pregnant.'

'Well, you do now,' Saffy said. 'And there aren't any witnesses to the fact that I've only just told you.'

She was winning. She could see that from the look on Marsh's face.

'Maternity leave is nine months. I *have* heard of employers who try to ditch staff in order to avoid paying it. Mostly in the court reports.'

Marsh tried a laugh. 'You're not pregnant! This is like that story you told poor Dermot about your father having a heart attack. You're lying.'

'No,' Saffy said, pulling her jersey dress around her tightly, taking a weird pleasure in showing Marsh the tiny bump. 'No, I'm not.'

Marsh sat back and tented her fingers. 'I'll give you three months' salary. Take it or leave it.'

Saffy remembered a negotiation tactic Marsh herself had taught her to play. It was called 'The Next Person Who Talks Dies'.

'Oh, don't try to play that stupid little game with me.' Marsh rolled her eyes. 'I'm so much better at it than you are.'

But apparently she wasn't because she was the one who spoke next.

'Four months' salary. That's my final offer.'

'Six. And a reference. And I keep the Audi.'

'Don't make me laugh!'

Saffy had one final card to play. 'Okay, Marsh, I won't. Greg hasn't signed a contract for the White Feather ad yet, has he?'

There was no way Greg would pull out of the shoot but Marsh didn't know that. Her nostrils flared again, this time quite a lot. Saffy's mobile rang. She checked the screen. It was Jess.

'It's Greg.' She stood up. 'Excuse me, I have to take this.'

'No,' Marsh said flatly, 'you don't.'

Saffy sat down again, gratefully. Her legs were shaking but she managed to keep her voice steady. 'I'll need all that in writing. I'll type my own reference and send it over to you to sign before I leave.'

Marsh shrugged, turned away, uncapped her Mont Blanc pen and scribbled a quick note. She handed it over. 'I'm disappointed in you. For a while back there, I thought you were really something.'

Saffy stood up. 'Really? Well, I thought you were having an affair with some hot young guy, not sleazing around with a middle-aged, married man and then treating him like shit in public. But there's no accounting for taste.'

God, these hormones were fantastic. It was like being possessed by Joan Rivers. 'And I'm not talking about *your* taste. I can see what you see in Mike. I just have no idea what he sees in *you*.'

Saffy deleted her emails and the personal file on her hard drive, typed a glowing reference for herself and emailed it to Marsh. Ant had been right. This was an impersonal space. There was nothing to clear out except for a couple of books, her dusty gym bag, two umbrellas and Liam's football slippers. He'd left them behind that day he came into the office.

She took them down to the kitchen and put them in the recycling but then, after a minute, she went back and retrieved them. She stuffed them into a Jiffy bag with a ten-euro note and scribbled Liam's name and Joe's address on the front.

She found a blank postcard in her drawer and drew a pretty bad piggy bank on the front with a marker then she turned it over and tried to think of what she could say to let him know that she loved him, even though she had only known him for such a short time. Then she remembered the postcards her dad had written to her. It didn't matter really what she said, as long as she said it from the heart.

Dear Liam, I know I owe your swear pig quite a bit. I'm not sure how much but this should cover it. You left your slippers in my office. I hope they still fit! I'm sorry I had to go without talking to you properly. Keep up the swimming and don't take any you-know-what from Alex. Love, Saffy

'Will you put this in the post for me?' Saffy asked.

Ciara was red-eyed. She must have found out about what had happened. She always knew everything.

'Su . . . uh . . . uh . . . uh . . . ure,' she wheezed. 'Sorry. Bloody asthma. Kicks in when I'm uh . . . hup . . . set.'

Saffy went around the reception desk to hug her. 'I'll see you and Vicky on the outside,' she said. 'It'll be like *The Shawshank Redemption*. And this will cheer you up: you know that Ant heard Marsh having sex with Simon in her office?'

'Yeah.' Ciara brightened. 'That or else she keeps a ch . . . hhhipmunk in there.'

'Well, it wasn't *Simon*,' Saffy whispered. 'It was *Mike*!'

Ciara's face broke into a huge grin. 'No!'

The phone rang and the last thing Saffy heard as the automatic doors closed behind her was the sound of Ciara, in stitches, trying to answer it. 'Hahahha hello Komodo. Can I hahhahaha help you?'

33

'There's a trampoline and I patted a baby donkey. He was called Ciunas. That's the Irish for "be quiet". He didn't have toenails. Just one big one, called a hoof. Luke wants the phone now.'

Luke came on the line. 'Grandad says I'm allowed Snickers. Do we have a divorce yet?'

Jess frowned. She had told her parents not to give the twins crap to eat. It was going to take her months to wean them off it when they got back.

'Sweetheart, please tell Grandad you are *not* allowed Snickers and no, of course we're not divorced, you have to be married to get divorced anyway.'

'Oh.' Luke sounded disappointed. 'Jack's mum has a divorce and now he has two houses and two dads and Santa brings him two presents. I'm not sure about the Tooth Fairy. He came last night when Lizzie's front tooth came out.'

Jess put her hand over her mouth. Lizzie had lost her second tooth and neither of them had been there! She might be there for the next one, or Conor might be there, but they wouldn't be there together. From now on, all the special moments in the twins' lives would be divided up and portioned out.

Conor was the fairest person she knew. He wouldn't fight her for custody or be pushy about access. She would get Christmas morning and the Easter Egg Hunt, though he was much better at the clues. And she would have to give him something back. Weekends maybe and a couple of weeks in the summer holidays. She leaned her head against the banister and pressed the phone hard against her ear until it hurt. She needed to feel something other than panic, and this pain would do.

'There was all this blood,' Luke was saying, 'but it wasn't red it was brown. And Lizzie can poke her tongue out through the hole. Will Daddy be living in our house when he gets back from his holidays?'

Jess took a breath. 'We'll see! And guess what? I'm coming

down to pick you up on Saturday and we'll all come back to Dublin on the train!'

She sounded, she thought, like Saffy. Her voice had that awful fake brightness Saffy's had when she talked to the twins. 'That will be fun, won't it?'

Luke didn't answer. He was gone. He must have dropped the phone. She could hear him whooping in the distance.

'Luke? Hello!' Jess looked out through the smeared glass panel in the front door, as though he might be out there, in the garden instead of miles away in Cork. 'Hello? Hello?'

The grass had grown about a foot since Conor had cut it last. It looked wild but at least it was hiding the clutter of plastic toys that always littered the lawn. A silver lining for every cloud.

Jess had been reading a book on how to be happy while she sat with Saffy's mother. Len, the hippy boyfriend, had left it behind one evening. It was simple. Look for the good in everything. Count your blessings every night. Plant something. Keep it alive. Be kind to strangers. Exercise three times a week. Anyone could get the hang of it. Apparently.

She listened to the distant voices on the other end of the phone. Her mother calling the dog, her father laughing. Lizzie shouting, 'It's my go! It's my go!'

'Mum! Dad! Luke! Lizzie!' Jess raised her voice until it was almost a shout. 'Can you hear me? I'm still here.' But nobody came.

'Just raise your arms and tilt your hips forward, suck your stomach in. Oh yes! Hold that!'

The beautician moved the spray gun up and down Greg's legs. He felt the cool mist follow the line of his muscles. It felt good. In fact, it felt great. He had enjoyed every single minute of the last few days, even the boring bits. Standing still for an hour while the model maker clipped millimetres off each feather in his wings, trying on four different loincloths while the Wardrobe women bickered over which one was sexier, waiting for twenty minutes between takes while all the extras were herded into their first positions – he had loved every moment of it.

'This must be pretty boring,' the beautician said.

'Nah, not really.' Greg shook his head. How could he be bored when he was the most important person on set? The focus of everyone's attention? The one the whole thing hung on?

The beautician turned the spray gun off for a moment and bent forward to clear a streak from behind his knee with cotton wool. Behind her, in the full-length mirror, above her sizeable but shapely bottom, he could already see that the fake tan, in four different shades, was giving him David Beckham's body.

He was naked except for a strategically placed sock. Angels didn't have tan lines. She gave it a little tug now, to straighten it.

'Perfect, Mr Glesson. Can you turn around, bend over slightly and put your hands flat against the wall?'

'Sure.' Greg gave her a lazy smile then turned slowly, clenching his buttocks, tightening his calves.

'Mmmmm,' she said. 'That's lovely.'

He grinned to himself. He knew it was. He had it back, his mojo, his Elvis dust, his shine. He had thought for a while that he'd lost it for good but now he had been given a second chance, and this time, he wasn't going to mess it up.

Conor wasn't expecting to see Becky again before he flew back to Dublin. He had mailed his edits over first thing, waited a few hours and then called to see if she had everything she needed.

'Thank you, I do. And I have some good news. I sent the first ten chapters over to the publisher already and he read the first couple of pages and mailed me back to ask me not to send it out to anyone else. It doesn't mean that he'll take it but it's a good sign.'

'Bloody hell! That was fast!'

Becky laughed. 'Is that a good "bloody hell" or a bad "bloody hell"?'

'It's a great "bloody hell". Well done!'

'Well done, you. Listen, we shouldn't count our chickens but I don't think a little celebratory lunch would count. I was supposed to be meeting an editor today but she's cancelled. Are you around? We could go back to the Vietnamense? I mean, if you're free. If you're not rushing back to Dublin or anything.'

'No. I mean, yes. Lunch would be great. I was thinking of staying around for a couple of days.'

He had planned to check out and book an evening flight back to Dublin but he could change his plans.

He had dressed up for lunch. A pair of new jeans he'd bought in a shop on Oxford Street and an old blue cotton shirt he'd pressed badly using the hotel room iron. He looked down at it critically as he sat on the leather sofa at the reception of Douglas, Kemp & Troy. Maybe he should have used the hotel laundry service.

At first, Conor didn't realise the receptionist was talking to him. 'Mr Fah-hee.' Her cut-glass accent made his name sound Arabic.

'That was Ms Kemp. She's been called into an emergency meeting and it looks like a long one so she's had to cancel lunch. She's asked me to apologise.'

'No problem.' He stood up. What was he supposed to do now? Wait for her to be free? Go to the restaurant on his own? Go back to the hotel?

He was standing outside the building, looking up and down the hot, busy street, wondering what to do when Becky came running down the steps.

'Conor! I'm glad I caught you.' She wearing a short-sleeved navy dress and high shoes. She put her hand on his arm. 'I'm so sorry about lunch. I was really looking forward to it. One of our most important authors is having a meltdown. He's up there now, tearing his famous hair out, threatening to change agents. The other partners are on holiday so I have to talk him down.'

'Hey, don't worry about it. Lunch is for wimps. Or is that breakfast? I can never remember.'

'You're so nice, Conor.' She squeezed his arm. 'You really have no idea just how *nice* you are.'

He didn't know what to say to that, so he just smiled for a bit and she smiled back. He didn't care about lunch any more. He would be quite happy to stand around with her hand on his arm being smiled at like this for the rest of the afternoon.

She snapped out of it. 'Oh God, what am I doing out here? I'd better get back up there. His hair is probably the only reason people buy his books. Look, I'm not sure how long this will take but, if I get out alive, would you like to meet later? I could drop by the hotel. We could go out for drinks or stay in for drinks or . . .'

'That would be . . .' Before Conor could think of what that would be, she stood on tiptoe, kissed him quickly on the lips then hurried over to the stairs. He watched her bare, brown legs as she took the steps two by two and finished the sentence in his head.

. . . dangerous.

'First positions, please.'

A hundred women with long hair and a body mass index of less than twenty in short gauzy white tunics were lined up, ten abreast, at the back of the field. And very nice breasts they were, too, Greg had to concede, surveying them, from a safe distance, through the window of the honey wagon.

On all the other set-ups, he'd had his own, personal chemical toilet. But this was the last scene and they were officially in the middle of nowhere, though if he craned his neck he could see the roof of Woodglen, where he and Saffy had their wedding reception.

He had given her a week to consider his proposal, his second proposal, when you thought about it. And he did think about it, he thought about it a lot. Saffy had always been dead against having children so he'd never really given it any serious thought. But, now that it was a possibility, he found himself warming to the idea.

Kids were all right. What you saw was what you got. When they were pissed off, they cried. When they were happy, they laughed. You didn't have to bullshit them. They were fun to hang out with. Look at Lizzie. He'd rather be stuck in a lift with her than with most grown women. Except, possibly Jennifer Aniston or Angelina Jolie. Though not the two of them together, obviously.

Then there was the whole genetic thing. Making a film would be pretty cool. But it would only really be around for a few months before it went to DVD. A child would be out there in ninety years' time, possibly more. They were making new medical discoveries every day. Look at the ear they grew on that mouse.

And look at women. Most of his fans were women, right? And what did women love, apart from hot guys? Babies. All the greats were popping them out. Pitt, Cruise, Affleck. Though Ben really needed to put that baby down for a while and get out there and do a few more auditions. That other Affleck dude, Casey, was creeping up on him.

Saffy getting pregnant was great timing. A little baby was the perfect reason for them to start all over again.

He had been single for a couple of months now and it was scary. Girls had *changed*. What had happened to the female population? All they thought about was *sex*. It was only six years since he'd hooked up with Saff but since then sex had become a whole different ball game. He blamed the internet.

He had thought Tanya was out there but they were all like that, now. That blonde model, Alyssa, could have run an Ann Summers store from out of her bedside locker. And she'd wanted to do a threesome, which he thought sounded okay until he realised she meant *with another man*. It was time to settle down.

Ben Rosen was tracking through the extras on a dolly. The script said that they were supposed to flow around his camera in a wave of polished limbs and glossy hair but they were marching past in regimented lines.

'Cut!' Rosen came out from behind the camera and ducked under the canopy where Ant and Vicky were watching on video assist. He had a quick look at a playback of the shot.

'Good job!' he yelled at the crew. 'That was totally off the hinges! Check the gate.'

'Off the hinges is right. Those women look like Soviet troops,' Ant hissed to Vicky. 'Tell the pony-tail to do it again.'

For the hundredth time in the last two days, Vicky wished that Saffy was here. Simon and Nervous Dermot were too busy gaping at the skimpily dressed extras to care about what was going on.

She stood up and went outside to find Dylan Rick. Rosen had

made it clear at the start that nobody was allowed to talk to him directly. All comments had to be channelled through his assistant.

'It's not that I don't want feedback from you guys,' he'd assured them. 'This is your baby and it's a collaborative process. But I gotta stay focused, you know? So I can't have more than one voice in my head at the one time.'

But somewhere along the line, probably at the point when Nervous Dermot had hijacked the casting, Rosen had lost interest. Vicky was starting to suspect that the only voice he was hearing in his head was his own. And what it was saying was, *Take the money and run.*

She had raised issue after issue with Dylan. The extra that kept looking straight at the camera. Greg's performance, which was way over the top. The fact that Rosen was supposed to be shooting close-ups on every shot to give them flexibility in the edit but wasn't.

Dylan smiled and nodded and said 'sure thing' a lot and then absolutely nothing happened. It wasn't going to be a terrible ad – Rosen was too egotistical to make one of those – but it was going to be mediocre and that was probably worse.

She found Dylan standing near the gate to the field. He had spread a magazine on the ground to protect his shoes. He was standing on a picture of Jessica Alba in a bikini, talking on his phone. A dozen cows were clustered by the electric fence, watching him with interest.

'He didn't,' Dylan was saying. 'Shut up. You did? Shut up!'

Vicky tugged his sleeve. 'Dylan, I'm sorry to interrupt you,' she whispered, 'but I need you to get Ben to do the last shot again.'

He held up a 'one minute' finger at her. 'Get out!' he said into the phone. 'Shut up!'

Vicky stood with the cows, waiting for him to finish. She desperately wanted a drink but Ant had told her that if she drank on this shoot he'd never speak to her again and, as she was the *only* person he spoke to, she knew that would probably ruin his life.

It took five minutes for Dylan to wind up his call. By then,

Vicky knew, the camera would have been taken off the dolly, the track would have been broken up and Rosen would be already setting up the next shot. It was too late. Again.

Greg stood with his arms outstretched while the Wardrobe girl attached his wings.

'Last set-up,' she said. 'Bet you'll be glad to be shot of these fecking feathers.'

The truth was he'd be sorry to give his wings back. He'd enjoyed being an angel. Acting had its ups and downs. Getting paid twenty-five grand to stroll around in a loincloth being gazed at by a bunch of hot woman was definitely an up.

He had been hoping he'd get to actually fly but apparently the budget didn't cover it so the ad was going to end with him drifting off into the sunset in a hot-air balloon with all the women waving up at him.

Tony, the first AD, helped him onto the back of a quad bike, tucking his feet into cotton slippers so they didn't get muddy on the trip across the field.

As they pulled up by the balloon, Greg recognised the guy who was chatting to Ben Rosen. It was that asshole that had been dating Saffy. Greg had only seen him once, standing in the supermarket car park with his arm around her, but he never forgot a face. Especially when it had a crooked nose and a uni-brow.

'So when we shout "roll", Joe,' Rosen was saying, 'I need you to crouch down in the basket so we're only seeing Greg.'

'It's a gondola,' Joe said, 'we call it a gondola, not a basket.'

'Whatever. You don't have to be completely out of shot, we can retouch you out in post-production but the less we see of you, the better.'

'Sounds good to me!' Greg said, climbing off the quad bike.

He let the first AD take off his blanket. Then he stood with his chest out, looking Joe up and down. It was more up than down, really. The dude was well over six feet. He wished he was wearing his boots instead of the slippers.

'Greg, this is Joe,' Ben Rosen said. 'Joe will be taking you up today. You're in safe hands. Apparently he's one of the best.'

'That's not what I've heard.' Greg folded his arms.

Joe raised an eyebrow but, to Greg's disappointment, he didn't seem to know who he was. He turned his back and vaulted into the basket/gondola thing and began fiddling with some dials.

Vicky watched the first AD help Greg climb the stepladder so he could get into the balloon. His fake tan was streaking and his wings were crooked. Why had nobody done final checks? She stuffed another sausage roll into her mouth and tried to swallow her irritation with it. Her favourite shot, the one where the angel flew, had been taken out at the last minute. Rosen had promised her the balloon shot would look just as good but Greg was so small he was barely visible above the high wicker sides of the gondola. This was too much. She looked around for Dylan and saw him, back over by the gate, talking on the phone again. Rosen was a few feet away talking to the lighting cameraman. She gulped down the sausage roll and walked up to him. 'Ben, I know I'm not supposed to speak to you directly, but we're going to have to redo Greg's fake tan. And we need to get someone from props to put a box in the gondola for him to stand on. He looks tiny.'

Rosen didn't look at her. 'Relax. We can fix his height in post.'

'Okay, but can we just have one shot of him standing on a box because—'

'Back off, willya? I'm in the middle of something here!'

As Vicky walked away she heard him hiss at the lighting cameraman, 'Jesus H. Christ. Can someone ask Dylan to get the Wicked Witch of the West out of my hair?'

'Your hair?' Ant came over and planted himself in front of Ben Rosen. He put his hand in his pocket and pulled out something shiny.

'Oh my God!' Nervous Dermot nibbled his knuckles. 'He has a knife!'

'You call that greasy rat's tail *hair*?' Ant sneered, waving the shiny thing.

It was, Vicky realised, the nail scissors from his Swiss Army penknife.

Rosen stepped back nervously. 'Cool down, Bud. You're not supposed to talk to me! You're supposed to talk to Dylan.'

'Yeah? Well, you're not supposed to insult *her*. She has more talent in her little finger than you have in your entire body. You fraud! You fake! You phoney fuckwit!'

Ant lunged at him and grabbed the pony-tail in one hand. He started to hack at it with the nail scissors but, before he could cut it off, Simon rugby-tackled him and knocked him to the ground.

Rosen turned to the crew. 'Did we get that on camera?' He said. 'Were we turning over? That guy was trying to slash my throat!'

Dylan Rick appeared, moving swiftly across the field as if he was on wheels. 'Time out, everyone!' He put his arm around Rosen.

'One more shot, Ben. One more shot and I'll get you out of this sheep shit. We'll go straight to the airport. We'll do the edit in New York. I'll book Virgin, first class. You can have a massage. You've got about ten minutes before the light goes. Just get the shot.'

Simon stood up and let Vicky pull Ant to his feet.

'Get him out of here.' Dylan hissed. 'And don't bring him back.'

Vicky led Ant over to her car and opened the door for him. She cleared a pile of magazines and a jumper and some sweet wrappers off the passenger seat so he could sit down. Then she went around to the driver's side and got in.

'I'm sorry about the mess.' She picked a Flake wrapper from between the seats and stuffed it into the glove compartment. 'I know you hate mess.'

He shook his head and pressed his lips together.

'You were amazing back there, Ant, just amazing! Thank you for standing up for me! Nobody's ever stood up for me like that.'

She knew Ant didn't like human contact but she couldn't help it. She leaned over the gear stick and put her arms around him and hugged him really hard against her chest. He was shaking.

'What's the matter?' She pulled back and looked into his face. He was blinking at her rapidly, as if he was trying to tell her something through eyelid Morse code. Dot dot dash. Dash dash dot. Dash. 'Ant! Are you hurt? Do you need anything?'

'Yes,' he said. 'I do. I've been waiting six years, eleven months and twenty-two days for you to do that. I need you to do it again.'

'First positions everybody!' The extras formed a circle around the balloon. 'Quiet on set!'

Joe did some final checks on his instruments, and then he turned around to give the first AD the thumbs-up. The little actor guy in the angel costume was freaking him out. He kept staring at him. His face was almost orange and one of his eyes was twitching. He looked kind of deranged.

'Make a habit of screwing round with the married ladies, yeah?' the angel said suddenly.

Flying made some people paranoid. If this guy was one of them, Joe thought, he'd rather deal with it on the ground. Being in an enclosed space a few hundred feet up in the air with someone who was flipping out was a bad idea.

'I think you're mixing me up with someone else,' he said calmly.

'Let's not play games, dude,' the orange guy said. 'I know who you are and you know who I am. I'm Greg Gleeson.'

'Sorry, I'm sure you're famous but I—'

'I'm Saffy's husband. Remember me now?'

Saffy. Joe felt a mixture of pleasure and pain hearing her name spoken. Apart from a brief conversation with Liam, where he had explained that they wouldn't be seeing her again, he hadn't allowed himself to even think it since that night in Wicklow.

When he'd had the call for the White Feather job he'd checked to see if she'd be on the shoot. He'd only taken the gig because he'd been told she wasn't working at the agency any more. And now he was face to face, well, chest to face really, with her *husband*. He was angry and Joe didn't blame him.

'No,' he said, 'I don't make a habit of screwing around with married women. I'm sorry, okay? If I'd known she was married nothing would have happened.'

'Joe, thirty seconds to lift-off!' the first AD shouted from below.

'What about pregnant women?' Greg was still glaring. 'Make a habit of screwing around with them?'

Joe shook his head. 'Look, I don't know what your problem is. I'm happy to sit down and talk to you about it sometime but right now we've both got a job to do here so can we cut the talk and get on with it?'

'Pull the rope and roll!' Ben Rosen shouted.

'I've got one more question. What's it like shooting blanks?'

Joe turned around. 'What?'

'Saffy told me you had the snip.'

'She told you *what*?'

The first AD watched the angel's fist connect with the balloon guy's jaw. *Smack*. Then both of them disappeared under the rim of the gondola.

'Holy crap!' he said to nobody in particular. 'Is it a full moon or something?'

Saffy parked her car on the Vico Road and looked out at the rain. Bray Head had disappeared. The sea was a blurry grey smudge below. She had intended to go down to Killiney to watch the swimmers for a while but she was afraid that she would slip on the rocks and that would be dangerous for the baby. What was she going to do about this baby?

Time was running out. She was supposed to give Greg her answer tomorrow and, if it was 'no' she would have to go to London next week.

She closed her eyes and tried to imagine herself and Greg as parents. She could picture Greg, naked from the waist up, holding a child and looking like an Athena poster but when she pictured herself, she could only imagine dropping it or spilling hot coffee on it or leaving it on the roof of her car and driving off.

It wouldn't remember any of this when it was older but it would hate her anyway. She would try to make everything perfect and she would fail. She would fail in every way she could imagine and other ways she hadn't imagined yet. And it would get hurt and it would be lonely and it would blame her. It would look at her the way she had looked at her mother when she was a teenager and she would know that sometimes it was thinking, *I wish I hadn't been born.* How did people have children? How did they deal with the fear?

A guy with a rolled-up towel under his arm walked past smoking and Saffy leaned out her window. 'Hi!' she called after him. 'Excuse me! Could I have a cigarette?'

'Nice car.' He grinned.

That was another thing that would have to go if she had a baby: the Audi. You didn't see many baby seats in the back of TTs.

He passed her a cigarette. She didn't want to ask him for a light in case he wanted to chat so she waited till he had walked on and reached down to push in the cigarette lighter, but it wasn't there.

She suddenly remembered Liam fiddling with it the very first time she'd met him, the day she gave him a lift back from school, when he'd bled all over her car. She remembered Joe cleaning up the blood with the blue towel. But, before she could remember any more, she stopped herself. The remembering had to stop. She had to move on.

She stuck her hand under the seat and her hand closed around the lighter. Then her fingers touched something else. She pulled it out. It was the plastic folder she'd shoved there the day she'd read her father's letters. She had forgotten all about it.

It was full of photographs. They seemed to be shots from her mother's modelling days. Saffy had seen pictures like them before but not these exact ones. Jill looked pretty and very young – hardly more than sixteen or seventeen. These must be the first shots she'd ever had done.

There was a separate bundle of photographs held together with a rubber band that snapped when Saffy touched it and the pictures spilled into her lap. Her mother was a year or two older in these pictures and she wasn't pretty. She was beautiful.

They weren't modelling shots, they were portraits, taken in an ordinary garden, and Jill wasn't posing, she was simply looking at the camera, smiling and letting it look at her and Saffy knew, suddenly, that her father had taken them.

She flipped through them. The last one was a portrait, too, but it was full length. There was a man with his arm around her and his other hand resting on her very pregnant belly. It was her father.

She leaned back in her seat and pressed the cigarette lighter and lit her cigarette. She thought of the frames she'd left on her mother's window sill at the hospital. She smiled. She had tried to create a picture of all three of them and now she had one. She hadn't quite arrived yet but it looked like she would be there any day.

They had been happy once, her mum and her dad. He was her *dad*, now, not her father. They had been happy for nearly three years. *I thought we couldn't be happier, then you came along and I found out I was wrong*, his letter had said. Just because she didn't remember it, just because it hadn't lasted, didn't mean it hadn't happened.

Saffy had always told herself that her father walking out was the worst thing that could have happened to her. Actually, there was something much worse. They could have chosen not to have her at all.

She dropped her cigarette butt out of the window, narrowly missing a cocker spaniel that was walking past. The owner, a woman with a poo bag dangling from one arm and a phone to her ear, glared at her. But Saffy didn't notice. She was typing a text to Greg. It was one word long. And the word was: YES.

34

Saffy was late for Greg. As she followed a concave waitress through the lunchtime crowd at 365, she realised that this was a first.

'Babe!' He stood and stretched his arms out and she walked into them and he held her tight for a long minute.

'Dress-down Friday?' He grinned at her saggy T-shirt dress and flip-flops. He was dressed in tight, inky-blue Diesel jeans and a startlingly white shirt. He was wearing his wedding ring again and she was wearing hers along with the engagement ring, though she was going to have to ask him to exchange it for something smaller. She could do serious damage to a baby if she tried changing a nappy with it on.

'You look beautiful, Babe,' he said as he let her go. 'You've got that whole glow thing going on, seriously.' They sat down and he poured her a glass of champagne from an open bottle.

Saffy shook her head. 'I shouldn't drink.'

'Come on. All the supermodels drink champagne when they're pregnant. And we need to celebrate.'

'I'm not sure we should celebrate just yet. Marsh fired me.'

The waitress was back. She managed to touch Greg four times while she handed him his menu and not to look at Saffy at all when she passed over hers.

'You know what?' Greg said when she'd gone again. 'It's cool that you've been fired because now you can come to LA with me.' He was grinning. 'I got the part in the Elmore Leonard picture. Farrell dropped out again. It's not one hundred per cent confirmed but they want me to go over next week to do a screen test. It starts shooting in February!'

Saffy looked at him, confused. 'Greg, the baby's due in February . . .'

He laughed. 'People have babies in America!'

'But what about my mother?'

'Your mother will be fine by February. I have a sick sense about it.'

He held up his champagne glass.

'The glass is half full, okay? Your mother is going to get through this. We're going to have a little baby. I'm going to get my foot in the door of Hollywood. And I'm going to have the Chicken Caesar without the anchovies in the dressing. Hold the croutons.'

'What?' her sluggish, pregnancy brain couldn't keep up. Then she realised that he was ordering his lunch.

'Hold. The. Croutons,' the waitress said, somehow managing to make little cubes of fried bread sound incredibly dirty. 'And for you?' Her eyes drifted to Saffy and then back to Greg. She was looking at him hungrily. But she probably was hungry. She looked as if she hadn't eaten for years.

'I don't want anything.'

The waitress hunched up her bony shoulders and shook her lollipop head. 'You have to have something. There's a minimum charge of twenty euro.'

'I'll pay the minimum charge. I just don't want to eat anything.'

'I'm sorry. That's not possible.'

'I've changed my mind. I do want something,' Saffy said. 'I want you to stop drooling all over my husband for a couple of minutes so we can have a private conversation. Is *that* possible?'

The fattest part of the waitress was her bottom lip. It began to tremble now and she turned on her heel and fled.

Greg patted her arm. 'That was a bit harsh.'

'I can't help it, Greg. It's my hormones. What's her excuse?'

'Babe, she has hormones too.'

Saffy broke a breadstick in two and held one half between her fingers like a cigarette in the hope that it would help her to feel calm. She had made her decision. She was going to keep the baby. She was going to go back to Greg. The hard part was supposed to be over. But now, suddenly, there were a whole bunch of new decisions to be made.

'You haven't thought this through, Greg. The baby might be

overdue. And even if it isn't, even if it's born in LA in February, what happens then? You'll probably have to go on location . . .'

'. . . for six months. To Mexico. You love Mexico, Saffy. Remember that amazing holiday we had in Puerto Escondido? Remember the beach and the sunsets and the mojitos?'

Saffy did remember. She also remembered the American couple in the next room who got amoebic dysentery and the French guy who was bitten when he tried to feed a tamale to a feral dog.

'I loved it for a two-week holiday, Greg, but it's a third-world country. I'm not sure it's top of my list of places to take a newborn baby.'

'Look, I don't have it all worked out yet.' Greg topped up his champagne. 'But we'll figure it out. We'll make it happen and it'll be great. It'll be an adventure!'

She began to mash the breadstick into the tablecloth with her thumb. 'This whole Hollywood thing would be easier if I wasn't pregnant, wouldn't it?' She didn't want to look at him. She was too scared that she might be right.

Greg put the bottle back into the bucket. 'Whoa! Hold on a second! I never said that!'

But he didn't have to say it. It was there in his face.

'Be straight with me, Greg,' she said in a small voice. 'Please. It's not too late to change your mind.'

He frowned and ran a hand through his hair. 'I don't know. Maybe we could have planned it a bit better but—'

His mobile rang. He made a helpless face. 'Sorry. I really have to take this. It's Lauren.'

He leaned back in his chair and grinned at the ceiling. 'Lauren, Babe! Yeah! Course I can talk. They don't allow mobiles in here but I'm sure they'll make an exception for me.'

Saffy bumped into the waitress outside the Ladies and cadged a cigarette after apologising for being so rude.

'S'okay. You're probably a Taurus, right? Sign of the bull?'

Saffy was a Capricorn but she nodded.

'My mum's a Taurean,' the waitress said. 'She can be a real cow, too.'

The rusting fire escape at the back of the restaurant was a smoking area for staff. There was probably a pretty terrace somewhere for customers but Saffy didn't care. This was an emergency. She lit the cigarette and took a drag. There was that delicious nicotine fizz again, in the tips of her fingers and her toes. Then she had a thought. What about the baby's fingers and toes? Did it have any yet? Was this cigarette going to damage them?

She pushed the thought away. Why was she worrying about harming the baby? The baby almost certainly wasn't worrying about all the ways it was going to harm her. She made a mental list of them. For a start, she would be unemployable for the next year.

She would lose her body, no question. Some women, like Jess, got cute bumps. Saffy was not one of those women. She had already put on ten pounds. She was going to turn into a whale. People were going to watch her waddling past and think, *A man actually had sex with her?* And, if Marsh was right, no man would ever want to have sex with her again.

If she went to Hollywood with Greg she would be stuck in some soulless LA suburb with the baby while Greg hung out in Oaxaca with Maggie Gyllenhaal or Sandra Bullock.

'I see you've been mining for diamonds. That why you didn't return my calls?'

She turned around. It was the Australian guy – Doug. He was wearing his chef's uniform and his trademark grin. He nodded at her ring and whistled.

It had occurred to Saffy that she might run into him here but she hadn't cared. It was all so long ago now. It all seemed so unimportant.

'And you've taken up smoking.' He shook his head. 'You *have* been busy. I've been busy, too, but I found time to call you.'

'Yes,' Saffy said tiredly, 'you did. But I'm guessing that, since we slept together, you've been painting terrible pictures and shucking unfortunate oysters and chasing unavailable women, not getting married, getting separated, getting fired, getting pregnant, nursing a sick parent and . . .'

She saw the look on his face and realised she had, at last,

managed to scratch the surface of his Teflon ego but it didn't feel as good as she thought it might have. She sighed. 'Oh God. Ignore me. I'm pregnant. The hormones are making me very ratty.'

He raised one eyebrow. 'You were always pretty ratty. But hold on a second, *we slept together*? Why did nobody tell me?'

'What do you mean?'

'I mean, you hoovered up my legendary chocolate soufflé, knocked back almost an entire bottle of my twenty-five-year-old Armagnac and cried snotty streaks all over my sofa while you told me the story of your life. Sleep? I couldn't get you to shut up. I went to bed after about three hours and you followed me in and got in beside me. I thought you might put a sock in it then but you didn't. You were going on and on about your father at that point so I just slipped in my ear plugs and left you to it.'

'We *didn't* have sex?'

Doug gave her a dirty look. 'Darl, if we'd had sex, you would have returned my calls.'

She looked up at him and something loosened in her chest and she realised that she had been afraid. She had thought she had gone off the rails when she'd broken up with Greg on Valentine's night and everything she had done since then was, in some way, overshadowed by fear that it might happen again.

'You're absolutely *sure* about that?'

'Sure I'm sure. But if you ever want to have sex when you're a yummy mummy, you know where to find me.'

The word 'mummy' did something to the backs of Saffy's knees. She put her hand on the railing to steady herself.

'But no talking next time,' Doug said. 'Or crying. Well, you can cry if you like, but only with gratitude.'

He turned to go back inside. The light behind him lit up his hair for a second, like a coppery halo.

'You should give up the smokes if you're pregnant,' he said over his shoulder. 'They're really bad for your baby.'

Saffy let the cigarette drop from between her fingers. It fell in a tiny constellation of sparks, into the yard below.

'Yeah,' she smiled up at him, 'you're right.'

*

Conor stopped at a chemist in Covent Garden and bought a bottle of aftershave and a packet of condoms. He felt like an idiot for buying them but not as much of an idiot as he knew he'd feel if he got into a situation where he needed them and didn't have them.

It had been years since he'd bought condoms. He wondered why there were so many kinds. Wondering about that stopped him from wondering what it would be like to go to bed with Becky. He had forced himself not to think about it for nearly two weeks now, it was a losing battle.

It was a stiflingly hot day. He walked back to the hotel. He undressed, took a shower and got dressed again. He sat on the end of the bed and watched some cricket on TV, even though he had no idea of the rules. He tried to figure them out and that distracted him for a while but then it stopped working.

He took the condoms out of the bag and put them in the drawer of the bedside table. Then he moved them to the bathroom cupboard. He took the packaging off the aftershave and put some on. Then he poured some down the sink so Becky wouldn't think he'd bought it specially if she saw the bottle.

He forced himself to leave the room, walking up to Old Compton Street and along Frith Street to Soho Square. Part of him wanted her to call while he was gone. But part of him was relieved when he checked with Reception and she hadn't.

He took the condoms out of the bathroom cupboard and wrapped them in a tissue and put them in the bin. He tried to read a book for a while. He made himself a gin and tonic from the minibar. It was the first drink he'd had in his room. He had another one. Then he felt hungry and ordered an omelette from room service. He must have dozed off. When he woke up his mobile was ringing. He was smiling before he answered it.

'I thought you weren't going to call.'

'I had to.' It wasn't Becky, it was Jess. His first thought was that something bad had happened.

He sat up. 'Is everything okay?'

'Everything is fine.'

'Are the twins all right?'

'They're great. They're still with my parents in Cork. They miss you.'

'How's Saffy's mother?'

'She's awake. She's not making any sense at all but apparently that can happen and they have the pneumonia and the sepsis under control. They'll be able do a marrow extraction in a day or two to decide when she goes back on chemo. How are your edits going?'

'I'm finished. I got them off this morning.' *Shit!* Why had he told her that? He waited for her to ask him when he was flying back to Dublin but she didn't.

'That's good,' she said after a pause. 'So what are you doing now?'

'Nothing really.' God, this was awkward. 'I was just having a rest. Look, tell Luke and Lizzie I love them and I'll be back soon. I'll text you when I've booked the flight.'

'Listen, Conor, I remembered something.'

'Yeah?' He hoped it was something quick. Becky might arrive any minute.

'Remember when you came home with the hamster and you said it was Brendan and that you'd found him at Greg and Saffy's place?'

'Yeah?'

'And I didn't believe you? Well, it came back to me. A couple of months ago, I brought Luke over there and he had Brendan in his *pocket*. I put him in my bag in case Saffy freaked out. He must have escaped. That's how he got to Trump Towers!'

Conor cradled the phone under his ear and went over to the minibar. He unscrewed the cap on a tiny bottle of gin and took a gulp. What was her point? Where was this going? And how long was it going to take for her to get there?

'So it *was* Brendan, Conor. It was the *real* Brendan all the time!'

Of course it was Brendan. There was only one Brendan.

'I'm sorry I didn't believe you,' Jess said.

'Forget about it. It doesn't matter.'

There was a knock at the door. Was it room service? Or Becky? He was only half-listening to Jess.

'There's something else. I read your book last night. I went through your emails and I found it and I stayed up all night reading it. And I loved it, Conor. There was so much of you in it. And me. And the twins. And I was wondering if I could take you out to dinner somewhere nice so I can tell you how brilliant it is and how sorry I am for making it so hard for you to write it.'

He tried to take all this in but it was too confusing. There was another, more urgent knock.

'Sure. Look, I'll call you when I get back. I have to go now. There's someone at the door. I've got to go. Bye, Jess.'

'Bye, Conor,' she said. 'I'll see you soon.'

Conor hung up and threw the phone on the bed. He checked himself in the mirror. Then he took a deep breath and opened the door.

Standing in the corridor, in a blue summer dress and flip-flops, was Jess. She looked beautiful but it wasn't how she looked that hit him. It was the way she was looking at him. He couldn't remember the last time she had looked at him like that.

She tucked her hair back behind her ears and gave him a nervous smile.

'I told you I'd see you soon!'

He swallowed. 'I didn't realise it would be *this* soon. I thought you were calling from Dublin.'

'I'm sorry. I had to come. But if you tell me to turn around and go home, I won't blame you. I've been such a bitch. I'm sorry, Conor.'

She looked at the floor. 'This is not an excuse but I've been so scared for the last few months. Ever since you got that first letter from the agent.'

The agent who could appear any minute! Conor scanned the corridor.

'Scared of what?'

A man in a suit with a briefcase came out of the room opposite. Jess waited for him to go before she answered.

'I feel so stupid saying this. Scared of things changing. Of not being enough for you any more. For the longest time I was all you wanted, you know? And I got used to that. And it freaked me out that you were going to have this whole new part to your life and that I wasn't involved in it. And I took it out on you.'

She looked up at him and her lovely eyes were brimming with tears.

'I'm so proud of you, Conor, for putting up with that shitty school all these years and for breaking up that fight and for getting up in the middle of the night to write your book. And I hope it gets published and I hope it's a bestseller but, even if it's not, I want you to start another one. Because you know what?' She started to laugh. 'You're so much better at writing than you are at teaching. This is what you're supposed to do, okay?

'Okay.' The lump in Conor's throat prevented him from saying any more. It meant so much to hear her say that.

'And there's something else I want . . .'

'What is it?'

She stepped inside the door, kicked off her flip-flops, and pushed the door closed with one bare foot. Then she pulled her blue dress over her head and began unbuttoning his shirt. 'It's this.'

Jill dreamed she was walking on water. It was so easy that she couldn't believe she hadn't tried it before. Then she lost her footing and the water gave way and she slipped beneath the surface. She woke up drenched with sweat. She was hooked to a tangle of wires. Two cool jets of oxygen hissed from plastic tubes beneath her nose.

It was late afternoon. Sadbh had been sitting by the bed when she'd fallen asleep but she was gone now. Her eyes were gluey with sleep. Her mouth was furry and sour but her mind was clear. She held her breath and waited for the fog of words to descend but it didn't.

'I am here,' she said out loud. Her voice was rusty but it did what it was told. The words that had slipped away like fish before when she tried to find them now swam into shoals of perfect sense. 'Here I am.'

She lay perfectly still, afraid to move in case this delicious clarity disappeared. She looked around the the room, finding names for what she saw: 'Door. Locker. Book. Water jug.

Window sill. Photograph.' She sat up to see it properly and, for a minute, she thought that she was still dreaming.

It was a picture of her with Rob and Sadbh and Sadbh was grown up. But that was impossible. Rob had left when she was barely walking. She stared at the three of them, shoulder to shoulder. A snapshot of the life they were supposed to have had. The life he had destroyed when he left. Then she realised it was an illusion. There were two photographs, one slightly in front of the other.

She had created her own illusion after he had gone and she had shared it with Sadbh. The little white lie that he had simply abandoned them. That he had just walked out and never looked back. For some reason, she had thought that it would help both of them to survive without him. Sadbh grew up believing it, and, after a while, Jill had started to believe it herself. And then it was too late to change her story. It would have been too confusing for Sadbh anyway.

He had sent money every month for eighteen years. She had hated him for keeping his word. She wanted him to stop so she could hate him more, but he didn't. She wouldn't let herself spend a penny of it, not even in the beginning when she was desparate. She meant to give it to Sadbh some day, along with his cards, when the time was right, but that time had never come.

Rob had broken Jill's heart and she had wanted to break his and she had succeeded. She could read the pain between the lines of every one of those breezy little notes he'd written. *Love, Dad.* In the beginning, it comforted her to think he was suffering but, as the years passed, his dogged attempts to connect with a girl who couldn't even remember what he looked like just made her sad.

All those birthdays, all those Christmases he had missed and all the moments in between. The trips to the zoo. The new school shoes. The sleepovers. The weight of all that time balanced against the couple of kilos of paper and ink that when added together weighed less than Sadbh had when he had last seen her.

Not a day goes by that I don't miss you, Sadbh, Rob had

written in that first letter. *You're the first thing I think of when I wake up and the last thing I think of at night.*

She had slept with that letter under her pillow for weeks. Re-reading one line over and over. *I loved your mother. I still do.* And then she had put it away with his cards. She had kept every single one.

When the final letter came from his friend to say he'd died, she had gone to a counsellor. Once a week for six months, she had sat on a kind of beanbag in a shabby room above a bicycle shop in Blackrock opposite an older woman with a terrible grey perm. She had cried and agonised about whether or not to tell Sadbh the truth. In the end, she had been too afraid that, if she did, she would lose her daughter. And she very nearly had.

She had set out to break Rob's heart but she had ended up breaking Sadbh's as well. She had had no right to stop her seeing her father. She knew that now. She had always known it, deep down.

There was no clock in the room. Jill had no idea how long she had been awake or how soon her daughter would come. The familiar exhaustion of illness began to creep up on her. What if this clarity of thinking was gone before she had time to tell Sadbh how sorry she was. She stared at the door, willing Sadbh to come. There were so many things she should have told her daughter years ago. She had wasted so much time. She didn't want to waste another minute.

35

At some stage, Saffy had started counting the number of steps it took to get from the door of the hospital to her mother's bed. It was usually somewhere between eighty and a hundred. It never seemed like enough to cover the vast divide between the real world and the weird parallel universe where sick people lived.

Out there, if someone was injured or bleeding or crying, she would have automatically stopped to help. In here, she had learned to just keep walking. Past the blonde woman sobbing in the corridor in Casualty (eighteen steps). Past the bald man in pyjamas doubled up groaning outside the X-ray department (thirty-one steps). Past the red-faced woman in a wheelchair whispering to herself outside Haematology (forty-four steps).

It took fifty-eight steps to get to the lift. It should have been fifty-six but she had to step aside to let a woman pushing a boy in a wheelchair get in first. He was in his teens and he had lost all of his hair. He had a biker's black leather jacket draped over his blue pyjamas.

'All I'm trying to tell you,' the woman squinted at the lift buttons and jabbed one, 'is that Jesus loves you.'

'I don't want Jesus to love me.' The boy rolled his eyes. 'I want Scarlett Johansson to love me. Or Beyoncé. Or the hot blonde one out of Girls Aloud.'

The woman gave Saffy a long-suffering look. But, Saffy thought, he had a point. What teenage boy wants to be loved by a man in his thirties with a beard? She was afraid to meet the woman's eyes in case she laughed so she looked down at her feet instead.

The woman was wearing sensible open-toed sandals. The boy had on navy slippers that reminded her of Liam. She stared harder at the floor to block him out. She missed him. She had thought she would get used to it but she hadn't.

The lift stopped and an elderly lady with a sweet wrapper stuck to one leg of her Zimmer frame got in, followed by a man in loafers with leather tassels. As the doors began to close, someone else stepped in. Someone wearing Caterpillar boots spattered with tiny flecks of blue and white paint. Saffy stared at them. They looked familiar.

'Please don't go to America,' the voice was familiar too.

'I'm not going to America,' the old lady said. 'I'm going to Geriatrics on the second floor.'

'I met that actor guy who says he's your husband. He told me you got back together and that he's taking you to LA.'

'You must be mixing me up with somebody else,' the lady insisted. 'My husband passed away in nineteen ninety-two, and he wasn't an actor, he was an estate agent.'

'Saffy, look at me, please.'

Saffy looked slowly from Joe's boots up into his eyes. His hair had grown and he had a couple of days' stubble and a purple bruise on his chin. She wanted to put her hand to his face but she knew that if she touched him once, she wouldn't be able to stop.

'I know you're having his baby,' he said, 'but please don't go to the States with him. Not until you hear me out first.'

Saffy swallowed. 'Greg told you I was pregnant?'

'He told me.' Joe nodded. 'And then he hit me. Or I hit him. I can't really remember who hit who first. I was pretty angry but I wasn't angry with *him*, I was angry with myself, at the way I treated you.'

'But you didn't do anything wrong, Joe.'

'Yeah? What about not allowing you to explain your side of the story? What about dragging out all the old self-pity I had about Shelley screwing around behind my back and blaming it on you?'

'Can you take this elsewhere?' the man with the loafers said. 'There are children and old people present.'

'I'm not an old person!' the elderly lady said. 'Seventy is the new fifty.'

'Yeah. And I'm sixteen,' the boy in the wheelchair said. 'And I'm enjoying this.'

Joe took Saffy's shoulders. 'What about that night I let you drive all the way back to Dublin after you heard your mother was sick?' he said softly. 'I can't believe I did that. What about not even calling you or texting you to find out if she made it?'

'She did.' Saffy's eyes filled with tears but they were happy tears. 'She did make it.'

Jill was healing slowly and all the confusion was gone. Mr Kenny had said he would start chemo again in a week. And Saffy felt as if she was healing too. Every time she came to the hospital, her mother was sitting up smiling, watching the door, with another missing fragment of her father. Something small she remembered. That he used to whistle 'Penny Lane' when he was shaving. That he loved cowboy movies. That, when he was a boy, he had a dog called 'Grin'.

The lift stopped again and two nurses got in.

Joe rubbed his eyebrows with his thumb and forefinger.

'When your package arrived for Liam, you know what I did? I took it away from him. I wasn't going to even let him open it. I've been such an asshole!'

One of the nurses giggled.

'Sh!' the boy in the wheelchair said.

'I had baggage. I had Liam and I expected you to take him on and you did. But I wasn't prepared to take on your baggage.'

The lift doors opened again and the man with the loafers and the old lady got out.

'It's my fault,' Saffy said. 'I should have told you I was married. But I was too scared. I thought if you knew, you wouldn't want me.'

'Not want you? Are you crazy? I want you so badly it hurts.'

The boy in the wheelchair was watching them like a table tennis match but Saffy didn't care.

She smiled. 'Really?'

'It hurts here.' Joe clutched his head. 'And here.' He grabbed a handful of his shirt over his heart. 'And here.' He clapped a hand to his groin. 'And I don't know what I'll do if you go to LA . . .'

'I'm *not* going to LA,' Saffy said as the doors closed again.

'You're not?'

She shook her head. Greg had tried to change her mind that day in the restaurant, after she'd handed him back the rings. But his heart wasn't in it. The Hollywood break meant more to him than anything else. His career came first. That was how it had always been, she realised, she just hadn't seen it. And that was fine when it was just the two of them. But it wasn't fine any more, not with a baby on the way.

'I'll need you to pay maintenance when you get sorted out,' she'd told him. 'And I need you to promise that, even if you're in the States, you'll be a part of this. I grew up without knowing my dad; I don't want that for our child.'

'Greg is going to LA,' she told Joe now, 'but I'm staying here. We're getting a divorce.'

He grinned. 'You are?'

The lift stopped on the fourth floor and the doors opened. Saffy could see the sign for Jill's ward at the end of the long corridor. A tiny white feather danced in the updraft from the lift shaft.

The woman pushed the boy in the wheelchair out.

'Wait for the next one, love,' she said to a man with a toddler who was waiting to get in. 'It's over eighteens in there.'

'*Great*,' the boy in the wheelchair grumbled, looking over his shoulder as the doors closed behind them. 'Now we'll never know what happens next.'

Lakeview
Butterhill
Blessington
County Wicklow
Ireland

Dear Frank,
You wrote to me in 2005 to tell me the sad news that my dad, Rob Reilly, had died. I'm really sorry it's taken so long to thank you for your kindness. I didn't actually get your package till late last year when I came across a pile of postcards and two precious letters from my dad.

I had no idea that Dad had ever written to me. I grew up thinking that he didn't want to be part of my life. I am still getting used to the fact that he was trying to stay in touch with me for all those years and that he never stopped hoping that we'd meet.

I would have given anything to see him even once, before he died but I'm so grateful to have his letters and postcards because, even though I have no clear memories of Dad, I feel as if I recognise his voice when I read them. I think that somewhere in my heart, I have never really forgotten him.

I wanted to let you know that I will be in the UK in July. I'm bringing my mum over to Bristol. She still has family there, though she hasn't seen them in a long time. Mum is recovering from a long illness so I don't think she'll make it as far as Wales this time but I'm going to drive over to Swansea with my fiancé, Joe.

If you're free it would be great to meet you. And I would love to visit Dad's grave or the place where his ashes are scattered so I can say a proper 'goodbye.'

Yours,

Sadbh Martin

P.S. I forgot to thank you for the photographs. I have the one of Dad in the garden framed on my kitchen wall with some pictures of my stepson Liam and my three-month-old baby, Robert. He has his grandfather's eyes!